Pamela Evans was born and brought up in Hanwell in the Borough of Ealing, London, the youngest of six children. She is married and has two sons and now lives in Wales. She has had eight novels published, which are all available from Headline, including *A Barrow in the Broadway* ('a long, warm-hearted London saga' *Bookseller*), *Lamplight on the Thames* ('a good story and excellent observation of social change over the past forty years' *Knightsbridge and South Hams Gazette*), *Maggie of Moss Street* ('a good traditional romance and its author has a feeling for the atmosphere of postwar London' *Sunday Express*), *Star Quality* ('well peopled with warm personalities' *Liverpool Post*), *Diamonds in Danby Walk* ('a heart-warming family saga' *Newtownards Chronicle*), *A Fashionable Address* ('very readable' *Bella*) and *Tea-Blender's Daughter*.

D1332435

The Willow Girls

Pamela Evans

KNIGHT

Copyright © 1994 Pamela Evans

The right of Pamela Evans to be identified as the Author of
the Work has been asserted by her in accordance with the
Copyright, Designs and Patents Act 1988.

First published in 1994
by HEADLINE BOOK PUBLISHING

First published in paperback in 1995
by HEADLINE BOOK PUBLISHING

This edition published 2002 by
Knight an imprint of The Caxton Publishing Group

10 9 8 7 6 5 4 3 2 1

All rights reserved. No part of this publication may be
reproduced, stored in a retrieval system, or transmitted,
in any form or by any means without the prior written
permission of the publisher, nor be otherwise circulated
in any form of binding or cover other than that in which
it is published and without a similar condition being
imposed on the subsequent purchaser.

All characters in this publication are fictitious
and any resemblance to real persons, living or dead,
is purely coincidental.

ISBN 1 84067 413 X

Typeset by CBS, Felixstowe, Suffolk

Printed and bound in Great Britain by
Mackays of Chatham plc, Chatham, Kent

Caxton Publishing Group
20 Bloomsbury Street
London WC1B 3JH

To Max, with love

PART ONE

Chapter One

Clock-watching was the main preoccupation of the women in the machine shop at the aircraft components factory. Wistful cries of 'Roll on knocking off time' could be heard even as they arrived for work and echoed throughout the day in all parts of the room.

Long hours of repetitive labour performed under artificial lighting slowed the hands on the clock. Around mid-afternoon every day Nina Dent could have sworn they stopped moving altogether. Today seemed particularly endless. Warm weather and bad ventilation produced such debilitating torpor she barely had the strength to pull down the handle of her machine.

Sunshine beating against the blacked-out windows didn't help matters either; it thickened the atmosphere even more and augmented the mingled smells of oil, grease and sweat, whilst the punishing din of the machines was a constant assault to the eardrums.

Looking around her, Nina noticed that most of her workmates were similarly affected. Some were staring blankly into space; others were yawning; one woman was fiddling with the curlers poking from the front of her turban; a few more were settling down after a

3

prolonged trip to the cloakroom. Nobody even had the energy to sing.

Periods of mass lethargy were only to be expected in Nina's opinion. Even the most diligent worker couldn't help but flag at some point during the shift, which was probably why the management allowed them to listen to the twice-daily sessions of 'Music While You Work', well known for its cheering effect.

'Come on, ladies, get a grip of yourselves now,' said the foreman, shouting to make himself heard above the clatter as he moved authoritativelyamong the machines. 'I've seen more life in a butcher's shop window.'

Vowing not to look at the clock again until she had drilled at least another fifty holes by which time the hands *must surely* have moved on, Nina drew on what little vitality she had left and called to those within earshot, 'How about a song, girls? All together now. One . . . two . . . three . . .'

Without further ado she launched into a rousing chorus of 'I've Got Sixpence'.

The response was slow but eventually most people were joining in, later assisted by half an hour of popular music from the BBC broadcast over the loudspeakers. The singing had its usual reviving effect and production began to resume its former momentum. Slowly, painfully, the seconds dragged by until, at last, it was five minutes to finishing time which meant they could get ready to go home.

In the crowded cloakroom, overalls were shed against an exuberant discussion by the younger women of plans for the evening, enthusiasm for their social life undiminished by the arduous working day.

'A few of us are going up the Palais tonight, Nina,' said a young married woman called Doris. 'Do you fancy comin'?'

'No, not tonight, thanks,' said Nina, struggling to remove the impregnated grime from her hands at the washbasin.

'I suppose you'll be helping your mum in the pub?'

'That's right.'

'Again tonight!' exclaimed Flo, a sprightly grandmother who had been called up for war work when the government had raised the registration age for women.

'Yes, again tonight,' said Nina lightly, 'what's wrong with that?'

'Nothing's *wrong* with it, ducks,' said Flo kindly, 'but it's such a long working day for you. It would do you good to have a night off, to go out and have some fun . . . a young girl like you.'

'You sound just like my mum,' replied Nina. 'She's always telling me that. But I enjoy helping her in the pub, honestly. It doesn't seem like work to me.'

'After drilling 'oles in this dump all bloomin' day, I don't suppose it does,' agreed Flo.

'And at least you get to meet people,' remarked someone waiting in the queue for the washbasin.

'Depends who you mean by people though, dunnit?' said Doris who was an authority on local nightlife. 'The Willow's all right as pubs go . . . but it's ever so short on talent. All the tasty young servicemen are up the Palais looking for girls.'

'Don't you be so sure about that,' grinned Nina, her blue eyes shining wickedly as she dried her hands on a grubby roller towel and ran a comb through her reddish-gold hair in front of a tarnished mirror on the wall. 'We do get the occasional punter in with his own teeth.'

'You be careful you and your mum don't kill each other fightin' over him then,' joked Flo, causing a roar of laughter.

'Well, I don't mind admitting that I'm hoping to get off with a nice rich Yank tonight,' said Doris, who didn't hide the fact that her evenings weren't spent pining away at home while her husband was away in the army. 'You should come along with me, Nina. A hunky GI would really show you how to have a good time.'

'Don't listen to her, Nina,' said Flo laughingly. 'All she'll do for you is get you a bad name.'

'Come off it, Flo,' objected Doris. 'I'm only suggestin' that the girl has some fun while she can. Here today gone tomorrow, as they say.'

'Cheerful soul, ain't you?' remarked someone.

'I'm only saying what everyone else is thinkin',' said Doris breezily. 'With all these flamin' doodlebugs about, you never know when you've done your last jitterbug.'

'I hope your old man never finds out what you've been getting up to while he's away,' said Flo.

'Don't worry about him,' Doris exclaimed, hanging her overalls up on one of the overloaded pegs on the muddy-green wall. 'He won't be at the back o' the queue if there's any willing mademoiselles around out there in France.'

'He's away fighting a war, not on a ruddy holiday,'

Flo pointed out without malice for she liked the flighty Doris.

'There's a name for people like you, Doris,' said one of the more serious-minded in an acid tone. 'You ought to have more respect for your marriage vows and the fact that your husband is away fighting for his country.'

'Mind your own business,' she retorted, affronted. 'At least I don't go out enjoyin' myself on the quiet . . . like some people.'

'I hope you're not suggesting that I do that?'

'Of course I'm not, you silly cow!' said Doris, who didn't think a sanctimonious old matron stood much chance of riotous hedonism. 'All I mean is, not everyone is as open as I am about it.'

'That's no excuse.'

'Like I said, it's my business what I do after work,' asserted Doris.

'Now, now, you two,' admonished Flo. 'No squabbling.'

'Anyway, it's only a bit o' fun,' continued Doris, ignoring Flo and glaring at her detractor. 'Stayin' at home of an evening gives me the screamin' willies with all these bombs about. At least going out dancing helps to take your mind off things.'

This drew a murmur of agreement. Despite the altercation between the two women, camaraderie among the workers in general was good. They worked hard and most of the young single ones, and a few of the married ones too, liked to play hard. After a punitively long shift many of them would rush home, have a meal, get washed and changed and go out dancing or to the pictures, and still be on duty at the factory again early the next morning, air raids notwithstanding.

Nina had certainly found her workmates to be a mixed bunch when she first came into war work. Having been brought up in a public house, she was no stranger to a coarse turn of phrase but she'd been shocked by the vulgarity of some of the women, and the casually explicit way they talked about sex had been a revelation.

Back at the machines the factory hooter sounded, liberating the day shift to make way for the night workers. With a new lease of life, the women streamed towards the time clock, jostling with the night shift who were trying to clock in.

Cards duly stamped, they trooped through the factory gates in a crowd, chattering and laughing. Nina walked with a group, talking and enjoying the fresh air, albeit that it was permeated with acrid smoke from the flying bombs that had wreaked havoc on London this last few weeks. There was such a long queue at the bus-stop, she decided to walk home with a few of the others.

The evening sun was low in a hazy blue sky streaked with yellow and pink. Its cruel light spread across the ubiquitous bomb sites in the rubble-strewn streets. Even the once lustrous privet hedges were encrusted with brick dust, and many of the trees were stripped bare by the bomb blasts, the leaves rotting prematurely on the ground.

Her companions went their separate ways at various points, leaving Nina to complete the last part of the journey alone, a slim, freckle-faced eighteen year old dressed in a frayed blouse and a dirndl skirt she'd made out of an old frock. At the Broadway she walked along

King Street, glancing idly in the dusty shop windows then turning into a sidestreet that led to the river, its oily waters crowded with commercial craft.

Smoky tug boats, with lighters in tow, chugged to and from the wharves in the warm summer evening. Along with Thames sailing and motor barges they carried a diverse range of goods including coal, brewing materials, processed food and flour.

The tide was just beginning to ebb and she paused for a moment to watch a family of ducks perched on some driftwood on the edge of the muddy foreshore, preening their feathers. Moving on past piles of debris, which had been a row of houses until the other day, she came to some pretty old cottages, a few small factories and a boatyard. Then there were some large superior houses, wasteground dotted with trees, and a long-established bomb site bright with purple rosebay willow-herb.

When the graceful old contours of The Willow came into view, close to the eponymous tree overhanging the riverbank, she felt warm with relief that it had not fallen victim to the daily quota of flying bombs. The Willow was Nina's anchor – her comfort and security.

Since 1869 The Willow had been a public parlour to the local people as well as the lightermen, bargees and boatmen of the floating river community. It was a spacious, solid building on three floors with bay windows at the front overlooking the river, with Hammersmith Bridge in view to one side and Chiswick Eyot to the other. There were public entrances to the property from the river side and also from the street, with a private door at the side of the premises. Near both public entrances stood a colourful pub sign picturing a willow tree.

Before the war it had been one of the most elegant pubs on the river, being white-rendered with shiny black paintwork, the garden at the side fairy-lit at night. Now, in these dangerous and austere times, with no materials available to carry out maintenance, the white walls were darkened by soot and bombdust, the paintwork had peeled almost to the bare wood and the gardens were blacked out after dark. Even the ivy that covered some of the walls was nearer to black than green.

Tilly Dent was in the saloon bar wiping the tops of the stained wooden tables when she heard her daughter come in through the private entrance. The beer shortage meant that Tilly opened for business much later than in pre-war times so the evening session hadn't yet started.

'I'm in here, love,' called Tilly, an attractive peroxide blonde of thirty-six with stunning blue eyes and a shapely figure she carried with aplomb.

Nina appeared through a door behind the wooden bar counter which curved around to the adjacent public bar.

'Hello, Mum. Phew, am I glad to be home!' she said, lifting the counter flap to get through to the bar and collapsing into one of the brown-painted Lloyd Loom chairs. She sighed with the sheer joy of being home amidst soothing familiarity, breathing in an amalgam of scents: beer, wood, polish, lingering cigarette smoke, sawdust from the public bar. 'I'm absolutely starving.'

'Had a hard day, love?'

'Not 'alf. I'm cross-eyed from drilling holes.'

'I'll bet.'

'But the girls are a friendly bunch and that helps to make the time pass,' said Nina, who usually managed to look on the bright side of everything. 'How was your day?'

'I'm nearly boss-eyed an' all from soldering electrical parts together for hours on end, but it wasn't too bad,' replied Tilly. 'It's not often we don't find something to have a laugh about at the factory.'

Tilly had taken over as licensee of The Willow when her husband, Joe, had been called up into the army. As the shortage of drinks of every kind meant she was forced to cut her business hours drastically, doing away with weekday lunchtime openings altogether until things improved, she also managed to work a part-time shift in a war factory.

In her role as publican she was aided by a trusted local man called Syd who was past the age of enlistment. He was her cellarman-cum-barman and general helper. She also had an extra pair of hands in her daughter.

'A few of the girls on my shift are going out dancing tonight,' Tilly went on to say. 'So there'll be some ripe tales to tell tomorrow.'

'Some of them from my place are going up the Palais tonight too,' remarked Nina chattily. 'They asked me to go with them, as a matter of fact.'

Tilly frowned. 'Why don't you go then, love?' she

11

suggested, taking a pile of clean ashtrays from the bar counter and setting them out on the tables. 'It'll do you good to have a girls' night out.'

'No . . . I don't fancy it.'

'Look, Nina, you mustn't feel you have to stay at home to help me every night,' said Tilly anxiously. Her daughter was a real asset to the business. Her extrovert personality and sunny nature made her a favourite with the regulars, many of whom had watched her grow up for she'd been born here. But after labouring at a machine all day it wasn't right for her to be working every night too. 'Syd and me'll manage here without any trouble.'

'How many more times must I tell you? I enjoy working here, so stop going on about it.' This was no lie for The Willow was much more than a place of business to Nina. It was her spiritual retreat after the harshness of the factory. Surrounded by the bonhomie of a crowded bar, she felt relaxed and happy and was equally comfortable sharing a joke with the punters as she was listening to their problems. 'You'll soon know if I get fed up with it.'

'That's true enough,' said Tilly with a wry smile, for her daughter had been brought up to speak her mind which was probably why they got along so well together. Having set out all the ashtrays and tidied the high wooden stools into a line alongside the bar, she went round to the other side of the counter and rinsed the cloth she had been using in the sink below the bar. 'You're certainly no shrinking violet.'

'I wouldn't be your daughter if I was, now would I?'

grinned Nina, glancing idly round the empty bar-room with its polished wooden floor and heavily embossed wallpaper that had once been red and cream and was now a dull maroon shade.

The walls were liberally hung with mirrors advertising the products of the various breweries with whom they did business. A dominant feature of the room was a wide marble fireplace, cold and empty at this time of year with a brass firescreen covering the opening and a vase of dried flowers on the mantelpiece. There was a wireless set mounted on the wall at the end of the bar and a piano stood in the corner.

Deciding to go upstairs to the flat, Nina rose and made her way through the bar to their private hallway at the back. Her mother patted her arm fondly as she passed. 'You're such a help to me, Nina,' she said softly. 'I'm proud of you, and so will your dad be when he comes home.'

'Never mind all that,'said Nina with an affectionate grin. 'I'm only doing what I want to do.'

Tilly gave her an impulsive hug and Nina responded warmly. Whilst the Dents were not given to cloying sentimentality, they were a caring and demonstrative family. 'Come on, then,' she said, 'let's go and have somethin' to eat before we get ready for opening. I've got some mince cooking on a low light.'

'Smashing,' said Nina.

Their living accommodation was on the first and second floors. The rooms were spacious with high ceilings and sash windows. There was a living room with a dining table in the bay, a sitting room at the back which was only used on special occasions, a kitchen, bathroom and three bedrooms, the third of which was used for live-in staff in pre-war times and was now something of a junk room. The attic room was used for storage.

They ate a hurried but companionable meal by the open windows looking out over the river. Perched on the sideboard was a wireless set which was emitting good news about events overseas.

'Sounds to me as though the Germans have more troubles than the ones we're givin' 'em,' said Tilly, after hearing that there had been an attempt by German officers to murder Hitler.

'It does too,' agreed Nina.

'Our boys have really got them on the run an' all,' continued Tilly, leaning her head back slightly as she enjoyed a cigarette after her meal.

'It certainly seems like it,' agreed Nina, when the newsreader said that the Allies were driving the Germans from Normandy and forging ahead across France.

'Stands to reason they'll do well with your dad among their numbers somewhere, dunnit?' joked Tilly.

'Naturally,' smiled Nina.

'Those damned Nazis who are working at the bomb-launching platforms at Pas-de-Calais don't seem to be in any sort of bother though, do they?' said Tilly as the air raid siren began to wail for the umpteenth time that day. 'Judging by the amount of bloomin' doodle-bugs they still keep sending over.'

'Mm.'

14

'If it gets too dodgy we'll go down the cellar till the All Clear.'

'See how it goes,' said Nina.

Although both women behaved rather casually on hearing the ominous rasp of a winged robot scuttling across the sky, an acceleration of speech and movement as they began to clear the table betrayed a certain tension.

'I'll see to the dishes while you get yourself ready to open up, if you like,' offered Nina.

'Ta, love,' said Tilly, glancing at her pretty daughter who had no need of powder and lipstick to make her look presentable. 'Oh, what it is to be young. One day it'll take you longer than two minutes to get ready.'

'Stop fishing for compliments,' laughed Nina. 'You know very well you still look smashing. Everyone says so.'

As the flying bomb passed overhead, its roar growing fainter, they went to the window and watched the missile clattering eerily across the clouds in the distance, flame spurting from its tail as it headed upriver. They waited until it was out of sight then winced at the explosion which rattled the windows and sounded quite close.

'It seemed to be heading Winnie's way,' remarked Tilly, referring to her sister who lived in Chiswick. 'I hope her and her family haven't copped it.'

'I'd say the explosion was much further away than that,' commented Nina.

'Let's hope you're right,' said Tilly, frowning deeply. 'I might not get along with that stuck-up sister o' mine and her snooty husband and daughter but I don't wish them any harm.'

'Course you don't,' said Nina, returning to the table to continue with the task in hand. 'Now go and put your war-paint on. If we don't have the doors open dead on time, they'll start breaking 'em down.'

'They will an' all,' laughed Tilly. 'Having to wait till eight o'clock for me to open up is punishment enough. If I'm a second late, my name will be mud.'

Nina gave a companionable nod but she knew it would take more than a spot of unpunctuality in these chaotic times to diminish her mother's popularity. She was one of the most well-loved pub landladies this side of the river.

Seated before her dressing-table mirror, Tilly poked her little finger into an almost empty lipstick tube, teased some of the scarlet substance out of the corners with her nail and spread it over her lips. The cosmetics shortage was one of the hardest of wartime deprivations for her to bear. She'd sooner go without food than have to face the punters without a nice touch of make-up to brighten herself up. In her opinion a landlady owed it to her clientele to bring a touch of glamour into the bar, something that the passing years and the scarcity of every type of beauty aid made increasingly difficult.

Adding a touch of rouge to her cheeks, she turned her attention to her hair, sweeping the sides up in fashionable style and securing them with her precious hair grips, leaving the back to fall into a loose pageboy.

She stood up and looked at herself in the full-length

mirror on the wardrobe door. Her white blouse fitted snugly over her full bosom and was tucked into a floral cotton skirt which she wore with wedge-heeled sandals, her legs having been painted with gravy browning earlier since she didn't have a pair of stockings.

A sudden feeling of exhaustion overwhelmed her and she was forced to sit down on the edge of the bed. Oh, how she longed to slip between the sheets and sleep away her aching weariness. It seemed so long since she hadn't felt tired. As much as she enjoyed her work in the pub, at this precise moment she didn't feel able to walk across the room, let along work the evening session downstairs.

You're not the only one doing more than one job in wartime, she admonished herself. Get up, you lazy cow, and get moving. You know how much it means to Joe to keep this place in business until he comes home.

Joe was the fourth generation of Dents to own The Willow. His great-grandfather had built it back in 1869 and it had been handed down to succeeding generations ever since. Joe had taken over after his father's death some years ago, having worked in the business before that.

Despite the very best endeavours of several breweries to take it over, The Willow remained a privately owned free house. It was important to Tilly and Joe to be free to stock their pub from whichever brewery they chose even though the present crisis meant they bought drink wherever they could find it.

The property was leasehold and had been built on land owned by the Cavendish family to whom they paid annual ground rent. Based on a friendship between Joe Dent's ancestor and one of the Cavendishes back in the last century, it was an agreement that had been in existence between the two families for as long as the pub. The ground rent was merely a small token amount and the lease was renewed at the appropriate times as a matter of course.

Taking a deep breath and forcing her tired eyes to stay open, Tilly gave a vigorous yawn, stretched her arms with a groan and dragged herself to her feet. 'Into the breach again, old girl,' she muttered wearily, and hurried downstairs just in time to open the door to Syd who was reporting for duty.

Within minutes of the doors being opened, The Willow was crowded with locals and river people, the whole building reverberating with noise and laughter. Whilst pulling pints and opening bottles, Tilly, Nina and Syd chatted to the customers, joined in the badinage, listened to gossip and offered comfort to those who had lost loved ones in the air raids. Drinks had to be rationed to be fair to everyone but people stayed whether their glasses were empty or not, so congenial was the atmosphere. Drinking receptacles of every type were in short supply and those who didn't bring their own, took the risk of not being served.

The main topic of conversation this evening was the good news from across the Channel with the air raids in second place. Everyone had their own doodle-bug story to tell and tales of narrow escapes came thick and fast.

As darkness fell and the blackout curtains were

drawn across the windows, the boisterous dialogue of the darts players in the public bar was drowned out when one of the regulars got vamping at the piano in the saloon bar. The whole place erupted into a rousing version of 'Roll out the Barrel'. The bombs seemed less frightening, hardship was temporarily forgotten.

Standing aside from all this for a moment, Nina felt a moment's pleasure so acute it brought tears to her eyes. This is what running a pub is all about, she thought, bringing people together, helping them to forget their troubles, for a short while at least. For a good publican there was much more to the job than just selling drinks.

Her mother *was* The Willow in Nina's opinion. Without her it wouldn't enjoy a fraction of its popularity. Dad was an adequate landlord – in peacetime he kept a good cellar and was popular enough with the customers. But Tilly had that something extra that made people choose The Willow over other pubs in the area in which to socialise. Nina remembered her father once saying that his wife could turn a temperance society meeting into a party.

Watching her holding court among the clientele on the other side of the bar, Nina could see exactly what he had meant. She had a natural affinity with her fellows and could be all things to all people – friend, flirt, mother. Amorous male customers never overstepped the mark with Tilly. A seasoned diplomat, she would please them by accepting their advances in a lighthearted manner whilst making it very obvious they would not be welcome outside the bar.

The job of landlady necessitated she be entertaining, good-humoured, and able to stand her ground with troublemakers of whom The Willow had its fair share. Tilly was an expert in all these areas but Nina thought that perhaps her greatest gifts were her warmth and humanity – they were why people loved and respected her.

She came back behind the counter with a tray of dirty glasses. 'You look tired out, Nina love,' she said, rinsing the glasses in the sink. 'Why not go up to bed? You have to be up earlier than me in the morning for your shift.'

'And miss all this . . . no fear,' laughed Nina.

'It's music to the ears, innit?' said Tilly. 'A crowded bar and the sound of people enjoying themselves.'

'It certainly is.'

'Some people would hear a bloomin' awful racket . . . but we hear music,' she remarked thoughtfully.

'Yes, that's exactly how it is,' said Nina.

'When it begins to sound just like a racket, I'll know it's time to leave the licensed trade.'

'I suppose you will.'

Nina considered it an asset to have been brought up in a pub. Even though only on the periphery while she was growing up, the atmosphere had spilled over into the home. She could remember as a child occasionally being affected by the herd instinct and wanting to be the same as all the other children at school: to live in an ordinary house with parents who weren't working every night.

But most of the time she'd enjoyed being different.

Had been proud to be known as 'The Girl from The Willow'. She recalled sneaking into the bar during opening hours on many occasions. What a fuss the customers had made of her! It had been worth the tellings off she'd been given when her parents had found out.

As she'd grown older she'd realised that she had the same natural gift for this business as her mother – that special something that put her at her best in a room full of people.

Working in a pub would be degrading to some girls, she knew that. But The Willow was the family business in which she'd grown up. When the war ended and people were free again to choose their occupation, Nina could think of nothing she'd rather do than help her parents run this place.

Chapter Two

The only sounds in the Wilcoxes' living room were the wireless tuned low to Arthur Askey singing 'The Bee Song', and the click of Winnie's knitting needles.

Her husband Cedric was sitting in an armchair reading the newspaper, having just returned from a Home Guard meeting. Their daughter Alice was perched on the sofa mending a worn patch in one of her office blouses. The wireless was only on in case there was a news bulletin. Cedric didn't approve of light entertainment programmes.

Straining her ears, Alice heard the end of the variety show which was followed by a programme of dance music by Geraldo. Almost without her realising it was happening, she began humming along softly to the tune of 'Don't Sit Under the Apple Tree'.

Frowning darkly, her father looked up from his newspaper. 'What is that noise, Alice?' he asked, squinting at her myopically over the top of his spectacles.

'I was humming.'

'Well, I'd prefer it if you didn't when I'm trying to read,' he said crossly.

'Sorry, Daddy,' she said with dutiful contrition.

'I should think so too.'

'The tune they are playing is rather catchy,' she explained. 'It made me want to hum.'

'I do hope you're not getting to like the dreadful dance music they keep putting out on the wireless.'

'As if I would,' denied Alice with her customary compliance. 'It was just that one song that caught my attention.'

She had been raised on a strict diet of classical music in keeping with her parents' idea of what was suitable for the lower-middle-class daughter of a senior bank clerk. She was taught that popular songs were only for the stupid and degenerate. Piano lessons at an early age and enforced practice throughout her childhood had made her into a competent pianist but she would never risk engaging the wrath of her parents by indulging an occasional desire to buy the sheet music of popular songs.

'I should jolly well hope so too,' said her mother, a formidable woman past the age for compulsory war work but currently employed part-time in the offices of a grocery store to avoid any possibility of not being seen to do her bit. Ignoring the fact that women from all backgrounds had been directed into essential employment in war factories, she added, 'That sort of music is only to the taste of the hoi-polloi . . . common factory girls and the like.'

'Some of the women at the bank like dance music, I think, Mummy,' ventured Alice with an unusual show of daring. Although a grown woman of twenty, she was totally dominated by her parents and had been so effectively indoctrinated with their narrow views as to believe them to be her own.

'You don't have to tell me that,' retorted Cedric, who had fought in the Great War but was not eligible to do so in this one, much to his relief. A tall, pallid man with thinning hair and a long face, Cedric worked at the same bank as Alice and was not ashamed of having relied heavily on nepotism to get her a job there. 'I've heard the shameless talk that goes on among the women when they should be working. All they seem to care about is going out enjoying themselves at dances . . . and finding men.'

'Yes, they do seem to like to . . .' began Alice.

'And as for all that muck they plaster on their faces if they can get hold of it,' Cedric continued as though his daughter hadn't spoken.

'Disgusting,' agreed Winnie with a disapproving shake of the head.

'I really think it's scandalous the way this war has destroyed moral standards,' ranted her husband.

'So do I, dear, but the important thing is for us not to let our own standards slip,' said Winnie, glancing proudly at the man to whom she had been married for over thirty years. She considered him to have been an excellent catch, having worked in the same steady job for his entire working life, excluding his military service in the First World War.

'And as for some of these comedians they allow on the wireless,' he went on, ignoring her remark.

'Shocking.'

'Mindless drivel,' he declared. 'I'd even go so far as to

call some of it gutter humour, the sort of thing you would expect to hear in some place of disrepute.' He sat thoughtfully for a moment. 'In that public house of your sister's, for instance.'

Winnie flushed defensively. She always had the uneasy feeling that her younger sister's line of business reflected on her personally somehow, even though they hardly ever saw each other.

'I don't think Tilly's pub is actually disreputable, Cedric dear,' she said, biting her lip. 'In fact, I think it's probably one of the better kind of public houses. It's in quite a pleasant position on the river anyway.'

'All public houses are dens of iniquity,' announced Cedric, who was from a puritanical background and disapproved of all forms of entertainment. 'If I had my way, I'd close the lot of them.'

'Quite so,' murmured Winnie, who felt she'd done enough in defence of her sister's profession.

Cedric turned his attention to his daughter. 'I hope you're taking note of all this, Alice? Don't ever let me hear that you go into such places.'

'There's no chance of that,' she said truthfully for on the rare occasions as a child when, with her mother, she'd visited her aunt and uncle at their pub, she'd felt most uncomfortable in their company.

Her aunt and uncle had been far too jocular for her taste – always laughing and joking and upsetting her mother who would spend the entire visit tight-lipped with disapproval. And who could blame her when her younger sister behaved like a tart? Alice had seen her playing up to the men in the bar from the hallway on her way upstairs one day when the door had been left open.

As for her cousin, Nina . . . well, she'd been an embarrassment, dragging Alice outside to the pub gardens and making friends with the children of customers, not to mention the scruffy individuals who lived on the barges. Alice hadn't known where to put herself, she'd felt so out of place. Looking back on it, she didn't think any of the Dents had a serious bone in their body – life was one big joke to them. It had put Alice off pub people for life.

'Don't you let the current moral climate influence you, Alice,' her father was lecturing.

'Of course she won't. She's far too well brought up for that,' intervened Winnie, aghast at such a suggestion.

She looked with pride at her daughter whom she considered to be tastefully dressed in a drab grey skirt and porridge-coloured jumper. Her light brown hair was parted to one side and fastened with a slide in schoolgirl fashion around a small face which was exceptionally pale because she was never encouraged to go out after work except to do her stint of compulsory fire watching. Although an extremely pretty shade of pale blue, her eyes lacked sparkle and were lifeless from years of domination.

Winnie was fifty-three years old – seventeen years older than her sister Tilly. They were the daughters of a draper's assistant, and from a humble but fastidiously respectable home on the outskirts of Hammersmith. Winnie, like her mother before her, had always considered a good reputation to be of paramount importance and had gone to some pains to find herself a man with a steady job and a good name in the community. Tilly had been the rebel, the one to let the family down with her outgoing ways. Trust her to marry a publican! Winnie thought. The vulgar lifestyle suited her extrovert nature perfectly.

'Anyway, it's time for you to make the cocoa now, please, Alice,' came Winnie's polite but insistent request.

'Yes, of course, Mummy,' said Alice, putting aside her sewing and rising.

'And there's a little piece of the cheese ration left in the larder,' continued Winnie. 'You can cut some bread to go with it.'

'All right,' said Alice, trotting obediently from the room.

She had just lit the gas under the kettle when the siren went. She heard groans of 'Oh, not again' from the other room and her own sentiments matched theirs completely. Life had been one long air raid since the robot bombs had started coming over at all hours of the day and night. No one bothered much about the daytime raids but the Wilcoxes usually went into the shelter when the siren sounded during the evening.

The distant throb of a flying bomb didn't send her into an immediate panic, she was far too well trained. She calmly performed the air-raid duties that had been assigned to her by her parents. She turned off the gas taps and electricity at the mains, checked that the stirrup pump was easily accessible near the buckets of earth and water on the front doorstep, then hurried back to the kitchen.

Winnie and Cedric were passing through on their way out to the shelter in the back garden. Cedric was carrying some blankets for it was damp and cool in the Anderson even on the warmest evening.

'Come along, Alice,' commanded Winnie in a carefully composed voice for it was not family policy to show personal feelings. They believed in keeping a stiff upper lip at all times.

'I'm right behind you, Mummy,' said Alice, following her out of the door.

They picked their way across the garden in the dark to Winnie's complaints about having to wait until after the All Clear for her supper. Stopping in her tracks suddenly, she said, 'Oh, drat, I've forgotten to bring my knitting.'

'Never mind about that now,' said Cedric irritably. 'We probably won't be in the shelter for long.'

'But I'll go mad down there with nothing to do,' wailed his wife.

'You'll just have to put up with it this time!'

'I'll go back and get it for you,' offered Alice.

'No, no, I'd better go myself,' insisted Winnie. 'I'm not quite sure where it is . . . it could be in one of several places. I'll probably be able to lay my hands on it quicker than you.'

'Oh, for pity's sake,' sighed Cedric furiously. 'Forget about the damned knitting for once.'

'No. I'm not going to do that, Cedric,' she said. 'I'll only be a minute.'

'Make sure you're no longer then,' he ordered.

Nina waited with her father by the shelter

entrance, listening to the sound of her mother's footsteps across the garden, acutely aware that the hum in the sky had become a grating roar and was no longer distant.

'I suppose I'd better go and see what's happened to your mother,' said her father after a few minutes, handing Alice the blankets.

'Shall I go, Daddy?' she offered. 'I don't mind.'

'No . . . I'd better do it,' he said with obvious reluctance. 'I can't think what's keeping her . . . all this nonsense about knitting.' He sighed. 'It's all so damned unnecessary.' He glared at Alice. 'Well, don't just stand there. Get into the shelter.'

Obedient to a fault, Alice felt her way into the clammy interior, her stomach churning at the sound of the aircraft which now seemed to be directly overhead. 'Please keep it going . . . please don't let it stop,' she appealed to some higher authority, for she knew that when the robot ran out of fuel it would stall and make its lethal descent.

What on earth are they doing? she wondered, alarmed by her parents' continued absence. A spluttering noise overhead sent a bolt of fear through her body. With every muscle clenched, she waited, the silence like knives to her nervous system.

After a few agonising seconds the earth shook with a thunderous explosion. She was sent crashing to the floor, banging her head on the bench on the way down and losing consciousness.

'Mummy . . . Daddy!' was her bewildered cry when she came to and had recovered sufficiently to scramble to her feet, grazed knees smarting, head throbbing.

Clambering out of the shelter, she froze at the scene before her. All the houses in the row had disappeared and in their place was a heap of rubble spewing flames and smoke. With her throat and chest smarting and her eyes streaming from the blaze, she stumbled across the garden in search of her parents, tripping over smashed bits of furniture and feeling the crunch of broken glass under her feet.

Somewhere between the shelter and what had once been the house, she stopped, paralysed by what she could see in the lurid glow from the conflagration. Her parents were lying together in a grotesque heap on the ground where they had been blown by the blast.

Her mother was sprawled out against her father, her head thrown back and legs wide apart. Her skirt had been blasted up over her waist so that her enormous flannelette knickers were hideously displayed in the uncertain light.

Even as Alice went down on her knees to her parents, her intuition told her that they were both dead. Numb with shock and trembling all over, she instinctively adjusted her mother's skirt. The air was already full of the clang of fire bells.

Chapter Three

Approaching The Willow on her way home from work the following evening, Nina was alarmed to see her mother walking towards her along the towpath. It must indicate something serious because Tilly was usually much too busy at this time of day to take a constitutional. Please don't let it be Dad, she prayed. Not the dreaded telegram from the War Office . . .

Compared to this terrifying possibility, the news that an aunt and uncle she'd hardly known had been killed, came almost as a relief.

'Me and Winnie never got on,' her mother was saying tearfully as she sat down on a decrepit wooden bench and lit a cigarette, 'but it's shaken me up somethin' awful. She was my sister after all.'

'You're bound to be upset,' said Nina, slipping a sympathetic arm around her mother's shoulders. 'What about Cousin Alice? Is she . . . ?'

'She's fine . . . Grazed knees and a bit of a headache, that's all,' Tilly informed her. 'She was in the shelter when the bomb fell.'

'That's one blessing then.'

'Mm.' Tilly drew thoughtfully on her cigarette. 'Alice

is at our place now, as a matter of fact. She was waiting for me outside when I got in from work this afternoon. She's nowhere else to go, poor dear, there's nothing left of the house. She stayed at a rest centre last night.'

'The poor thing must be devastated.'

'Bound to be,' agreed Tilly with a nod of the head. 'But being a Wilcox she ain't showing it. I honestly don't think that girl knows how to let herself go.'

'The famous Wilcox grin and bear it routine, eh?'

'She isn't doing much grinning but she certainly seems to be bearing it . . . a real chip off the old block.' She puffed on her Craven A. 'That's why I came to meet you. Wanted to put you in the picture without her being there, to warn you that she'll be living with us. I've already cleared the spare room for her.'

'That's fine with me.'

'I don't think it's gonna be easy, having her there.'

'We'll manage.'

'Yes, we will. But will she?' said Tilly, frowning. 'She's told me straight out that we're a last resort. She'd not stay with us if she had any alternative.'

'Charming!' exclaimed Nina.

'It isn't really her fault,' defended Tilly. 'She's been brought up to think she's a cut above.'

'Oh, well, we'll just have to be patient with her . . . at first anyway,' said Nina, sensitive to her cousin's loss. 'Snooty bitch or not, she must be feeling rotten and we're all she's got now.'

'I knew I could rely on you to make her welcome.' Tilly stood up, ground out her cigarette-butt under her shoe, blew her nose and adopted a purposeful air. 'Well, we'd better get back and have something to eat before we get ready to open up. It goes without saying we'll have to put on a cheerful face for the customers. Mustn't depress 'em with our problems . . . most of 'em have quite enough of their own.'

Noticing that her mother's eyes were bright with tears as well as resolution, Nina gave her a reassuring hug. 'Don't worry about Alice fitting in with us, Mum,' she said. 'I'll do my best to make her feel at home.'

'That's my girl.'

'You never know . . . once Alice and I get to know each other we might even get to be like sisters,' said Nina. 'I've always wanted one.'

'Anything's possible, I suppose,' said Tilly doubt-fully.

With arms linked companionably, mother and daughter walked home along the riverbank in the summer evening.

'I want to make it clear right from the start,' Alice announced aggressively as the three of them dined on sausage and mash a little later, 'that I don't want to live in a public house. I'll be moving out as soon as I can find somewhere else.'

'At least you're honest about it, I'll say that much for you,' said Nina, amazed at her cousin's steely composure, and certain that she, herself, would have been inconsolable in like position.

'More importantly,' continued Alice, tight-lipped and ashen, 'while I am staying here, I will not help in the bar under any circumstances whatsoever.'

'Fair enough, love,' said Tilly indulgently.

'You mean . . . you'd not even be prepared to help out in a crisis?' queried Nina.

'Definitely not,' confirmed Alice, her voice shaky but adamant. 'I shall pay you for my board and lodging from my wages from the bank so you'll have no right to expect me to do anything more than my share of the domestic chores.'

'Naturally we wouldn't *expect* it of you,' explained Nina, stifling her irritation in respect for her cousin's bereavement. 'But living at a pub isn't like living in an ordinary house – it's a working home. Life tends to be dominated by what's going on downstairs in the bar.'

'I shall not allow my life to be affected by it at all,' Alice stated categorically. 'The pub has nothing to do with me. I'm merely a lodger.'

'You might find yourself wanting to muck in with us later on when you're used to being here,' suggested Nina.

'I certainly will not!' declared Alice.

'There's nothing like a spot of bar work to cheer you up,' insisted Nina, grinding her teeth but keeping her temper. 'It would certainly put some colour back in your cheeks.'

'Not 'alf,' agreed Tilly, with a tentative grin. 'Some of the things you hear behind the bar are enough to bring you out in heat bumps.'

'I want nothing to do with any of it,' stated Alice.

'What exactly do you have against pubs?' asked Nina with genuine interest.

'Leave it,' intervened Tilly, throwing her daughter a cautionary glance. 'If Alice doesn't want to help in the bar, she doesn't have to. She's upset . . . let her be.'

Nina met her mother's eyes in surprise. 'I only wondered . . .'

'I'll tell you what I have against them,' cut in Alice, sounding nervous but resolute. 'They are magnets to the dregs of society. Dens of iniquity, every last one of them.'

'I beg your pardon,' defended Nina hotly. 'The Willow is a respectable house . . . a valuable asset to the community.'

'How can any public house be respectable,' snorted Alice, 'if it's full of drunks and lechers.'

'What with the beer shortage and all the local young men away at the war, we're a bit short on both at the moment,' said Tilly, taking refuge in humour.

'That isn't the point,' said Alice, who had never seen the funny side of anything in her life.

'If there were no degenerates, what would people like you exercise their disapproval on?' Nina couldn't resist asking.

'Now then,' warned her mother.

'And anyway, ours is a family pub, Alice,' Nina continued, moderating her tone to please her mother. 'A place for people to meet in a friendly atmosphere. You'll soon see how respectable we are.'

'I've no intention of seeing anything of the kind,' said Alice, two spots of colour rising on her pallid cheeks. 'I shall not set foot in that part of the premises. I shall stay up here of an evening.'

Tilly looked at Alice with compassion in her eyes. 'Don't worry, love,' she said gently, 'no one is going to force you to do anything you don't want to do. Of course you can stay up here in the flat if that's what you would prefer. This is your home now.'

Naturally protective of her mother, Nina experienced a moment of painful empathy as she watched the reassuring hand Tilly placed on Alice's arm across the table impatiently brushed aside by the younger woman. Nina could cheerfully have murdered Alice but, receiving a strong message from her mother's eyes, exercised self-restraint.

It wasn't like Mum to allow herself to be so blatantly insulted without putting up a fight. It must be because of Alice's awful situation, Nina decided. Her mother's popularity had always made her seem almost immune to the nastier side of human nature, but she was vulnerable to Alice. Oh, yes. For some reason that young woman had the power to wound her, Nina could see it in her mother's eyes.

She felt a sense of foreboding, as though nothing would ever be the same again. She didn't know why or how but she was suddenly convinced that Alice's coming into their lives was going to change everything. She also knew with equal certainty that she herself would not be able to tolerate her cousin's superior attitude for very long. If her manner didn't improve fairly soon there would have to be some strong words. Alice Wilcox was going to have to learn that she couldn't hurt people and get away with it – just bereaved or not!

* * *

'I don't know why you let Alice treat you so badly, Mum!' exclaimed Nina, during a quiet moment in the saloon bar one evening a month or so later. 'It isn't like you to let anyone walk all over you. You certainly wouldn't let *me* get away with it.'

'It's because I feel so sorry for her,' explained Tilly, turning away quickly and emptying a bag of coppers into the till. 'Just imagine how you'd feel if you lost your parents and your home all in one fell swoop.'

'Yeah . . . I know it must be awful for her,' admitted Nina, 'but does she have to be so foul? I've tried to be nice to her, I really have. I'd like to be friends but she just won't have it.'

'I know how difficult she is, love. I've seen the way you've tried and I'm proud of you,' said Tilly.

'She's so arrogant, I'm sick to death of it. I don't know who she thinks she is . . .'

'Try to be patient for a bit longer,' entreated Tilly. 'Give her a chance to get used to us. She's obviously grieving for her mum and dad, even though she doesn't show it. I don't think she means to be so hurtful.'

There was something about Alice her mother wasn't telling her, Nina was sure of it.

'All right, I'll try,' she sighed.

It was a Monday evening, usually the quietest night of the week in the pub. Tonight, however, there was quite a crowd in. Further reductions in beer supplies had forced Tilly to cut her opening hours even more which meant everyone arrived at about the same time. The public bar, in which Syd was serving, was packed with bargees playing darts, while the saloon bar was peopled mostly by men from the local factories and some elderly male residents. Women were more in evidence at The Willow at the weekends.

Nina had to admit to being relieved that Alice never came into the bars. At least there was somewhere she could speak to her mother in private and let off steam about her cousin, who had made life upstairs a misery these last few weeks with her superior manner and spiteful tongue.

As a crowd gathered around the piano and no one needed attention for the moment, Nina said, 'You can go upstairs for a break if you like, Mum. Put your feet up for ten minutes. I'll manage here.'

'No, you go,' said Tilly, looking towards the door. 'Someone's just come in I wanna have a word with . . . it's that bloke who can sometimes get hold of fags on the quiet. You go up and give Alice a bit of company.'

'My company is about the last thing she seems to want,' said Nina sadly. 'But, okay, I'll give it a try.'

'Fancy a cup of tea, Alice?' asked Nina, peering into the living room to see her cousin sitting in an armchair listening to the wireless.

'Tea?'

'Yes, tea, why so surprised?'

'Isn't tea a bit tame for you of an evening?'

'Of course, I forgot, I normally have a gallon of gin in my break,' she said with withering sarcasm.

Alice turned pink but didn't reply.

'You work in a bank but I don't expect you to have your pockets stuffed with pound notes,' said Nina with asperity.

Her cousin remained silent and cocked her head towards the wireless as though listening intently.

'So, do you want to join me in a cuppa or not?' said Nina showing signs of impatience. 'Only it's a waste to make a whole pot just for one.'

'Oh . . . all right then,' Alice condescended.

Curbing a desire to drag her cousin out of her chair and shake her till her ears dropped off, Nina marched into the kitchen, fuming. If she could cope with a pub full of bargees at closing time, she was more than a match for a prissy bank clerk with delusions of grandeur. If only her mother would allow her to speak out, though. Pub life was a team effort. If Lady Muck thought herself too grand to go into the bars, the least she could do was to offer to make the workers a cup of tea in their break.

'Sorry, Mum, but I can't stay silent any longer,' she muttered to herself, and marched back into the living room to switch off the wireless.

'What's going on?' asked Alice.

'It's time you and I had a proper talk.'

'Oh . . . what about?'

'About your attitude towards my mother and me. Particularly my mother.'

Alice sat perfectly still, staring ahead of her. 'I don't know what you mean,' she said haughtily. 'And I'm certainly not going to enter into any heated discussion with you when I'm trying to relax.'

The supercilious tilt of her head severed Nina's last shred of self-control.

'Right, that's it, madam!' she exploded. 'If you're not prepared to discuss this of your own accord, I'll *make* you bloody well listen.' She grabbed her cousin by the arms and pulled her to her feet, staring into her face. 'I've just about had enough of your airs and graces.'

Alice looked worried but didn't struggle or say a word. She just stood looking at Nina with a mixture of bewilderment and distaste.

'Look, we all know it must be awful for you . . . losing your parents and everything,' Nina said, panting slightly with rage. 'But that doesn't give you the right to treat us like something you've trodden in!'

Alice's face was expressionless, her eyes a vivid blue against her pallor but dull and emotionless, her thin lips set in a hard line. When Nina released her hold on her, she didn't move away.

'My mother's a good and caring woman,' Nina said, her voice shaking with temper. 'She simply doesn't deserve the treatment you're giving her.'

'Your mother is a tart,' announced Alice suddenly.

Nina was too shocked to speak for a moment. 'Don't you dare say such a terrible thing!' she said vehemently at last.

'It's true,' said Alice, her voice sharp with acrimony. 'I've seen her on my way upstairs, flirting with men over the bar, leading them on . . .'

'How dare you?'

'You've only to look at her to see what she is. She's all

paint and peroxide,' said Alice, cheeks flushed now, eyes gleaming with spite.

Suddenly Nina's palm tingled with the force of the blow she'd just dealt to the other woman's cheek. She stared in horror as Alice staggered backwards, holding her face.

'Don't you ever insult my mother again,' Nina raged. 'Allowing the customers to chat her up is all part of a landlady's job, you stupid bitch! Everyone knows it doesn't mean anything. She'd never be unfaithful to my father, not in a million years.'

'How do you know?' snorted Alice.

'Because I know my mother, and I know the way the pub trade works. If you were to involve yourself in our life instead of skulking outside it, trying to find fault, you'd see the way things are for yourself.'

Alice looked at Nina in silence. Her flush had faded and she had reverted to her normal mushroom pallor, eyes becoming dull and lacklustre again.

'If you'd only take the trouble to get to know my mother,' Nina continued, determined to make her point, 'you'd realise that she is a naturally friendly and warm-hearted person . . . but that's something you'd know nothing about, isn't it? You coldhearted cow!'

Alice began to tremble. For the first time Nina saw a glimmer of emotion in that closed little face of hers. Her lips twitched, her eyes shone with tears. Even as Nina perceived the change, Alice's expression reverted to normal.

'My mother has asked me to be patient with you,' Nina went on. 'She's prepared to put up with your appalling behaviour because she feels sorry for you . . . that's the sort of person she is. But I've had enough, and if you so much as say one wrong word to her in future, you'll get more than just a slap across the face, I can promise you that. You've insulted her for the last time, lady . . . *do you understand?*'

Alice gave Nina a strange look then turned and hurried from the room, leaving her cousin trembling, eyes hot with tears. The stuck-up bitch asked for it, Nina told herself. So why do I feel as though *I'm* the one who's done wrong?

Alice sat on her bed shaking all over. Her muscles ached with tension and her stomach was churning. Why didn't the bomb take me when it took my parents? she asked herself miserably. Life was so dreadful without them. She hated living with Nina and Aunt Tilly – felt so uncomfortable with their way of life. Their confidence shattered hers so completely that she protected herself with a superior attitude. She may not have been able to stand up to her parents but, fortunately, she was able to articulate the opinions they had taught her to defend herself against her cousin and aunt.

But none of this helped now and Alice found herself wishing she was dead. Self-pity had plagued her since her parents' death. Deprived of a safe existence within the strict guidelines in which she'd been raised, she felt lonely and afraid. Being too inhibited to express her grief to anyone or relieve her despair with tears, she had a constant ache in the pit of her stomach. The only relief she found was to give way to a violent resentment and jealousy of her aunt and cousin for their easygoing ways and close relationship from which everyone else was excluded.

Why didn't she just leave and get a place of her own? Accommodation wasn't easy to find in London but there might be more places about with so many people having fled the capital since the onset of the flying bombs. She earned a good salary, could afford a reasonable rent.

The truth of the matter was she just didn't have the courage to strike out on her own, and there was no one at the bank she knew well enough to lodge with. Alice had never been able to make friends, maybe because her parents had always discouraged it; they hadn't wanted her corrupted by the ways of modern women.

With them gone she didn't feel as though she belonged anywhere. Sometimes her isolation was so hard to bear, she found herself lowering her sights and wanting to belong with Aunt Tilly and Nina at The Willow. Pure desperation, of course, which must be curbed if she was to fulfil the plans for her future which had been drummed into her from a child.

She would marry into the same respectable lifestyle in which she had grown up. Somewhere there was a man who would take her away from this atmosphere in which she felt so incongruous. And he certainly wouldn't be the sort to be found in a public house!

Much to her annoyance, her conscience was beginning to bother her. Perhaps she shouldn't have resorted to calumny about her aunt just because she'd wanted to hurt her cousin and dent her intimidating self-assurance? Nina was sure to repeat the incident to Aunt Tilly who would probably give her notice to leave, then what would she do?

A tap at the door recalled her to the present.

'Can I come in?' asked Nina, poking her head round the door.

'Well . . . er . . . if you like,' said Alice, standing up uncertainly.

'Look, now that we've had a good old barney and cleared the air, how about both of us making an effort to get along?' suggested Nina in a conciliatory manner.

Alice was completely taken aback. She'd expected icy hostility from her cousin after the altercation. Despite herself she felt warmed. 'Well . . . I . . .' She was embarrassed and unable to respond in the way which her heart dictated.

'I know you must be having a rough time,' said Nina, who never bore grudges. 'And I'm sure you didn't mean those terrible things you said about my mother.'

'Maybe not,' mumbled Alice, staring at the floor.

'I know you don't like living here with us,' said Nina mildly, 'but I honestly think you'll be a darned sight more miserable if you move out. Even if you were to find anywhere with so many places being bombed, it would be hellishly lonely for you. So why not stop fighting us every step of the way and put up with the way things are, for the time being anyway?'

'Well . . .'

'You don't have to like us,' Nina pointed out bluntly. 'Just try not to show your dislike every single minute we're together. Mum and I aren't thick. We know how you feel about us . . . we don't need to be constantly reminded.'

When her cousin didn't reply, Nina moved closer to her with an encouraging smile. 'Come on, Alice. How about it then, eh? We can't go on like this, living in such a horrible atmosphere.'

'Why don't you just ask me to leave?' asked Alice.

'Because I don't like the idea of you walking the streets with nowhere to go. Anyway, I really think it will be better for you to stay with us. Blood is thicker than water, whether you like it or not.'

Alice chewed her lip. 'It's no good expecting me to join in pub life because I can't,' she said. 'I simply don't have it in me.'

'I'm not expecting that,' Nina assured her. 'All I ask is that you make an effort to be civil, especially to Mum. I meant what I said earlier. I'll get really stroppy if you don't treat her right in future.'

'Okay.'

'Good,' Nina raised her arms to give Alice a hug but her cousin stepped back quickly as though anticipating her action. Nina shrugged and turned away to the door. 'I've gotta get back to work now. I won't have time for that cup of tea after all.'

Outside the door, she sighed with relief. It had been worth swallowing her pride to smooth things over. She'd been shocked by her own violence just now, especially towards someone with Alice's problems. That girl was a puzzle, though, she thought, recalling how her cousin had shrunk from her attempt at an embrace. Oh, well, it takes all sorts, she told herself silently, and hurried downstairs to the bar.

Alice felt tears gush down her cheeks in a scalding tide. Trust the Dents to make her feel worse by being kind instead of giving her what she deserved and telling her to get out! It was such a relief to cry though, like warm water running over her and melting away the tension. She climbed into bed fully dressed, pulled the covers over her head, and cried herself to sleep.

News of the liberation of Paris a few days later brought crowds in to The Willow in party mood, confident that the final victory wouldn't be far behind. A version of the 'Marseillaise' was belted out, followed by 'Roll out the Barrel' and all the usual favourites, the evening culminating in a hearty knees up. The only slight dampener to the proceedings was the shortage of beer. Tilly was forced to ration everyone to one drink.

Nothing could have lowered the mood of optimism though. Even the chilling rumours of a V2 bomb shortly to be launched by Hitler paled into insignificance against the good news from across the Channel.

When everyone had gone and the bar was still and silent, tables wiped, ashtrays emptied and towels draped over the pump handles, Tilly seemed in sombre mood.

'What's the matter, Mum?' asked Nina as they made their way upstairs. 'You seem a bit quiet.'

'Mm . . . I've been thinking about yer dad,' she sighed.

'So have I. It must be all this talk about France.'

'Yeah. It's made me wonder whereabouts he is over the water,' she explained, 'and what he's doing.'

'I wonder if he's anywhere near Paris?'

'Wherever he is, I wish he would come home soon.'

'I'm sure it won't be long now.'

'I do hope not,' was her mother's wistful reply.

Chapter Four

'Word's just come down the line for us to take a ten-minute breather,' said Infantryman Baz Paxton to his mate Joe Dent one September afternoon as they crouched in the undergrowth, hidden behind a wooded area surrounding the extensive grounds of a country château.

'Thank Gawd for that,' said Joe, perching on a grassy hillock and lighting a Weight. 'I'm dying for a smoke.'

'Looks like the Krauts have scarpered,' said Baz, peering through the trees towards the building, reputed to have been used as a billet for German officers until the recent enemy retreat. 'There's not a sign of life in there anywhere.'

'We've really got 'em on the run now,' agreed Joe.

'I reckon it's all over bar the shouting,' remarked Baz, sitting beside his friend on the damp ground and lighting a cigarette.

'Could be 'ome in time for Christmas at this rate,' said Joe.

'Maybe . . . with a bit of luck.'

Despite their positive mood, they had not lost touch with the reality of the situation. The Allies were advancing swiftly but they still had to take on the heavily fortified Siegfried Line. Having swept across France and Belgium, they were now about twenty miles from the German border.

Their current mission, when they received the signal, was to storm the building in front of them to make sure it was empty before it was made into a temporary headquarters for the British Army.

Having been together all summer through some really intense fighting, the two men had become close pals despite their difference in age. Now they sat smoking in companionable silence, the earthy scent of approaching evening filling the air, pine cones and beech leaves littering the ground around them. To either side of them the other members of their platoon were talking in low voices, most taking comfort in tobacco.

'I was just thinking about Brussels,' remarked Joe.

'Yeah . . . you don't forget a thing like that,' said Baz for they had been among the British troops to liberate that city to ecstatic scenes on the streets.

'One of the few memories of war you don't wanna forget,' said Joe.

'Not 'alf,' agreed Baz.

'I wonder what my missis is doin' now?' sighed Joe, whose main topic of conversation was his wife and daughter.

'Getting ready to open that pub of yours at this time of day, I should think,' said Baz, who had heard so much about the Dent family he felt as though he knew them personally.

'Last time I heard from her she was having to open even later 'cos of the beer shortage.'

'In that case she's probably sitting down writing a letter to you,' said Baz encouragingly.

'By the time it gets through to me, the bloomin' war will be over.'

'You won't care about letters then,' grinned Baz.

'Too right I won't. I can't wait to get home to her.'

'You married blokes are all the same,' remarked Baz teasingly. 'All you wanna do is get back to your wives . . . but when you're at home with 'em you spend all your time trying to get out with your mates.'

'It's only natural for a bloke to want male company,' said Joe. 'My Tilly likes to go to the pictures with her women friends an' all, but we're always there for each other to come home to.'

'Only teasin',' said Baz.

'Marriage is a great institution, mate. You should try it.'

'Do leave off, I'm much too young for that sort o' caper.'

'I suppose you are,' agreed Joe casually. 'Mind you, you're twenty. I was married by the time I was your age.'

'More fool you,' said Baz lightly. 'You won't catch me tying myself down for years yet . . . not until I've made something of myself.'

'Oh, of course. I forgot about your plans to be a millionaire.'

'You can scoff,' retorted Baz, 'but I'll do it, mate, you just wait and see. Maybe I'll not end up as a millionaire but I'll have my own business and enough dosh to live comfortably, don't you worry. I'm not gonna be stuck in a dead end job for the rest of my life, that much I do know. If the war has done nothing else it's made me realise how precious life is. You've gotta make the most of it.'

The son of a labourer from a poor home in North London, Baz was a young man of great spirit. Tall and strong, with shandy-brown eyes and curly chestnut hair, he was a fine figure of a man. Resourceful too. Even as a schoolboy he'd had his little earners. As well as a paper and a milk round, he'd polished cars for the nobs up West, run errands, cleaned front doorsteps, even collected the money for the tallyman when he'd needed a hand.

Anything legal considered, that was his motto, no matter how degrading or hard. Had the war not forced him into a factory until his call up, he'd probably have made enough money by now to start up in some sort of pukkah business.

'How do you plan to get started?' asked Joe with genuine interest. He was very fond of this cheerful young bloke who'd shown such mettle on the battlefield. He was the sort of chap Joe would have been proud to have as a son – he would trust him with his life.

'By workin' hard to get the dough,' Baz explained. 'I'll take on anything and work day and night if necessary.'

'Married life would cramp your style, then,' said Joe. 'Wives want their man at home of a night.'

'That's why I intend to stay single,' said Baz breezily.

'Once you're burdened with that sort of responsibility you can kiss ambition goodbye.' He finished his cigarette and stubbed the dog-end into the ground. 'One day, when I'm an established businessman, I might consider it.'

'All the nice girls will be snapped up by then,' laughed Joe.

'A not-so-nice one'll do me fine.' Baz grinned, white teeth gleaming against his tanned skin, grimy and weatherbeaten now beneath his steel helmet.

'You're a case, you are,' laughed Joe. This sort of lighthearted banter relaxed them. Even though things were going so well for the Allies, there was still a lot of tension about. 'My Tilly would take to you. You must come over and meet her when we get back to Blighty.'

'Try stopping me,' said Baz.

The sergeant's voice, telling them to prepare for the signal, halted their conversation.

'Here we go again,' said Baz as they waited with rifles at the ready. 'This one'll be a doddle though, the buggers are long gone.'

When the signal came the unit poured through the trees and edged across the overgrown lawns towards the house. Tensing at the sound of a shot nearby, Baz looked up to see a sniper in a tree, peering at him through the foliage, the barrel of his gun pointing down. 'Why, you slippery bastard,' he said aloud, intercepting the other man's bullet with one of his own.

'That's him sorted, eh, Joe?' he muttered, moving on across the wet grass, nerves jangling.

Sensing that his friend was no longer beside him Baz

turned. Bile rose in his throat at what faced him. His friend was sprawled in the long grass, eyes wide and lifeless, his uniform soaked with blood across the chest.

Baz had thought he was too battle-hardened to be overly affected by death, but he was wrong. Swallowing the lump in his throat, he bent down and closed his friend's eyes before removing the dog tags from around his neck to give to the officer in charge. He knew that this was one image of war he would never, *ever*, forget.

By the time news of Joe's death finally reached The Willow it was the afternoon of Christmas Eve. All three women had finished work early that day and were at home when the telegram arrived. Nina and Tilly were adding holly and mistletoe to the crumpled, pre-war paper chains in the bars while Alice was upstairs making mince pies with such dubious makeshift ingredients as raw dates and cooked prunes.

Never had she felt more of an outsider than she did when watching her aunt and cousin take this blow together. They wept loudly and unashamedly for a long time then slipped into comforting platitudes about what a fine, brave man he was to give his life for his country.

Alice longed to tell them that she knew how bad it felt because she had been through the same thing when her parents had died. She wanted to sympathise with and comfort them. But they seemed to want only each other so she just stayed quietly on the sidelines, making tea.

As the time approached for the pub to open and they were both still deep in despair, she said, 'Shall I put a notice on the door of the pub . . . saying it will be closed tonight?'

They both stared at her incredulously, almost as though she'd suggested setting the place on fire.

'Why on earth would you do that?' asked Tilly.

'Well, because of a family bereavement, of course. I thought . . . I mean, neither of you is in any state . . .'

'My Joe would turn in his grave if we didn't open the pub on a Christmas Eve on his account,' explained Tilly. 'I'm the legal owner of The Willow now and it's my duty to run the place as he would have wanted.'

'But . . .' Alice gave up. She didn't think she would ever understand these people.

'It's our busiest night of the year,' Tilly continued, her voice still thick with emotion but very decisive. 'The punters will have been looking forward to it for weeks. I've managed to get a bit more stock in for Christmas, and some holly and mistletoe from a barrow boy. We'll not disappoint our customers.'

'Won't you find it hard to face them?' asked Alice worriedly.

'Hard but not impossible . . . business will carry on as usual,' said Tilly. She looked at the clock. 'We might be a bit late opening up though, Alice, so would you mind popping downstairs and explaining the situation to Syd when he arrives? Tell him to hold the fort till we get down there.'

'I'll give a hand tonight if it'll help,' Alice heard herself say, much to her own astonishment.

Nina only just managed to keep a grip of her emotions

when they sang 'The White Cliffs of Dover' which had been one of her father's favourites. It was almost closing time and people were mellow and relaxed. At ease in the warm and cheerful ambience they were able to forget Hitler's lethal V-bombs temporarily, as well as their disappointment that this was yet another wartime Christmas Eve.

The joyfulness of the occasion exacerbated Nina's own sadness but she was certain they had done the right thing in carrying on as normal. When they'd first received the news she'd thought she would never smile again. Opening up for business had forced her into it.

Her mother was over at the piano singing with the rest. It was her way of coping. Alice was standing near to Nina behind the bar. She was still an odd, withdrawn sort of girl for all that she had improved since the showdown back in the summer and was no longer so ill-mannered. She couldn't pull a decent pint and was far too reserved to make a good bar-maid but at least she'd made an effort down here for the first time this evening. And to be fair she'd been a great help, washing glasses and serving bottled beers. Poor old Syd seemed to be getting slower by the minute which wasn't surprising since he was well into his seventies now.

'You'd never guess how bad she must be feeling, would you?' said Alice, glancing across at her aunt.

'She's a true professional, that's why,' Nina explained.

'And you too,' said Alice. 'I don't know how you manage to look as though you're having a whale of a time when you obviously feel like hell.'

'Putting up a front is all part of the job,' said Nina.

'Anyway, it's our way of dealing with it . . . both Mum and I would crack up altogether without something to keep going for.'

'Yes, I can imagine.'

Nina gave her cousin a wry smile. 'I gather that our trade still doesn't give you the same sort of buzz?'

'Definitely not. I don't have the right sort of personality.'

'You'd soon loosen up if you did more bar work,' said Nina.

'I might pull a better pint with practice but the repartee isn't something I'm cut out for,' Alice said, adding quickly, 'and nor would I want to be.'

'To each his own,' said Nina. 'Anyway, thanks for your help this evening. It made a lot of difference on such a busy night. Poor old Syd is getting to be more of a liability than an asset these days.'

'That's all right,' said Alice. 'It was better than sitting upstairs on my own on a Christmas Eve.'

'You can go upstairs now if you like,' said Nina. 'There won't be much to do now and you must be dead on your feet, not being used to it.'

'Are you sure?'

'Positive.'

'All right then.' She didn't move away immediately. 'I'm really very sorry about your father.'

'Yes, I know you are . . . and thanks,' Nina gave her an involuntary hug. 'Merry Christmas, Alice.'

'Merry Christmas to you too,' Alice said, feeling unexpectedly moved.

* * *

Alice was still feeling emotional when she got into bed. What was happening to her? She wouldn't go so far as to say that she'd enjoyed helping out in the bar this evening, but she hadn't loathed it as much as she'd expected. In fact, it had felt rather nice to be part of a team instead of being isolated within her own little world. There was a sense of achievement in having gone through with it too, for the idea of being on show behind the bar at The Willow had been tantamount to appearing nude in the street to a woman of Alice's inhibited nature.

Now that it was over, she felt buoyant with success and warm towards her aunt and cousin. My God, she thought with a sense of shock, I must be getting to like being here, and that won't do at all. It's time I made a real effort to leave or I'll get too comfortable and end up like Nina and Aunt Tilly – a glorified barmaid.

Nina was glad to see the back of the festive season. Christmas Day was the only day of the year that The Willow didn't open for business and the time hung heavy upstairs in the flat. Only small presents were exchanged as everything worthwhile was either rationed or overpriced on the black market. Nina gave Tilly cigarettes and some scent she'd managed to get from a spiv. Alice was also given perfume with a bar of chocolate from Nina's sweet ration.

The emaciated turkey Tilly had obtained through one of the regulars brought little joy since neither Nina nor her mother felt like eating anything. However, as wasting food was one of the worst of all wartime sins, they went through the ritual of Christmas dinner with the help of a bottle of sherry they'd put by for the occasion.

Boxing Day was a blessed relief because they opened for an hour at lunchtime and the evening session was busy. On New Year's Eve they always put on some sort of entertainment. Decent pub turns were as hard to come by as everything else with so many performers away in the forces. The ones who were left were either third-rate or ancient.

However, with the assistance of an elderly female singer who warbled her way through all the wartime favourites accompanied by her partner on the accordion, the New Year of 1945 was seen in with all the usual Willow gusto.

January brought freezing weather, a coal shortage, and a scarcity of everything except V2-bombs which dropped without warning causing violent explosions and leaving nerves stretched like cheese wire.

In March, reports from abroad held the definite ring of victory when the Allies crossed the Rhine. Still wary because of past disappointments, however, people treated the news with caution, their feet kept firmly on the ground by the sobering announcement from the Minister of Food soon after that rations would probably have to be cut. The security margin of food stocks had already been shipped to the liberated countries, apparently.

By Easter, however, when the V2-bombs had subsided and street barrows were packed with daffodils and violets, a mood of optimism was rife in the shabby

London streets and every newspaper carried headlines of hope and the promise of an end, at last, to the long dark years.

People whose wartime jobs had forced them to leave town were beginning to return home. Some Londoners were even thinking about getting their houses done up, though the government's new ten-pound limit on house repairs drove them to use off-duty servicemen for some amateur decorating.

Life went on much as before at The Willow as the three women waited for peace, the beer and glass shortages continuing to make life doubly difficult. Along with the rest of London they were shocked at the death of President Roosevelt on the eve of Victory. Few people would forget his contribution to the war and the comfort of his broadcasts back in the bad days.

Closer to home that spring there was a noticeable change in Alice. She began to take more interest in her appearance and to go out in the evenings. She coyly admitted to seeing someone called Dudley but he was kept well hidden. Until one day in late-April when she asked if she could bring him home for Sunday tea.

Dudley Harding was the chief cashier at Carter and Reed, a department store in Hammersmith. He had worked in the accounts department of the firm before the war and had been made chief cashier on returning there after being invalided out of the army. The store had been short staffed and desperate for anyone with experience.

He had come into Alice's life like the answer to a

prayer via her counter at the bank where he was a customer. He was tall, fair and immaculate with pale grey eyes that seemed to Alice to shine with intelligence.

His most attractive attributes were his refined manners, his cultured accent, and his place among the bank account classes, his being respectably in the black. The instant she perceived these virtues she fell deeply in love with his status and decided that he was the man for her. He was her route back to civilised life.

Fortunately for Alice, who had neither the looks nor the personality to cope with competition, he was not particularly good looking. He was rather too pale and sickly in appearance to attract much female attention, and the chest wound that was responsible for his early return from the war caused him to stoop a little.

There was a certain presence about him, though, Alice thought, with his smart clothes and spectacles adding a dash of class to his appearance. Spurred on by her urgent desire to return to her former way of life, she set about winning his heart with flattery and friendliness.

Only when she had procured a proposal of marriage did she feel secure enough to let him meet Aunt Tilly and Nina. She swelled with pride when she introduced him because he politely handed her aunt a bunch of daffodils and said how delighted he was to meet her.

The formalities over, they started on a high tea. Tilly had opened a tin of salmon she had been saving for the Victory celebrations and they had caraway seed cake to follow. Dudley was being the perfect gentleman. Oh, yes, he knew how to behave.

'I must say, Mrs Dent, it's very good to meet you at last,' he was saying in the most charming manner. 'Alice has told me so much about you.'

How diplomatic of him to please her aunt in this way, thought Alice, because she had told him almost nothing about her home circumstances.

'That's more than she's done about you,' said Tilly with her usual candour. 'She's been very mysterious.'

Alice turned scarlet and looked most uncomfortable. 'Well . . . I . . .'

'She was just choosing her moment,' put in Nina helpfully because she could see that her cousin was squirming. 'A sensible move, in my opinion.'

Alice threw Nina a grateful look. 'Yes, it doesn't do to be too premature about these things.'

'I take it then that you're serious about each other?' said Tilly with unnerving frankness.

Alice looked as though death would be a blessed relief. 'Auntie . . .' she said in a reproving tone.

Tilly threw her a sharp look. 'Just because I'm your aunt and not your mother, doesn't mean I don't feel responsible for you, you know.'

'That's perfectly understandable, Mrs Dent,' Dudley said smoothly. 'And just to put your mind at rest, Alice has invited me here this afternoon because we have something important to tell you.'

Up went Tilly's brows. 'Oh . . . have you now?'

'Yes, I've asked Alice to marry me and she's accepted.'

'We're going up West to get a ring next weekend,' said Alice, beaming.

'Blimey, that's quick!' exclaimed Tilly involuntarily.

64

'You haven't known each other five minutes.' She narrowed her eyes shrewdly. 'I hope you're not . . .'

'What wonderful news,' intervened Nina swiftly, giving her mother a disapproving look as poor Alice changed colour yet again. 'Many congratulations to you both.'

'Yeah . . . yeah . . . of course,' said Tilly, still looking somewhat bemused.

'Have you set a date for the wedding yet?' asked Nina, smiling warmly at her cousin.

'We will as soon as we can find somewhere to live,' said Alice. 'We're going to buy a place.'

'That'll cost you a packet,' said Tilly in her forthright manner. 'Prices have rocketed with the end of the war in sight.'

'Fortunately, we should be able to afford a modest place in a decent area, Mrs Dent,' Dudley said blandly.

'Oh?'

'Yes, I earn a very good salary.'

Tilly was thoughtful for a moment, then she gave a broad smile and said, 'In that case, dears, I think a toast is in order. I've got some sherry stashed away for Victory Day. We'll have a drop o' that to celebrate.'

'So, what do you think of Alice's little bombshell?' Tilly asked later downstairs in the bar.

'I'm pleased for her, of course,' said Nina thoughtfully. 'It's what she wants . . . marriage to someone steady and reliable like Dudley.'

'What did you think of him, though?' asked Tilly.

'Well, he's certainly good husband material,' said

Nina. 'A steady job with excellent prospects . . . he's clean and well-mannered . . .'

'Yes, I know all that, but you haven't answered my question.'

Nina looked into her mother's shrewd eyes, knowing she couldn't lie to her. 'To be perfectly honest, he gave me the creeps,' she admitted. 'Ugh! I don't know what it was about him . . .'

'Mm, I know what you mean . . . he had the same effect on me.'

'Too sure of himself perhaps?' suggested Nina.

'Yeah, a bit too smooth for my liking.'

'The poor chap,' commented Nina, 'it's mean of us to judge him. He's obviously a thoroughly decent type and highly suitable for Alice.'

'Maybe we shouldn't take too much notice of first impressions.'

'Perhaps he'll grow on us.'

'I do hope so,' said Tilly. 'Anyway, I don't suppose we'll see much of them after they're married.

'Probably not. But we'll have to try to get on with him for Alice's sake when we do. It wouldn't be fair to spoil things for her,' said Nina.

'Course it wouldn't. And as long as he's good to her, that's all that matters, isn't it?' said Tilly, wishing nevertheless that she didn't feel so uneasy about her niece's intended.

Chapter Five

'Are you ready, Nina?' asked Tilly, her voice reverberating against the stone walls of the cellar.

'Yep, I'm ready.'

'Right then. One ... two ... three ... lift!' said Tilly, and the two women staggered across the room carrying a heavy crate of brown ale between them, their shoes scraping against the stone floor.

They moved alongside a row of wooden barrels raised a foot or so from the ground for convenience when tapping on a wooden horsing frame set in concrete against the whitewashed wall. Pipes attached to the barrels ran up the wall and through the rafters, carrying the beer from cellar to counter by means of a suction pump. Wooden crates of bottled beer and empties were stacked around.

It was bitterly cold down here on this January afternoon, the air musty with the smell of damp and beer-soaked wood; the thud of footsteps rattled eerily overhead as people in the street walked across the drayman's trap-door in the pavement.

Needing to take a breather, the two women set the crate down at the foot of the wooden steps that led up to the bar through a trap-door in the floor behind the counter.

'Cor blimey, Nina, we'll have muscles like navvies if we don't find a reliable man soon,' puffed Tilly. 'Old Syd might have got a bit doddery towards the end but at least he always turned up for work . . . the ones we've had since he popped off have all been worse than useless.'

'They certainly have,' agreed Nina breathlessly, 'and we can't really do without some male muscle in this job.'

'That's a fact,' tutted Tilly. 'I reckon I'll get trouble with me ticker if I have to do much more liftin' and carryin'.'

'We're bound to find someone suitable soon,' said Nina, bending over to grip the side of the crate, and grabbing the iron stair-rail with the other hand. 'In the meantime, let's get this lot upstairs. It'll soon be time to get ready to open.'

Only Nina and her mother lived at The Willow now. Alice had married Dudley last autumn and they had bought a house in Turnham Green.

Nina's job at the factory had ended with the war eight months ago and she now worked solely in the pub. Her decision to stay in the trade had delighted her mother who needed a full-time bar-maid with the resumption of normal opening hours, albeit that drink was still in short supply and they couldn't offer their customers a pre-war choice.

VE Day at The Willow had been a lively affair with everyone doing the conga along the riverbank beneath a sky lit with fireworks. Stock had run out early so they had closed the pub and Tilly, Nina and Syd had gone up West to celebrate with a crowd of regulars. Almost as though choosing his moment, old Syd had passed on peacefully in his sleep after the celebrations.

Finding a suitable replacement for him had proved surprisingly difficult. Easy enough to employ someone, with thousands of ex-servicemen looking for work, but getting a man they could rely on wasn't so simple. The first had been caught with his hand in the till, the second had been helping himself to the stock, and this latest joker had the habit of only turning up for work when he felt like it, which left Tilly and Nina doing all the heavy work.

Heaving the crate up into the bar, they got to work on the bottling up. Then they checked the glasses were clean and polished, put a fresh supply of glass cloths ready for the next batch of dirties, and hurried upstairs to smarten themselves up.

Their first customers were a couple of regulars, the Johnson brothers, who had been Thames bargees for more than forty years.

'A treble scotch and twenty Players, please,' said the elder brother, Jack, giving Tilly a wicked grin.

'A pint of bitter and five Weights is nearer the mark,' she laughed.

'That'll have to do then, won't it, love?' he said good-humouredly.

'One of these days you'll come in here and I'll actually be able to sell you what you want.'

'Gawd knows when that'll be,' said younger brother

Tom, a weatherbeaten man with wild, dark eyes and an unruly beard. 'Makes you wonder if things'll ever pick up, dunnit, with all this talk about rations being cut again?'

'It really does . . . and the wheat content in bread is gonna be reduced,' said Tilly, carefully pulling the pump handle down and holding the glass under the tap. 'They reckon our loaf will be as dark as it was back in forty-two.'

'Not much of a reward for winning the war, is it?' said Jack mournfully. 'High income tax . . . precious few jobs for our boys to come home to . . . food shortages . . . You can't even get a decent pint of beer.'

'It'll take time to put things right,' said Tilly, handing him a packet of five Weights and taking his money. 'It isn't just a British problem, there's a world food shortage.'

'The first thing we need to do in this country is get the bleedin' Socialists out,' said Tom. 'They're making a right pig's ear of it.'

'Give 'em a chance, mate,' said his brother heatedly. 'They've only been in power for six months.'

'Now, now, you two,' admonished Nina, laughingly. 'If you start on politics it'll only end in a fight.'

The brothers didn't heed her warning but continued the debate between themselves at a table as other customers came in and needed attention at the bar. Tilly had gone upstairs to get some more coppers for the till when a stranger appeared.

'A pint of bitter, please,' he said, smiling broadly at Nina.

'Certainly, sir.'

'Is your mum about, ducks?'

She eyed him quizzically, wondering how he knew who she was. He was tall with laughing brown eyes and a wide mouth that was grinning at her from under a trilby hat tilted jauntily at an angle. 'Yes, she's just popped upstairs. She won't be long.'

'Good.'

'You seem to know us,' she said enquiringly as she filled his glass.

The smiling eyes became serious. 'I've heard so much about you, I feel as though I do,' he explained. 'I was an army pal of your dad's. He carried a photo of you and your mum with him everywhere . . . you've grown up since it was taken but not so much that I can't recognise you.'

'Oh, I see.' Her smile was now wide and welcoming.

'I was with him when he died as a matter of fact.'

'I'll go and tell mum to hurry,' she said, feeling very emotional at this unexpected news.

'So how long have you been back then, Baz?' asked Tilly later on when the pub was closed and the three of them were having cocoa upstairs in the flat.

'Only a few months,' he told her. 'It's taking them forever to get everybody demobbed.'

'Months?' said Tilly in surprise.

Seeing the question in her eyes, he said sheepishly, 'I know I should have come to see you before but . . .' He paused, inhaling deeply on a cigarette. 'Well, to tell you the truth, Joe and me were best mates and I was really

71

gutted when he died. I just couldn't face talking about it.'

'What made you come today?' Tilly wanted to know.

'Conscience, I suppose,' he admitted. 'I knew I mustn't put it off any longer. I'd have been letting Joe down if I hadn't come to see you.' He looked from one to the other. 'You two were his life . . . he never stopped jabbering about you.' He gave a half smile, his eyes glazed with memory. 'I used to tell him to change the record sometimes. "Not Tilly and Nina again," I'd say.' He paused for a moment then coughed to hide his own response to this recollection. 'Anyway, I think you ought to know that he died like a hero, and it was so fast he couldn't have felt much pain.'

'How did it happen?' asked Tilly tremulously.

When he came to the end of his brief account, she was in tears.

'Oh Gawd,' he said, looking deeply concerned, 'I've upset you. Perhaps I shouldn't have come?'

'Don't be so daft.' She sniffed. 'I feel better now that I know . . . and it's so good to know that Joe was with a friend when he died.' She blew her nose. 'Your coming to see us means a lot.'

Baz threw Nina a questioning look, seeking reassurance. Having been raised in an all male household, he wasn't used to dealing with delicate feminine emotions. His mother had died when he was a lad and he'd lived with his father and younger brother. 'The last thing I wanted to do was to upset either of you.'

'Don't worry, you haven't,' Nina assured him shakily,

her own eyes brimming with tears. 'We're crying because we're so pleased to see you.'

'Oh, that's all right then,' said Baz with a kind of baffled relief. He stood up, looking at them uncertainly. 'Well, as long as you're okay, I'd better get going or I'll miss the last train back to Tottenham.'

'Oh,' cried Tilly with regret, 'can't you stay for a bite of supper with us? It's only cheese on toast but we'd love to have you.'

'Sounds nice but I don't fancy walkin' home and I can't afford to splash out on a taxi.'

'You're very welcome to stay here for tonight,' offered Tilly. 'We've a spare room since my niece left to get married and we'd enjoy having you.'

'Okay, you've talked me into it,' he said, grinning and sitting down again.

Nina offered to get the supper while her mother chatted to their guest.

'So what are you doing with yourself now you're finally demobbed?' asked Tilly when her daughter had disappeared into the kitchen.

'Nothin' regular.'

'One of the great unemployed, eh?' said Tilly with a sympathetic nod. 'Shame. But I'm sure things will perk up soon.'

'Don't worry about me, I'll never go short,' he told her.

'How come?'

'Oh . . . by doing a bit of this and that, you know,' he explained. 'I'll turn my hand to anythin' to make a few bob. House decorating . . . fetching and carrying for market traders . . . collecting for rentmen . . . van-driving. You name it, I'll do it.'

'What was your job before the army?' she asked chattily.

'I was in a factory,' he said. 'But I'm not going back to that. If I do, I'll still be clocking on when I'm forty.'

'Gonna make your fortune, are you, son?' she smiled.

'I've plans, yeah. That's why it suits me not to have a steady job . . . it would cramp my style too much.' He grinned. 'Your Joe used to take the mickey out of me somethin' terrible about my big ideas.'

Tilly was thoughtful. 'As a matter of fact, I'm looking for an amiable young fella like yourself as a barman-cum-cellarman,' she told him. 'The chap I've got at the moment is about to get his marching orders because he keeps letting me down. I need a man about the place . . . someone to do the heavy work as well as keep the punters happy.' She gave him a sharp look. 'I couldn't pay you a fortune but the money would be regular. Interested?'

'No thanks, Tilly,' he said without hesitation. 'Like I said, a steady job would tie me down. I can make more as I am now. I'm tryin' to get enough behind me to start up in proper business when things pick up in the country in general.'

'You could still do some of your sidelines if you worked for me,' she pointed out. 'And you'd make a lot of useful contacts. You get to know a lot of people working behind a bar.'

'Mm, there is that,' he said, but still sounded doubtful.

'We could make it a temporary arrangement, if you

like,' she persisted for she had taken a real liking to Baz. He was a natural for bar work with his extrovert personality and down-to-earth charm. It could be the perfect short-term solution for them both.

'Would that be fair to you, though?' he said, because he wanted to be honest with her. 'I mean, you'd go to the trouble of teaching me the job and I'd be off as soon as it suited me.'

She shrugged her shoulders. 'I accept that will happen, but at the moment I urgently need someone . . . so you'd be doing me a favour.' She eased her shoulders in a circular movement, her face creased with pain. 'Nina and I are killing ourselves doing work we're not built for.'

'Mm, I suppose you must be.'

'I'd accept the fact that it wouldn't be forever and I'd keep an eye out for someone permanent,' she assured him.

'You would?'

'Definitely.' She paused. 'All I would ask is that while you are working for me you're reliable and turn up for duty when you're supposed to, whatever sidelines you're running in your spare time.'

He smoked a cigarette thoughtfully. As well as feeling he ought to help out, he wouldn't mind some temporary pub work . . . as long as she didn't get any ideas about his being on the permanent staff.

'You could live in if you like, save travelling to and from Tottenham,' Tilly was saying.

'Looks like you've got yourself a new barman then,' Baz said.

Nina came into the room just at that moment and was told the news by a beaming Tilly.

'Welcome to The Willow,' Nina said with a devastating smile that made Baz aware of another very good reason for taking the job. She was lovely and he wanted to get to know her a lot better. 'I hope you'll be happy working here with us.'

'I'm sure I will,' he said, meeting her eyes.

You will if I have anything to do with it, she thought, for the instant she'd clapped eyes on him in the bar that evening she'd known he was the man for her.

It was Saturday night and The Willow was packed to the doors. An ex-sailor was playing the piano and the words of 'You Are My Sunshine' rose from the crowd around the piano above the general hubbub of conversation and laughter.

Each time Nina and Baz brushed past each other behind the bar, they lingered for a few seconds more. As Nina took some change from the drawer in the till, Baz's hand closed over hers.

'How about us having a night out together, Presh?' he said in low tones, the shortened version of 'precious' having become his pet name for her.

'We can't both take the same night off,' she reminded him.

'We can if we take a Monday – it's never very busy then. I'll get my brother George to stand in for me.'

'We'll mention it to Mum after we close,' she suggested.

'She'll be as good as gold about it . . . don't you fret.'

'You've got her eating out of your hand, that's why,' laughed Nina, receiving a frisson as, turning so that her back was out of view of the customers, she felt his hand slip tantalisingly over her bottom. 'She can't refuse you anything.'

'Can you?' he whispered, his mouth close to her ear.

'Don't push your luck,' she teased. 'And keep your hands to yourself or you'll have the customers talking.'

'They can't see,' he said in low tones. 'And you know you like it.'

She certainly couldn't argue with that. It was two months since Baz had come to The Willow, and it had been a period of immense happiness for them all.

The Dent household had been transformed by his chirpy presence, his sense of fun filling the place with new life. He made ordinary everyday life feel like a party despite almost every commodity being put back on wartime levels. Always ready with a smile and a joke for the customers, he had been an instant hit in the bar. Nina hadn't seen her mother looking so happy in a long time. Mealtimes became occasions of delightful badinage between the three of them.

As for Nina herself, she was experiencing joy at a more personal level. There was nothing lukewarm about her feelings for Baz; she wanted him with a ferocious passion every waking moment, and to make her happiness complete, he reciprocated. Already, she could not imagine life without him, and they would fall into each other's arms the minute they were alone.

'I'll leave you to ask Mum about us having Monday night off then,' she said, reluctantly removing his hand.

77

'There won't be a problem, I promise you.'

'There will be if we don't get on with some work, though!'

As predicted there was no trouble about their having a night out together. Since anyone within a mile of Nina and Baz could see what was going on between them, Tilly was fully aware of their love affair and thoroughly approved.

They went to the West End to see Ingrid Bergman and Cary Grant in *Notorious*, and had supper at Lyon's before getting the bus back to Hammersmith.

'I've had a lovely time . . . you've spoiled me rotten,' said Nina as they walked along the towpath under the stars, brilliant in the cold clear night.

'You're worth it.'

'What a perfect thing to say, Baz,' she said, melting.

'I mean it,' he continued earnestly. 'If I could afford it, you'd have every single thing you've ever wanted.'

'Oh, Baz, I do love you.'

'And I love you too.'

Baz was no expert on women. He'd had girlfriends but had never felt like this about anyone before. Nina fascinated him. He wanted to be with her every minute – to talk with her – to look after her – to make love to her . . .

They slipped into the shadows of some wasteland on the edge of a bomb site and fell into each other's arms.

Hooter was a canny local man of advanced years who lived on the fringes of villainy. His appellation came not from any abundance in his nasal region but from his 'nose' for what was occurring on his patch, legal or otherwise. Nothing happened on this manor that he didn't know about.

One day in April he came in to The Willow to see Baz.

'I hear you like to earn a bit o' dosh on the side,' he said, as Baz poured him a pint.

'Long as it's legal, yeah. I don't touch anythin' dodgy though.'

'I can put a steady supply of casual jobs your way . . . all strictly legit.'

'How come?'

'I've got contacts,' explained Hooter sipping his beer and resting his beady eyes on Baz. 'I know everyone worth knowing round 'ere . . . and there's always someone wanting something done.'

'There's plenty of blokes eager to earn a few quid doing it too, I reckon,' Baz pointed out.

'Not all of 'em want to get up early in the morning or get their hands dirty though,' said Hooter. 'Rumour has it you ain't afraid of either.'

'That's right.'

'So you and me could do each other a bit o' good.'

'If they're such good little earners, why don't you keep them for yourself?' enquired Baz.

'I used to when I was younger, mate,' Hooter explained, 'but I'm getting on a bit now. I'd sooner just take a percentage.'

'Ah, I guessed your percentage would come into it sooner or later,' said Baz, taking the money for the man's drink and putting it in the till.

'Naturally. I've gotta live, same as anyone else,' said Hooter.

'Course you have, mate.'

'You pay me when you get paid for the job.'

'That sounds fair enough to me, but how do you know you can trust me?'

'Tilly speaks highly of you and that's good enough for me.'

'On the subject of Tilly,' Baz said thoughtfully, 'I can't take on anything that'll interfere with my work here. I wouldn't want to let her down, you see.'

'It's up to you to make sure you don't then.'

'But that's my only condition,' said Baz. 'As far as the work is concerned, I'll consider anything legal.'

'Good. Well, like I said, I can put plenty o' work your way,' said Hooter. 'But for starters it's a market job. A mate o' mine, a fruit and veg man in Shepherd's Bush market, wants some help with his stall for a couple of weeks.'

Baz handed him his change, frowning. 'I dunno about that. I have to be on duty here for the lunchtime session.'

'That's not a problem,' explained Hooter. 'He only wants someone for a few hours early mornings . . . and I do mean early . . . to go to market for him and set up his barrow and look after it till he gets there. His missus is ill and he has to see to her and get the kids off to school of a morning before he can go to work.'

'Well, in that case, it sounds right up my street,' said Baz eagerly. This could be just the break he'd been looking for, the chance to earn some real money.

'If my mate's pleased with the way you do this job, I'll put you on to as much work as you can manage.'

'What I can't do I'll pass on to my brother,' said Baz.

'Okay. As long as he's straight and reliable,' warned Hooter.

'They don't come straighter than George,' Baz assured him.

'This could be the start of something big, George,' Baz told his brother the following afternoon over a cup of tea at the kitchen table in the shabby flat in Tottenham that George shared with their father.

'You reckon so?' said George, a stockily built man with brown curly hair and soft hazel eyes.

'Certain of it,' said Baz. 'A steady run of odd jobbing could earn me enough to get started in a proper business.'

'I'm pleased for you, mate.'

'But I need you to come in with me on it, bruv,' said Baz, ''cos I won't be able to do all the work . . . not while I've got this job at the pub.'

'Why not just take on what you can comfortably handle?' suggested George sensibly.

'No. I don't wanna turn any offers down or they might stop coming my way,' Baz explained. 'If you come in with me we'll make a good little team.'

George was doubtful; he didn't have his brother's drive and tenacity. In fact, he was a quiet, unambitious man, currently unemployed and earning a little occasional money as an amateur painter and decorator. 'I'm not sure, Baz,' he said, worried. 'You know I don't like responsibility.'

'But you won't have any,' Baz assured him. 'I'll organise everything. All you have to do is help with the work.'

'Are you sure?'

'Course I'm sure,' said Baz firmly. 'I'll have to stay on at the pub for a while because I need steady money coming in. This means I won't have as much time as you. It'll be a chance for both of us to earn some decent dough.'

'Count me in then,' said George, more amenable to the idea now he knew he could lean on his brother.

'Good man,' said Baz, giving him a friendly slap on the back.

'Will you tell Tilly about it?' asked George.

'Yeah, sure I will,' said Baz. 'Why wouldn't I? She's a good mate of mine so she'll be pleased for me. She knows how much I want to get started on my own in business. As long as it doesn't interfere with my work at the pub, she doesn't give a damn how I use my spare time.'

'That's all right then.'

'We're on our way, George,' said Baz excitedly. 'I really think we're on our way.'

Chapter Six

It was an enormous relief to Nina to have broken the news to Baz.

'You've no idea how worried I've been about telling you,' she said, as a sudden burst of sunlight changed the sludge brown waters of the Thames to olive green. They were sitting together on a quiet stretch of the riverbank one June Sunday afternoon. 'I wasn't sure how you'd take it.'

'Silly girl,' he said affectionately. 'You should have known I'd be behind you on a thing like this.'

'We'll have to get married more or less straight away though,' she told him anxiously. 'I'm turned three months, you see, having taken all this time to pluck up the courage to say anything . . . it'll begin to show soon.'

She fixed her eyes on the brilliant colours of a dragonfly, skimming across the river surface, as she waited for him to reply, tensely nibbling at a blade of grass. When he remained silent she turned to see the unmistakable signs of tension in his profile; his jaw muscles were taut, his skin a chalky white.

Fear and pride rose in equal proportions. 'Don't feel you have to marry me, Baz,' she said, trying to sound calm. 'I'll manage if you'd rather not.'

'Don't be daft, of course I want to,' he assured her. 'And I know it will have to be quick.'

'Oh . . . good.' She still sensed a certain reluctance. 'Anyway, all this has done has moved things forward a bit. I mean, we would have got married anyway, eventually.' She cleared her restricted throat. 'Wouldn't we?'

He looked into her face, her eyes translucent and awash with love for him, the red lights in her hair picked out by the sun. 'Course we would, Presh,' he said at last, slipping a reassuring arm around her shoulders and drawing her closer to him. 'No doubt about that.'

'You seem a bit tense.'

'Naturally it's come as a bit of a shock. It isn't every day I hear I'm gonna be a dad,' he explained gently, 'but it's all gonna be all right, don't you worry about a thing.'

'Thank goodness for that!' she said with immense relief, for the thought of facing this alone was a daunting prospect indeed. 'The first thing to do is to tell Mum. She'll go up the wall, of course, but even that isn't so scary with you beside me. Oh, Baz, I've been feeling so bad. You've been so wrapped up in your sidelines lately, I've hardly seen you outside work. I thought you might have gone off me.'

'Shush,' he said, stroking some stray strands of hair from her face. 'You know I'd never do that. I've been working hard to build a future for us, that's all.'

'Oh Baz,' she sighed contentedly, 'have you really?'

* * *

'I'm trapped, George,' Baz confessed to his brother a week or so later, having escaped from a household fraught with wedding talk to refresh himself in the comfort of male company. 'I don't wanna get married, I'm just not ready for it.'

'I don't see how you can get out of it now, mate,' said George in his slow drawl. 'Not unless you can persuade her to get the problem seen to. There's plenty who'll see her right if you're prepared to pay.'

'No, I don't want that, not for Nina.'

'It would solve the problem.'

Baz shook his head. 'No I couldn't let her do that,' he sighed, observing his brother across the kitchen table through a pall of cigarette smoke. 'I haven't the heart to tell her I don't want to get married. It would devastate her.'

'Surely she must have guessed?'

'Not a chance. I pretend to be as pleased as she is.'

'That doesn't seem a very sensible way to go into marriage,' said George, frowning. 'What chance will it stand if it starts off with pretence?'

Baz puffed on his cigarette, shaking his head. 'What else can I do? I just can't bear to hurt her, George, she's very special to me.'

'You're saying you love the girl then?'

'Course I love her,' he said, aghast at any suggestion to the contrary. 'I love her to bits. There's no one else for me.'

'So where's the problem then?' asked the baffled George.

'It's obvious. Marriage'll wreck my plans.'

'Why?'

''Cos I'll be tied hand and foot with a wife and kid to account to and support,' he explained gloomily. 'I need to be free to get myself off the ground, to come and go as I please. I was planning to give up the job at the pub soon and concentrate on the earners we get from Hooter, but I can't give up steady money now. Not with a wife and child to feed.'

'What exactly did you have in mind for Nina then, before this happened?' George was curious to know.

'To carry on as we were, I suppose,' said Baz. 'I'd have married her in the end but not yet . . . not now. I need time, George. Time to get some money behind me to set up in business proper. That's the time to get married, when I've something concrete under my feet.'

What George lacked in dynamism he made up for in common sense. 'Seems to me it's a clear case of having your cake and wanting it too,' he said.

'No preaching, please.'

'It has to be said, bruv, and the way I see it,' his brother said thoughtfully, 'you've two choices. You either face up to your responsibilities and make the best of things . . . or you disappear. Make a run for it.'

Nina's wedding day was the happiest of her life. It wasn't how she'd always imagined it would be, of course; there were none of the trimmings her cousin Alice had had – no church, organ or long white dress. It was a brief register office ceremony with a small reception afterwards back at The Willow. She looked lovely, though, having used all her clothing coupons on a pale green summer suit and small feathery hat.

Nothing could have spoiled the day for her, not the drenching rain nor the fact that Baz was late arriving at the register office. Not even Alice and Dudley's superior attitude. Baz made her feel like the most cherished woman in the world and her happiness was complete.

'I'm so happy, Baz,' she said, as they sat by the rainsoaked windows of the riverside hotel where they were to spend their wedding night. 'Thank you for making it such a wonderful day for me.'

'Thank *you* for marrying me,' he said with sincerity. 'I must be the luckiest bloke alive.'

This stretch of the river just outside Richmond was less commercial than where they lived, its green and gentle banks hazed with a light mist on this unseasonal summer's day. Moisture dripped off the elms and sycamores in the hotel gardens as the rain continued to fall.

'It must be costing you a fortune for us to stay here,' she said.

'Worth every penny,' he told her. 'Can't have you spending your wedding night at The Willow with your mother in the next room . . . we'll have quite enough of that in the future.'

'I shouldn't think we'll have to stay there for long, though,' said Nina in her usual positive manner. 'We'll soon be able to afford a place of our own.'

'Course we will,' he said, sharing her optimism. 'Given time we'll have everything we want . . . and more too.'

Baz was genuinely happy. Once he'd faced up to his obligations, after his talk with George, he'd realised that marriage didn't have to be the end of everything. Quite the reverse. With Nina beside him, no challenge would be too great. After all, what did he want to improve his position for except to give her and the baby a good life? He slipped his arms around her, smiling into her eyes.

'The future is going to be so good for us, Presh,' he said, holding her to him and breathing in the sweet scent of her hair. 'So very, very good.'

'Sorry I'm a bit late, Til,' puffed Baz one evening in the February of the following year as he hurried into position behind the bar, still dressed in the old clothes he used for his house decorating jobs.

'Where the hell have you been?' asked his mother-in-law, leading him to the back of the bar and pretending to be busy at the till so that they could talk without being overheard. 'We needed a new barrel put on and some crates brought up from the cellar.'

'I'll do it right away.'

'You're too late, mate,' she hissed. 'I had to ask one of the regulars to help me. Nina's busy with the baby. I had to leave the bar unattended.'

'Not many in tonight, though, is there?' he pointed out hopefully. 'The freezing weather is keeping 'em at home.'

'Don't try and wriggle out of it that way,' she warned him. 'I pay you to be here in time to do everythin' that needs doing in the cellar before we open, as far as that's possible. I don't expect to have to do your work myself.'

'Sorry, Til,' he said again. 'I wanted to finish the painting job I was doing tonight. I was so near the end I didn't want to have to go back tomorrow.'

'I thought you were collecting rents for someone.'

'That was last week,' he explained. 'Jack of all trades, me.'

'That's not what I've been callin' you this last hour or so!'

'I'm really sorry, Til,' he repeated with feeling.

'Sorry isn't good enough, Baz,' she informed him. 'I told you when I took you on that I don't mind what you do in your spare time as long as you're on time for duty here. It leaves me right in the cart when you're late. Nina helps me out when she can but the baby is taking all her time at the moment – naturally. He isn't two months old yet.'

'It won't happen again, Til, I promise,' he said.

'You said the same thing last week and the week before,' she admonished forcefully. 'You're letting this so-called spare time work rule your life . . . and mine.'

'I need the extra money.'

'You need the regular money that I pay you an' all,' she said.

'What's that supposed to mean?'

She turned to him and looked deep into his eyes. 'Look, son, I know how hard you're working to make something of yourself and I admire you for it, but I'm trying to run a business here. I can't do that efficiently with you constantly letting me down.'

'What else can I say but sorry?'

'We're pals, you and me, Baz,' she persisted because she wanted to make him understand the gravity of the situation. 'And I think the world of you. But I've gotta make a stand. I mean, look at it from my point of view. If you don't pull your weight here, I shall have to replace you. I need someone I can rely on.'

'Okay, Til, point taken,' he agreed. 'I'll not let it happen again.'

'Righto, Baz. We'll leave it at that for the moment,' she said. 'Now, for Gawd's sake go and smarten yourself up. Those clothes you've got on are enough to put the punters off their beer.'

When Baz climbed the stairs much later on, after he'd finished work, he could hear the familiar sound of the baby screaming. Did all babies cry as much? he wondered. He couldn't remember the last time he'd had a decent night's sleep.

He was frozen to the bone and exhausted as his crippling work schedule took its toll. If he wasn't working in the pub he was distempering, collecting, standing in for some market stall holder. He'd even worked all night painting the inside of a factory for the owner while the place was empty. Still, at least he had transport now; only a battered old van but it meant he could get about without relying on London Transport. Petrol rationing was still a bit of a nuisance but with care he usually managed to make his coupons last.

Nina was sitting in an armchair in their living-room feeding the baby when he went in. Wearing a red woollen dressing gown which clashed with her hair, she looked pale and strained. The room, which had once been Baz's bedroom, was cold and damp, the fire hidden from view by a fireguard strewn with steaming nappies. Nina's room had become the marital bedroom.

"Ello, Presh,' he said, kissing the top of her head and feeling her stiffen against him.

'Hello,' she said icily.

'Anything the matter?' he asked, vaguely remembering that she'd been a bit offhand earlier when he'd rushed upstairs to get changed.

'No,' she said in a tone to indicate the opposite. 'Is there any reason why there should be?'

'Not that I know of, but you're obviously in a lousy mood,' he said, wondering how this sullen, lacklustre woman could be the same effervescent girl he had married.

She looked up at him, her eyes hot with tears. 'Is it any wonder I'm in a mood, with you buggering off and leaving my mother to do the work she pays you for?'

'Oh, she told you.'

'She didn't have to,' she snapped. 'I went downstairs to find out where you were. When you hadn't appeared up here I thought you might have come back home and gone straight to work or something. And I found Mum doing her nut because you hadn't turned up for duty again.'

'I was only an hour or so late,' he said lamely.

'Only an hour or so?' she shouted. 'How much more irresponsible can you get?'

'I'm not being irresponsible,' he insisted, sinking wearily into an armchair on the other side of the hearth. 'Just the opposite in fact. Everything I do is for us . . . you, me and Joey . . . so that we can have a decent life in the future.'

'A decent life?' she shrieked, hating the person she had become but driven on by her husband's inexorable refusal to face facts. Her new responsibilities weighed heavily upon her. Parenthood was a serious business requiring a mature attitude. Why couldn't Baz accept it as she had had to? 'We'll have no life at all if you don't stop messing Mum around. She'll be forced to take on someone else and she can't afford to pay two of you. Then where will your precious sidelines get us, eh? Can they keep us . . . can they?'

'Well, not fully. Not quite yet,' he was forced to admit. 'Just give me a bit more time.'

'Time won't put food in our stomachs or clothes on our backs if Mum has to sack you,' she said. 'I'll not sponge off her, Baz. She's having enough trouble making the pub pay while everything is still in such short supply.'

He was shocked at her suggestion. 'Sponging off anyone isn't my style and you know it.'

'All right, maybe I do know that,' she conceded. 'But you are gonna have to change your ways. I don't want to live with my mother forever. I want a place of our own. We'll never get that if you lose your regular money.'

'We'll get a place, don't worry,' he said emphatically. 'Better than you've ever imagined an' all.'

'An ordinary place will do for me,' she told him.

'I want the best for you.'

'You're a dreamer, Baz,' she said in exasperation. 'And that was all very well when you were single. But things are different now you've a child to keep. You're a father, it's time to grow up.'

'They're more than just dreams,' he reminded her.

'Ambitions then.' Her tone softened, becoming conciliatory. 'There's nothing wrong with having ambition, Baz, it's very commendable. But you have to be realistic too. Having a job at the pub and doing the sidelines just isn't working out, so something will have to go. And we both know what that must be.'

'I'll take on fewer odd jobs,' he suggested.

'That won't do any good,' she said grimly. 'You'll still get too involved with them and let your work at the pub suffer. No, Baz, the sidelines must go altogether.'

'But if I give them up now, I'll spend the rest of my life as a barman,' he said miserably.

'And what's so terrible about that? Anyway, you're hardly just a barman, are you?' she reminded him brusquely. 'You're the son-in-law of The Willow, remember. Mum will retire one day . . .'

'And I get to run the place on the strength of being married to the boss's daughter?' he said sarcastically. 'Well, thanks a bunch.'

'Other men wouldn't say no.'

'I'm not other men,' he interrupted fiercely. 'I'm me, Baz Paxton. I want to make my own way . . . to provide for you and Joey in my own way.'

'Oh, come on, Baz,' she said in a cynical tone, 'at least be honest about it. This isn't about Joey and me.' She lifted the snuffling child on to her shoulder and gently patted his back. 'It isn't even about money. It's about you and your ego – your selfish craving to be a bigshot.'

'I'll make some cocoa,' he said because her accusation was something he had never considered and he didn't want to face the possibility that she could be right.

'Go on, walk away from the argument,' she yelled, becoming almost hysterical. 'But the problem won't go away. If you love me and Joey and care anything at all about our marriage, you're going to have to face up to reality. And that means giving up your odd jobbing and settling down to your real work in the pub.'

He stopped at the door, the truth refusing to be suppressed any longer. She couldn't possibly know the enormity of what she was asking him to do. It was like having the spirit and energy physically beaten out of him. But now he reluctantly accepted the fact that it was something he must do. His love for her gave him no choice.

'All right, you win,' he said in a subdued manner. 'I'll not take on any more sidelines.'

Chapter Seven

'Another cup of tea, Nina?' invited Alice.

'Yes, please,' she replied, sitting back and watching her cousin pour from a china pot into a wafer-thin cup.

'So how are things at The Willow?' asked Alice.

'Fine.'

'How's Baz?'

'He's okay. How's Dudley?'

'Marvellous. Did I tell you he's had another rise in salary?'

'Several times.'

'Oh.' She turned her attention to seven-month-old Joey who was sitting on his mother's lap. 'He's really coming on, isn't he?'

'He certainly is,' agreed Nina, kissing his head. 'He's a real poppet.'

They were in Alice's sitting room, neat and tasteful with a piano and a gold-coloured suite standing on best Axminster surrounded by polished lino. Since Dudley's fat salary meant they could afford to pay black market prices, they didn't have too much trouble in finding nice things.

'Must be very awkward for you,' said Alice with a

syrupy smile as she handed Nina her tea.

'Awkward?' she said in an enquiring manner.

'With all of you being crowded together at your mother's place.'

'We manage.'

'You'd like a place of your own though, I expect,' said Alice complacently.

'No, of course not,' snapped Nina sarcastically, throwing her cousin a withering look. 'I just love tripping over my mother every time I use the kitchen. And I'm thrilled to bits not to have any privacy or independence.' She paused, fighting against tears. 'And do you know the thing I enjoy most of all?'

'Er . . . no,' said Alice, wary of her cousin in this mood.

'Being invited to your place for tea so that you can rub my nose in it and bore me to death about your lovely house . . . your new furniture . . . your *wonderfully* successful husband!'

Alice turned scarlet. 'I didn't meant to upset you.'

'Oh, come on. I can't believe you're that dim.'

'What am I supposed to do – pretend poverty?'

'Don't be ridiculous,' said Nina hotly.

'Well then . . .'

'There is a middle ground, you know. Can't you see that I'm sick to death of having your acquisitions shoved down my throat? How well things are going for you. How brilliant Dudley is at his job. Baz might not be in the same league financially but at least I married him for love.'

'Meaning that I didn't marry Dudley for that reason?'

'You'd not have given him a second glance if he'd come to empty your dustbin,' Nina stated categorically.

'You've no proof of that,' objected Alice. 'Anyway, so what if it's true? Like is attracted to like, it's a fact of life.'

'Which explains why you and I don't get along too well, doesn't it?' said Nina, standing up with the baby. 'And right now I can do without the company of someone with whom I have nothing in common apart from a distant genetic connection.'

'Nina, don't be like that.'

'Cheerio, Alice. See you when I'm in a more patient mood. Don't bother to see me out.'

Nina left her cousin staring miserably at her feet. Slamming the front door, she put Joey in his pram and marched down the path, her nerves jangling. Halfway down the avenue, she stopped, recognising her own selfishness with shame. Alice was tactless and insensitive; at times she was about as much fun as tight shoes on a long walk with her endless bragging. But she didn't deserve to bear the full brunt of Nina's personal wretchedness. It wasn't Alice's fault that her cousin's marriage was falling apart and Nina didn't seem able to put things right.

Hurrying back to the house, she rang the doorbell.

'Sorry I blew my top, love,' she said when a bewildered Alice answered the door. 'Put it down to the time of the month. Er . . . do you think I could come in and have that cup of tea after all?'

'Course you can,' said Alice, with a puzzled smile.

* * *

Dudley Harding was a very methodical man who ran his entire life to a strict routine. He left home at seven-thirty in the morning and arrived home at seven at night, except Fridays and Saturdays when he was later. Each week of the Hardings' lives was identical and he didn't like the rhythm upset. He insisted on the same food on the same day each week: cold meat on Mondays, fish on Friday, meat pie on Wednesday, and so on. A sudden change of menu could have him sulking for days so Alice made sure it never happened.

They made love every Saturday night, after a concert or a theatre visit, regardless of their mood. This schedule was altered only if either was ill. Should Alice feel the need at any other time, her impulses were suppressed to the point of denying their existence, since she had been raised to believe such feelings unseemly in a decent woman.

She considered her life with Dudley to be completely satisfactory. She shared his need for an orderly life – it gave her back the security she had grown up in. As a provider he couldn't be faulted. They never went without anything through lack of funds. Whilst not a man requiring a hectic social life, most weeknights they stayed home and listened to the wireless or read books, Dudley enjoyed genteel, cultural pastimes such as the well-reviewed plays and classical concerts to which he and Alice went regularly.

As his wife, she didn't consider it her place to know anything more than the basic details of his work and wouldn't dream of asking what his salary was. He earned enough for them to live to a high standard and gave her whatever cash she needed; that was quite enough for her.

On the evening of her cousin's outburst, as she and Dudley relaxed in their living room and she was meditating on having made such a good marriage, she found herself wondering why she still felt compelled to impress her cousin – constantly to prove herself equal.

Why was it that Nina, who was married to a loud-mouthed chancer who didn't have two ha'pennies to rub together, still had the ability to make Alice feel inferior? How could it be that Nina, who had nothing in comparison to Alice, seemed to have everything?

It occurred to her that her craving for respect from her aunt and cousin was more than mere snobbery; she wanted them to be proud of her. Why did they have such peculiar values that they did not recognise how well she had done for herself?

Could it be jealousy perhaps? After all, she had a comfortable life and financial security while they worked long and unsocial hours for a meagre living in that ghastly pub of theirs.

She was recalled to the present by her husband's voice.

'It's five minutes past ten, Alice dear,' he told her, putting down his newspaper on his lap, his cool grey eyes resting on her critically.

'Why, so it is,' she said, glancing at the polished oak clock on the mantelpiece. 'I'm sorry, dear. I'll go and make the supper at once.'

'Well, we do usually have it at ten on the dot of a weeknight, don't we?' he reminded her in a mildly admonishing tone. 'You know that's when I like it.'

'Yes, of course,' she said, rising. 'I must have forgotten the time, I really don't know why.'

She did though . . . she was deeply preoccupied with a truth that refused to be stifled even as she put the milk on the gas-stove to boil and sawed into a loaf of the awful dark bread they were forced to eat these days. It wasn't jealousy that prevented Nina and Aunt Tilly from being overly impressed by her achievements. Neither of them was capable of such a negative emotion. The reason they were not envious of her, or anyone else for that matter, was because they were infuriatingly self-sufficient. They didn't need her as she needed them.

This realisation both annoyed and astonished her. It was irritating to discover that even after making an upward move from The Willow, she was still unable to cut herself off from them; she still felt driven to pursue the close friendship with them which continued to elude her.

She was still mulling over the situation when she went into the other room with the supper tray.

'Did you have anyone interesting in tonight?' asked Nina that same evening over cheese sandwiches and cocoa in Tilly's living room after Baz and Tilly had finished work downstairs.

'No,' said Baz dully.

'Just the regulars,' said Tilly. 'Old Albert nearly had a fit when he came in because someone else was sitting in his chair. He was late and we didn't think he was coming in.' She smiled at the memory. 'I'll have to pin a bloomin' great Reserved notice on that chair.'

'I miss being down there on a regular basis,' said Nina who at the moment only helped out when they were really busy, while Joey was still taking up so much of her time. She did it for love rather than money. Her mother could only afford a token payment with stock still not being back to normal, and this reflecting in the takings.

'As Joey gets bigger you might feel like coming back a few evenings a week regular when he's in bed,' said Tilly. 'I'll be able to afford to pay you a proper wage once stock levels improve and trade picks up.'

'That would be a great help,' remarked Nina chattily. 'Money doesn't go anywhere when you've got a baby . . . even his little rompers cost the earth.'

'That's if you're lucky enough to find anything decent in the shops to buy,' remarked Tilly.

'Mm. Two years since the end of the war and rations are still being cut,' complained Nina.

'We still have to queue for every bloomin' thing,' said her mother.

Nina finished her cocoa and turned to her husband. 'What do you think about my working regular evenings when trade picks up, Baz?'

'It's up to you,' he said in an insouciant manner.

'We could certainly do with the extra cash,' she pointed out.

'As long as Joey won't suffer by it.'

'That goes without saying. I'll only be downstairs.'

'There you are then.'

'You don't seem very interested.'

'You do what you like,' he said coldly. 'I would never stop anyone doing that.'

'Meaning that I would?'

'If the cap fits . . .'

Resentment flared as they exchanged icy glares.

'I'm going to bed,' said Baz.

'You've not finished your sandwich,' said Tilly in concern.

'I don't want it,' he said, and marched from the room without another word.

A few minutes later, Nina followed.

With a worried sigh, Tilly took the uneaten sandwiches to the kitchen and covered them with a cloth. Food was too short to waste so much as a crust of bread.

Baz was unbuttoning his shirt, his fingers trembling from the effect of the quarrel, when his wife charged into the room, her eyes blazing.

'You never waste an opportunity, do you?' she accused.

'What are you on about?'

'You know very well what I mean,' she replied, sick with misery at yet another fiery altercation. 'You never miss a chance to remind me that I stopped you doing your odd jobbing.'

'I wasn't reminding you of that . . . not especially.'

'Yes, you were. And it wasn't me that stopped you, it was circumstances,' she said through clenched teeth.

'At least you didn't have to worry about the price of

Joey's clothes when I was doing it,' he pointed out.

'I would have done, though, if you'd kept it up and lost your steady money – and you know it!'

'I know nothing of the sort,' he retorted. 'All I know is that you keep reminding me what a lousy provider I am. How expensive everything is . . .'

'That was just conversation, I wasn't getting at you.'

'And I wasn't getting at you when I said I wouldn't stop you doing what you wanted,' he claimed.

'Yes, you were.'

'No, I wasn't, you're paranoid. The slightest thing and you're having a go at me.'

'Huh! Hark who's talking. *You're* always going on at *me*.'

Joey started to cry.

'Now you've woken the baby,' she said, close to tears.

'Go on, blame me for that, too. You blame me for everything else.'

'Who's being paranoid now?'

She lifted Joey from his cot beside their bed and tried to pacify him by rocking him gently in her arms. But he wouldn't be mollified.

'I'll have to go and make him a bottle,' she said. 'He doesn't usually have one at this time but it might settle him.'

'Here, give him to me. I'll have him while you do it,' said Baz.

Pacing the bedroom floor with his son in his arms, Baz was close to tears, the pain of hurting his wife a physical ache in the pit of his stomach. Why did he keep doing it? Why didn't he try to put things right instead of sniping back at her when she gave him a hard time? It wasn't her fault his dreams had come to nothing. He was responsible for what had happened.

The baby's screams softened into little snuffles. 'I wouldn't be without you for all the money in the world, little fella,' he said softly, kissing Joey's head and breathing in his sweet milky scent. 'It's just that . . . well . . . it would have been nice to have been able to give you a better start in life, that's all.'

When Nina returned with the bottle, the baby was fast asleep in his cot and Baz was in bed.

'He's gone off, out like a light,' he whispered.

'That's good,' she replied wearily. 'It couldn't have been a bottle he wanted then.'

'Attention, I reckon.'

'Yeah, probably.'

'I'm sorry I said all those horrible things earlier,' he said, drawing her to him as she got into bed.

'Me too.'

'Friends again then?'

'Yeah.'

But somehow a barrier remained between them which neither seemed able to dispel. They went to sleep back-to-back, each feeling desperate and hardly able to believe that this terrible thing was happening to them.

Tilly couldn't get to sleep. Her nerves were in ribbons and her head was pounding with the memory of the quarrel she'd heard from the other bedroom earlier. To have seen the young couple on their wedding day, no one could have believed that things would get so bad between them.

They'd been so right for each other; even Nina's untimely pregnancy hadn't seemed to matter. Love's young dream they'd been then: radiant, caring, sensitive to each other's needs. Now they were like two fighting cats, watching each other and waiting for the opportunity to inflict the next wound.

The saddest thing of all was knowing that the basic ingredient was still there, despite everything. You could feel it like electricity when they were both present in a room. Admittedly, it manifested itself more as hatred than love but at least it hadn't been destroyed. Neither had their relationship paled into tired indifference as it might have without the passion that had attracted them to each other in the first place.

She was positive the problem stemmed from Baz's having to settle for less than he'd hoped for. He felt thwarted and inadequate as a provider while Nina was feeling guilty because she had squashed his dreams, even though she would never admit it. It was a vicious circle. Had circumstances allowed Baz to prove himself before he was burdened with the responsibility of marriage, things would have been a whole lot different. But it hadn't happened that way and he had to accept it.

There was nothing Tilly wouldn't do to help them save their marriage but sadly she accepted the fact that there wasn't anything anyone could do except the couple themselves.

Turning over on to her side, she prayed that they

would find a way through their problems for she had seldom seen two people with stronger feelings for each other.

Chapter Eight

The quarrel began the same as all the others; a seemingly innocuous comment hit a raw nerve and set them at each other's throats. This time, however, things got out of control.

Six months had passed – six months of tacit resentment interspersed with savage scenes like the one that erupted that bitter January afternoon.

It was Sunday. Tilly had taken advantage of the fact that they opened later in the evening and gone to visit her friend Hilda, the landlady of The Five Bells in Fulham whom she knew from attending Licensed Victuallers meetings. Nina and Baz were alone in the flat except for Joey, now just turned a year old and able to totter about.

Nina was busy in the kitchen preparing tea when Baz appeared in search of matches to light a cigarette.

'More money going up in smoke,' she snapped, astonishing herself with the remark for she had no real objection to Baz's smoking.

'Even begrudge me a smoke now, do you?' he said icily. 'Gor blimey, I get little enough pleasure.'

'So do I . . . and whose fault is that?' she retorted,

swept along by a violent need to hurt him for all the pain she was feeling.

'Oh, mine, of course,' he said sarcastically. 'Isn't everything that's wrong with the world my fault?'

'You said it.'

'It's a wonder I haven't turned to drink, living with you, you miserable bitch.'

'And who's made me that way, eh?' she countered, bordering on hysteria as the strain of the last few months took its toll on her nervous system. 'You have. With your moodiness, your insinuations.'

'Oh, shut up!'

The kettle she was filling under the tap was slammed down on to the wooden draining board. She swung round and lunged at him, clawing his face with her fingernails. 'I hate you . . . I hate you!'

'Why, you spiteful cow!' rasped Baz, touching his smarting face and seeing blood on his fingers. 'You're out of your tree . . . round the bend . . . mental!'

'Well, if I am, you've driven me to it,' she said, trembling now and sobbing loudly, terrified of what was happening to her.

'That's right, blame me. Blame me for every bloody thing!'

'I just can't take any more, Baz . . . I can't,' she wept, going for him again and pummelling his chest with her fists. 'No more . . . no more . . . no more.'

An ear-splitting shriek brought them both to silence. Turning, they saw Joey standing in the doorway, scarlet with howling, still only a baby but old enough to be afraid of what was going on around him.

With a flash of heightened perception, Baz saw his marriage illuminated in that scene, almost as though he was viewing it from the outside. The fear on his son's face registered with agonising clarity as did the anguish in his wife's eyes and the blood on his own hands. He knew they had come to the end of the road . . . none of them could take any more.

In the early hours of the next morning, while everyone was sleeping, he threw some things into a holdall and crept quietly down the stairs and out of the private door. He left two letters on the kitchen table, one addressed to his wife, the other to his mother-in-law.

Baz was always up before Nina in the mornings so she didn't find it unusual to wake up and find herself alone. When there was no sign of him in the flat when she shuffled down to the kitchen, she assumed he was doing something downstairs in the bar or the cellar. She had made some tea and was about to take a cup up to her mother when she noticed the letters on the table. With a knot of fear in her stomach, she opened the envelope bearing her name.

Darling Nina
Before we destroy each other completely, and ruin Joey's life into the bargain, I am leaving. I'm not proud of what I'm about to do but I don't know what other course to take. My staying around certainly isn't doing anyone any good. I still love you and don't want to keep hurting you. I just can't cope with the situation between us.

Somewhere along the line we seem to have lost our way. It's all my fault, I know, perhaps I just wasn't ready for marriage. I'm so very sorry.

I enclose some money and will send regular payments, so you need have no worry about how you are going to support yourself and Joey. I know I've been a dead loss as a husband but I won't let you down over this. It will probably be hard for you to believe this, but I really do love you.

Baz.

Her heart pounded horribly, her skin was suffused with icy perspiration. She rushed to the bathroom and was violently sick. The pain of the last terrible months with Baz was as nothing compared to the agony of losing him. Some thread of normality snapped inside her, blinding her to everything but her own desperation. She tore into her mother's bedroom, quivering all over and close to hysteria.

'He's gone, Mum,' she wept, shaking the sleeping woman by the shoulders and thrusting the letter into her face, her personal trauma rendering her insensitive.

'Gone . . . who's gone?' muttered Tilly sleepily.

'Baz . . . he's left me and Joey.'

'Don't be daft, Baz wouldn't do a thing like that,' she said, sitting up in bed in bewilderment.

'He has . . . look at this!'

Tilly yawned and rubbed her eyes, then read the letter. 'Oh my Gawd,' she muttered, swinging out of bed and dragging on her dressing gown. 'The fool . . . the silly bloody fool!'

'I have to go and find him, Mum,' gasped Nina, grey-faced and trembling. 'Joey's asleep in his cot. Will you look after him till I get back?'

'Course I will, love. But did you ought to go after him?' said Tilly, trying to gather her wits for she was still not fully awake. 'I mean, he could be anywhere by now.'

'I have to get him back,' Nina sobbed, her voice guttural with emotion.

'Calm down,' said Tilly, suddenly alert to her daughter's mental state. 'You're not going anywhere until you've calmed down.'

'I must.'

'Nina love, no. Don't go . . .'

But she was already tearing down the stairs and out into the freezing day in her dressing gown and slippers. With tears streaming down her face, she ran wildly through the rime-covered streets, her voice echoing in the frosty air as she cried out Baz's name. People on their way to work turned and stared at this poor deranged creature; some giggled with embarrassment, others shook their heads with pity.

Around the Broadway and along King Street she sobbed his name, her voice strangled with weeping. Covering the same ground over and over again, she wandered the backstreets.

Then, near the station, she saw him . . . striding along in his dark overcoat and trilby hat. Breathless, and with a stitch stabbing into her side, she ran to catch him up, grabbing him from the back.

'Oh, Baz, thank God I've found you,' she gasped. 'Thank God!'

'Ere, what's going on?' said the man, turning to reveal that the only way in which he resembled Baz was in the clothes he was wearing. 'What's your game? I'm a respectable married man?'

'Sorry . . . I thought you were someone else,' she mumbled, hurrying on her way.

She never remembered walking to the riverside; she was barely aware of being there by the bombed site of the lead mills, staring into the dark, choppy waters. Nor did she feel the piercing wind blowing through her dressing gown, or the gentle hand on her arm.

'Come on, ducks,' said old Albert kindly. 'You come along with me. Let's get you 'ome to The Willow. You'll catch your death out here.'

When Nina woke she felt heavy and dull-witted. She knew something was wrong but what it was escaped her for a moment. Then it all flooded back and she wanted to cry out with pain. But she felt too slow, too tired. Hardly able to move a muscle.

The room was dark and the curtains were drawn. What time of day was it? What was going on? She called her mother who appeared almost immediately and switched on the light.

'Ah, you're awake,' she said.

'Where's Joey?' was Nina's first question.

'Asleep in my bed. I didn't want him to disturb you.'

'What time is it?'

'Just turned seven.'

'Shouldn't you be downstairs?'

'Hilda's lent me one of her barmen to stand in for a

couple of hours. Being a Monday it isn't all that busy.'

'What's happened to me, Mum? I feel peculiar.'

'The doctor gave you something to knock you out.'

'Oh, yes . . . I vaguely remember him coming.'

'I had to call him in, love,' explained Tilly, sitting by the bed and taking her daughter's hand. 'You weren't yourself at all when Albert brought you home, I was afraid you might go off again.'

'Sorry for worrying you,' said Nina, vaguely recalling her local marathon. 'I shouldn't have taken off like that . . . I didn't know what I was doing.'

'Are you feeling any better now?' asked Tilly.

Nina gave her a wry look. 'I don't think I'll ever feel any better.'

'No, I don't suppose you do at this moment.'

'What an idiot I was, though, rushing round the streets looking for him,' she said, her hysteria having turned to aching bitterness. 'It wouldn't have done any good if I had found him, would it? He doesn't want me.'

'It's marriage he doesn't want, I think,' said Tilly.

'Me . . . marriage . . . what's the difference?' said Nina wearily. 'My God, what a hypocrite he turned out to be, eh? All that rubbish in the letter about still loving me.'

'Mm.'

'You don't walk out on someone you love, do you, Mum?' she said, her voice slowed by the drugs. 'The least he could have done was to spare me the humiliation of trying to justify his actions.'

'I'll get you a cup of tea, love,' said Tilly, who could cheerfully have murdered Baz Paxton at that moment but deemed it wise not to say so.

'Thanks, Mum,' said Nina, starting to cry again.

In the kitchen, Tilly re-read the letter that had been addressed to her.

> Dear Til,
> Sorry to leave you in the lurch. I've brought enough crates up from the cellar to see you all right for the next few days and left everything in good order down there. I hope you don't have too much trouble finding a replacement for me. I know you'll hate me for going off like this but I can't see any other way. Look after Nina and Joey for me.
>   Baz.

Tilly's fury knew no bounds. She put the letter in her apron pocket and poured Nina's tea. How dare Baz Paxton walk out on his responsibilities and calmly issue her with instructions to look after them for him! She was bitterly disappointed in the man for whom she had felt true affection – the man she had begun to think of as a son.

He'll wish he'd never been born if I ever come across him again, she thought, her hand trembling slightly as she took a cup of tea in to Nina.

Six months later Tilly did come across Baz again. He telephoned, asking her to meet him outside Lyon's Corner House at Marble Arch.

'You've got a bloody cheek!' she said after he'd led her inside and ordered afternoon tea.

'I know.'

'I'm surprised you dare face me,' she ranted, 'since you've proved yourself to be such a coward.'

'You've every right to be cross.'

'Cross ain't the word for how I feel about you, mate,' she expostulated. 'I'm bloody furious!'

'Yes, I expect you are.'

'Have you any idea what you've done to my daughter. Have you?' she raved.

'Well, I . . .'

'You almost sent her mental, that's what you did,' she cut in. 'My Nina has been on the verge of a nervous breakdown.'

He chewed his lip, his eyes full of remorse. 'Oh, dear. She took it really bad, then?'

'How the hell did you expect her to take it?' exploded Tilly. 'She was broken-hearted, Baz. It made her ill. In fact it's been touch and go with her this last six months, though she's done her best to hide it.'

'I see.'

'You don't see at all,' she rasped. 'That girl's been through hell.'

'And now?'

'Now I think she might have turned the corner.'

'Thank God,' he said.

'It's certainly no thanks to you,' she told him.

'You've every right to be upset,' he said sheepishly. 'I know I've done a terrible thing. I thought it was best for both of us.'

She sipped her tea and smoked furiously, the teacakes remaining untouched on her plate. 'I hope you haven't asked me here because you want me to help you get back with her, 'cos I won't do it. I won't have her upset. You've made your bed, you lie on it.'

'That isn't the reason I asked you to meet me,' he informed her in a subdued tone.

'Oh?' She observed him over the rim of her cup, seeing him properly for the first time since she'd been here and realising that her daughter wasn't the only one to have suffered. He had lost weight and gained worry lines around his eyes which no longer held their old sparkle.

'I want Nina back,' he explained gravely. 'I won't pretend I don't. I miss her something awful. As bad as things got between us, she'll always be the only woman for me.' He drank his tea, meeting Tilly's eyes. 'But I'm not going to ask her to have me back.'

'She wouldn't, mate,' Tilly retaliated, 'so don't kid yourself.'

He flinched as her remark hit home. 'That's one thing I'm not doing, Til, kidding myself.'

'Just as well.'

'Look, can you stop blasting off at me just for a minute and hear what I have to say,' he begged. 'Please?'

She inhaled on her cigarette. 'All right, go on then.'

'I'm certain that things would only have got worse if I'd stayed, and they'd be as bad again if I were to go back,' he explained. 'Because I'd always have this sense of frustration at not being able to prove myself.'

'You shouldn't have been so free and easy with your pleasure if you weren't prepared for the consequences, should you?' she snapped predictably.

'I'm surprised to hear an intelligent woman like you stating the obvious,' he said. 'Don't you think I haven't told myself that a million times over? Anyway, with respect, I didn't actually have to tie Nina down, you know.'

'No,' sighed Tilly. 'I don't suppose you did.'

'What use are recriminations to any of us now?' he asked rhetorically. 'Nina and Joey are better off without me so that's the way it has to be. I accept that. Apart from sending money, I'll stay out of their lives altogether.'

'So, what do you want of me then?' asked Tilly.

'I want you to keep me informed about them,' he explained.

'Ooh, I dunno about that, Baz. If you want to know about them, Nina is the one you should approach.'

'And upset her all over again? Not likely,' he said. 'We both need a clean break which is why I never put a letter in with the money I send every month. I think it will be easier for us both if she doesn't know where I am.'

'At least you're regular with the money, I'll say that much for you,' conceded Tilly.

'The least I can do.'

'The *very* least,' she said with grim emphasis.

'Maybe later on,' he continued, 'when Nina and I are both stronger, we can meet now and then. Perhaps I can get to know Joey a little. But not yet, it's still too delicate. So if I give you my address, could you let me know if anything happens that you think I should know about? Not everyday matters, of course. Just if she's ever in trouble at any time and you think I might be able to help.'

'My name will be mud with Nina if she ever finds out I'm collaborating with the enemy,' Tilly said, unable to stifle a grin and realising that she was still very fond of Baz, despite what he'd done.

'In that case we'll have to make sure she knows nothing about it.' He handed her a slip of paper. 'This is where you'll find me. I'm staying with George and Dad at the moment but I'll be moving on once I can afford a place of my own. I'll ring you with any change of address.'

'But . . .'

'Don't worry, I'll put the phone down if Nina answers,' he assured her. 'And I won't write letters because Nina will recognise my writing on the envelope.'

'All right, son, I'll do it,' agreed Tilly with a heavy sigh.

He smiled for the first time but, to Tilly, it was a pale imitation of the wicked grin that had once captivated The Willow customers.

'You're a pal, Til.'

'None of your soft soap now,' she said with a hard look. 'You're still well in the doghouse with me.'

Nonetheless, they chatted in a more relaxed manner over a cigarette.

'Have you gone back to your odd jobbing?' she asked.

'Yeah.'

'How's it going?'

'Not bad. I'm still waiting for the good times to come, though.'

'Aren't we all?'

Two things were largely responsible for Nina's recovery: her little son and her work at the pub, both of which prohibited outward signs of depression.

Even in the dark days immediately after Baz's departure, when she had wanted to hide away and wallow in self-pity, she had managed to put on a cheerful face for Joey of whom she felt doubly protective in Baz's absence. Fortunately, he was too young to fret for his father and soon appeared to forget all about him.

Nina began to work regular evenings in the pub. Baz's payments meant she could live in reasonable comfort so the money she earned paid for extras, and the actual job itself kept her sane. Although, initially, she found it hard to take the customers' pitying looks and studious avoidance of Baz's name, she gradually rediscovered her enjoyment in her work. Behind the bar during a busy session she was not a failed wife, discarded and alone, but a woman people enjoyed talking to; she felt popular and needed.

Ostensibly she was as warm and lighthearted as before. In reality there had been profound changes. She was much less naive now – even cynical. Some good had come from what had happened, she told herself; at least it had strengthened her and made her more independent. In a strange sort of way there was comfort in having reached rock bottom because she knew that nothing could hurt her this deeply again.

Oddly enough, the one person in whose company she felt comfortable these days was her cousin, Alice. Being so short on tact, her dialogue often touched a tender spot but at least she didn't pretend that nothing had happened, or try to play the ministering angel.

Listening to her droning on about material things had a therapeutic effect on Nina in that it gave her a sense of normality. Even Alice's boastfulness didn't grate on the nerves quite so much, maybe because in her ultra-sensitive frame of mind Nina could see it for what it was – a lack of confidence on her cousin's part.

'It must be terrible to be deserted by your husband,' Alice said one afternoon in the autumn, not long after the birth of her first child, Malcolm.

Nina had called round to visit with Joey and they were having tea and biscuits in the sitting room. Joey was playing on the floor with some wooden building bricks, the baby was asleep in a crib in the corner of the room.

Her cousin was so blatant, Nina managed a wintry smile. 'My God, Alice, you certainly know how to turn the knife.'

'I was only trying to be sympathetic,' she protested.

'All right, I'll forgive you,' said Nina lightly.

'What I mean is, I don't think I could cope if that happened to me.'

'You'd have to, wouldn't you? Since there isn't a choice.'

'Admittedly. But I think I'd probably go to pieces.'

'Rubbish. You're as tough as old boots when it comes to it,' said Nina. 'Look how you coped with your parents' death . . . not so much as a tear shed in public.'

'I was falling apart inside though,' Alice admitted.

'But you didn't show it, which means you were coping.'

'Yes. But having to pick up the pieces after your husband walks out on you would be worse than bereavement, I should think,' she said. 'I mean, there's humiliation and rejection to cope with too.'

'Yes, that's true.'

'Frankly, I admire the way you've kept yourself together.'

'I went berserk at first,' confessed Nina. 'I tore round the streets in my nightclothes looking for him. I was right out of my mind for a while.'

'Really? I didn't know that.'

'No, it didn't reach the elite avenues of Turnham Green. Mum made sure of that.'

'Well, you certainly seem to be in control now.'

'Working helps, and my mother is very supportive.'

'I can imagine. Aunt Tilly is a real brick,' agreed Alice. 'I'm sure my own mother in like circumstances, bless her, would have been in a worse state than me because of the scandal.'

'Thank God my mother isn't like that!'

'It would have been a bit different for us, though,' remarked Alice, nibbling a ginger biscuit.

'You being respectable avenue people, of course,' said Nina, with tongue in cheek. Alice was so transparent it was hard not to tease her.

'That's right,' she replied, missing the joke.

'Even us publicans have standards, you know.'

'Oh, Nina, you know that wasn't what I meant,' corrected Alice, flushing as she finally caught on. 'What

I was trying to say was . . . well . . . you and Aunt Tilly don't worry about what people think of you, so it doesn't matter.'

'Nobody likes being the subject of gossip,' Nina informed her, 'but it's a tiny discomfort compared to the way I feel about losing Baz.'

'You still love him, then?'

'God, yes.'

'That will pass in time . . . or I suppose that's what the experts would tell you.'

'They may well say that but I wouldn't put money on them being right in my case.'

'Like that, eh?'

'Very much so.'

'Would you have him back?'

'Never,' exclaimed Nina harshly.

'But if you are still in love with him . . .'

'I still wouldn't.'

'How can you be so sure?' asked Alice. 'You don't know how you'd feel if you saw him again.'

'At this moment in time, I know exactly how I'd feel,' said Nina.

'You do?'

'Yes, I'd want him back more than anything. But I wouldn't take him back. He's hurt me too badly . . . destroyed my trust and respect for him . . . and it wouldn't work for us without that.'

'No.'

'It's taken this to make me realise that loving someone is one thing, liking them is quite another. I used to think it was all part of the same package.' She paused, then began thinking aloud. 'Perhaps that's why it all went wrong . . . because we stopped liking each other.'

'Might there have been faults on both sides?' asked Alice.

'Undoubtedly. I'm not saying it was all his fault, not by any means.'

'Oh.'

'But just to walk away from the problem like that . . . that's what is unforgivable in my book.'

'I expect I'd feel the same if it was Dudley.'

Nina gave a wry grin. 'Well, since your steady and reliable Dudley is never likely to leave you for any reason other than death, you've nothing to worry about, have you?'

'No, I suppose not,' said Alice, the mild barb in her cousin's tone completely lost on her.

PART TWO

PART TWO

PART TWO

Chapter Nine

'A light ale for me, please, Nina dear,' said an elderly man in baggy grey flannels and a sports jacket, white hair tidied with Brylcreem. 'And a glass of Guinness for the wife.'

'Coming up, Percy,' she smiled, taking a bottle from the shelf behind her and unscrewing the stopper. 'And how are you on this fine summer evening?'

'Not so dusty, thanks, ducks . . . and yourself?'

'Very well, thanks,' she said, carefully pouring the light ale into the glass at the correct angle to avoid producing too much of a head.

'Where's your mum tonight?'

'She's having a day off.'

'Left you in charge of the shop, has she?'

'That's right,' she said, pouring the Guinness.

'It's nice that Tilly can go out with an easy mind,' he remarked chattily as he handed her some coins. 'She can be sure things will run like clockwork around here with you in charge.'

'Well, I'm not so sure about clockwork,' she said modestly. 'But, yes, she can take time off knowing that she won't come home to find her business in ruins.'

'Has she gone anywhere special?' he enquired conversationally as she handed him his change.

'Yes, as a matter of fact she's gone to the Festival of Britain with her friend Hilda,' Nina told him. 'They've been gone all day.'

'Cor, I bet they're having a high old time,' grinned Percy. 'Me and the missus went last week. It was smashing, something to please everyone there. Fountains . . . a tree walk . . . even open air dancing under floodlights. Just like something you see in the films.'

'I know, I took Joey last week,' Nina told him. 'He loved it. I couldn't get him out of the funfair, though.' She rolled her eyes affectionately. 'He wanted to go on everything.'

'I can imagine. He's just at the right age to appreciate that sort of thing.'

'I'll say. He'll be five in December,' she said. 'He starts school next month, when they go back after the summer holidays.'

'Get away,' he said, shaking his head in disbelief. 'The time doesn't half fly, dunnit? It don't seem five minutes since you were trottin' off to school for the first time.' He smiled, remembering. 'Your mum was that tearful . . .'

'Time marches on, eh, Percy?' said Nina, adding laughingly, 'And talking of marching . . . you'll get your marching orders from your wife if you stay here chatting to me for much longer.'

Grinning, he went over to join his wife at a table while Nina turned her attention to a younger man.

'Evenin', Nina, how's it going, love?' he asked.

'Not so bad, Johnnie, thanks. The usual pint of brown and mild?'

'Yes, please, and I'll have a gin and orange and a couple of lemonades to take outside, too.'

'Got the family with you tonight, then?' she remarked.

'Yeah. It's such lovely weather me and the wife thought we'd give the kids a treat,' he explained. 'They enjoy watchin' the boats on the river. The main attraction of the moment though is the swing you've just had installed in the pub garden.'

'We thought that would be a hit with the little ones,' she said, setting his drinks down on a round tin tray. 'It's nice for the whole family to be able to go out and have a drink together of a summer's evening, isn't it?'

'Not 'alf. Long as you don't make it too comfortable for them,' he laughed, 'or I'll never escape without bringing the whole bloomin' brood out with me.'

'I can see you letting that happen, too,' she said with friendly sarcasm because John was a real man's man whose evenings were often spent playing darts with his mates in the public bar. 'That wife of yours lets you get away with murder.'

'She's glad to get me out of the house so she can listen to the wireless in peace.'

'I'll believe you, thousands wouldn't.'

As he reached into his pocket for some money Nina said as an afterthought, 'I've got some crisps in, if you're interested?'

'Blimey, things *are* beginning to look up,' he grinned.

'That'll really make the kids' day. Can you spare a packet for the wife too?'

'Certainly I can for one of my favourite regulars,' she said, producing four packets of potato crisps from a large tin under the counter. 'There you go then . . . one each.'

He went off happily with the tray and Nina continued serving, assisted by a barman called Dick who had been with them since Baz left three and a half years ago.

Reflecting on those years for a moment, she could see that her life had altered quite considerably. To their mutual benefit she had relieved her mother of some of the responsibility of the pub. Nowadays they were more like partners than landlady and barmaid.

Nina knew she was making a good job of it and felt very much in control. Experience had made her an expert in the art of handling people. She'd learned to sense the mood of the customer and to judge whether a jokey or serious approach was appropriate. In this line of work, there was no point in being offended by the odd spot of harmless vulgarity. But she took after her mother in her attitude to drunkenness or foul language. No one ever offended twice in her presence.

Things were still fairly grim in the country as a whole with some food items remaining on ration, income tax almost as high as in wartime, and the housing shortage still acute despite the proliferation of prefabricated houses.

But she could see some signs of improvement. Petrol and clothes were no longer rationed, and although many commodities were still not freely available, at least the five-shilling limit for restaurant meals had been abolished.

The Willow's turnover had been looking healthier lately as stock became marginally less of a headache to obtain. It was the Festival of Britain, though, which had opened on the South Bank of the Thames in May of this year, that had been a real tonic to everyone. Nina could see new hope and energy in the customers as they glimpsed an end at last to the grey years of austerity.

Already the drab streets were splashed with colour as front doors were newly painted and window boxes planted with brilliant displays of geraniums, pansies and marigolds. People decorated their interiors in bright contemporary style with jazzy wallpaper and carpets of a hectic design.

Nina was optimistic for the future and reasonably happy with the present. She had a son she adored, a job she enjoyed and a mother who was her closest friend. Having come through her wrecked marriage emotionally scarred but sane, she thought she had earned the title of 'survivor'.

She still couldn't think of Baz dispassionately, though; the memory of that black Monday was still too vivid. The halcyon days before their relationship had turned sour were remembered only with aching nostalgia. Even now, she sometimes cried herself to sleep with the sheer hopelessness of loving him. Occasionally, however, she could go all day without thinking of him at all so there had been some progress.

A sudden flurry of customers recalled her to the present. Whilst busy serving, she also dealt with a number of other queries. Someone wanted to know the date of the next darts match, Dick asked her if there was a spare set of dominoes anywhere for the public-bar crowd, the pianist informed her that the piano needed tuning so could she please get the tuner in? Running a pub was excellent training in doing six things at once.

The pub was closed, the cashing up finished and Nina was unwinding with a cup of cocoa upstairs in the living room when her mother arrived home, brimming with enthusiasm for the Festival.

'Honestly, Nina, I really think this country is gonna be right up on top again before very long,' she said, having painted a colourful picture of her day out.

'If our takings are anything to go by I think you may be right,' Nina happily informed her.

'Really?'

'Yes, they're up again tonight so I think we can now call it a steady improvement.'

'Oh, that is good news,' exclaimed Tilly.

Alice, Dudley and their two little boys arrived at The Willow in style one Sunday afternoon the following spring.

'Well, what do you think of it?' Alice wanted to know as Nina, Tilly and Joey stood outside the pub looking at the Hardings' latest acquisition.

'Cor,' exclaimed Joey, bursting with admiration. 'It's smashing . . . and it's *red*!'

Both Nina and Tilly were forced to agree that the

new Ford was indeed 'smashing'. It certainly brightened up the street in which there was only one other car parked and that was black.

'Lucky things,' said Joey, looking at his cousins with childish envy. 'Can we have a car, Mum?'

'No,' said Nina simply.

'Oh,' he said, his disappointment evident. 'Why can't we if they've got one?'

'Because I said so,' she told him firmly.

'It isn't fair,' he complained sulkily.

'That's quite enough of that sort of talk,' warned his mother.

Alice made a timely intervention. 'How would you like your Uncle Dudley to take you for a ride in it with Malcolm and Teddy?' she suggested pleasantly.

'Ooh . . . yes, please, Auntie Alice,' he enthused.

'Take the children round the block a few times, will you please, Dudley?' she instructed.

'All right, Alice dear,' agreed her weed of a husband who always seemed to Nina to be on his last legs, with his wheezy chest and bloodless complexion. 'But listen to me now, all of you children . . . you must be very careful. I want no sticky fingers on the seats or mucky shoes on the floor. Just don't touch anything.'

'No, Father,' chorused his sons, who were three and a half and two and a half. Nina always felt rather sorry for them because they had been landed with the unfortunate combination of their mother's prim personality and father's pallid appearance.

As the car rolled out of sight, the three women went upstairs to the flat and congregated in the kitchen while Tilly started to prepare tea.

'Things are going really well for you then, Alice,' she said.

'I can't complain.'

'I shouldn't think you'd dare,' said Tilly without a trace of envy. 'Every time we see you you've got something else new.'

'It's all Dudley's doing,' Alice proudly informed them. 'He's such a wonderful provider.'

'Yes . . . we can see that,' said Tilly thoughtfully.

'Actually we've decided to have the boys privately educated,' announced Alice proudly.

'Get away!' said her aunt.

'Yes, we're going to get their names down for Grove House as day boys as soon as possible.'

'Blimey,' said Tilly, for that school was one of London's most prestigious. 'Your mum would have loved that.'

'They'll be proper little . . . er . . . gentlemen then,' said Nina.

'I hope so,' said Alice. '"Manners maketh man" and all that . . . but, of course, the main object of the exercise is to get them decently educated.'

Taking the tea caddy from the cupboard, Tilly asked Alice to lay the table in the other room while Nina cut and buttered some bread.

'So are you going to have a go at driving the new car, Alice?' enquired Nina, as her cousin gathered cups and saucers from the dresser.

'Of course not,' said Alice, shocked at such a suggestion. 'I wouldn't know where to start.'

'You could learn.'

'Oh, no, I prefer to be driven, thank you very much.'

'I'd jump at the chance, if it was me,' said Nina.

'Would you really?' said Alice, feeling oddly deflated by her cousin's enthusiasm for something she had never even considered. 'Don't you think that driving a car is a male preserve?'

'Hardly,' disagreed Nina, 'since women were driving everything from ambulances to aeroplanes during the war.'

'Well . . . yes. But generally speaking in peacetime,' Alice continued more hesitantly, 'it's usually the man of the family who takes the wheel.'

'Women drivers are in a minority, I grant you that,' conceded Nina. 'But I've noticed a lot more of them about just lately. I'd do it like a shot if I could afford a car.'

'You know what our Nina's like, Alice,' Tilly pointed out kindly, perceiving her niece's change of mood. 'She'll have a go at anything.'

'Yes,' agreed Alice with a mixture of annoyance and envy. 'I really think she would too.'

'Beats me where Dudley gets all his money from,' Tilly confided to Nina when they were washing up the tea things after the visitors had left.

'He does seem to be coining it, I must say.'

'The way they live, you'd think he was a company director or something. Not an accountant . . . and an unchartered one at that.'

'I've often thought the same thing myself,' confessed Nina. 'I mean, the sort of position he holds would

135

command a good salary but I wouldn't have thought it would run to private education as well as all the rest of the trimmings they seem to take for granted.'

'Mm. It's curious.'

'Must be something to do with the fact that he's been with the firm so long,' suggested Nina.

'Maybe,' said Tilly, frowning. 'But whatever the reason, he certainly must be making a packet.'

'Good luck to them, I say,' said Nina, drying a cup and hanging it on a hook on the dresser. 'That sort of thing means a lot to Alice.'

'It certainly does,' said her mother, emptying the enamel washing-up bowl and drying her hands. 'I just hope she doesn't get hurt somewhere along the line.'

'Oh, what makes you say a thing like that?'

'Nothing in particular, it's just that Dudley doesn't ring true with me somehow. He never has.'

'I've never been able to take to him, either,' admitted Nina, 'but I'm sure you've nothing to worry about so far as Alice is concerned. He's obviously a good husband.'

'Yes, I know that, but still . . . oh, I dunno.'

'You worry too much about Alice,' said Nina.

'Her heart's in the right place even if her priorities are a bit confused,' replied Tilly swiftly.

'That's true,' said Nina, noticing once again how eager her mother was to leap to Alice's defence. What was it about her cousin that inspired such protectiveness?

Nina and Tilly might not have been in the same financial league as the Hardings but business improved to such an extent over the next year that they were able to invest in a television set on which to watch the Coronation of Queen Elizabeth II.

They made a real occasion of it at The Willow – decked the place out with flags and bunting and shared their new toy with their customers by setting it up in the saloon bar.

In the evening they put on a special party night, employing some of the best turns on the pub circuit. The male singer got everyone joining in with 'Down at the Old Bull and Bush', expertly assisted by their resident pianist, Charlie, at the piano. The bar-maids they now employed at the weekends came in to help out with the rush on this special occasion.

Balloons hung from the ceiling and a selection of savoury nibbles were laid out, sandwiches, sausage rolls and crisps, with compliments of the management. The bars were packed to the doors and when the balloons floated down it was the signal for a knees up, before the assembled company congaed out to the garden for the fireworks.

Joey, whose favourite prank was to slip downstairs into the bar and see how long he could stay there before he was chased back upstairs by his mother, had a wonderful time. The customers made a real pet of him and when the constable on the beat called in on his rounds, the boy was spirited out of sight among them.

'What a night, eh?' Nina said to her mother later on as they sat in their dressing gowns drinking cocoa.

'Mm.'

'Joey had a whale of a time, did you see him?'

'Yeah, bless him.'

'I think we can safely say the whole thing was an unqualified success.'

'Mm,' agreed Tilly, though her tone was strangely lacking in sparkle. 'I haven't done the cashing up yet but I'm sure we must have done well.'

'Bound to have done. The place was heaving and the till going like the clappers all night,' agreed Nina excitedly.

'Yes.'

'It's good that the increase in trade last year wasn't just a flash in the pan, isn't it?' enthused Nina. 'It really bodes well for the future of The Willow, don't you think?'

There was a peculiar silence.

'Mum . . .'

Tilly stared into her cup, avoiding her daughter's eyes.

'Mum,' said Nina again, finally realising that all was not well with her mother and remembering also that she had been quieter than usual these last few days. 'Mum, what is it? Has something happened?'

The older woman chewed her lip, then with a worried sigh she said, 'Yes, I'm afraid it has, love.'

'What? What is it?'

Wearily Tilly went over to the sideboard and picked up her handbag. 'This came the other day,' she said, drawing out an envelope. 'I didn't want to spoil the Coronation celebrations for you by mentioning it. But now it's all over you'll have to know, I suppose.'

'Know what?'

'Well, it seems there isn't gonna be a future for us at The Willow.'

'No future? Don't be silly. It's our business, our home.'

'Not for much longer, apparently,' Tilly informed her gravely.

'But I don't understand.'

'We have to get out of here.'

'Get out!' exclaimed Nina, aghast. 'Why on earth would we have to get out? We own the place . . .'

'We own the building but not the ground it stands on,' Tilly reminded her through dry lips.

'Isn't that why we pay ground rent?' said Nina, her stomach churning.

'Yes, but it seems the Cavendish family no longer wish to continue with the arrangement.'

'But how can they just stop?' Nina asked in bewilderment for she was not familiar with the details of her parents' affairs.

'Simple. They're not going to renew the ground lease this time,' Tilly explained solemnly, handing her the letter. 'Here, read it for yourself. You'll see that our days here are numbered.'

Chapter Ten

Having read the contents of the letter, Nina thought she was probably better equipped to deal with the problem than her mother.

'Don't worry too much about it, Mum,' she said protectively. 'I'll soon sort it out.'

'I don't see how you can,' said the other woman worriedly. 'I mean, legally we don't have a leg to stand on. Our arrangement with the Cavendish family is a personal one . . . there's never been anything in writing to say that they have to extend the ground lease beyond its current term.'

'What a ridiculous state of affairs,' was Nina's response.

'Yes, it is. I can see that now,' admitted Tilly ruefully. 'But there are some things you just take on trust.'

'Not when your home and livelihood are at stake,' riposted Nina.

'The lease has always been renewed as a matter of course before. It was a gentleman's agreement between your dad's great-grandfather and the head of the Cavendish family when the pub was built, and it's been handed down through the generations,' explained Tilly.

'The story goes that the two men were drinking pals.'

'You'd have thought Dad would have had the sense to put things on to a firmer footing when he took over, wouldn't you?' reproved Nina, shocked and angry at her parents' carelessness.

'I don't suppose he thought it was necessary,' said Tilly miserably. 'He just paid the ground rent annually as a routine job. It probably never occurred to him that the arrangement might not continue indefinitely.'

It was pointless to ask her mother why she had been so negligent about something so crucial when she'd become the owner, because Nina knew the answer. As a landlady Tilly stood alone; her gift for entertaining the punters was the backbone of the business. But her skills didn't stretch to administration. Nina had been having doubts about this for some time, ever since she'd become more involved in the running of The Willow. This latest development was proof of her mother's casual attitude towards paperwork.

'You really should have taken this up years ago, you know, Mum,' she admonished sternly.

'Course I should. It's obvious to us all *now*,' said Tilly with a touch of asperity.

'Fortunately,' continued Nina, 'from what you've said, it's more than likely just a misunderstanding and nothing to worry about. The Cavendishes probably have the ground lease on more than one property. They'll have got us mixed up with someone else or failed to realise that we have a special connection with the family. After all, why would they suddenly change a policy that has been in existence for yonks?'

142

'One of the oldest members of the Cavendish family has popped off since the lease was last renewed,' said Tilly meditatively. 'I remember reading about it in the local paper a few years ago. This Captain Jasper Cavendish who signed the letter must have taken over the running of the estate.'

Nina glanced at the letter. 'He's put "retired" after his name so he must be an ex-army man.' She sighed with relief. 'That's the explanation. He's obviously been away a lot in the past and isn't au fait with the way the estate is run.'

'Yes, that must be what it is,' said Tilly, brightening.

'No doubt about it,' confirmed Nina. 'What else could it be? The Cavendishes have a reputation for being decent, fair-minded people. They wouldn't pull a stroke like this unless it was a mistake. I'll write to this Captain Jasper bloke first thing in the morning explaining the situation . . . I'm sure there won't be any problem.'

'Let's hope you're right.'

One morning a week later Nina was in the cellar hammering a wooden spile into the keystone in the centre of a beer barrel to let in a small amount of air. Then she knocked the brass tap, which was attached to the beer pipe, into the shive at the end. It was on occasions like this, when the cellarman was unexpectedly absent, that she was glad she knew how to put a new barrel on tap.

Today had got off to a bad start. Joey had faked everything from ear-ache to appendicitis to get out of going to school because of an arithmetic test. By the time she'd made sure he really was pretending, they were late and had to run all the way to school.

No sooner had she returned home, with a stitch in her side and a throbbing headache, than Dick's wife had telephoned to say that he was sick and wouldn't be coming to work and to tell Nina that a new barrel of bitter needing putting on tap. Her mother had already gone out shopping and to deliver last night's takings to the bank so the job had fallen to Nina.

The cellar was cold and damp despite the warm June weather outside. Dark patches of mould suffused the white walls in odd corners. It was always cool down here. Only in exceptionally hot weather did they need to use an electric fan to maintain the temperature at the low level necessary to keep the beer in good condition.

Having tapped the barrel, she turned her attention to the bottled beer and had just dragged a crate of stout over to the steps when she heard the telephone ringing upstairs in the hall. She cursed, leaving what she was doing to scale the steps. At this rate she was going to be ready for bed by lunchtime.

'May I speak to Mrs Paxton, please?' asked a well-spoken male voice.

'Yes, speaking.'

'Jasper Cavendish here.'

'Oh . . . hello.'

'I'm ringing in reply to your letter,' he told her smoothly.

'Good,' she said cheerfully, glad she hadn't been kept waiting too long for his response.

'You say in your letter that you are the daughter of the licensee.'

'That's right. I'm acting for her in this matter.'

'So I gather.'

'The business about the ground lease not being renewed was all some sort of misunderstanding, I assume?' she said confidently.

'It certainly was not!' he informed her firmly.

'Oh!' She was unnerved but tried not to show it. 'I must say I'm very surprised to hear this because . . . as I said in my letter . . . there has been a special arrangement between the two families since our pub was built.'

'A change is long overdue then, isn't it?' he said coolly.

'I don't see why,' she replied, trying not to be intimidated by his sangfroid.

'Then let me spell it out for you,' he said unemotionally. 'I have taken over the Cavendish family estate following the death of my grandfather and I wish to reclaim the land on which your public house is built.'

'But you can't do that!' she told him. 'I mean, The Willow has been in my family for generations.'

'It's high time the site was put to a more practical use then,' he said.

'More practical use?' she echoed quizzically. 'What on earth do you mean?'

'The Willow is to be demolished and the site used for housing,' he informed her briskly.

'Oh, no. That really isn't on,' she protested, her voice quivering with emotion.

'Whyever not?'

'I should have thought that was obvious.'

'Not to me it isn't.'

'Well, because The Willow is an important part of the community,' she pointed out desperately, 'and that's not the only thing. The actual building is of historical interest too . . . it's part of London's heritage. You can't knock it down, you just can't!'

'Surely you're not suggesting that a creaky old public house should take priority over living accommodation . . . in the middle of a housing shortage?'

'There wouldn't be space for many houses on our site,' she said dully.

'Flats, Mrs Paxton,' he corrected blandly. 'The idea is to build a block of flats on that site.'

'You mean, you're going to knock down a building of historic value just so you can put up a modern block of little boxes?' she asked incredulously.

'Not me personally,' he informed her evenly, 'but I believe that is the intention of the developer who is interested in purchasing the site from me.'

'Oh, I see.' Now she understood what was behind all this. The Willow's site was prime building land. But it wouldn't be the hard-up homeless who would benefit from its demolition; it would be the privileged few who could afford to pay high prices for luxurious riverside accommodation.

'Anyway, you've plenty of time to find somewhere else to go before the lease actually runs out,' he told her in an insouciant tone.

'And what are we supposed to pay for "somewhere

else" with? All we own is this pub. It's not only our home, it's our living.'

'If you've been running a successful business for a long time, surely you must have something behind you?'

'After years of crippling austerity? Don't make me laugh!'

'Perhaps one of the breweries will be willing to help you?' he suggested airily. 'They'd probably be only too pleased to have such experienced people manage one of their houses.'

She was too upset by this suggestion to reply.

'Anyway, as I've said, there are still a few months left on your lease,' he pointed out glibly. 'Long enough for you to find alternative accommodation.'

'We're not going anywhere, mate,' she informed him with sudden decision. 'Not in a few months . . . or years . . . *not ever*.'

'That attitude won't help you one bit,' he said haughtily. 'Our solicitor has checked out the legality of the situation. The land belongs to us. We are perfectly within our rights not to rent it out if we no longer wish to do so. No court in the land can alter that.'

'I'll fight you every inch of the way,' she declared.

'To win a war one has to have power, my dear,' he said arrogantly. 'Ideals and determination aren't enough . . . power is what matters.'

And before she could reply to such brutal logic, he hung up.

Rain poured down from the leaden September skies,

dimpling the river, misting the bank and drenching the crowd gathered at the street entrance to The Willow.

'The weather would have to do the dirty on us, wouldn't it?' muttered Nina to her mother who was standing beside her holding a banner which read SAVE THE WILLOW.

'Yeah, typical. I'm sure more people would have turned up if it had been dry,' said Tilly, rivulets of water trickling off the biscuit-coloured rain-hat that matched her mac.

'No doubt about that,' agreed Nina, clad in raincoat and headscarf.

'Maybe we ought to postpone it till next Sunday?' suggested Tilly.

'We can't do that,' protested Nina. 'Not with a reporter from the local paper promising to be there with a photographer. We can't afford to miss that sort of publicity.'

'I suppose not,' agreed Tilly, who was only being realistic. 'I'm just worried that half of this lot'll drop out on the way 'cos of the rain.'

Joey appeared, swathed in yellow oilskins and Wellington boots. He too was carrying a banner.

'Can we get going now, Mum?' he asked excitedly. This sort of adventure was right up his street.

'Yes, I think we're just about ready, son,' she confirmed, shouting to the others: 'Is everybody ready?' and receiving an affirmative reply.

'Right, let's get this show on the road then.'

With Joey at one side and Tilly at the other, Nina led the march towards the Broadway carrying a banner on a pole, her supporters marching along in the rear. THE WILLOW FOR OUR COMMUNITY – PEOPLE BEFORE PROFITS – DON'T DESTROY OUR LOCAL read their placards. Behind came a motley crowd of local musicians, heartily banging and blowing to the tune of 'There is a Tavern in the Town'.

For three months Nina had worked tirelessly to gather public support for her 'Save The Willow' campaign. Before resorting to such drastic measures, however, she had gone to see Jasper Cavendish and begged him to change his mind. She'd even suggested that she and her mother try to raise the money to buy the land but when he told her the asking price she knew it was beyond their reach. When it had become obvious that the man had as much humanity as she had legal right to stay on at The Willow, she'd turned to other means.

As well as getting up a petition in the pub, she'd gone out door knocking to swell the number of signatures. She was given short shrift by those who disapproved of alcohol, of course, but many people were only too keen to add their voice to a campaign against a historic London landmark falling victim to the bulldozers.

Having received such a positive response, she was disappointed on delivering the petition to the Town Hall to be told that there was nothing they could do. She was even more downhearted when the Member of Parliament for the area was of the same opinion.

A breakthrough had come when she'd gained the interest of an enthusiastic young reporter on the local paper. Doug Smith had agreed to write a piece about the campaign provided she staged some sort of an event to add colour to his article and persuade his editor to give him more space, possibly on the front page. He'd suggested she go for something dramatic which would make interesting reading as well as a point.

He'd been delighted with her idea of a protest march from The Willow to the Cavendish family house near Ravenscourt Park and had agreed to be outside the house at four o'clock this afternoon with a photographer.

Nina had spared no effort in organising the occasion, informing the police of their intentions and leaving nothing to chance except the weather which had been typically unco-operative.

Now, exhilarated with belief in her cause and optimism in the outcome of this demonstration, she led her band of supporters in an orderly manner. They plodded through narrow terraced streets into leafy St Peter's Square and on into King Street, heading towards Ravenscourt Park. In a salubrious avenue near the park, they came to a halt by the double gates of the Cavendish mansion which was set back from the road in extensive grounds.

An enthusiastic welcome from Doug Smith awaited them. 'Quite a good turn-out considering the weather,' he said cheerfully, red hair flattened damply to his head, spectacles streaked with rain.

'Not too bad,' agreed Nina. 'It would have been better attended without the rain but that's one thing none of us can do anything about, isn't it?'

'True . . . but we can use it to our advantage, Mrs Paxton,' he said with a wicked grin.

'We can?'

'Sure.'

'How?'

'You know the sort of thing . . . sturdy protesters brave the weather for their cause . . . courageous marchers get a soaking for the sake of their community,' he explained. 'It's all good sales-boosting stuff for the paper. It might help to get the editor on our side too.'

'You're a ruddy con man, do you know that?' laughed Nina.

'Only in a very good cause, though.'

'You're just the sort of man we need on our side,' she told him.

The marchers were beginning to walk up and down with banners erect, chanting, 'The Willow forever.'

'Let's get some photographs done before the rain washes all the writing off the banners,' suggested Doug.

'Good idea.'

'We'll take a good selection and choose the best of the bunch.'

'Okay.'

'Now then, Mrs Dent, can we have one of you with your daughter and grandson . . . that's it . . . hold the banners facing the camera so that the slogans can be seen . . . okay fine . . . now move over so we can get some of the marchers into the picture . . . . lovely . . . Mrs Paxton, if we can have one with you handing me the petition . . . terrific . . . okay, hold it right there.' He turned to the photographer. 'Righto, Bill. Make this a good one and we'll make the front page.'

A reel of film and several degrees of sogginess later,

Doug made a few final notes and told Nina and Tilly that he was pleased with the way it had gone and he was going all out to rouse public sympathy with his article.

'We'll shame the bugger into changing his mind,' he said. 'Jasper Cavendish is a big noise in certain circles around here . . . sits on all sorts of worthy committees.'

'His family have a very good name, I believe,' said Nina.

'Oh, yes. They're reckoned to be philanthropists.'

'He must be the rotten apple then.'

'Undoubtedly,' agreed Doug, 'and the other members of the family won't want their reputation tarnished by the suggestion that he isn't selling the site for the public good so much as to line his own pocket.'

'He doesn't seem to be particularly bothered by our presence here at the moment though, does he?' Nina pointed out, glancing towards the house in which there were no faces visible at the window. Not so much as a curtain twitching.

'Well . . . he wouldn't be, would he?' said Doug.

'What do you mean?'

'A bunch of protestors making a bit of a noise outside his house isn't much of a threat to him, is it?' Doug said. 'He's just sitting it out in there thinking he's got all the power, unaware this story is going into print. If it isn't made public at this stage, no one will query it and he'll get away with it.'

'You're right,' said Nina.

'You wait until it's splashed all over the paper on

Friday,' grinned Doug. 'He won't be able to ignore us then.'

Nina was trembling with anticipation when she called at the newsagent's to buy a paper on the way home from taking Joey to school on Friday morning. She was disappointed at first glance to see that the story hadn't made the front page, and stood outside the shop flicking through the pages. That was odd . . . there was no sign of it anywhere. Doug must have been too late for this week's edition.

He was most apologetic when she got through to him on the telephone.

'I'm so sorry, Mrs Paxton, I really am,' he said.

'Don't worry. As long as it gets into next week's edition.'

'Well, actually . . . um . . . there isn't any chance of that, I'm afraid.'

'When is it going to be in there then?' she was eager to know.

There was a silence; then a muffled sigh and the sound of him clearing his throat. 'Er . . . well . . . actually the editor has squashed the whole idea.'

'You mean it won't be in the paper at all?'

'That's about the size of it,' he confirmed.

'But what about all the time and effort you've put into it?' she said in astonishment. 'All that film you used . . . all the notes you took.'

'All wasted,' he explained mournfully. 'And the film has been destroyed.'

'But why, for heaven's sake?' she asked urgently. 'I

mean, even apart from my own personal interest, it would have made a good human interest story. People ought to be told about what's going on in their local community.'

'The reason is very simple,' he informed her gloomily. 'I didn't know when I took the story on that Captain Jasper Cavendish is a shareholder in the paper.'

'Oh, I don't believe it!' she exclaimed.

'It's true,' he told her. 'Talk about irony. Anyway, my editor showed him the story before we went to press out of courtesy, and . . . well, the rest is history, as they say.'

'It's so damned unfair!'

'I couldn't agree more,' he said, 'and I'd walk out if I didn't need the job so badly.'

'Is there nothing you can do?' she entreated.

'I'll continue to give you my personal support, of course,' he told her. 'But at a professional level there's nothing else I can do at all. I really am so very sorry.'

'It isn't your fault,' she assured him. 'You've been wonderful. Thanks for everything.'

But it was as much as she could do not to burst into tears at this cruel blow. All her hopes had been tied up in the story getting into print. Now she just didn't know which way to turn . . . and time was running out.

Chapter Eleven

'Isn't it about time you thought about getting married again, Baz?' suggested George Paxton one autumn evening when he was visiting his brother.

'Yeah, what about it, Baz?' said George's wife, Marge, who was sitting next to her husband on the sofa in Baz's flat above his television and radio shop. 'You can't beat married life.'

'And there speaks the voice of experience,' laughed Baz. 'All three months of it. You two love-birds are still just beginners, the novelty hasn't even begun to wear off. Anyway, I'm still married to Nina.'

'High time you got divorced and made a new start with someone else,' opined George. 'It's more than five years since you two split up.'

'It must be very lonely for you living on your own,' said Marge, a warm-hearted type with lively brown eyes and hair that was currently auburn but could be honey blonde or brown next week if the fancy took her.

'Yeah, it must be . . . and it isn't necessary for a well-set up bloke like you,' George chipped in.

'Stop nagging, you two, and have another drink,' said Baz swiftly because it still upset him to think of the way he had destroyed his marriage.

'No more to drink for me, bruv, I've gotta get up for work in the morning.'

'You certainly have,' confirmed Baz. 'I want you at the shop bright and early tomorrow. I'm going to the wholesaler's first thing and there's a bloke coming in to finalise a deal.'

'What on?'

'A television.'

'On the never-never?'

Baz nodded. 'So the paperwork will have to be done.'

'I'll do that if I'm not busy with a customer,' said Marge who worked as a part-time assistant in Baz's shop.

'I'm expecting some portable radios to be delivered while I'm out, too,' said Baz.

'That's good,' said George who was his brother's general helper in the business. 'We can't get enough of those . . . I've been turning people away.'

'Mm, they're very popular with youngsters,' agreed Baz. 'Especially the sets with shoulder straps. It's really "with it" for the teenies to have one of those draped round their neck.'

. 'What with those and record players, the kids have got it made,' said George.

'Bit different to when we were teenagers, eh?' said Marge who had grown up in the same street as the Paxton brothers. 'All we had was air raids and ITMA.'

'Thank God things are better now,' said Baz.

'Too true.'

The conversation was halted by the sound of the

telephone ringing in the hall. ''Scuse me, folks,' said Baz, leaving the room to answer it.

'Hello, Baz . . . it's Tilly.'

'Tilly!' he said in surprise, his heart quickening with a mixture of pleasure at hearing her voice and anxiety at the reason he was doing so. 'Nothing wrong, I hope?'

'I can't talk now,' she said in a low tone, 'but I need to see you.'

'Sure. Any time.'

'How about tomorrow afternoon about three at your place?'

'Suits me.'

'Whereabouts are you in the Portobello Road?'

'A few minutes' walk from Ladbroke Grove Station, towards Westbourne Park.'

'Don't worry, I'll find it.'

Baz hadn't realised just how pleased he would be to see Tilly until she appeared in his shop the following afternoon.

'Oh, it's so good to see you, Til,' he said, greeting her with an emotional hug.

'Ditto,' she sniffed, her eyes bright with tears. 'Even if you don't deserve it.'

Leaving George in charge of the shop, Baz took her upstairs to the flat and made some tea.

'Well, you're obviously doing all right for yourself,' she said, settling in an armchair in his living room. 'When you phoned me with your change of address I didn't realise it was a shop.'

'Only a little one but it's a start,' he said.

'So your hard work and determination have really paid off then?' she remarked, casting an approving eye around the room which, whilst not especially stylish, was pleasantly appointed with a comfortable three-piece suite, modern occasional furniture and a television set standing in the corner with its walnut-veneered doors closed across the screen.

'That's right. By working all hours I was able to save regularly and eventually I was able to rent a shop and get started properly,' he explained. 'Just like I always said I would.'

'Is it worth the price though, eh, Baz?' asked Tilly sharply.

He gave her a hard look. 'Don't let's drag up the past, Til. It won't alter anything.'

'I suppose not,' she said, and changing the subject added, 'So how come you got into the television trade?'

'Seemed a really safe bet. Being a new industry,' he explained, 'there's a growing demand.'

'I can imagine.'

'The telly has become a status symbol to some people.'

'And not havin' a set is another form of one-upmanship for others,' she grinned. 'Some snobbish types reckon it's a trivial pastime for people with low intellects. Honestly, Baz, you should hear some of 'em going on about it in the pub . . . not to mention my niece and her husband.'

'Luckily for me there are many more in favour than against,' he told her. 'There's a positive boom. In radios and record players too.'

'What happens about repairs?' she enquired chattily.

'Our set is always going wrong.'

'I call in a qualified repairman to do all that.'

'Sounds as though you've got it all sewn up.'

'Yep. Repairs . . . an arrangement with a hire purchase company . . . it's only a little shop but I've got it very well organised.'

'I can see that.'

Detecting a note of tension in her voice, Baz decided it was time to dispense with the chit-chat. 'Anyway, Til, I'm sure you haven't come here to talk about me.'

'You're right, I haven't,' she said, her expression darkening.

'So tell me about it?'

'There have been unexpected developments at The Willow,' she explained, 'and you said you wanted to be kept informed about Nina and Joey.'

'What's happened?'

'Looks like we'll all be moving out soon.'

'Leaving The Willow? I don't believe it!'

Having told him the whole story, she said sadly, 'Nina has nearly driven herself into the ground over this, poor girl. And after all her hard work we're going to lose the place anyway. We've come to the end of the line.'

'Not quite, Tilly,' said Baz thoughtfully. 'Not quite.'

'What do you mean?' she asked, narrowing her eyes.

'Leave it to me,' he said enigmatically. 'I think you'll be hearing from Captain Cavendish quite soon. With a very different proposition.'

'I don't believe we've met, Mr Baxter,' said Jasper

Cavendish as Baz was shown into his office within his luxurious house.

'No, we haven't,' was Baz's laconic reply.

'You said when we spoke on the telephone that you have some sort of a proposition to put to me?'

'That's right,' said Baz, taking a seat in a brown leather armchair by the window through which shafts of sunlight filtered, striking the corner of the leather-topped desk at which the Captain was sitting.

He saw a man of middle years with deep-set eyes, thin lips topped by a greying-black moustache and a network of red veins suffusing his face. Jasper Cavendish in turn ran a judicial eye over his visitor, noting the brash stripe on his suit, the dazzling tie. 'Before you say any more I have to tell you that I'm not interested in anything illegal.'

'All legal and above board,' Baz gave him a hard look. 'My name is not Baxter, by the way.'

'Oh, really? So why lie about your name if you have legitimate business to discuss?'

'You'd have refused to see me if I'd given my real name,' explained Baz candidly. 'Now that I'm safely inside with you, however, I can tell you that my name is Paxton. I'm Nina Paxton's husband.'

There was a brief hiatus while the significance of this registered with the Captain. 'Oh, no, I suppose you've come to plead that wretched woman's case?' he exploded. 'You're damned right I wouldn't have let you in.' He rose and glared at Baz, his scalp gleaming as cruel sunlight shone through his thinning grey hair. 'Get out, before I have you thrown out.'

'I'm not going anywhere,' said Baz calmly. 'Not before you've listened to what I have to say, anyway.'

'Oh, really!' puffed the Captain, his mottled complexion becoming plum-coloured. 'I'm a busy man, I've got better things to do with my time than listen to you. I've told your wife my position. I am not going to renew their lease and that is *final*.'

Baz remained cool. 'Summer nineteen forty-seven. The officers' mess at Chelsea Barracks,' he said in a slow, meaningful manner.

The Captain's face tightened. He narrowed his eyes at Baz. 'What *are* you prattling on about, man?' he said, a slight breathlessness contradicting his calm exterior.

'You know what I'm referring to.'

'Get out of here this minute . . . go on . . . *out*!' blustered the Captain, unable to hide his agitation. He marched over to the door and opened it with a flourish. 'Out . . . *now*!'

Remaining where he was, Baz continued, 'You were in charge of the mess funds until then, weren't you?'

Jasper Cavendish closed the door and walked slowly back to his seat at the desk. 'All right,' he said with an irritated sigh. 'Say what you have to say . . . but bear in mind that slander is against the law in this country.'

'I know that. In fact, I know a lot of things. You learn much more than how to pull pints when you work in a pub,' Baz informed him evenly.

'Really?'

'Oh, yes. People say things to a barman when they've had a few drinks that they'd never tell another living soul.'

'Do get to the point,' growled the other man impatiently.

'Okay. I was working at The Willow in the summer of nineteen forty-seven. We used to get a lot of army officers in around that time . . . they liked to socialise by the river on a summer's evening as a change from the mess.'

'Spare me the details.'

'There was a Major Barlow,' said Baz. 'He was a regular at that time.'

'Charlie Barlow,' gasped Jasper almost in a whisper.

'Yes. He liked a tipple did Charlie,' explained Baz, his eyes on the Captain's face. 'A real old boozer in fact . . . not that he could have got legless very often in our pub in those days 'cos booze was still short.' Baz drew slowly on a cigarette. 'Anyway, one night he came in to The Willow already tanked up and in a chatty mood . . . a real case of verbal diarrhoea.'

'Get on with it,' barked Jasper.

'Well, he told me there'd been a real hoo-ha in the barracks that day. Apparently mess funds had gone missing and one of the officers was strongly suspected of having stolen them.' He paused and the only sound in the room was the Captain's irregular breathing. 'Someone called Cavendish. Captain Jasper . . .'

'I'll take you to court over this,' interrupted Jasper.

'Why would you do that?' queried Baz. 'I'm only repeating hearsay. It was never proved and everything was kept quiet for the sake of the regiment but all the chaps knew you'd done it. Instead of a court martial you were asked to resign. Left under a real cloud apparently.'

'I'll sue for every penny you've got,' said Jasper, his voice ragged with fear.

'I think not,' said Baz calmly. 'You wouldn't want all that dragged up again, would you? Not now you've found a niche for yourself in civvy street . . . serving on various charity committees.' He leaned back his head and exhaled smoke very slowly. 'Particularly as you serve on some as treasurer.'

'I'll . . .'

'You'll keep quiet until I've finished, that's what you'll do . . . *old boy*,' commanded Baz, reducing the other man to silence.

'This thing with The Willow site is your insatiable greed all over again, isn't it, Captain?' he continued. 'Though I suppose I shouldn't call you Captain, considering the dubious circumstances under which you left the army. You had more money than you knew what to do with when you were in the Guards but you had to get your sticky little fingers on other people's dough too. It's the same now. You don't need the money you can raise by selling The Willow's site as building land, but you just can't say no to some easy dosh.'

'And you can, I suppose?' Cavendish muttered accusingly.

'I've an eye to making a few quid, yes,' admitted Baz. 'The difference between you and me, mate, is that I work for mine. And I have to grab every opportunity that comes my way because I have to survive without the comfort of family money behind me.'

'Have you quite finished?'

'Almost,' said Baz. 'All that remains is for me to spell out my terms.'

'Your terms?'

'Oh, come now, you must have known there would be a deal.'

Cavendish gave a nonchalant shrug.

'The deal is this,' said Baz. 'You sell my mother-in-law, Mrs Dent, the freehold to The Willow, at a price she can afford . . . but for enough so that she doesn't feel beholden . . . and I'll keep quiet about your past indiscretions.'

'You must be mad!'

'If you don't do this,' Baz cut in grimly, 'I'll make sure your army disgrace is known all over London. There won't be an organisation anywhere that will want you on their committee . . . nor a hostess who will have you as a dinner guest.'

'You're nothing but a cheap crook,' declared the Captain.

Baz gave a dry laugh. 'If that isn't the pot calling the kettle black, I don't know what is!'

There was an uneasy silence. Baz stared out of the window, watching some russet leaves flutter to the ground from an oak tree in the garden.

'Sell them the freehold, you say?' Jasper asked at last.

'That's right,' confirmed Baz meeting his gaze.

'Well, I don't suppose I have much of a choice, do I?'

'None at all,' replied Baz. 'Not if you want to hold your head up around here, anyway.'

* * *

A few days later, Tilly visited Baz in a much more cheerful frame of mind.

'Cavendish has offered to sell us the freehold,' she said excitedly as he made her tea upstairs in the kitchen. 'We had a letter this morning.'

'I thought you might.'

'You're a ruddy marvel, do you know that, Baz?' she told him. 'How did you get him to do it?'

'Just reminded him of a few home truths, that's all,' he explained. 'Nothing for you to worry about.'

'I won't press you for details then,' she said. 'But . . . oh, Baz, I'm so grateful. I don't know what we'd have done if you hadn't come to the rescue. Now, instead of us being thrown out, we keep the building and the land it stands on too. Just think what this means . . . no ground rent to pay, no more fear of eviction.' She threw her arms around his neck and smacked a kiss on his cheek. 'Thanks ever so much, love.'

'Does this get me back into your good books?' he said lightly, setting cups and saucers out on a tray.

She frowned. 'I'll never, *ever* forgive you for what you did to my daughter.' Her tone softened though. 'But . . . well . . . I think I might consider putting you back on my Christmas card list.'

'I'm glad I got involved then,' he laughed.

'I haven't told Nina that you sorted it,' she said. 'She doesn't even know that you and I are in touch. Shall I tell her now that the problem's solved?'

'No . . . it might spoil it for her if she knows I've had a hand in it,' he said. 'Leave things as they are.'

'She thinks old Cavendish had a change of heart on his own, but she's far too relieved to wonder why.'

As he poured boiling water into the teapot, Baz couldn't resist a question. 'Does she ever talk about me?'

'Not often to me, not now,' said Tilly. 'But she talks to Joey about you. Never says anything bad about you to him though. She concentrates on the good things, the fun you had in the early days.'

'Does he wonder why I left?'

'Not yet. He's still young enough to accept the situation as it is, without asking questions.'

'That's good.'

'It won't stay that way for much longer though, I shouldn't think. He's bound to get more curious as he gets older.' She gave Baz an affectionate smile. 'He's a fine boy, the image of you. He can charm the birds off the trees too.'

Baz leaned against the kitchen unit waiting for the tea to brew, aware of a familiar ache deep inside him. 'I'd love to see him, Til. Well . . . to see them both, really.'

'It's all coming home to roost now, is it, what you gave up?'

'I have regrets, I won't deny it.'

'It's a damned shame, the way things turned out for the two of you.'

'Yes.' He lapsed into thoughtful silence. 'It's been five years. Nina's had time to build a life for herself. Do you think it would be wrong of me to call in at The Willow some time? Nothing heavy, just to see her.'

'I honestly don't know the answer to that, Baz,' said Tilly. 'That's something you must make your own mind up about.'

Just when Nina thought she was over Baz, a memory would assail her with such poignancy she would wonder if she was ever going to get the wretched man out of her system.

A constant reminder was Joey who bore a striking resemblance to his father; even his mannerisms were achingly similar. The wicked gleam in her son's eye and a certain set of his mouth could sometimes throw Nina right off balance.

She found herself in the grip of just such a feeling one afternoon in the spring of 1955. The children were on their Easter holidays from school and Alice had invited Nina and Joey over for tea.

'Do I have to go, Mum?' asked Joey miserably.

'Yes, you do,' asserted Nina. 'So go and wash your hands and face and change into the clean clothes I've laid out for you on your bed.'

'Why do I have to go?' he asked sulkily, twisting his mouth in the same stubborn way his father used to.

'Because Aunt Alice has been kind enough to invite us, that's why,' she informed him briskly, to hide the fact that she was hurting inside.

'Aunt Alice doesn't expect Gran to go, does she?'

'No. That's because she knows that Gran likes to have a nap in the afternoon so that she isn't too tired to work in the pub at night.'

'Why can't I stay here with Gran then?' he persisted.

'Because she wants some peace and quiet. And anyway I want you to come with me,' she informed him, sitting at her dressing table and flicking the comb through her stylish feather-cut in front of the mirror. 'So go and get ready or it won't be worth going at all as I have to get back for opening time.'

'Mm . . .' he said thoughtfully.

'And don't be slow on purpose, Joey,' she said, reading his mind, 'because we're leaving here in ten minutes' time whether you're ready or not. There is absolutely no way you're going to get out of it.'

His mouth turned down at the corners, his eyes were distant. She could almost hear his thoughts as he struggled to work out a plan.

'But Malcolm and Teddy are such twerps,' he told her, getting to the crux of the matter.

'Now, Joey, it isn't nice to speak about your cousins like that,' she admonished, putting on some lipstick.

'It's true,' he went on. 'They don't like football . . . they don't go to Saturday morning pictures . . . they don't have a telly so they don't even know about that.'

'It isn't their fault their parents disapprove of those things, is it?' Nina pointed out.

'Why do they disapprove of the telly?' he wanted to know.

'Aunt Alice and Uncle Dudley think it's mindless entertainment only fit for their social inferiors,' explained Nina, quoting her cousin's very words.

'What does that mean?'

It means they're snobs, she thought, but kept that to herself. 'They don't think the programmes are any good,' she said, giving him a watered-down summary of Alice's harsh criticism of something of which she had no real knowledge. 'Now go and get ready, there's a good boy. We won't stay there long.'

'Promise?'

'I promise.'

His grin melted her heart. It was the Baz factor all over again. She concentrated her mind on the outing ahead. About the only part she was expecting to enjoy was the drive over to Turnham Green in the little Austin she had been able to afford as a result of the continuing upsurge in business.

Surprisingly enough, Alice's snobbishness, which had increased along with her material status, did not deter her from continuing to pursue a friendship with her aunt and cousin. Busy as she was, Nina didn't have the heart to refuse Alice's numerous invitations if she could possibly find the time. Alice was family after all!

This afternoon saw Alice at her worst. She had invited some neighbours to join them for tea and was at pains to hold her own in the struggle for social supremacy. Having thoroughly exhausted the wonders of Formica, Marley tiles, fitted carpets and self-service shopping, Alice and her cronies then embarked upon an orgy of disapproval of another modern phenomenon.

'Aren't those gangs of youths who hang about the streets dreadful?' exclaimed a woman with a perm that was so rigid it might have been styled with cement. 'Teddy Boys, I believe they call them.'

'Disgusting,' agreed Alice in an exaggerated whisper.

'One sees them hanging about on street corners as one passes in the car. Ugh! Those terrible Edwardian clothes and that awful haircut . . . a DA, whatever that's supposed to mean.'

'It's short for Duck's Arse, Aunt Alice,' announced Joey helpfully. 'Everyone knows that.'

His cousins giggled behind their hands and earned themselves a warning glare from their mother.

'Really, Joey,' reproved Alice, 'that isn't a very nice thing for a little boy to say, now is it?'

'It's what it means, though,' he said, childish sincerity mingled with a touch of devilment.

Alice threw his mother a reproving stare and turned to her friends. 'It's living in a public house, I expect,' she explained apologetically. 'He gets to hear things the rest of us miss.'

'You'd have to have been living on the moon just lately to have missed out on what DA means,' Nina pointed out with a mischievous grin.

She observed her cousin's embarrassment with a mixture of irritation and amusement. It was no more than the silly woman deserved. Whilst Alice didn't like to publicise the fact that her relatives were in the licensed trade, she couldn't resist bringing the two separate parts of her life together with the idea of impressing Nina with her affluent social circle. This sort of contretemps was usually the result. Would she never learn?

'Well, I certainly didn't know,' snapped Alice.

'Running a public house must be enormous fun,' said a woman with a French pleat and an attitude that indicated she'd sooner work in the sewers herself and was only trying to change the subject.

'I enjoy it,' said Nina simply.

'Fortunately we don't get any of those Teddy Boy creatures hanging about in the Avenue,' said Alice, keen to steer the conversation away from Nina's occupation.

'We get plenty of them round our way,' chirped Joey. 'Gran and I saw a gang of them in the Broadway on our way home from the pictures the other night . . . on Gran's night off.'

'He goes to the cinema at night?' asked Alice in a critical tone.

'Yes, if there's something suitable on in the holidays,' explained Nina. 'What's wrong with that?'

'Well, nothing. I . . .'

'The Teddy Boys ought to be locked up,' intervened French Pleat quickly, sensing a storm brewing between the cousins.

'I couldn't agree more,' said Alice obsequiously.

'The police can't arrest them if they haven't done anything,' Nina pointed out, 'just because they happen to be wearing drain-pipe trousers.'

It wasn't that Nina approved of these anti-social louts who carried such dubious hardware as coshes, flick-knives and bicycle chains which they used on one another and to wreck dance halls and cinemas. On the contrary, she was horrified by what she'd read in the papers of the havoc they caused. But the prissy relish with which Alice and her friends dealt with the subject infuriated her.

'The trousers are proof of their intentions,' stated Tight Perm categorically. 'The clothes they wear are the uniform of the degenerate. They're making a statement when they wear them.'

'Perhaps some of them just happen to like wearing those sort of clothes?' suggested Nina.

'Surely you're not defending them?' said Alice icily.

'Certainly not,' said Nina adamantly, 'but I find it hard to believe that every young man who happens to like wearing a drape jacket is a villain. Admittedly many of them are, but I don't like such rash generalisations.'

'You'd soon change your tune if a gang of them came into your pub, I bet,' said French Pleat.

'If they were being a nuisance, of course I would,' admitted Nina. 'Luckily they seem to prefer town centres to the riverside, and dance halls and cinemas to pubs.'

'I shouldn't think any place of entertainment is safe from them,' said Tight Perm.

'We'll be all right at The Willow,' said Nina confidently. 'There's too great a distance between us and the Broadway for them to want to bother us.'

These proved to be famous last words. One evening a week or so later, the doors of the street entrance to the pub thrust open and a group of Teds burst in, swaggered noisily over to the bar and ordered some drinks.

'You're all under eighteen,' said Nina, perceiving the gawkiness, the acne, the immaturity of their facial bone structure. 'So I'm afraid I can't serve you with alcoholic drinks.'

'I'm nineteen,' announced a boy with a greased quiff, sideburns and a DA, a long jacket with a velvet collar, drain-pipe trousers and a bootlace tie. 'And you just try and prove I'm not.'

'You'd have an army haircut if you were,' challenged Nina.

'I'm deferred from National Service,' he said with an insolent grin. 'I'm trainin' to be a brain surgeon.'

His mates fell about at this.

'That's enough of your lip, the lot of you,' intervened Tilly. 'You heard what the lady said . . . no booze.'

'Drop dead, Grandma,' sneered the one with the quiff who appeared to be the gang leader.

'Yeah, shut your gob, you silly old cow!' said one of his mates.

'Right, I'll soon sort you lot out,' said the fearless Tilly, moving along the bar and lifting the flap.

'Out the way, Tilly, I'll deal with this lot of scum,' said Dick, who was right behind her.

'Get lost, Grandad,' said one of the louts, receiving loud cheers and applause from his mates.

'Mum . . . Dick . . . stay where you are,' said Nina in a commanding tone. '*I'll* take care of this.'

At the strong note of authority in her voice both Tilly and Dick stood where they were.

The leader stared at Nina, daring her to oppose him, then walked over to the table where old Albert was sitting. 'Me and me mates wanna sit at this table, Grandad,' he informed him arrogantly, eyes resting defiantly on Nina. 'So on your way, mate.'

Nina was round the bar in an instant. 'Out! Get out

of here!' she shouted, pointing to the door and meeting the rebellious eyes of the leader.

'Have you got cloth ears or somethin', missus?' he said in a slow, threatening drawl. 'We ain't going nowhere . . . not until we've been served with some proper drinks, anyway.'

As Nina tried to grab his arm with the intention of helping him to the door, he reached into his pocket and drew something out. With a small flourish of his hand, he flicked a blade from a small knife which he held close to her face, eyes shining with malice.

'P'raps now we'll get some service round here, eh, lads?'

His mates cheered.

The silver blade gleamed in the light, close to Nina's throat.

Chapter Twelve

Into the shocked silence came shouts of outrage from all corners of the room.

'Bloody delinquents!'

'Villains!'

'Hooligans!'

But when the leader brandished the knife at the company in general, and bicycle chains were produced from under the Edwardian attire of the others, the atmosphere became hushed with fear.

'Come on now, lads, this is getting out of hand,' said Tilly, moving out from behind the bar counter to lend her daughter support. 'On your way.'

'I told you to leave this to me, Mum,' admonished Nina, her throat dry, legs about to cave in.

'Not likely,' said Tilly.

The leader turned his attention back to Nina, touching her chin with the blade before stepping back with the knife still pointing in her direction. Her heart thumped with terror and her skin was damp with sweat. She was painfully aware of the danger. Last year a youth had been murdered by a gang of Teds on Clapham Common.

'We all want a pint o' bitter, missus,' he said. 'So go

and pour 'em for us . . . *now* . . . or you'll really get to know how sharp this blade is.'

'No,' managed Nina, though her mouth was dry with terror.

'Better give it to 'em, Nina,' advised Albert shakily, supported by a murmur of agreement from around the room.

'Maybe he's right, love,' said her mother.

'Keep out of it, Mum, *please*.' Nina turned to the leader. 'You want alcohol, you go somewhere else for it. We are not serving you in this pub.'

'If you don't, you'll get more of this,' he said, lightly touching her chin with the blade again.

'And this,' said one of the others, swinging a bicycle chain.

Breathless with fear but managing to fake assurance, she said, 'You'd better go ahead and do it then . . . 'cos I'm not serving you.'

He was clearly disconcerted by this unexpected opposition. 'Get over there and start pulling some pints, missus,' he demanded, but she noticed a slight tremor in his voice.

She knew that her safety depended on what worried him most: being made to look foolish in front of his friends by backing down, or actually using the knife.

'I'm not going anywhere,' she said, her gaze meeting his in a challenge.

Tension rocked the room as he put the knife against her cheek. His mates were beginning to turn pale. Weapons were being slipped back into pockets as they realised that they could be accessories to a serious crime and, more importantly, recipients of the concomitant punishment. She felt the balance of power swing in her favour.

'Why don't you get out?' she demanded. 'You're not getting a drink in this pub.'

'Don't waste your time on 'er,' said one of his mates.

'No . . . she ain't worth it,' said another.

Slowly their leader lowered the knife and put it back into his pocket.

'We didn't want your lousy beer anyway,' he said with renewed bravado. 'Wouldn't wanna drink in a pub full of old codgers.' He turned to his friends. 'Come on, lads, let's get out of this dump and go somewhere a bit more lively.'

Swinging his shoulders, he led the crêpe-soled brigade to the door. Following them and seeing them safely off the premises, Nina turned towards the room heaving a loud sigh of relief. To her utter amazement, the entire company erupted into applause. At which point she burst into tears.

One November evening of the same year, Baz stood shivering on the riverside outside The Willow, the raw cold of the foggy night seeping into his bones. Many other times over the last couple of years he'd stood on this very spot in the dark, longing to go in and see Nina. Commonsense had always prevailed and he'd walked away telling himself it was all for the best but feeling bitterly disappointed.

Tonight, however, the need to see her again was particularly strong. Deeply apprehensive, he pushed open the doors of the saloon bar which was fairly crowded considering it was a winter weeknight. He made his way over to the bar feeling more nervous with every step.

'Evenin', squire,' said the barman.

'Evenin',' said Baz.

'What can I get for you?'

'A scotch, please.'

Dick took a glass from the shelf and turned to the optics. 'Brass monkey weather tonight, all right,' he remarked, turning round and putting the drink on the bar.

'Not 'alf.' Baz just couldn't bring himself to tell the man who he was and ask to see Nina. It was as though he had entered into enemy territory, where everybody was ready to castigate him for deserting his wife and child. 'You still manage to draw a crowd though . . . despite the cold weather.'

'Oh, yeah, it's a rare night we aren't busy at The Willow.'

'Too much to do for one barman, I should think?' said Baz, deviously probing for information.

The man was unwittingly accommodating. 'That's right, but I won't be on my own for long. It's the landlady's night off but her daughter will be coming on duty soon . . . when she's finished getting her little boy to bed.'

'I see.'

Baz swallowed the drink and immediately asked for another. He was dry-mouthed and inwardly quaking. This was not a good idea! He would drink up and leave.

He was probably the last man on earth Nina would want to see. He paid for the second drink and finished it in one.

'See you, mate,' he said, pulling on his leather gloves.

'You off already?' the barman said in surprise.

'Yeah . . . see you again sometime, perhaps.'

He was about to turn and walk away when he saw her. She appeared through the door at the back of the bar looking stunning, her halo of red-gold hair gleaming vividly against her emerald green jersey dress. He didn't move or speak, just stood where he was staring at her.

'Hello, Baz,' she said in an impersonal manner, almost as though he was just another customer. 'What brings you to these parts?'

'I . . . er . . . well . . .'

'It isn't like you to be lost for words,' she said briskly.

Meeting her eyes he saw a new confidence there – a harshness he had never seen in her before.

'No . . . um . . . er . . . I was just passing,' he managed at last.

'I see.' She turned to the barman. 'Isn't there anyone wanting service in the public bar, Dick?'

'Oh, right,' he said receiving the message and mooching off towards the other bar.

'You look wonderful,' said Baz.

'Thank you,' she replied graciously. 'I do what I can with nature's basic ingredients, you know.'

'You're so stylish now . . . your hair's shorter . . . it suits you.'

'Short styles are all the rage,' she informed him coldly. 'In this trade it isn't good for business to go about looking like a frump.'

'No, of course it isn't.' He studied her face, trying to identify this cool sophisticate with the spontaneous young girl he had known.

'Are you going to stand there gawping at me all night or are you going to do the decent thing and buy a drink?' she asked crisply.

'Nina, can we talk?'

'Sure, if you don't mind doing so in between customers.'

'You know that isn't what I mean,' he said.

'Do I really?' she said with undisguised hostility. 'Well, it's news to me. How would I know what you mean about anything? You're a stranger to me.'

'I must speak to you alone.'

'Not possible, I'm afraid,' she said tartly. 'It's Mum's night off. I can't leave Dick on his own.'

'Another time then.'

'I don't have much time to myself actually, Baz,' she said with more than a touch of asperity. 'Bringing up a child alone as well as helping to run a pub keeps me fully occupied.'

He cast down his eyes. 'I suppose I deserve that.'

'You must be the judge of that,' she told him sharply.

'Can I see you one evening away from here?' he implored. 'We could have dinner together, perhaps.'

'Why? What reason do you have for asking?'

'I just want to be with you . . . to talk to you.'

'Well, there's a novelty,' she said with a cutting edge

to her voice. 'I thought getting away from me was more your style.'

'I didn't expect you to be pleased to see me.'

'You'll not be disappointed then, will you?'

'Please have dinner with me one evening soon?' he persisted. 'On your next free night off perhaps?'

She gave a tight little laugh, shaking her head in disbelief. 'You really are the bloody end, Baz Paxton. You turn up here after nearly eight years and start trying to date me as though nothing has happened!'

'Please, Nina.'

She turned away and served a customer, her smile belying her inner turmoil. Having completed the business, she turned back to Baz.

'All right. Pick me up here at seven-thirty on Thursday evening,' she said in a cool, efficient manner. 'Now, if you'll excuse me, I have to go upstairs to make sure my son is all right.'

Instructing Dick to take charge for a few minutes, she left the bar. Once in the hallway, with the door closed behind her, her control faltered and she began to quiver from top to toe.

Seeing him again had devastated her. All those years of discipline counted for nothing against the strength of her feelings for him. Resolving not to let them destroy her, she hurried upstairs to try to recover her composure before she went back to face the customers.

'So you're a legitimate businessman now, then?' said Nina as they lingered over coffee in the restaurant of a

West End hotel on Thursday evening.

'That's right.'

'Which is what you always wanted.'

'Yes.'

'You must be feeling pretty damned pleased with yourself, having proved to everybody you can do it.'

'It was myself I had to prove it to,' he corrected.

'Well, whatever. But now that you've got it all out of your system, what comes next?'

'Progress, I suppose. The television shop is only a beginning. It was something I could get into without a huge amount of capital,' he explained. 'I started with just a couple of sets and gradually built up stock. It's an established business now but it's still only a very small shop.'

'Will you open another?'

'Maybe, or I might go into something entirely different . . . if I come across the right opportunity.'

'Oh, really? Do you have anything definite in mind?'

'No, not yet,' he said, 'but I'll know what I'm looking for when I see it.'

Nina had behaved with cool courtesy towards him throughout a superb meal. Now, as it drew to a close, she thought it was time to bring matters to a head.

'So, Baz, you've spent a fortune wining and dining me . . . you've brought me up to date with what you've been doing since I last saw you . . . now I'd like to know what all this is really about.'

'I still love you, Nina,' was the simple reply.

'Oh, no, not that,' she said, raising her hands in protest. 'Don't do this to me, Baz, it isn't fair.'

'I didn't intend this to happen, believe me,' he said, shaking his head. 'When I called in to see you the other night . . . all I wanted was to see you again, really . . . but as soon as I clapped eyes on you . . . I knew . . .' His voice was unsteady with emotion and he cleared his throat. 'I knew that you're still the only woman for me.'

'Stop it, Baz, please.'

'I can't help the way I feel, Nina,' he said ardently, leaning forward and looking into her face. 'I'm older now, the circumstances are different. I know I could make you happy if you'd give me a chance. I really do love you.'

She stared at him across the starched white table linen cluttered with bone china crockery and crystal wine glasses. 'The word love rolls off your tongue so easily,' she said.

'It's what I feel.'

'Isn't real love supposed to make you want to be with someone no matter how bad things get? Not disappear when the going gets tough and stay away for the best part of eight years.'

'I've stayed away because I thought it was the best thing for you.'

'Too ashamed to do anything else, more like!'

'Yes, there was an element of that too,' he admitted candidly. 'I'm not proud of the way I've behaved.'

'I should damned well hope not!'

'Many a night I've stood outside The Willow trying to pluck up the courage to come in and see you.'

'My heart bleeds for you.'

'You've changed,' he said. 'You've become hard.'

'Hardly surprising, is it?'

'I suppose not.'

'You suppose not?' she rasped, her eyes hot with rage. 'Have you any idea what I went through after you left?'

'We couldn't have gone on as we were . . . you must have known that.'

'No, but we could have talked about it . . . tried to work something out,' she told him. 'You don't just run out on someone you love. It was cruel . . . unforgivable.'

'Everything you say is true,' he admitted. 'I know I must have put you through hell. At that time it seemed as though I was hurting you more by staying.'

'Nothing could have been as bad as your going off like that,' she told him. 'I wanted to die. If it hadn't been for Joey . . . well, I'm not sure I could have gone on.'

'I felt bad too,' he sighed. 'But I just couldn't take any more of the way things were between us.'

'Obviously.'

'I didn't enjoy walking out like that,' he pleaded, 'and I've never stopped missing you.'

'I don't need this sort of talk, Baz,' she said. 'I've made a life for myself and Joey. I won't let you come back and wreck it.'

'I won't wreck it, not this time. I want you back, Nina,' he told her urgently. 'You and Joey.'

'You must be off your chump if you think I'd even consider it.'

'It'll be different this time,' he said. 'I'll make it up to you.'

'No, Baz,' she said determinedly. 'No . . . no . . . no . . .!'

'Don't you feel anything for me at all?' he asked.

'Oh, yes, I feel something for you all right,' she said. 'But most of the time it feels like hatred.'

'Just give me a chance to change all that.'

'If you had come back and asked me this in the first year after you'd left, I'd probably have been persuaded. I wanted you that bad.' She moistened her dry mouth with a sip of coffee. 'But when I began to emerge from the hell you'd left me in, I'd changed. I might not have been happy but I was in control. And I never want to lose control again.'

'I'd respect your independence.'

'You don't understand, Baz,' she cut in swiftly. 'It goes much deeper than my independence. I can't forgive you, you see, and without that we'd be back where we were before you left.'

'In time you would learn to trust me again.'

'No, I honestly don't think I would. So there can be no reconciliation.' She brushed her brow with her hand. 'Please don't upset me by trying to change my mind. I really don't want any of this.'

He knew she meant what she said and he had no right to pursue her on this question. 'All right, Nina,' he said sadly. 'I'll do what you ask.'

She gulped her coffee, knowing that she had just passed through a crisis. She wanted him back with a kind of desperation, but it couldn't work. She was carrying too much bitterness and it would continually come between them.

'However, because I don't think it would be right for me to stand between you and your son, I'll agree to your

185

seeing Joey on a regular basis. If you wish.'

'I'd really like that.'

'You've provided well for him all these years, I'll say that much for you, but I'll only agree to your seeing him on my terms.'

'Oh?'

'If you're not happy with my conditions we'll have to fight it out in court,' she said brusquely, her emotional turmoil urging her to hurt him. 'Though I'm not sure the law would be too sympathetic towards an absentee father.'

'Hey, calm down. You know I would never resort to the law on something as personal as this,' he said. 'As far as I'm concerned the only rights I have over Joey are the ones you allow me to have.'

'Right . . . so long as we understand each other.' She took a deep breath to try to calm her turbulent emotions which were causing her to over-react to everything he said. 'You must realise that I have Joey's interests to think of. I've been both mother and father to him. I've tried to give him stability. I don't want my authority undermined just because you've come back on the scene.'

'Okay, I respect that. So what do you have in mind?'

'I'll agree to your seeing Joey regularly so long as it doesn't interfere with any arrangements I have made for him or with his schooling,' she said assertively, 'and only if he wants to see you.'

'You think he might not want to, then?'

'I'm not sure. He's nearly nine . . . old enough to have opinions of his own even if they are childish ones.'

'Old enough to think of me as a right bastard?'

'I've tried not to let my own feelings influence the way I've dealt with his questions,' she explained. 'I've told him that these things happen between grown-ups sometimes ... that it can't be helped ... all that sort of thing. But when it comes down to it, Baz, you left us and he knows it. He's very protective of me. Boys often are towards their mothers.'

'He'll probably give me a hard time then?'

'My guess is that he'll either hate you or hero worship you,' she said. 'Either way you're going to need a whole lot of patience. So if you're not prepared for that, then I'd rather you didn't take it on at all. Don't start seeing him if you're going to give up at the first hurdle.'

'I understand.'

'Another thing . . . please don't try to use this situation to get at me,' she said in a businesslike manner. 'I want no more talk of our getting back together. You will collect him from The Willow and bring him home again. That is all. The only contact you and I need have will be concerning our son.' She gave him a hard look. 'Is that understood?'

'Don't worry, I won't bother you. I've done enough damage.'

'Good. And while we're in the mood to put our affairs in order,' she continued in a formal manner, 'there is no need for you to support me financially any longer. Provided you continue to supply money for Joey, I can manage.'

'Oh . . . but I'd like to continue to pay maintenance for you as well,' he said, frowning.

'And I'd rather you didn't.'

'But I can afford it,' he persisted. 'I'm doing well.'

'So am I,' she told him. 'The Willow is really on the up now. Mum and I are able to draw a good salary.'

He looked deeply depressed. 'It means a lot to me, to be able to help you in that way.'

'And it means a lot to me to be independent,' she replied.

'At least I felt I wasn't failing in my duty completely when I was supporting you financially.'

'As far as I'm concerned, you no longer have a duty to me . . . only to Joey.'

'You are still my wife . . .'

'Only on paper, and we can soon alter that if you wish.'

'You mean divorce,' he said grimly.

'That's right,' she said. 'I'm not expecting to get married again myself so things can stay as they are for the time being as far as I'm concerned. I've heard divorce is awfully long and drawn out. But if ending our marriage legally will help you to accept the fact that it is over between us, then it might be the best thing.'

'No, no,' he said quickly, 'there's no need for anything as dramatic as that.'

'Okay then. Now, about your seeing Joey . . . may I suggest Saturday or Sunday afternoons, say once a month?'

Chapter Thirteen

'You haven't managed to get your feet back under the table at The Willow, then, Baz?' remarked George one Sunday the following autumn when Baz was having lunch with him and Marge in their new house at Acton. 'Even though you're seein' the boy regularly.'

'What a thing to say,' objected Baz sharply. 'You make it sound as though I'm using our meetings as some sort of leverage ... and that's the last thing I'd do.'

'Sorry, bruv, no offence meant,' said George with genuine contrition. 'You know me, it's just my way.'

'Okay.' Baz gave his brother a small grin to indicate that he was forgiven. George's heart was in the right place even if he was short on savoir-faire. Still unhappy with responsibility, George relied on his wife and brother to ease him through life. Both accepted his shortcomings in this respect since he had abundant kindness and loyalty.

Baz considered him to be an asset in his business, his diligence and commitment making up for a certain lack of acumen. It was obvious to anyone that Marge was the brains in their marriage. She had made the decision to buy this house and organised the mortgage. All that was required of George was to sign on the dotted line and supply the deposit. The latter was no problem because Baz made sure his brother shared generously in his own success.

He was very fond of them both. George was his only close blood relative since their father's demise, and Marge was more like a sister than a sister-in-law. She made their home open house to him and this meant a lot to Baz. Having all grown up together in North London, he'd counted her a friend long before they had become related.

'How are things going with young Joey now?' she asked, pouring some mint sauce over her roast lamb.

'Oh . . . about the same,' he said with a gloomy sigh.

She gave a sympathetic sigh. 'No improvement at all then, after nearly a year?'

Sprinkling salt and pepper over his food, he said, 'No, he obviously can't stand the sight of me.'

'It's odd that he still agrees to see you, isn't it?' she said thoughtfully. 'If that's the way he feels.'

'That's because he enjoys making me suffer, I should think.'

'What exactly does he do to make your meetings so awful?' she enquired, observing Baz with interest.

'He's sulky . . . uncommunicative . . . ill-mannered.'

'Is it worth persevering, then?' wondered Marge who had recently become a blonde and wore her hair backcombed around her face in the latest Italian style. 'There doesn't seem to be much point if you both have such a miserable time.'

'I'll stick it out as long as he still wants it,' said Baz.

'I won't be the one to give up.'

'And you'll go on letting him get away with murder the whole time, I suppose?' she chided disapprovingly.

'I'll have to be patient with him if I want him to learn to like me,' Baz pointed out. 'He does have good reason to hate my guts after all. I did walk out on him and his mother.'

Marge put down her knife and fork and leaned forward, her cheeks suffused with an angry flush as she addressed her brother-in-law. 'You make me so mad sometimes, Baz,' she told him hotly. 'All right, so you walked out on your wife and child . . . and it was a lousy thing to do . . . but does it mean you're going to have to spend every second of the rest of your life feeling guilty about it and licking the boots of that boy of yours?'

'Of course not but . . .'

'I don't know the intimate details of what went wrong between you and Nina, of course,' she continued in strident tones, 'but I've always believed that these things take two. I find it hard to believe that she was *completely* blameless in the break up of your marriage.'

'It was me who walked out.'

'Maybe if she'd been different, you might have stayed.'

'It wasn't her fault.'

'Okay, carry all the blame on your own shoulders if you feel you must,' she said with feeling. 'But please, Baz, don't let young Joey treat you like dirt. You're worth more than that. You might have done wrong by him and his mother but you still have a right to some happiness, every bit as much as they have.'

'Marge, love,' admonished George mildly, 'it isn't any of our business.'

She reached across the table and rested her hand on her brother-in-law's. 'Sorry, Baz, I spoke out of turn. But the three of us go back a long way and it upsets me to see you punishing yourself.'

'I know, Marge,' he said, giving her hand an affectionate squeeze.

'Even apart from that, giving in to Joey all the time isn't going to do him any good,' she opined, 'and it certainly won't help your relationship with him.'

'I know you mean well, Marge,' he said. 'But do you think we could change the subject?'

'Sure.' After a brief pause she said, 'Has George told you that I've booked a course of driving lessons?'

'No.'

'Well, I have. Isn't it exciting? I'll be able to run errands in the firm's van when I've passed my test.'

'Oh dear,' said Baz with a look of feigned horror. 'I don't know if I'll be able to stand the worry of knowing you're out on the loose in the van.'

'I'll be perfectly all right,' she said brightly.

'You will, yes . . . but what about the van?' he teased.

Her reply was a sharp kick on the ankle. They finished the meal in fine bantering form until it was time for Baz to leave to collect Joey for their monthly outing.

Baz and Joey had been to a cinema in the West End to see *The King and I*.

'Well, what did you think of it?' asked Baz, as they

192

emerged into Leicester Square.

'Rubbish,' declared Joey. 'I wanted to see "Rock Around the Clock".'

'So you've said . . . at least a dozen times,' said Baz. 'And I've told you why we didn't go to see that . . . because Teddy Boys are causing trouble at every cinema where it's showing.'

'I'm not afraid of them.'

'No, but you wouldn't enjoy being caught up in one of their riots, I'm sure,' said his father. 'Apparently there's jiving in the aisles and fireworks being let off . . . not to mention plenty of bad language.'

'You're old fashioned.'

'Very probably,' Baz said in the controlled manner he had learned to adopt towards Joey's insolence.

'Glad you admit it.'

'Where would you like to go for tea?'

'I'm not bothered,' Joey replied with studious indifference.

This was the sort of behaviour Baz had come to expect from his son. Today, however, as a result of Marge's plain speaking at lunch, it seemed completely unacceptable to him.

'Okay, as you're not bothered, we'll do what I say,' he said, grabbing the boy's hand and leading him forcibly to the car he'd parked in a side street.

'Where are we going?' asked Joey as Baz drove out of the West End.

'To my place.'

'I don't wanna go there,' he wailed, 'I wanna have my tea out.'

'You're too late, mate. You've lost your chance.'

'I wanna go home.'

'You'll go home when I say so,' Baz informed him.

Back at his flat Baz made a pot of tea, cut some bread and spread it with butter, put it with a pot of jam on the table in the living room and told Joey to get on with it.

'I'm not eating that rubbish,' said the boy. 'I always have something nice on a Sunday.'

Baz gave him a hard look. 'Are you sure you don't want it?' he asked, glancing towards the table.

'Yeah.'

'Right, you'll have nothing at all then,' he announced, removing the food from the table and marching into the kitchen with it.

Returning, he poured himself a cup of tea and sat in the armchair.

'I'll tell my mum about this,' muttered Joey.

'You won't need to because I intend to tell her what an oik you are when she's not around.'

'Don't you dare upset my mum,' the boy said vehemently.

'She's a right to know how you behave when you're out of her sight.' He hadn't emphasised his difficulties with Joey to Nina because he had seen the problem as his own punishment for the sins of the past. Marge's common sense had given him a wider perspective.

'I hate you,' announced Joey miserably.

'You've made that very obvious.' Taking his tea, Baz moved from the armchair and sat down opposite his son at the table. 'And while we're on that subject, let's have this out in the open once and for all, shall we?'

'I . . .'

'Quiet,' boomed Baz. 'You listen to me for a change.'

'But . . .'

'Shut up. I don't want a peep out of you until I've finished speaking.'

Finally reduced to silence, Joey stared goggle-eyed at his father.

'Okay,' said Baz, 'I accept that you have every right to hate me because of what I've done. It was a very bad thing to do and it means that I don't have the right to bring you up.'

The boy sat in silence, his face paper white against his navy blue jumper.

'I left for reasons you are far too young to understand,' Baz continued. 'I deeply regret it but I cannot change it. I may have lost all rights in your upbringing but I do have a right to courtesy from you because *I* treat *you* in a decent manner.'

'Huh!'

'Do you realise that you're letting your mother down by behaving like an ignorant lout? She's doing her best for you. The least you can do for her is to behave properly when she's not with you.' He paused, looking at his son closely. 'Don't you think I have a point?'

Joey shrugged his shoulders. 'I'm not rude to other people.'

'Don't be rude to me then.'

'I don't have to like you just because you're my father.'

'And I don't have to like you just because you're my son.'

'Oh!' That side of the argument obviously hadn't occurred to him.

'How can I like you when you always behave like such a cretin?'

'I don't care if you hate the sight of me!'

'Look,' said Baz patiently, 'I've organised these meetings because I thought it might be a good idea for us to get to know each other better.' He paused for a moment and took a deep breath. 'It isn't working out so if you'd rather not see me again, just say the word and we'll call it a day.'

The boy didn't reply.

'Well?' said Baz.

'I don't really know,' mumbled Joey at last.

'If we do continue to see each other though,' Baz continued evenly, 'you'll behave properly. One more rude word out of you and I'll disappear off the scene altogether.' He sipped his tea. 'It's entirely up to you, I'm easy either way. Think about it and let me know.' He stood up. 'Now get your coat and I'll take you home.'

Joey didn't move.

'Come on, chop chop. I haven't got all night.'

'Can I have a slice of bread and jam, please?' he asked.

'You said it was rubbish.'

The boy stared at his hands in his lap, fiddling with his finger nails. 'Well . . . um . . . I suppose that wasn't really true,' he mumbled, looking up at his father uncertainly. 'I'm ever so hungry and I would like something to eat . . . please?'

Encouraged by this volte-face, Baz was tempted to

relent and take him out to the espresso bar round the corner. But his better judgement told him to stand firm or he'd be back at square one. Joey might never learn to like his father but he'd damned well learn that he could only push him so far.

Baz went to the kitchen and returned with the food. 'Dig in,' he said.

'Thanks,' muttered Joey sheepishly.

Father and son didn't exactly become bosom pals after that but there was an improvement. At Joey's request the meetings continued, and, although he still kept his distance from his father, his manners were better. He had never called Baz anything, presumably because he found it impossible to say 'Dad'. Baz ended this embarrassment by inviting him to use his christian name which Joey seemed to find acceptable.

The pattern of their meetings changed very much for the better one weekend in December. Joey couldn't make Sunday afternoon that week because he'd been invited to a friend's birthday party, and Baz wasn't free on a Saturday because it was their busiest day in the shop and he didn't think it fair to leave George and Marge to cope alone.

Baz said Joey was welcome to spend Saturday with him but it would have to be either in the flat or the shop so he would be on hand to keep an eye on things. To his surprise Joey accepted. Once having sampled the atmosphere of Portobello Market, he preferred to spend part of every Saturday at his father's place instead of their formal Sunday outings.

Being a natural extrovert like his parents, Joey soon made friends with the stall holders, chatting to them and running errands. The fruit and vegetable section of the market was in the immediate vicinity of Baz's shop but further along there were stalls offering clothes, leathergoods, spices, fish, meat, and a multitude of other goodies. There were secondhand stalls and bric-a-brac barrows; fortune tellers and flower-sellers.

The mainstay of the market was the antique trade and the number of dealers working here had grown rapidly since the beginning of the decade.

Another culture that was growing fast in the area was noticed by Joey who had a very enquiring mind.

'There are a lot of black people round here, aren't there?' he said.

'Mm . . . quite few.'

'Why so many here?'

'They all move into the same area to be near their friends and relatives, I suppose,' said Baz. 'It's only natural.'

'Some people call 'em spades, don't they?' said Joey.

'Some ignorant people do, yes,' said Baz. 'Don't you let me ever hear you calling them that.'

'Why not?'

'Because it's insulting. How would you like it if people called you names?'

'They do. Some kids at school call me Stuffing.'

'Paxton . . . Paxo . . . stuffing,' said Baz with a grin. 'How did you guess?'

'Because that was my nickname when I was at school too,' he said, experiencing a sudden frisson at this unexpected reminder of his paternity.

'Cor . . .'

'But that's done in a friendly way and is quite different to calling people names just because of their race or colour.'

'Okay, I won't do it,' said Joey in a matter-of-fact manner.

The market boosted business for Baz because it drew crowds to the area. Joey was curious about this too.

'Do you like selling televisions?' he asked one winter afternoon when they were having buttered crumpets for tea upstairs in the flat. They were sitting at the table in the window, looking down into the crowded street, the dusk ablaze with colour and light from the stalls. Distant strains of music from the buskers could be heard above the loud vitality of the traders at work.

'It's a living,' replied Baz.

'Would you rather be doing something else then?' asked his son.

Baz thought about this for a minute. 'Yes, I think I would.'

'What?'

'I don't know.'

'How do you know you want to do it if you don't know what it is?' asked Joey.

'Well . . . one day I might come across a business proposition that will excite me,' Baz explained, 'and if that ever happens I'll stop selling televisions.'

'Oh.'

'What about you . . . what do you want to do when you leave school?'

'Work in the pub with Mum and Gran,' Joey said without hesitation.

'That isn't very ambitious, is it?' said Baz. 'Don't you fancy something a bit more adventurous?'

'Oh, yeah. I fancy being a rock 'n roll star like Elvis,' the boy grinned, 'but as that isn't very likely, I'll settle for a job at The Willow.'

'Surely you want to stretch your wings further than that?'

'No, why should I?' queried Joey. 'Mum was brought up there and she enjoys working there now. I'm looking forward to it. I can't wait until I'm old enough.'

This conversation worried Baz and set him thinking seriously about Joey's future. He felt he needed a private discussion with Nina about it but this was no simple matter since she discouraged anything other than superficial chit-chit when he called to collect and deliver the boy. There was one way he could speak to her without Joey being present, however. So he called at The Willow one Monday evening early in 1957 and broached the subject over the bar.

'Have you ever considered the idea of having Joey privately educated when it's time for him to go up to the seniors?' he enquired, after she'd served him with a drink.

'Yes, I've thought about it from time to time,' she said meditatively. 'Why do you ask?'

'I think it might be a good idea to send him to a good boarding school,' he said. 'I'll pay the fees.'

'What's brought this on?' she asked, somewhat taken aback.

'He's getting to the age when we have to think of his future,' he said. 'Boarding school will broaden his mind . . . his being an only child and living at the pub.'

'Growing up here didn't do me any harm,' she pointed out.

'No, that's true,' he admitted, 'but let's face it, Nina, neither of us had much of an education. It would be nice to think we'd given him a better start than we had. I'm not rich by any means, but I'm doing all right, I can afford it.'

'Boarding school though,' she said doubtfully. 'It's a bit drastic.'

'I don't think so, not really. After all, it isn't unheard of for publicans to send their children away to school . . . at least it gets them away from the pub environment for a while.'

Whilst Nina couldn't bear the idea of sending Joey away, she could see some sense in what Baz was suggesting with her son's future in mind.

'Yes, that is a valid point,' she was forced to admit.

'His horizons are very narrow at the moment,' he continued. 'All he wants to do is to go into the family business when he leaves school.' He paused for a moment then added quickly, 'Not that there's anything wrong with that, of course, but I think he should at least have the chance to get some qualifications . . . just in case he wants to do something else when the time comes.'

'I must admit I've had similar thoughts myself over the years,' she admitted. 'But there was never enough money to do anything about it until recently. I was thinking more in terms of his being a day boy somewhere local, though.'

'Boarding school would give him more all round benefit, I think,' said Baz. 'It would teach him independence and confidence to make his own way in the world.'

'Mm, maybe. I'm not sure how he'll feel about the idea, though,' she said. 'He'll probably hate you for suggesting it.'

'I can live with that if you and I decide it's the best thing for him. I stopped trying to be popular with him some time ago.'

'Well . . . look . . . I'll think about it and have a chat with Mum. And Joey.' Her tone changed suddenly and became brisk and formal, reminding him of his place outside the family circle. 'I'll let you know what we decide.'

'Okay.'

'Now if you'll excuse me, I have customers waiting to be served.'

Smarting from her abrupt manner, Baz finished his beer and left, feeling excluded and lonely. Just when they appeared to be together on something, she put up the barriers with him firmly on the other side. Would her refusal to let him back into her life ever stop hurting? he wondered, as he drove back to Ladbroke Grove.

Nina was thinking much the same thing as she called time that night. Seeing Baz regularly when he came for Joey was a terrible strain. Having to keep him at arm's length so that nothing was allowed to develop between them left her emotionally drained.

It now occurred to her that he would only have cause to come here in the holidays if Joey went away to school. The prospect should have been a comforting one but instead it made the future seem very bleak indeed.

Chapter Fourteen

Nina found herself in a difficult period of adjustment that autumn after Joey went away to school in Dorset. The place seemed desolate without his youthful exuberance and she agonised as to whether or not she'd done the right thing in agreeing to let him go. But once his cheery epistles began to arrive in the post, filled with chatter about his new friends, her doubts were diminished. If pub life had taught her son nothing else, it had taught him to mix.

The licensed trade had entered a period of change too these last few years with the general improvement in the economy. Following the end of building restrictions, which had given priority to housing and industry, new pubs were appearing in and around London to replace those that had been bombed.

Many of the new hostelries were far removed from 'locals' like The Willow. They were smart and modern with brightly coloured interiors furnished with Formica tables, plastic-covered chairs and juke boxes filled with American hits instead of a piano. In tune with the general reaction against austerity they were often much more brightly lit than their predecessors.

Nina and Tilly had found it necessary to modernise The Willow but had been careful not to destroy the character of the place. As the living standards of most of their customers had improved dramatically since the end of the war, the local had to keep in step. The shabby old furniture in the saloon bar had been replaced with comfortable chairs in red with cream Formica-topped tables; the old brown lino that had served them right through the war was discarded in favour of a warm, red-patterned carpet on which stood a new piano in place of the battered old honkytonk one.

Up-to-date radiators now supported the log fires in their battle against bitter winter draughts that whistled through the old building. Even the public bar boasted a television set and modern floor tiles.

Outside, the landscape had not remained unchanged either. The Great West Road had opened in 1956 and split the community in two. Public gardens now covered the bombed site of a number of factories near The Willow, and smart riverside flats had been built nearby, the latter being popular with city commuters. This meant a change of clientele. They lost some customers who now lived the other side of a busy road – and gained new ones from the luxury flats.

However, Nina was far too busy to dwell upon any of these innovations. As the soft golden autumn headed towards winter her mother fell victim to the Asian flu epidemic that was wreaking havoc across the country. For the first time that Nina could remember, Tilly was forced to take to her bed. Brenda, their part-time bar-maid, also succumbed which left Nina overworked and praying that Dick wouldn't fall sick.

Most of the regulars were sympathetic to her difficulties and patient about the drop in the standard of service. But not everyone was so co-operative as she discovered one Saturday evening when a social function in a local hall provided them with a rush of business during the interval.

'Any chance of us getting served in this lifetime?' asked a youngish, well-spoken man in blazer and flannels, impatiently tapping a coin on the counter.

'Are you running a pub here or a waiting room?' chipped in one of his friends.

'I'll be with you as soon as I can, sir,' said Nina, flushed but outwardly calm as she worked at the pumps and optics while Dick was busy in the other bar.

'You should employ more staff if you intend to give a service,' admonished Blazer.

'I'm so sorry. I've got people down with Asian flu,' she began.

'We all have problems,' interrupted Blazer haughtily. 'We come in to a pub to forget about them. We don't want to be lumbered with other people's.'

'I only have one pair of hands,' she reminded him.

'There's plenty of other pubs around here only too eager to take our money,' was Blazer's surly retort.

Nina glanced at the sea of faces on the other side of the bar, all vying with each other for her attention. 'Well, sir, if you're in that much of a hurry, may I suggest you try your luck at one of those?' she said with icy politeness though her cheeks were flaming. 'As much as I would like to I really can't work any faster, neither am I responsible for the Asian flu epidemic.'

'Can I give you a hand to clear the decks?' enquired a refined male voice beside her.

Turning, she found herself looking into the face of a good-looking stranger. 'Well . . . er . . . I'm not sure,' she muttered, feeling somewhat taken aback.

'I hope you don't mind my taking the liberty of coming round to this side of the counter,' he explained with perfect diction, 'only I can see that you're really up against it. And some of them are starting to get stroppy.'

'There's always someone who'll jump at the chance to complain,' she said in a low voice, adding a measure of orange to some gin in a glass.

'I do have some bar experience,' he continued. 'A friend of mine has an hotel. I've helped out as a favour when I've been staying there.'

'Um . . . I . . .' A clamour of voices demanding attention seemed suddenly to press in on her from all sides. 'Well, thank you, I could really do with an extra pair of hands.'

His name was Lester Tibbs, he told her later when the pub was closed and they were sitting by the saloon bar fire relaxing with a drink. He was thirty-five and had just moved into Acorn Court, a new block of exclusive flats.

'My office is in the West End so this area is highly convenient for work, whilst still being away from the crowds.'

'I don't know so much about that . . . it seems to be getting busier than ever around here lately,' she remarked. 'What with all the new buildings and more and more cars on the road.'

'The waterfront has a kind of peacefulness about it, though.'

'Oh, yes. I've always considered myself fortunate to live on the river.'

As he sipped his drink, Nina ran an approving eye over him. He was tall and slim with a mass of fair hair fashionably cut and brushed back from his forehead. He was impeccably dressed in a pale grey Italian-style suit with a snowy white shirt and blue silk tie. As for his face . . . well, stunning was the only suitable adjective. He had the most perfect features she had ever seen on a man. His lips were pink and bowed, his teeth pure white. Long lashes curled around bluish-grey eyes. He really was exceptional.

'So, what line of business are you in?' she asked conversationally.

'Property,' he said, leaning back and smoking a cigarette.

'An estate agent?'

'Commercial premises mostly,' he explained.

'Luckily for me you seem able to turn your hand to other things,' she smiled. 'I really do appreciate your help this evening.'

'It was a pleasure,' he said smoothly. 'A nice change from my usual work.'

'You saved my life, anyway,' she told him. 'One of the drawbacks of being a privately owned house is that you can't hand that sort of problem over to the brewery.'

'No . . .'

'Which reminds me, how much do I owe you for your efforts?'

'Don't be silly,' he said.

'Well, if you're really sure,' she said graciously, because to insist seemed insulting.

'Of course I'm sure,' he said. 'I'm usually around in the evenings and weekends and I'll gladly help out again until one of the invalids is back on duty, if you need a hand.'

'It's kind of you but I couldn't let you work for nothing,' she said, feeling embarrassed, 'and I'd feel awkward offering you barman's rates.'

'Don't give it another thought,' he assured her, his eyes meetings hers disturbingly. 'Just look on it as my doing a favour for a neighbour.'

'Well, in that case,' she smiled, 'all I can say is, thank you very much.'

'How about tomorrow lunchtime?' he enquired.

'A helping hand would be very welcome,' she told him. 'We're always packed to the doors on a Sunday lunchtime, usually with men, so it can get pretty boisterous.'

'I'll be here when you open,' he said, reaching across the table and briefly touching her hand before rising to leave. 'You can rely on it.'

'I'll look forward to it,' she said, somewhat bewildered by the effect he was having on her.

'I'm not at all sure I like the idea of a complete stranger being on our side of the bar when we haven't even checked his references,' said Tilly the next morning

210

when Nina took her breakfast in bed and told her about their temporary helper. 'You make sure you keep a firm eye on the till.'

'That's a bit cynical,' tutted Nina.

'Maybe it is . . . but when some bloke we've never set eyes on before comes in off the street and offers to work for nothing, it makes sense to be cautious,' said Tilly, wheezing loudly for the flu had left her very bronchial. 'Different if it's a regular but there's a whole lot of villains out there, Nina. You've been in the pub game long enough to know that.'

'Lester Tibbs is no villain, I can promise you that,' she protested. 'He's educated, a man of means. It's written all over him.'

'Villains come in many disguises,' Tilly reminded her as Nina put the tray on the bedside cabinet while she propped up her mother's pillows. 'They don't all use bad language and dress like spivs.'

'You don't need to tell me that,' Nina pointed out. 'Not after the Jasper Cavendish affair.'

'Of course. I'd forgotten all about that bit o' trouble.'

'Lester is as straight as a die, I'd stake my life on it,' insisted Nina. 'A real gentleman . . . such lovely manners.'

'Sounds as though it's you I should be worryin' about, not the takings,' smiled Tilly.

'I should be so lucky,' laughed Nina. 'A man like Lester could have anyone. He's got everything . . . good looks, charm, money.'

'A real smoothie by the sound of it,' said Tilly.

'He's sophisticated certainly,' admitted Nina. 'A bit

different to the down-to-earth types we're used to.'

An attack of coughing halted Tilly's conversation for a while. 'The sooner I'm out of this ruddy bed and back downstairs the better,' she gasped when the hacking finally subsided. 'Before this bloomin' Tibbs bloke sweeps you off your feet altogether.'

'No chance of that,' Nina was quick to deny. 'I'm once bitten and twice shy in that direction.' She placed the tray in front of her mother. 'Come on, eat your breakfast while it's hot. I'll go and get your cough mixture.'

'Thanks, love,' said Tilly thoughtfully. She just couldn't wait to meet the 'amazing' Lester Tibbs.

During the next week Nina had cause to wonder how she would manage without Lester who was always there when she needed him. As soon as Tilly was well enough to get up and sit in a chair Nina took him upstairs to the flat and introduced them.

'He's certainly a charmer,' was her mother's verdict after he'd gone. 'Nearly as good-looking as Rock Hudson.'

'Better,' laughed Nina.

Nina and Lester had fallen into a pleasant routine. After they'd closed the pub and Nina had settled her mother for the night, they would unwind together with a drink by the dying embers of the log fire in the saloon bar. She looked forward to their little tête-à-têtes and was flattered by his interest in her.

'You're a very attractive woman,' he said one night over a gin and tonic.

'Tell me more . . . tell me more.' She laughed to keep the mood light.

'That husband of yours must have been mad to let you go.'

'It wasn't quite as simple as that,' she told him.

'These things never are.'

'Is that the voice of experience?' she asked.

'I've had my share of relationships, sure.'

'Have you ever been married?'

'No, I've never gone quite that far,' he said, his eyes meeting hers in a most provocative manner.

She steered the conversation on to Joey, hoping that a more maternal mood might defuse the sexual tension between them. It was a long time since she'd found a man physically attractive. This one had her feverish with desire and she wasn't sure she could handle it.

'You must have been quite young when you had your son,' he remarked in a complimentary manner.

'Yes, I was just out of my teens,' she told him. 'Back in the days before youth culture.'

'I remember it well.'

'Nowadays youngsters have their own fashions, their own music . . .'

'Even their own television shows like "The Six Five Special".'

'That's right.'

'It won't be long before your Joey is interested in all that.'

'He is already.'

They fell into a comfortable silence until Lester started talking about the pub. 'From what you've told me, I get the impression that you and your mother have an excellent partnership,' he said chattily.

'Oh, yes, we make a good team.'

'Partnerships don't always work so well, though, do they?' he remarked. 'Not even between relatives.'

'We're not legal partners,' she informed him.

'Oh, really?'

'No. My mother's the landlady, it's her business.'

'Yes, I've seen her name over the door. I thought perhaps you might be a part owner?'

'No, nothing like that. It's just a personal arrangement,' she explained. 'It's something that has progressed over the years into a sort of partnership. Maybe that's why we got along so well . . . because there's nothing in writing.'

They talked some more along these lines. His interest in the business pleased her. It showed that he was as curious about her life as she was about his.

'I shall miss our nocturnal chats,' she remarked as she saw him out. 'Both Mum and Brenda are on the mend. They'll be back on duty by the weekend.'

'We shall continue to see each other, though, I hope,' he said.

'So do I,' she said uncertainly. 'You'll be coming into The Willow for a drink, I expect?'

'I didn't mean that,' he said smoothly. 'I'd like us to see each other . . . "date" as they say in America.'

'Oh.' Naturally she was flattered but there was a certain hesitancy too. Relationships were synonymous with pain to her. It had been fun having Lester around to boost her ego and make her feel like an attractive woman again. It was good to know that her libido hadn't died the death after all this time . . . but did she want anything more than that? 'That would be nice but let's not make any firm arrangements until my mother is right back on form. I can't go very far until then, anyway.'

'That's fine with me,' he said, with one of the winning smiles which made her want to throw caution to the winds.

All thoughts of Lester were pushed into the background a few days later.

The day her mother was due to return to work, Nina woke up feeling peaky and by the afternoon was in the full throes of Asian flu, confined to bed and unable to think of anything beyond her aching limbs and blinding headache.

'I was planning to go to the doctor to get a jab too,' she confessed to her mother, for an Asian flu vaccine had recently become available.

'A bit too late for that now,' said Tilly.

'I'm sure Lester will give a hand downstairs in the evenings if you're pushed,' Nina suggested weakly through the blistered lips of her fever.

'There's no need. Dick and I can manage now that Brenda's back,' said Tilly.

Nina felt too rotten to care what happened in the pub. For over a week she felt at death's door, the influenza complicated by congestion of the lungs. Even when she was able to take a tentative step out of bed, she felt too weak to do anything other than sit in an armchair by the fire.

An abundance of flowers, fruit and chocolates arrived

from Lester but he didn't visit her because he hadn't had the vaccination. This suited Nina because she didn't feel up to seeing anyone except family. Alice, who had predictably taken preventative measures, came to see her cousin regularly.

'So you've found yourself a new man then?' she said lightly one foggy winter afternoon as the three women sat by the fire in the living room.

'Honestly, Alice, you make it sound as though I picked him up in some bargain basement,' said Nina.

'Judging by this lot,' said Alice, waving her hand towards the offerings adorning the sideboard, 'he's more of a Harrods or Fortnum's man.'

'You've some really weird ideas, Alice,' said Nina, with a watery smile.

'There's nothing weird about a man who sends presents. I'm very glad you've found someone at last,' said her cousin with her usual disregard for tact. 'It's high time you had a man in your life.'

'He isn't *in* my life, as you put it,' said Nina irritably.

'He'd like to be, though,' put in Tilly. 'That's obvious.'

'He feels sorry for me because I'm ill,' said Nina because she felt too feeble to bother about the implications of Lester's attentions. 'Once I'm well again it will all stop.'

Instead he grew more attentive. Gifts continued to be lavished upon her and as she grew stronger he delivered them personally, showing his thoughtfulness by staying only until she seemed to tire. She was grateful for this for she couldn't remember ever having been left so run down before with flu.

Even when she returned to work, she still wasn't on form. The December increase in trade in the run-up to Christmas, which she usually enjoyed, exhausted her. Having Lester in the background, eager to take her out in his Jaguar in her spare time, was so therapeutic!

They usually went up West to the theatre or cinema and dined out afterwards. Although she made light of it to her mother and Alice because she didn't want them jumping to any premature conclusions, Nina enjoyed his company enormously. Lighthearted entertainment was just what she needed while at this low ebb. His pampering was so wonderfully relaxing, she stopped trying to resist it.

One night in December, after they'd been to Wyndham's Theatre to see *The Boyfriend*, Lester invited her back to his flat.

'Phew, this is really something!' she said, as he showed her into a spacious lounge with huge windows overlooking the river, its inky waters splintered with light from the riverside buildings.

'You like it then?' he said, as she studied the soft blue carpet, the sleek grey chairs and sofas, the tasteful paintings on the wall, the fashionable bar curving across one corner.

'It's terrific,' she replied, but although she was being truthful it was not an ambiance in which she could feel comfortable for any length of time. It was too clinically stylish with white and grey walls, spindle-shanked standard lamps, skinny sofas.

His kitchen made the one at The Willow seem like a museum piece despite their attempts at modernisation.

217

'I'm impressed,' she said, 'it's a housewife's dream.'

'What about a pub landlady's dream?' he asked casually.

'You'll have to ask my mother about that,' she said lightly.

'You run the pub with her, though,' he said. 'You must have a say in any major decisions.'

'What do you mean?'

'Well, for instance, if you particularly wanted a kitchen like this, would you be able to persuade her to have one put in?'

'It would be a joint decision,' she explained, feeling uneasy. She had a strong suspicion that he wasn't talking about kitchens at all but was using this situation to pump her for information about her relationship with her mother and how much influence she herself had in the running of the pub. But why would he want to do that? Unless he was serious about her and was planning a future for them together, in which case he would want to know how dispensable she was to her mother.

But he had already changed the subject. 'If you think the kitchen is slick, just wait until you see the bathroom.'

He led her along the parquet-floored hall and opened a door.

'Wow . . . it's blue,' she said, running her eye over a gleaming cornflower creation. 'I've never seen a coloured bath before.'

'Smart, eh!' he said.

'Gorgeous. Even my cousin Alice doesn't have one of those yet. She'll be green when I tell her.'

218

Back in the lounge he led her through a glass door on to a balcony looking out over the river. 'Oh dear,' she laughed, as they stood huddled together in the cold looking at the stars, crystal clear in the sharp night air. 'I feel as though I'm playing the lead in a Noel Coward play.'

'You're prettier than any of his leading ladies,' he said.

'Thank you,' she said, feeling vaguely disturbed. She enjoyed flattery as much as anyone else, but right now his abundance of it was making her nervous.

He poured some drinks and sat next to her on the sofa, drawing her into his arms and leaving her in no doubt as to what was on his mind.

'Oh dear,' she said shakily, 'I've obviously given you the wrong impression by coming back here.'

'We're both mature adults . . . you must know how I feel about you.'

'Yes, of course,' she said, drawing away.

'What's the matter then?' he wanted to know.

'I suppose I'm just not ready to sleep with you yet,' she said, managing to sound assertive.

'Oh . . . I see.' He was silent for a few moments and his irritation was a tangible force in the room. But when he touched her face with his finger and turned her towards him, he looked composed. 'Fair enough, Nina, I'll not rush you.'

Suddenly she felt completely at sea in his company; as though he was a stranger she had just spoken to in a bus queue instead of a man who had plied her with attention for the last few months. In what must have been the ultimate in bad timing, she found herself wishing he was someone else . . . *Baz of all people*. That man had broken her heart and almost destroyed her sanity but when she'd been with him it had never felt wrong. Even in the really bad times she had never felt out of place with him. Not like she did at this moment.

It'll be right with Lester too, eventually, she told herself. These things take time.

One Saturday afternoon in December, Baz was at the wheel of his van in Acton High Street, on the way to deliver a television set to a customer, when all the Christmas preparations around him imbued him with a crippling sense of loneliness.

How could anyone ignore the wretched season when every shop window blinded you with its decorations, the Salvation Army blasted out their programme of carols, and the entire population seemed duty bound to pour into every shopping centre in London and shop till they dropped? Christmas was all very well for religious types, for families and couples. But there was no place in the great annual bunfight for a loner like him.

Not that he was completely on his own. He had George and Marge who would make him more than welcome at their table. A sudden memory of the few Christmases he'd spent at The Willow filled him with piercing nostalgia. They hadn't had so much to make merry with in those days but by God they had partied!

He rarely saw Nina now that Joey was away at school. He'd managed to resist the temptation to pop in to The Willow on the pretext of having a drink. She'd made it clear that she wanted him to leave her alone and he reckoned he owed her that much.

Joey would be home for the holidays next week, though. A mixture of affection and excitement at seeing the boy again coursed through him, only to be followed by the dull ache of reality as he remembered the tension that had still existed between them at half term. Their meetings continued to be an improvement on those early fiascos. Joey was never bad-mannered now, in fact he was sometimes quite pleasant company, but Baz was always painfully aware that beneath the façade of civilised behaviour, his son hated his guts for the sins of the past and saw their meetings as a way of confirming this.

In melancholic mood, Baz found himself in agreement with what his brother George was always telling him: that he needed a serious relationship with a woman, a partner, a raison d'être. Meeting women wasn't a problem even though most of those in his age group were married with children. He had his own personal dating agency in Marge who insisted on introducing him to a string of emotional convalescents, women who were recovering from broken relationships of one sort or another. All of them had been nice people – he almost got involved from time to time. But, somehow, beyond the initial physical attraction, there didn't seem to be anything much on which to build – it just never felt right.

His thoughts took a different turn as he wondered what might please an eleven-year-old boy as a Christmas gift. The only thing he did know for sure was that his son's expectations would be a damn sight higher than his own had been at that age. A simple catapult or a bag of marbles would have been enough to send him to dizzy heights. These days it was all pop music and record players.

The world had certainly moved on since he was a boy, he thought, as he sat in a traffic jam outside the Lilac Cinema. In those depressed days you could have walked in the road in a High Street like this without getting mowed down. Now it was a complete log-jam as more and more people could afford their own transport.

Not everyone is doing so well though, he thought, noticing something at the entrance of the Lilac Ballroom adjacent to the cinema. There was an agent's board nailed across the doors bearing the message LEASE FOR SALE. Glancing up to the ballroom windows above the cinema, he perceived the dusty emptiness of dereliction and the agent's message repeated in several places.

He was intrigued. A dance hall should have been a resounding success in a heavily populated area like this which was very well served with public transport. So what had gone wrong?

His nerve ends tingled with excitement as they never had when he'd started his television business. Taking a pencil from his pocket he scribbled the agent's telephone number on the back of a cigarette packet.

Chapter Fifteen

As Lester wasn't going into his office on New Year's Day, he suggested that he and Nina go out somewhere special to help her recuperate after the hectic New Year's Eve celebrations at The Willow. Since Tilly was amenable to her daughter's taking the evening off and Joey was spending the afternoon and evening with his father, Nina was able to accept the invitation with an easy mind.

Feeling lighthearted and looking stunning in a black coat with a white fur collar and cuffs over a plain black dress with satin trimming, she waved goodbye to Tilly and Joey from the window of Lester's Jaguar soon after the pub closed after the midday session.

'I've got tickets for the early performance of *Dry Rot* at the Whitehall,' he informed her as the car rolled away.

'That's the farce with Brian Rix, isn't it?'

'Yes. I thought a spot of nonsense might be just what the doctor ordered.'

'Definitely.'

'I've booked a table for dinner this evening at a little place I know with a small dance floor . . . so we can dance the night away if you wish?'

'Lovely!'

After an enjoyable interlude watching a hilarious succession of misunderstandings and absurd innuendo, they took a stroll through the West End to work up an appetite.

Over dinner she said, 'I'm having such a good time, Lester. You certainly know how to treat a girl.'

'I do my best,' he said, smiling into her eyes.

She had never been more aware of his sex appeal than she was today. He looked dazzling in a dark suit with a pale grey silk waistcoat, his white shirt enhancing the smooth texture of his skin.

'It's so good to get out and relax after the Christmas rush at the pub,' she remarked, 'and today has worked out really well since Joey's with his father. I don't like to go out too often when he's home for the hols. I see little enough of him.'

'How long have you been divorced?' he enquired chattily.

'Baz and I aren't divorced,' she explained. 'Just separated.'

'Oh, really?' he said in surprise.

'Didn't I mention it?'

'No. I just assumed you were divorced, as you've not been together for years.'

'We've never got round to it . . . it hasn't seemed necessary since neither of us has wanted to remarry.'

'I see.' He ate his fish in thoughtful silence. 'Does your husband have any sort of claim on The Willow,' he finally asked.

'Well, no, of course not, since my mother owns the place and not me,' she said, puzzled by the question. 'Why do you ask?'

'No reason,' he said casually. 'I was just making conversation.'

This latest show of interest in her private affairs made her realise again how serious he was about her. He obviously had marriage in mind and was considering the obstacles. She herself was not unaware of the complications. There was her involvement at the pub, and Joey, and the long drawn out process of divorce proceedings. But for the moment she didn't allow such negative thoughts to spoil the pleasure of feeling chosen and special to someone.

The small band was playing 'Love Letters in the Sand' as they smooched slowly around the floor.

'You're looking lovely tonight, Nina,' he said, moving back slightly and casting an approving eye over her dress which hugged her figure, the dark colour enhancing the gold lights in her hair.

'Thank you. You're looking pretty good yourself.'

'I'm flattered to hear you say so,' he told her softly.

Mellowed by the wine and the romantic atmosphere, she was feeling pleasantly aroused. After a couple more drinks and some more close dancing, she was positively aflame. Since the feeling was mutual, they skipped coffee and went back to his place.

Closing the door behind them, they fell feverishly into each other's arms and left an untidy trail of clothing all the way to the bedroom.

* * *

'Mum's got a boyfriend,' said Joey, as Baz drove him home.

'Has she now?' Baz felt himself reeling from a ridiculous stab of jealousy. 'Is it anyone I know?'

'I don't think so,' replied Joey. 'He's new to the area. His name is Lester Tibbs . . . he lives in Acorn Court.'

'What's he like?'

'Seems all right.'

'Well, that doesn't tell me much, does it?'

'He's quite well off, I think,' Joey continued thoughtfully. 'Gran says he spends a lot of money on Mum. He's always giving her presents and taking her to expensive places.'

'Really?'

'Yes. They've gone to the West End today.'

'That's good,' said Baz, trying hard to mean it. 'Your mother deserves to have some fun. She works very hard.'

'That's what Gran says.'

'And how do you feel about it?'

'It doesn't really affect me since I'm away at school most of the time,' said the boy. 'As long as he's good to Mum, that's all that matters to me.'

Tears sprang to Baz's eyes at this further evidence of his son's loyalty to his mother. For all that Joey gave him a hard time in defence of her, Baz was proud of his devotion. He changed the subject because it hurt to hear about Nina and her new man. Unreasonable and hopeless as it was, he still wanted her back.

They chatted about this and that, but as they drew up outside The Willow, Baz said, 'Actually, I've something important to tell you.'

'You've got a girlfriend?' surmised the boy incorrectly.

'No, nothing like that.' Baz smiled. 'But I'm changing my line of business.'

Joey observed his father quizzically. 'You mean you're not going to be dealing in televisions and radios any more?'

'That's right. I'm selling the electrical retail business to fund my new project which is in a bigger league altogether.'

'What is it?'

'I'm taking over a derelict dance hall in Acton.'

'A derelict dance hall?' was Joey's astonished reaction. 'That doesn't sound much like progress to me.'

'Ah, but it is,' his father said enthusiastically. 'You remember I once told you that I would know the right business opportunity for me when it came along because it would excite me?'

'Yes.'

'This is the one, son, the challenge I've been waiting for.'

'Are you sure?' Joey said doubtfully.

'Positive,' replied Baz fervently. 'The idea of bringing the Lilac Ballroom back to life and making it into one of the most popular nightspots in West London gives me a real buzz.'

George and Marge were much more circumspect about the idea.

'You must be out of your tree to wanna take on a dump like this!' was the way Marge put it a few days later as the three of them climbed the rickety stairs into the ballroom. 'It's no better than a barn.'

'Now maybe. But it won't be once I . . .'

'Cor, what a bloomin' mess!' cut in the forthright Marge, standing on the dance floor and casting a disapproving eye around the vast expanse of dilapidation. 'It doesn't even have a decent floor . . . and the stage is falling to bits.'

'Yes, it does need quite a bit of work,' conceded Baz.

'Needs demolishin' more like,' corrected Marge.

'It was used as a dancing school before it became a ballroom, and a gymnasium before that,' Baz carried on regardless. 'What I plan to do is make it into a pukkah ballroom like the Palais with all the trimmings. Sprung floor, decent bands, soft lighting, a glamorous ladies' powder room with plenty of mirrors . . .'

'It'll cost a fortune,' George sagely pointed out.

'Which is why I have to sell the television business,' explained Baz. 'My credit with the bank is good and they've agreed to give me the finance I'll need on top of what I get for the business . . . so I'll be able to make this place into a palace.'

George shook his head mournfully. 'It'll be a massive job, Baz. You're moving into a different league.'

'Which is exactly what I've always wanted to do.'

'If it's such a sure-fire winner, why didn't the previous owners make a go of it?' queried Marge.

'Because they tried to do it on the cheap,' he said, waving his hand towards the chipped floorboards, the bare light bulbs dangling from the ceiling on ugly wires, the torn lino surrounding the dance floor. 'I mean, look around you. Would you wanna pay money to spend an evening here?'

'No fear,' said Marge.

'I've been talking to the manager of the cinema downstairs,' Baz went on. 'He told me that the people that had this place never booked any professional musicians, only amateurs. They spent money advertising to get the punters in but didn't provide anything to make them want to come back a second time.'

'Youngsters follow the pack. They go where their mates go,' Marge wisely pointed out.

'Exactly. And the leaders of the pack are drawn towards a place where there's a band that can play their sort of music,' said Baz. 'Anyway, I'm not just going to cater for youngsters. There'll be something here for everyone. We're going to open every night of the week and some afternoons too.'

'Get away,' said George.

'Yeah. We'll have tea dances for retired people as well as rock and roll for the kids at weekends,' said Baz eagerly. 'The Lilac will be the trendiest ballroom in London.'

'There's no chance of talking you out of it then?' said George.

'None at all. And if you two are going to be working with me on the project, it would help if you could show a bit more enthusiasm.'

They thought about this for a minute, then Marge said, 'We'll have to have carpet round the dance floor.'

'And on the stairs,' said George.

'You could rent the place out to a dancing teacher on Saturday mornings to help make it pay,' said Marge, beginning to warm to the idea. 'There's always a demand for dancing lessons.'

'We could have an old time night once a week too,' suggested George.

'Oh, yes, Baz . . . by the time we've finished you won't need to spend a penny on advertising,' proclaimed Marge. 'Dance halls sell themselves just by being there . . . once they get a reputation for being trendy.'

Baz grinned. 'I take it that you two are converted then?'

'Not 'alf,' they chorused.

Tilly and Nina were having breakfast in the living room one morning in March. Tilly was reading a piece in the newspaper about Elvis Presley reporting to a Memphis Draft Board for a two-year stint in the armed services.

'His fans'll be none too happy,' she said, 'with their idol disappearing off the scene until 1960.'

'Mm,' said Nina absently, yawning heavily as she stirred her coffee.

'You look as though you need to go back to bed,' remarked Tilly.

'I feel like it too,' confessed Nina, wearily lifting her cup to her lips. 'I don't feel as if I'll last until lunchtime.'

'All these late nights you're having are bound to have an effect, you know,' warned Tilly with motherly concern.

'That's one of the drawbacks of working unsocial

hours,' said Nina. 'If I didn't spend some time with Lester after I've finished work at night, I'd only get to see him on my night off and Sunday afternoons. He's out at work all day during the week.'

'Seems to be getting really serious between you two,' said Tilly.

'Yes, I think it is,' said Nina. 'He's great fun to be with. I feel like a young girl again.'

'I'm ever so pleased for you,' said her mother, buttering some toast. 'It's good to see you looking so happy.'

Indeed, it gave Tilly a lot of pleasure to see her daughter with a new lease of life. Since the New Year she'd spent an increasing amount of time with Lester and there was a new radiance about her – even if she was a bit bleary-eyed in the mornings. Lester Tibbs certainly didn't do things economy-style. Flowers and chocolates were still very much in evidence and he had given Nina a gold pendant recently. His generosity also extended to Tilly who was treated to chocolates and lashings of courtesy whenever he called for Nina.

So why did she have such a bad feeling about him? He'd done nothing to deserve it and seemed genuinely fond of Nina. It wasn't as though a man of his standing would be interested in the fact that Nina would inherit The Willow one day either. But try as she might Tilly could not erase this nagging sense of unease. Maybe he was just a little *too* charming.

This sort of sixth sense came to Tilly uninvited and was totally without foundation, she told herself. After

231

all, the similar doubts she'd had about Alice's husband had proved to be unfounded. The couple had been married for thirteen years and Dudley had never put a foot wrong. This was a comfort. If she'd been wrong once, she could be so again – and she did so want to be wrong about Lester, for Nina's sake.

'He'll be popping the question soon then?' she suggested.

Nina smiled. 'Any minute now, I should think. He's taking me out to dinner at The Ritz on my next night off . . . says he has something very important to talk to me about.'

'It's the real thing for you, is it?'

'There'll never be another Baz for me, of course,' said Nina wistfully. 'He was the real love of my life. But Lester and I are good together. I'm pretty sure we can make a go of it.'

'I'll have to start looking for a replacement for you, I suppose,' said Tilly, keeping her tone light so as not to spoil her daughter's happiness. 'I can't imagine a man in Lester's position wanting his wife to be out working in the evening.'

'No, I can't imagine it either,' said Nina, frowning. 'The problem is, I don't want to give up work. I'd like to stay involved . . . but it will probably have to be to a lesser extent.'

'Best wait and see how he feels about it, eh?'

'Mm,' nodded Nina. 'Anyway, I'll only be living around the corner in Acorn Court, and there are a lot of other things to sort out too . . . not least my getting a divorce from Baz.'

'Yes, that's the most important thing,' agreed Tilly.

'Should have been done years ago, of course,' said Nina. 'Still, it should be quite straightforward.'

'I don't think there's any such thing as a straightforward divorce, is there? It's always a dreadful business from what I've heard about it.'

'Well . . . let's wait until Lester actually proposes, shall we? Don't want to jump the gun.'

'It's more or less a foregone conclusion, though, I should think.'

'Oh, yes, I think so too,' agreed Nina happily.

With his usual panache, Lester had chosen the perfect setting for a marriage proposal, Nina thought, as they dined in the luxurious ambiance of The Ritz beneath glittering chandeliers, with waiters moving silently among the tables and blending discreetly into the background. Not for Lester a small intimate restaurant – he preferred to do things on a grand scale. He was looking particularly handsome this evening in a dinner jacket, and Nina was in green satin.

They were sipping wine between courses when he came to the point.

'As I have already mentioned to you, Nina, I've something important I want to ask you.'

'Fire away,' she said, smiling warmly at him across the table. 'You have my undivided attention.'

'It's something I've been thinking a lot about these last few months,' he said, his manner becoming serious.

'Yes?'

'And I'm now ready to offer you a proposition.'

'What is it, Lester?' she said, already knowing the answer.

'I would like to buy The Willow,' he said, his voice rising eagerly.

'What!'

'I thought it best to discuss it with you before approaching your mother,' he said calmly, as though he had not noticed her shocked expression. 'As you have such a say in what goes on.'

Nina was too stunned to speak for a moment. 'You want to buy The Willow?' she muttered at last, looking completely bemused.

'That's right. The idea came to me soon after we started seeing each other,' he explained. 'I got to thinking about its market potential – inevitable in my line of work – and then it came to me. Why don't I buy it myself?' he explained exuberantly. 'I haven't said anything to you before because I wanted to be sure it was a good bet . . . and to work out an acceptable offer.'

'Oh, I see,' she said, smiling weakly as she realised what he had in mind. 'You're thinking of you and me running the place together to relieve my mother of the responsibility . . . and she'd have the money to buy a place to live and more time to enjoy herself?' She shook her head. 'It's very generous of you, Lester, but I don't think she'll agree.'

'What on earth are you talking about?' he asked, looking genuinely baffled. 'We wouldn't be running it. Good God, no. I'd put a manager in. I'm not a publican. Naturally I would continue with my other business interests.'

Her eyebrows came together in a frown. 'I don't understand,' she said.

He put down his glass and leaned towards her. 'It's simply a business investment for me,' he explained evenly. 'I want to modernise the place . . . completely update it.'

'We have modernised.'

'Hardly,' he said critically. 'I plan to change the place altogether. Americanise it. Have a cocktail bar put in and a bowling alley built over the gardens. Its situation on the river is a big attraction . . . people will come for miles.'

'Destroy the character of The Willow altogether, you mean?' she said, aghast.

'Sure,' he said without compunction. 'This is a new age, Nina. People are hungry for anything new – especially anything American. Everything from filmstars and pop singers to gadgets and hamburgers. There's no point in clinging on to the past. Young people are the ones to cater for these days. They're the ones with pockets full of money to spend, and they're not interested in oak beams and elderly people talking about the old days, married men playing darts and dominoes to get away from the wife and kids. They want the new music, the latest hits on the juke box, a young and exciting atmosphere . . .'

'But The Willow is a family pub,' she cut in, horrified by what he was saying, 'catering for people of all ages.'

'And how many of your regulars sit at a table all night for the price of one glass of beer?' he asked.

'A few.'

'That seat could be used by a big spender.'

'My mother and I run a local,' she told him angrily. 'Vital to the community. During the war people still came even when we had very little to offer them in the way of drinks. They needed The Willow as a meeting place.'

'The war is over, Nina,' he said coldly. 'We're living in what people are calling the affluent society.'

'Not for everybody,' she said. 'Some people still can't afford to spend much when they go out.'

'They should stay at home then,' he said in an acerbic manner. 'And stop taking up valuable space in other people's commercial premises. Anyway . . . I'm sure you and your mother won't care what I do with the place if I give you a good enough price for it.'

Seeing him in a completely new light, she realised that she had never featured in his plans for the future at all. His interest in her private affairs had not been personal – he'd simply been snooping for possible obstructions to his business plan. In truth he was a stranger . . . someone she didn't know at all. She'd spent a lot of time with him, sure, she'd even shared his bed, but they had never got to know each other, had never really talked about anything worthwhile. It had all been fun and physical attraction.

'Our relationship isn't important to you, is it Lester?' she asked.

He sighed impatiently. 'Oh, really, why bring up personal matters when I'm trying to talk to you about business?'

'It's just been a casual thing for you all along, hasn't

it?' she persisted because she had a perverse need to hear him confirm this.

'Must you complicate matters?' he said crossly. 'We've had a good time together. I enjoy being with you. You are a very attractive woman . . .'

They were interrupted by the waiter serving the main course.

'All those times at your flat were just . . .' she began when they were alone again.

'They were terrific,' he finished for her in an unemotional tone, starting to cut into his steak.

'But they didn't mean anything to you, did they?'

'Of course they meant something to me. I'm not a complete moron,' he snapped. 'The sex was fantastic. You and I really make sweet music in that direction.'

'Sex . . . that's all it was to you then?' she said miserably.

'Sex is sex, my dear,' he said smoothly. 'You had a good time, didn't you?'

'Personally I prefer to call it making love.'

'Making love – having sex – what does it matter what you call it?' he said furiously. 'It all boils down to the same thing in the end – it's what adult couples do when the chemistry is right.'

'That isn't the way I think of it at all.'

'Look,' he said, putting down his knife and fork and looking into her face. 'It's been terrific between us. It still is. I've enjoyed every minute of our time together but . . .'

'But you never had any long-term plans for us?' she finished for him.

'Well, frankly, no.'

'God, I've been such a fool,' she said in a strangled voice. 'I trusted you . . . I really did.'

He leaned closer to her, his eyes narrowing in a face so full of animosity she barely recognised it. 'Look, Nina, we're both mature adults. I've done nothing to hurt you. On the contrary, I've spent a lot of money on you, given you a good time. I have never indicated that it would be forever. If you chose to see something that wasn't there, that's your problem.'

'Some things are just taken for granted in decent society,' she said.

'Oh, come now, you wanted an affair every bit as much as I did so don't start crying rape at me.' His manner was openly hostile now. 'You've been separated from your husband for a long time, you were looking for an affair . . . can you honestly deny that?'

'No, but when I slept with you I was making a commitment.'

He sighed again. 'Look, I don't want to end things between us because I like you and enjoy being with you,' he told her. 'We have a lot of fun together and I can see no reason why we shouldn't carry on as we are until such time as one of us wants to call it a day. But please don't ask more of me than that. I'm a self-centred bachelor. I like to come and go as I please and have no plans to change my way of life.'

Nina felt cheap and foolish. Painful as it was to admit, she knew that some of what he said was true. She had been at low ebb when he had come into her life. He'd cheered her up and reminded her that she was still a desirable woman. Their affair hadn't been about Lester at all – it had been about lust, loneliness and frustration. Above all it had been about Baz. She could see now that she still thought herself a failure because of her broken marriage and had wanted her relationship with Lester to be a success . . . something it never could be because it didn't have any real depth on either side.

'Well, you can't spell it out much plainer than that,' she said.

'No. So can we get back to the business we were discussing?'

'There's nothing to discuss,' she said, managing to compose herself. 'My mother won't sell The Willow to you, you can take my word for it.'

'I plan to be most generous in my offer for it.'

'She wouldn't let you have it for a million pounds, just so that you can destroy it.'

'Do give over. The Willow in its present form is a relic,' he stated categorically. 'A thing of the past.'

'There'll always be a place for family pubs like ours so long as people need other people,' she told him firmly.

'Call yourself a businesswoman!' he snorted.

'Yes, I think I can honestly claim to have earned that title,' she told him sharply. 'But that doesn't mean I have to be greedy . . . a soulless vulture grabbing from society. If we ever alter The Willow to attract wider custom, it will be done in keeping with the character of the place, to please our customers and not just to make a fast buck.'

'I take it the answer is no then?'

'Emphatically!'

'Oh, well, it was just an idea. I'll not lose any sleep over it.'

She unfastened the pendant he had given her and put it down on the table beside his plate.

'Oh, really, there's no need for such dramatic gestures,' he said cynically. 'Okay . . . so we don't have a business deal. That doesn't mean we have to become enemies.'

'I've learned more about you in the last half hour than in the whole time I've been seeing you,' she said. 'And now I realise we're worlds apart.'

She called the waiter over and asked him for her wrap.

'Surely you'll stay and finish your meal?' Lester ground out. 'I will be paying for it after all.'

'I'm sure you can afford it.'

The waiter brought her silk stole and held it for her before slipping quietly away.

'You'd better find yourself another local, Lester, because you're no longer welcome at The Willow. We may just be an old-fashioned community pub but we still have the right to choose our customers.'

And with that she turned and left, glad he couldn't see the hot tears running down her cheeks.

She cried all the way home in the taxi – tears of self-pity and anger and sheer damned humiliation. There was none of the grinding pain she had experienced when Baz had left her . . . none of the yearning for it all to be different. She'd not been in love with Lester, she had simply needed someone at that time. She'd made a fool of herself and that was what hurt.

The pub was still open when she arrived so she went in through their private entrance and slipped straight upstairs to change out of her finery into her dressing gown. She made a pot of tea and sat in an armchair with it, mulling things over. When her mother came upstairs later on, Nina poured out the whole story.

'Oh, Mum, I've been such a fool!'

'Not really,' said Tilly. 'You're human and you're only thirty-two . . . it isn't natural to live like a nun forever.'

'I suppose not,' she said, her eyes heavy and shadowed.

'Keep a grip, love,' her mother advised worriedly.

Seeing the fear in her eyes, Nina remembered a similar situation and the anxiety she had caused then.

'Don't worry,' she said calmly. 'Baz broke my heart. Lester has only dented my pride. There'll be no nervous breakdown, no rushing through the streets in my nightclothes.'

'Well, that's a relief,' said Tilly, drawing hard on her cigarette. 'I don't think I could bear to watch you go through that again.'

'I don't think I could,' said Nina. 'There isn't enough hurt left in me . . . Baz saw to that.'

'Oh, love, I'm so sorry,' said Tilly, her voice trembling with sympathy for her daughter.

'I'm all right, really,' Nina assured her. 'I might have made a fool of myself over a man twice, but there won't be a third time. Oh, no . . . never again!'

Tilly exhaled slowly, wishing her suspicions about
Lester had not proved to be correct after all.

Chapter Sixteen

'Let us in, mister, please,' begged a girl of about seventeen, accosting Baz as he elbowed his way through the swarm of people clustered around the entrance to the Lilac Ballroom. 'We're regulars . . . we always come on a Friday night.'

'If they've put the Full sign up, it's because the ballroom is packed to capacity,' he informed her. 'If we let any more in it'll be dangerous and we'll have the law on to us.'

'Aw, go on, mister, be a sport,' she begged, eyes shining persuasively through copious mascara, bosom rising pertly against a skin-tight black sweater which she wore with a red stand-out skirt and flat pumps. Her lacquered hair stood out around her face in bouffant style, and she was chewing gum energetically. 'Me and me friend won't make much difference.'

'We're only a couple o' little 'uns,' coaxed her friend, also working her gum with vigour.

'What about us?' came cries from the back of the gathering.

Reaching the glass-panelled doors at which a doorman stood on duty inside, Baz turned and addressed the group. 'We're full up, folks. I'm sorry. You'll have to get here earlier in future.'

'It's not fair,' someone wailed.

'We've come all the way from Wimbledon,' said another.

'And Wembley,' complained a young man in an Edwardian jacket.

'We had to get two buses and a tube to get 'ere,' mourned someone else.

Baz held up his hands. 'There's nothing I can do. I really am sorry.'

He tapped on the glass to Bob the doorman, and was swiftly ushered inside.

'Busy again tonight, Mr Paxton,' remarked Bob. 'I reckon we could have filled the hall twice or three times over.'

'That's the way we like it, eh, Bob?'

'It sure is.'

'Is my brother in?'

'He's in his office, boss . . . with his missus.'

Baz made his way up the thickly carpeted stairway which led into a foyer.

'Evening, Mr Paxton,' said Dilys, a mature lady who looked after the cloakroom. 'Packed out again tonight, innit? Gawd only knows where they all come from.'

'All over London, I think . . . fortunately for us.'

Slipping through the swing doors into the ballroom, it was as though he had entered another world. Beneath ever-changing coloured lights, youth en masse danced rock 'n' roll style to the Elvis Presley hit 'All Shook Up' which was being played at ear-splitting volume by the band on the stage. The punters jumped and jived, leapt and twisted. The hall was vibrant with the throb of unleashed energy.

It was all vastly different to the desolate ruin he had taken on just a few months before. The new sprung floor was flanked by softly lit alcoves, and a special lighting effect in the ceiling changed the mood at the touch of a switch. At the far end there was a comfortable lounge area where those taking a break could buy light refreshments.

Satisfied that everything was in order in the ballroom, he went into his brother's office where George and Marge were counting money at the desk. After commenting on another sell-out, Marge asked, 'Did you have any luck booking Billy Dark as a guest singer?'

'I've just clinched the deal with his agent over a drink.'

'Well done,' she said, adding lightly, 'we'll have to get plenty of smelling salts in for that.'

'You reckon we'll have a hall full of swooning girls to contend with, then?' smiled Baz.

'I don't know about the girls,' giggled Marge. 'But you'll certainly have to bring *me* round.'

The harmony that had existed between the three of them in the shop had continued into this business. A great deal of organisation went into the smooth running of an establishment like this. Behind the glamorous public image – the lights, the music, the glittering ambiance of a first-rate ballroom – was a team of people working long hours to make it all seem to happen by magic.

Baz enjoyed putting things into place behind the scenes, and was exhilarated by the end result, the sound of people enjoying themselves. He attributed the success of the ballroom to the fact that they catered for all tastes and age groups rather than relying on one section of the community for support. Open every day of the week, they provided facilities for everything from rock and roll to formation dancing.

'You're a bit past that sort of thing, aren't you, love?' teased George.

'Certainly not,' Marge informed him crisply. 'I might be over thirty but I can still dig the scene . . . especially when it comes to someone like Billy Dark.'

'The bloke's a creep,' said George playfully. 'I don't know what you women see in him.'

'Same thing that makes you men drool over Marilyn Monroe, I expect.'

'Changing the subject, you two,' said Baz on a more serious note, 'I've made a decision.'

'Oh?' they chorused, waiting for him to continue.

'I've decided that we're not going to stop with one dance hall,' he explained. 'We're going to have a chain of them before we're through.'

Although Nina was careful not to worry her mother by showing her feelings, the Lester Tibbs affair had left her with a profound sense of failure. It seemed to be further confirmation of her inability to sustain a relationship with a man.

Plagued by a feeling of inadequacy, she began to see her existence as narrow. After all, she'd never even had the normal adult experience of leaving home to get married since she and Baz had lived at The Willow. She considered the idea of widening her horizons by moving into a flat of her own, but the convenience of living on the job and the fact that she and her mother got along so well, made this seem a pointless exercise. So her restlessness persisted and she didn't seem able to dispel it.

Until one day in the spring when she received both a boost to her confidence and a possible solution to the problem. It came from one of their new regulars, a wealthy entrepreneur called Roy Marshall who had recently bought a house on the river.

'Do you ever fancy a change of scenery in your work?' he asked one evening when Nina was in charge because Tilly had gone out with her friend Hilda.

'I suppose we all do occasionally,' she said. 'But no, seriously, it would have to be something really special to tempt me away from here.'

'I suppose you could call what I have to offer really special.' He was a large, florid man of about fifty who wore Italian suits and brightly coloured silk shirts. Chunky rings adorned his fat fingers and his thick white hair was fashionably layered. 'It's certainly worth considering, anyway.'

'Are you seriously offering me a job?' she asked.

'More than a job. I'm offering you sunshine, luxury accommodation and complete responsibility in running a business . . . without the worry of ownership,' he announced.

'In that case, tell me more.'

'I've a bar in Spain and I'm looking for someone to run it for me,' he explained, leaning on the counter. 'I've been watching you in action this last few weeks, and frankly I'm impressed.'

'That's nice to know, thank you,' she said, somewhat taken aback.

'In fact, you're exactly the sort of person I'm looking for,' he continued. 'You're experienced in bar work, good with people, easy on the eye and mature enough to work on your own initiative.'

'You make me sound like a real smart arse!' she laughed.

'A dimwit is no use to me,' he told her candidly.

'You wouldn't want to go out there and run it yourself, then?'

He shook his head. 'Oh no,' he said emphatically. 'It's just a sideline. I've too many business interests here in London . . . hotels mostly.'

'Why set up in business abroad if you've so much going on here then?' she was curious to know.

'As a businessman, I'd be a fool not to. Spain is rich with opportunity at the moment,' he explained. 'There's so much trade out there now that more and more people are going abroad for their holidays.'

'I've heard that the tourist trade has opened up out there in a big way.'

'Package holidays are booming,' he continued, 'and there aren't enough bars to accommodate all the punters they take into Spain. Development is rife out there. My bar is quite new . . . this will only be its second season.'

'Do you have someone out there now . . . looking after it?'

'Yes, I have someone standing in but he's anxious to leave to set up on his own,' he explained. 'Everyone wants to get a piece of the action. Spain is a goldmine for anyone with a bit of savvy . . . Spanish . . . English . . . plenty of scope for everyone.'

'The job does sound appealing, I must say,' Nina confessed. 'I've never been abroad.'

'Travel broadens the mind, so they say,' he said, sipping his whisky. 'Now's your chance to find out for yourself and earn a good salary in the process.'

'What about the winter months, though?' she queried.

'I'd find a place for you here in the UK in one of my West End establishments – after you'd had a holiday,' he said.

'Mm, I'm very tempted but I have responsibilities here,' she said wistfully. 'For a start there's The Willow. There's also my son. I couldn't just swan off and leave everything.'

'But your boy is away at school, isn't he?'

She nodded. 'Yes, but he comes home for holidays and I like to see something of him. He's home next week for half term as a matter of fact.'

'I should think a young lad would be glad of the chance to spend his summer holidays in Spain.'

'Well, yes, I suppose he might be,' she agreed. 'But there's my mother to consider, too.'

'She seems a most understanding lady. I'm sure she'd not want to stand in your way.'

'That's the last thing she'd want to do but . . .'

'Look,' he cut in, 'all I ask is that you come and look at the place. Bring your son along too if you like. You said he has a holiday next week.'

'Go to Spain next week . . . just like that?' she said in astonishment.

'Why not? I'll pay all your expenses, of course,' he said. 'I'll organise everything if you say the word. The flight, the accommodation. We'll get you a visitor's permit if there isn't time for a full passport to be done.'

'But I'll feel obliged to take the job if you go to all that trouble and expense,' she said worriedly. 'And I'm really not at all sure . . .'

'You need feel under no obligation at all,' he assured her. 'I'm a businessman. The trip is just a fraction of my overheads. If the answer is no after you've spent a few days there, then I'll look for someone else, I promise.'

She still looked doubtful.

'Now what's the matter?'

'It's this place,' she told him. 'I can't expect my mother to manage without me for even a few days.'

'No one is indispensable,' he reminded her crisply. 'Anyway, the offer is there if you want it. Talk to your mother about it. Let me know what you decide.'

Tilly was all in favour of Nina's going on the introductory trip to Spain when she was told about it later that evening. She said that her friends from the Licensed Victuallers would help her to find a spare pair of hands for a few days.

'But it isn't as simple as that,' said Nina, worried by the implications of taking such a step. 'There's no point in my going all the way to Spain next week unless I'm seriously considering taking the job. It wouldn't be fair to Roy.'

'No, it wouldn't,' agreed Tilly. 'So if you like what you see, you must go ahead and snap the job up. It'll do you good to work away from The Willow for a while. I'll soon get a replacement for you.'

'It isn't that I want to leave The Willow or you. I mean, I'll miss you terribly,' said Nina, concerned for her mother's feelings. 'It's just that I've led such a narrow life. I've never been anywhere or tried anything different.'

'Exactly. And opportunities like this one don't come along every day,' Tilly said in a definite tone. 'If you decide to take the job you'll get no opposition from me. I'll be thrilled for you. Abroad, eh? Well, we *are* going up in the world. Even Alice hasn't done that yet!'

'She will before long, though, I bet. If it's the latest thing in one-upmanship,' laughed Nina.

'Poor old Alice.' Tilly smiled. 'She does leave herself wide open to ridicule with her airs and graces . . . still, there's no real harm in her.'

'No, course there isn't.' Nina was busy at the table getting the day's takings ready for the bank the next morning. On a sudden impulse she went over to the sofa where her mother was sitting and gave her a hug. 'Thanks for understanding how I feel, Mum. You're a real pal.'

'Never mind all that,' said Tilly swiftly, to hide her true feelings. 'You concentrate on getting a letter in the post to young Joey telling him he's off to sunny Spain for his half term holidays . . . he'll be thrilled to bits.'

Actually, Tilly was devastated by this development and dreaded losing her daughter to foreign shores. She could have howled at the thought of life without her. But Nina would never know about it. Her daughter needed to spread her wings and succeed at something in her own right, so Tilly would do all she could to encourage her.

Situated some thirty-five miles from Malaga, the old town of Marbella hugged the shore on the road to Gibraltar. Protected from cold winds by the barrier of the Sierra Nevada but exposed to the sea breezes, the Spanish hamlet seemed like a pearl set in gold to Nina's untravelled eye, the white buildings in perfect contrast to the golden sands.

Everything was so dazzling here compared to the greyness of home, with constant sunshine beaming from perpetual blue skies and sparkling on the aquamarine waters of the Mediterranean.

'So, what do you think of it so far?' asked Roy on their first evening as they dined alfresco beneath the fruit trees in Orange Square near the small hotel Roy had booked them into.

'Stunning,' she said.

'Smashing,' agreed Joey.

'Later in the year when the fruit is ripe the orange scent is quite strong in the square,' he informed them.

'That must be lovely,' she said, looking around at the lights shining through the trees as dusk fell, the coloured umbrellas of the cafés and bars, the dark-eyed Spanish waiters, the holiday makers strolling through the square in carefree mood and disappearing into the narrow cobbled alleys that led off this central area.

'If you take the job you'll be able to sample it for yourself,' he said.

'Go on, Mum,' urged her ebullient son. 'The boys at school'll be green about me coming here in the hols.'

'Stop trying to make up my mind for me, you two,' laughed Nina. 'I haven't even seen Roy's bar yet.'

'Tomorrow morning we'll put that right.'

'I can't wait,' said Nina.

She thought the bar was charming. It nestled on the edge of the sands near a sea of thatched umbrellas shading blue and white beach chairs. The structure was open-sided with a marble-tiled floor and a thatched roof with blue-fringed awnings and supports housing windbreaks that could be put into use in case of trade winds that occasionally blew across from Africa.

The bar counter was on a raised area with a balustrade, and was tiled with the blue and white patterned ceramics common to this area. Tables and chairs filled the lower floor to the side of an orange-fringed stage with a blue backdrop on which were spread two large, brightly coloured fans. Just in front of the platform was an easel with a board advertising a Flamenco dance show.

'The dancers look very young,' remarked Nina, glancing at a photograph of a group of young girls as she and Roy sipped coffee in the shade of the awning while Joey went to explore the beach.

'They are. In fact they're all still at school,' he explained. 'They're members of a local dance school. Put on a show here one evening a week during their holidays. This week is a holiday so you'll be able to see the show.'

'What a lovely idea,' she enthused.

'Yes, it certainly pulls in the punters.'

'Does the bar open every night?'

Roy shook his head. 'Only when there's some special entertainment on. You'd have a free hand to organise that as you see fit,' he explained. 'My current manager provides a meal to go with the dance show at a reasonable price. It would be up to you what you do about that, though naturally I would expect you to maintain a certain turnover.'

'Yes, of course.'

'Another good reason you should take the job is the hours,' he said, smiling. 'They're much less anti-social than you have now at the pub. Trade in a beach bar is primarily daytime. You'll be rushed off your feet serving coffee and light snacks as well as drinks, but you'll have most of the evenings to yourself. People go into town for their entertainment at night unless there's something special on here.'

'So I would be in sole charge here then?'

'Absolutely. Even down to the hiring and firing of staff,' he assured her. 'It will be just like your own business – except you'll have the security of a salary plus commission on overall sales.'

'I'd have to learn the language, of course.'

'Yes, that would be helpful to you.'

'I don't know how I'd manage to work in this heat,' said Nina, who was overwhelmed by the drastic difference in temperature to that she was used to.

'You'll soon get used to it. You'll probably get into the Spanish habit of taking a siesta in the afternoon. Which reminds me . . . the apartment that goes with the job is in one of the new luxury complexes overlooking the sea, less than five minutes' walk from the bar.'

'You've thought of everything, haven't you?'

'I have to if I want someone to spend a large chunk of the year away from home,' he explained.

'That's true.'

'I'm hoping you're beginning to find the idea irresistible?'

'I'll let you know for sure before we leave.'

The next couple of days flew past as Nina explored the area with Roy. They studied the competition and talked business while Joey enjoyed the beach under the supervision of Roy's bar manager. On their last evening Roy suggested they dine at his bar and watch the Flamenco dancing.

By day the bar was a welcome haven for sizzling sunbathers. By night it became magical with the aid of floodlights, flowers, and a stunning display of traditional Spanish dance. With a change of costume for every number these lovely young girls in breathtaking dresses, ribbons or flowers in their hair, twirled their bodies and stamped their feet in perfect harmony, heads raised proudly, hands moving gracefully.

Sipping coffee after a delicious meal of barbequed

steak and salad, with the sea shushing in the background and a brilliant spectacle in front of her as they watched the finale to the show, Nina made her decision.

'When do you want me to start, Roy?' she asked excitedly.

'As soon as you can,' he said, with a broad grin.

'Cor, smashing!' said Joey.

When Nina got back to London she was thrown into a hectic whirl of preparation, though she promised Tilly she wouldn't depart until they found someone to take her place. Thanks to Hilda's contacts in the trade, a mature lady called Mary was soon found to be suitable. This settled, Nina booked her flight and threw herself into the fun of shopping for clothes to suit the Spanish climate whilst spending some time in the bar showing Mary the ropes. Nina hadn't been as excited about anything in years.

'Are you all set then?' asked Tilly over breakfast on the day before Nina was due to leave.

'Almost. I've a few last bits and pieces left to get. I'd like to pop up West this morning . . . if you can manage without me here?'

'You don't work here anymore, remember?' Tilly reminded her playfully.

'Ooh, don't. You'll have me in tears,' grinned Nina.

'I must pop over to see Hilda this afternoon,' said Tilly chattily. 'The poor thing's hurt her back. Humping crates about, I expect. She's had to take to her bed.'

'What a shame,' said Nina sympathetically.

'I'll take her some liquorice toffees to cheer her up,'

said Tilly. 'She's very partial to those.'

'I'll run you over there in the car,' suggested Nina. 'It will give me the chance to say goodbye to her.'

'That's nice of you, love. I appreciate that.'

'What time would you like to leave here?'

'I'll have to get away by about three o'clock or I won't have any time to spend with Hilda before it's time to come back for evening opening.'

'Okay, I'll make a point of being back by then,' promised Nina.

Laden with last-minute essentials like sun tan lotion and toiletries plus some beachwear she'd not been able to resist, Nina came out of Selfridge's and hurried to her car which was parked in a side street, anxious to get home on time. Actually, she was cutting it a bit fine but the time just seemed to have disappeared while she was shopping. Oh, well, let's hope the traffic isn't too bad, she thought, piling her bags into the boot of the car.

An hour later, she still hadn't progressed much beyond Hyde Park Corner. Damn and blast! she fumed, glancing at her watch to see that it was just coming up to three o'clock. She was afraid her mother might wait too long for her to get back and leave it too late to walk or get the bus to Fulham. Nina was furious with herself for letting this happen. She hated to disappoint anyone, particularly her mother who was being so understanding about her going away.

Tilly was a woman of her word too and Hilda was

looking forward to seeing her. So when Nina still hadn't arrived home by three-fifteen she decided to go to Fulham on the bus. She wouldn't be able to stay very long but at least she wouldn't have let her friend down.

With her shopping bag filled with toffees, grapes and magazines, she hurried to the bus stop and joined the queue, hardly able to believe her luck when a bus came along almost at once. Last in line, she shuffled towards the boarding point behind the others and when her turn came, grabbed the rail and stepped up on to the platform. Before she had time to get the other foot on board, however, the vehicle moved forward, wrenching her shoulder painfully as she clutched the rail, her bag still hooked over her arm.

'Stop . . . please stop!' she screamed as the bus drew away with her clinging to the rail, her legs buckling under her and her hand slipping down the rail so that most of her body was off the platform. A sharp pain shot through her neck and shoulder as she struggled to maintain her hold as the bus gained speed, dragging her along with it.

Distantly, she was aware of a commotion inside the bus as the passengers realised what was happening and shouted for the conductor to stop the vehicle. The agony in Tilly's neck spread through her whole body making her feel sick and faint, her hand becoming slippery with sweat against the rail. Her grip was loosening. She struggled to hold on but just didn't have the strength.

She saw a shower of stars as her head hit the ground, followed by scorching pain all over as she crunched and bumped along the road, the contents of her bag spilling out as she fell. There was a moment of unbearable torture before she sank into oblivion. She lay motionless in the gutter, the silver wrappings of the liquorice toffees gleaming in the spring sunshine around her.

Nina couldn't understand what had happened to her mother. On arriving home to find that she wasn't there, she'd driven straight over to Hilda's with the idea of bringing Tilly back to The Willow in the car, only to be told that she had never arrived.

Now Nina was doing her packing while waiting for her mother to come home. She must have had a last-minute change of plan or something. It was odd that she hadn't phoned Hilda to let her know, though. Oh, well, she'll be back in a minute, thought Nina, feeling a tingle of excitement as she piled her pretty sun clothes into the case.

Ah, there she is now, she thought, hearing a knock at the door. She's forgotten her key again. Hurrying downstairs, Nina was shocked to see two policemen standing on the doorstep.

'Does a Mrs Matilda Dent live here?' one of them asked.

'Yes, she's my mother,' she said, a bolt of fear shooting through her.

'We found this address on a letter in her handbag.'

'What's happened to her?' she asked, feeling as though the breath had been sucked from her.

'She's had an accident,' said one of the constables.

'Oh. How is she?'

'She's in hospital.'

'Bad, is it?' She could hardly get the words out.

'Well.' He hesitated for only a few seconds. 'You need to get there as soon as possible.'

Nina and Alice sat either side of the unconscious woman's hospital bed, in a side ward because of the seriousness of her condition.

'It doesn't look like Mum lying there, does it?' whispered Nina sadly, for her mother was a mass of bandages, plasters and tubes.

'No, it doesn't,' agreed Alice who had come to the hospital immediately Nina telephoned.

'She'll have a blue fit when she comes round,' sniffed Nina, refusing to consider the possibility that her mother might not regain consciousness. 'You know how she likes to look her best to face the world . . . never even opens the front door to anyone without the full works on her face. Just wait till she realises she's been on show outside the house in such a sorry state.'

A doctor and nurse came into the room and Nina and Alice were asked to wait outside.

'Have the doctors told you anything?' whispered Alice fearfully when they were alone. 'I mean . . . er . . . she is going to come round, isn't she?'

'It's touch and go apparently.'

'Oh my God!' gasped Alice, her face pinched with worry.

'Try not to panic,' Nina said, her cousin's despair giving her courage somehow. 'Mum's a real fighter. If anyone can come through this, she will.'

'You think so?'

'Yes, I do.'

'I'm terrified,' said Alice.

'Me too,' admitted Nina.

'Aunt Tilly has always been so strong. It's frightening to see her so ill . . . so powerless.'

'They've told me that I must prepare myself for the fact that she'll probably be disabled if she does come round,' Nina informed her, 'but it's too early to know to what degree.'

'Oh, dear. Poor Aunt Tilly!'

'But let's get through this before we start worrying about anything else,' suggested Nina. 'Just let her live is my prayer.'

'Mine too.'

'Look, I have to make a phone call,' said Nina. 'So can you stay here in case anything happens? I won't be a minute.'

'Don't be too long, then,' requested Alice nervously.

For the first time Nina felt closely bonded to her cousin and liked the feeling. Impulsively, she threw her arms around her. 'Oh, Alice, I'm so glad you're around to go through this with me,' she told her.

'I don't know what I'd do without you either,' admitted Alice, tears sliding down her ashen face.

The two women clung to each other for a few moments before Nina hurried to the hospital reception area where there was a telephone for public use. With a shaky hand she dialled a number.

'Hello, Roy. It's Nina.'

'Hello there,' he said brightly. 'Are you all set for tomorrow?'

'No, I'm afraid not.' She gave him a brief account of what had happened. 'So I'm calling to tell you that I won't be taking the job after all.'

'But what about later on if your mother gets better . . .' he began.

'No, she's going to need me at home. I can't go away and leave her. I'm so very sorry.'

Chapter Seventeen

When her mother began to fret about her appearance, Nina guessed she must be on the mend.

'Ugh, what a sight! I look like a bloomin' corpse,' she wailed after looking at herself in her daughter's compact mirror. 'You'd better bring my make-up in next time you come visiting.'

'There isn't room on your face for much except lipstick,' Nina replied as only the centre of her mother's countenance was visible through the dressings. 'I should forget about it until your bandages are taken off.'

'That could be a while yet, and I must make an effort in the meantime,' Tilly insisted, propped up with pillows, her neck and arm still encased in plaster. 'Especially as so many people are taking the trouble to come and see me here in hospital.'

Indeed, the response to the news of Tilly's accident had been staggering, a true measure of her popularity. The room was swamped with cards, flowers, fruit and sweets, all given with genuine affection by customers, friends and neighbours. Even representatives from the breweries had come to see their favourite landlady.

'People come to visit you because they like you,' said

Nina. 'They don't care what you look like.'

'I care though,' replied Tilly. 'It's bad enough being stuck in hospital. Looking like death warmed up makes it a darned sight worse!'

Nina smiled. 'Okay. Alice is coming to see you tonight. I'll phone her and ask her to collect your warpaint from The Willow on her way here.'

'Ta, love.'

Although there was a marked improvement in her mother's condition, she was still far from well. The doctor had told Nina that she'd be in hospital for some time yet and when she did come home, it would be to a very different kind of life.

As well as suffering severe concussion and an assortment of broken bones, the blow to the head she'd received when she'd hit the ground had damaged her inner ear, upsetting her balance and causing severe giddiness. There was only a certain amount that could be done medically to control this condition. Apparently, a much more sedentary lifestyle was the key to her recovery.

She would have to get used to walking with the aid of a stick to help her balance and would only be able to stay on her feet for short periods at a time. In fact, she was going to have to take things very easily indeed in future with no stress or physical work. Nina wasn't sure if the full implications of this had registered properly with her mother yet, for it meant her career as a working landlady was at an end.

But now she was saying, 'Baz came to see me last night.'

'What, again? He must be one of your most regular visitors,' said Nina.

'He is, and one of my favourite ones too. Always good for a laugh is Baz,' she said. 'I've always had a soft spot for him, despite everything . . .'

'Yes, I know.'

'Mind you, he's changed a lot now that he's older,' she chattered on. 'He's quite the serious businessman these days. Doing ever so well for himself too. He's talking about opening another dance hall soon.'

'He's selfish enough to go right to the top,' said Nina sharply.

'Now then, Nina,' reproved Tilly. 'What happened between you and Baz was a very long time ago. I can't carry on hating him for it forever.'

'And I wouldn't expect you to,' she replied swiftly, annoyed with herself for over-reacting so visibly. 'Sorry . . . I was a bit hasty.'

'That's all right love,' said Tilly, moving speedily to a less emotive topic. 'So how are things at home?'

'Fine. Mary's proving to be a real asset. It's just as well we'd taken her on as my replacement as things turned out, isn't it? I don't know what I'd do without her now.'

Tilly's expression darkened. 'Oh, Nina, is there anything we can do about that job in Spain you lost?'

'Nothing. But I don't care about it, honestly.'

'Perhaps Roy Marshall might consider you for next summer or something?' Tilly went on. 'I feel terrible about you giving up that chance because of me.'

Nina took her mother's hand in hers. 'Look, if anyone

is to blame for your accident, it's me,' she assured her gently. 'If I hadn't been late back, you wouldn't have tried to go to Hilda's by bus . . . and you wouldn't be in that bed now.'

'That's a really stupid way of looking at it,' said Tilly.

'No more so than you blaming yourself for my not going to Spain,' said Nina. 'These things happen. I probably wouldn't even have considered the job had I not been feeling so low when it came up, and I don't regret not going in the least, I promise you.'

It was true. She'd been far too worried about her mother to feel disappointed about turning the job down at the time. And having to step into Tilly's shoes so suddenly had left her with little time to think about it since then, especially as she enjoyed being in sole charge of The Willow.

'When I'm back on form you can look out for something else abroad.'

'I don't want to go away now, Mum,' Nina told her firmly. 'The time for that has passed. I've accepted it and I'm very happy running The Willow in your absence.'

Tilly was thoughtful for a moment. 'I know everyone thinks I'm finished as far as my work at The Willow is concerned,' she said gravely, 'but I'll be coming back. I'll have to, it's my life.'

'We'll sort something out, don't worry,' said Nina, with a show of confidence she didn't really feel. 'You just concentrate on getting well enough to come home. We'll get round all the other problems then.'

Tilly was forced to change her mind about returning to

work when she was discharged from hospital. She hadn't realised just how weak she would feel outside the secure hospital ambiance – so faint and shaky and vulnerable. She could tolerate the lingering pain of her injuries and walking awkwardly because her shoulder had been left slightly deformed by a multiple fracture. She could even cope with the headaches and the exhaustion. It was the giddy spells that incapacitated her. It was the most frightening feeling to have the room spin around you, constantly to feel as if you were about to fall over.

In hospital she'd been protected and made to feel safe. The nurses had kept her cheerful. But being in the flat on her own for long periods while Nina was working downstairs, she became very depressed. She longed for her old way of life: at the centre of things, surrounded by people. But although she was prepared for the slow and painful process of getting down the stairs, she couldn't face the customers. She didn't want them to see her creeping around on her stick like some geriatric when she was only fifty. People were used to her being the life and soul of the party. They didn't want the depressing spectacle of an invalid hobbling about in the bar.

Mercifully, she didn't need assistance with her daily physical requirements, apart from a steadying hand from Nina getting in and out of the bath. She could even do a few light chores around the flat. But anything more strenuous than that would have her reeling and fumbling for a chair. The doctors had said that she must learn to live with the giddiness – that she would eventually be able to function in spite of it, provided she didn't aggravate the situation by over-exerting herself. She could have howled her eyes out at the thought that her days of normal living were over.

The worst part was being excluded from everything that was going on outside the flat. Nina was wonderful – no daughter could do more for her mother. But she never said anything of consequence about what was happening downstairs. Oh, there was plenty said about the pub running smoothly and mention was made of customers sending best wishes for her recovery. But where were all the dramas that running a pub entailed? The deliveries that were late, the awkward customers, the cloudy beer that refused to clear. For the whole of Tilly's married life, until now, this flat had buzzed with the trials and tribulations of pub life . . . as well as the joys.

Now Nina must be keeping them all to herself because the pub without problems didn't exist.

The aspect of her mother's illness that Nina found hardest to take was having to protect her from stress by keeping the day-to-day traumas of the business from her. It was such a strain not to be able to let off steam about such irritations as the persistent brewery rep who had given her earache or the customer who'd had one too many and got stroppy.

She missed being able to talk ideas through with her too – such considerations as whether or not they should drum up some extra trade by having a talent competition or start a dominoes team or continue with the Christmas club next year now that most people were able to afford the festive season. She longed to unburden herself about all these things but knew she must keep them to herself.

One night, a week or so before Christmas, she came upstairs exhausted after a really busy session and was surprised to see her mother sitting on the sofa in her dressing gown. She looked very pale and strained but thanks to a hairdresser who was willing to come to the house, her hair was well groomed.

'You're still up then, Mum? I expected you to be in bed and asleep by now.'

'I'm not tired and I fancied some company.'

'That's nice,' said Nina, putting the takings on the table ready to enter them in the book. 'I'll make some cocoa.'

'I've already done it,' said Tilly, pointing towards a tray of cocoa and biscuits on an occasional table.

'You should have left it to me,' said Nina, frowning.

'I think I can manage to heat some milk without collapsing, thank you very much,' came the tart reply.

'Well, yes, of course you can,' said Nina, uncertain of this strange mood.

'So come and sit down. Leave the money until the morning.'

Nina sank wearily into the chair by the fire, opposite her mother, making a mental note to enter the takings when Tilly was in bed. Life was so hectic at this time of the year, if she left even the smallest job over until the next day, everything piled up and she just couldn't cope.

'Had a busy night downstairs?' asked Tilly.

'Not half,' said Nina, adding quickly, 'But how's your evening been . . . what have you been doing?'

'Watching the telly as usual,' she replied. 'But I'd rather talk about what's been happening downstairs.'

'Nothing very exciting,' said Nina. 'All pretty routine. Old Albert sends his best . . . says he'll call in and see you one afternoon next week.'

'Was there some sort of trouble down there?' Tilly enquired. 'I thought I heard raised voices.'

'When does a pub not have plenty of those?' said Nina lightly.

'It sounded very much like an argument to me.'

'No . . . no,' she assured her quickly. 'Everything was fine down there, really.'

'Nina,' interrupted Tilly, her voice distorted with fury, 'this is my pub, *mine*, do you hear? So stop carryin' on as though it belongs to you . . . stop shutting me out!'

Nina was shocked by this outburst. 'Oh, Mum, I'm so sorry. I didn't mean to give that impression.'

'I might be a bit shaky on my pins but I'm not senile,' blazed Tilly. 'I know you had a rumpus down there tonight and I want to know about it. I don't want it kept from me as though I'm some child who isn't capable of handling it.'

'All right. There were a couple of blokes who'd had a bit too much, that's all,' Nina explained. 'They got on to religion because of the new Pope . . . well . . . you know what that's like to some people, worse than politics for getting tempers up. Anyway Dick and I sorted it, nothing for you to worry about.'

'But I *want* to worry about these things. *Don't you understand?* I want to know what's going on in the business. Being excluded from it is killing me.'

Tilly looked so forlorn sitting there in a pink dressing gown, Nina could have wept. She still found it hard to reconcile this delicate creature with the robust character her mother had been before the accident. The compensation the bus company had paid her for negligence on the part of their staff in an out-of-court settlement might have given her financial security but it couldn't give her back what really mattered: her health.

'I didn't think you were up to it, Mum,' said Nina. 'I've been trying to make things easy for you.'

'Can't you see how useless that makes me feel?'

'Now I can, yes. But it's difficult for me,' explained Nina. 'I mean, you can't deny that you need to be looked after at the moment?'

'I'll admit that, yes,' she said miserably. 'That's what's screwing me up inside.' She bowed her head and her shoulders began to shake. Her words were barely audible through her sobs as she gave vent to the feelings she'd been hiding behind a brave face all these months. 'I detest trying to battle with nature every day. I can't bear feeling so feeble . . . so utterly useless. I'm furious with my body for refusing to work like it used to.'

Nina went over and sat down next to her, slipping a comforting arm around the shuddering shoulders. 'There, let it all out. You've been so brave it will do you good to shed a few tears.'

'I've not been brave at all,' cried Tilly in despair. 'Not inside.' She pointed to her heart. 'In there I'm full of resentment. I feel as though I hate everyone else for being healthy when I'm not. I feel murderous towards that bus conductor for letting it happen, and yes . . . and this is the very worst part . . . in really bad moments I even find myself blaming *you* for what happened. I'm not a nice person at all, Nina, not when things don't go my way.'

'You're only human. Any of us would feel the same in your situation, I'm sure.'

'I mean, what's the point of being alive if I can't make some sort of a contribution?' Tilly lamented.

'But you *do* make a contribution,' Nina said emphatically. 'You're here. That's enough for me . . . and for Joey . . . and all your friends who come to visit you.'

But even as Nina spoke she knew she wasn't fooling anyone, not even herself. A giver like Tilly would never be able to settle for this empty, sheltered existence indefinitely. Something had to be done; something more positive than making sure she took her pills and didn't overdo things.

'Oh, Nina,' said her mother, blowing her nose, 'I'm so sorry to have burdened you with my feelings when you've more than enough on your plate. It just sort of came out.'

'If you can't tell me how you feel, who can you tell?' she said. 'Now let's drink our cocoa before it goes cold and I'll give you a blow by blow account of what went on downstairs tonight.'

* * *

Nina had a sleepless night worrying about her mother's state of mind. But after making a telephone call while Tilly was still in bed the next morning, she felt more hopeful about the situation.

'I was wondering if you might feel up to helping out with some of the paperwork, Mum?' she asked that afternoon over tea. 'Only I'm finding it a bit too much with everything else I have to do.'

Tilly was clearly surprised. 'Well, I'm not sure. I've never been all that good at that sort of thing.'

'I've had a chat with your doctor on the phone,' Nina continued. 'He seems to think it's a very sensible idea as long as you don't do too much. He thinks it would be good for you to have something to occupy your mind.'

'Oh, I don't know,' Tilly said doubtfully, illustrating her loss of confidence.

'Why not give it a try?' suggested Nina lightly. 'See how it goes. If you find it too much, I'll relieve you of it.'

'Well . . . all right then.'

'The doctor also thinks it's time you started getting out and about again too,' said Nina.

'Oh, does he now?' she said acidly. 'I just can't wait to go staggering down to the Broadway and end up on my bum because of a giddy spell!'

'That isn't what he meant,' said Nina. 'He meant outings with me in the car when I'm not working. You haven't wanted to up till now and I've not pressed you because I didn't think you were ready. But now I think you'll feel better for it.'

'I'm not at all sure . . .'

'Alice has passed her driving test now and she's always offering to take you anywhere you want to go. So is Baz.'

'Poor Baz,' remarked Tilly. 'He must dread coming to see me now that I'm home. The way you treat him, it's a wonder he hasn't died of frostbite!'

'I have to keep it formal between us. If I'm too pally he might get the wrong idea,' Nina explained. 'He might have won you over, and I think even Joey is beginning to see his good points, but it's easier for me if I keep my distance.'

'Oh, well, you know your own business best.'

'Anyway, don't change the subject,' admonished Nina. 'Now, about your going out . . .'

'Don't rush me, Nina, please,' begged Tilly. 'Let's see how I get on with the paperwork first. That's enough for the moment.'

'All right then,' Nina was forced to concede.

It was the evening of Christmas Eve. Nina was busy downstairs in the bar and Tilly and Joey were in the living room upstairs watching television. A Christmas tree shone in the window and bowls of sweets, nuts and fruit were set out around the room. The smell of Christmas permeated everything: pine needles, tangerines, freshly cooked pastry, the spicy aroma of stuffing for the turkey already prepared for tomorrow in the kitchen.

Tilly had spent some of the afternoon helping Nina make mince pies and sausage rolls. She'd had to sit down to roll the pastry and fill the pies but at least she'd done something to help. From downstairs she could hear the rise and fall of voices punctuated with gales of laughter.

'Can I have a sweet, please, Gran?' asked Joey.

'Go on then . . . but only one,' she grinned. 'You know the rules. Christmas starts for us when the pub closes on the night of Christmas Eve.'

'Would you like a toffee?' he asked politely, offering the dish to her.

'Not for me, son,' she said. 'But you can get me a glass of stout if you like.'

'Okay, Gran,' he said, and mooched off to the kitchen.

She was glad of a moment's solitude because she was having difficulty hiding the aching self-pity that was threatening to engulf her. This was the first Christmas Eve in over thirty years that she had not been downstairs to wish the customers a Happy Christmas. This must surely be the worst moment of all since the accident.

Joey returned carrying her drink on a tray and she thought how grown up he seemed lately. He was so confident and polite since he'd been away to school – a real credit to them. At twelve he was beginning to show the lankiness of incipient adolescence. No prizes for guessing who his father is, she thought fondly. His hair might be a shade or two lighter but apart from that he was Baz in miniature.

'Poured like a professional,' she told him, forcing a smile. 'Not too much froth on the top.'

'I'll be doing it for customers before very long,' he said. 'I won't have to stay up here in the flat many more Christmas Eves. I'll soon be old enough to be down in the bar, working alongside Mum.'

'That's true,' said Tilly. 'But when that time comes you'll probably want to do something else.'

'No, I won't.'

'Pub life is hard work and long hours, son,' said Tilly, frowning. 'A good education will give you the chance to do something else.'

'I know that, but I still want to go into the business with you and Mum.'

'Wait and see what else is on offer when the time comes,' advised Tilly, sipping her drink. 'It's much too early to start making those sort of decisions.'

'Would you like to be in any other kind of business, Gran . . . if you had the choice?' he asked chattily.

'Oh, no,' she said at once. 'The licensed trade is in my blood now. I wasn't born into it like you but I married into it and that's good enough.'

Joey sat down opposite her, chewing his toffee solemnly. 'I remember your telling me that Christmas Eve is your favourite night of the year in the pub,' he remarked conversationally. 'You know, with the decorations and the atmosphere and everything.'

'Yes, it's really special,' she said, tears burning her eyes. 'Everyone is in such a warm and festive mood.'

'So you must be feeling really fed up then that you're not down there this year?' he remarked.

'You don't know the half of it, son,' she said thickly.

'I'll creep downstairs later and have a peek, anyway,' he said.

'As you said, you won't have to find a corner to hide in for many more years,' she remarked.

He chewed thoughtfully. 'Are you not allowed to go down there at all, Gran, even if you don't do any work?' he asked. 'I mean, has the doctor actually forbidden it?'

'No, of course he hasn't done that,' she said. 'But as I can't work, there isn't any point in my going down.'

'You could go down and say hello to the customers though, couldn't you?' he suggested. 'You know, wish them a Happy Christmas and have a bit of a chat.'

'I could do, I suppose. But I wouldn't.'

'Why not?'

'Because . . . oh, you wouldn't understand.'

'I might.'

She was silent for a few moments, then she burst out, 'To be perfectly honest I don't want them to see me like this – creeping about with a stick.'

'Lots of them came to see you in hospital and you were much worse then.'

'It was different in hospital,' she said. 'You're expected to be below par there. But a pub is a place where people go to forget their troubles. They don't wanna be lumbered with some relic of a landlady when they've gone out to enjoy themselves.'

'I'm not sure you're right about that, you know, Gran,' he said with youthful sincerity. 'I mean, you're still the same person, aren't you? Even if you're not quite so light on your feet as you were, you can still talk to them and listen, show them that you care about them.'

The truth shook her to her very core. It had taken a twelve-year-old boy to see what she'd been blind to all these months. She'd been so immersed in self-pity, thinking of herself only as a victim in need of assistance, she'd forgotten that other people needed help too, even if it was just a listening ear in a crowded bar.

She struggled to her feet and limped slowly to her bedroom, leaning heavily on her stick. Because Joey knew that help was only acceptable to her if she asked for it, he didn't dare go to her assistance.

With trembling fingers Tilly patted her face with a powder puff, put on some rouge and lipstick, ran a comb through her hair and dabbed perfume behind her ears. After a quick look at herself in the wardrobe mirror she trekked back to the living room.

'I'd appreciate a hand with the stairs, if you wouldn't mind, please, Joey,' she said in a strong voice.

'Sure, Gran,' he replied, smiling as he hurried to her side.

She felt lightheaded and nauseous as she made the slow descent, gripping the banister with one hand and Joey's hand with the other. He was clutching her stick ready for when she got to the bottom. Trembling with a mixture of fear, excitement and sheer physical weakness, she felt beads of icy perspiration suffuse her skin all over. My powder will go all blotchy now, dammit! she cursed, deriving an odd moment of pleasure from the familiarity of the thought.

Pausing by the door to the bar counter area, she brushed her grandson's assistance aside. 'I'll go in under my own steam, thanks, son.'

But his enthusiasm was such that he darted impulsively through the door into forbidden territory and whispered something to his mother. Nina turned and, seeing Tilly in the doorway, gave a beaming smile.

'Hello, Mum,' she said. 'What a lovely surprise.'

'Well, if it isn't our Tilly,' said a man on the other side of the bar, his face glowing with delight.

'Ain't that a sight for sore eyes?' said the man standing beside him. 'Now my Christmas really is complete. Come round here and give us a kiss, Tilly love.'

Word quickly spread through the building and customers hurried to the bar, eager to offer her their personal welcome.

'About time too,' they said, crowding the counter.

'You've hidden yourself away for far too long.'

'Not 'alf!'

'Nina's been doing a grand job . . . you've taught her well . . . but the place just hasn't been the same without you.'

'Seeing you is the best Christmas present we could have.'

The compliments kept coming until they were interrupted by three hearty cheers followed by a rousing version of 'For She's a Jolly Good Fellow'.

Moved to tears but managing to retain her dignity, Tilly walked out from behind the counter into the crowded saloon bar. With the aid of her stick and a sea of helping hands, she went among her clientele to wish them the compliments of the season. It was a glorious experience – and one she knew she would never forget.

PART THREE

PART THREE

Chapter Eighteen

Shafts of June sunlight flashed across the bonnet of the silver Daimler as it left the heavy London traffic and rolled into the countryside.

'It's a lovely day for it, anyway,' remarked Baz to his passenger, who was looking extremely elegant in a royal blue and white Chanel-style summer suit with a white pill-box hat worn on the back of her fashionably full hairstyle.

'Yes,' was her laconic reply.

'Puts the mockers on the occasion if it's raining and we have to stay inside, don't you think?'

'Mm.'

'The boys tend to get edgy then too,' he said, indefatigable in his attempts at conversation. 'You know, with all the parents being forced together inside the school for the day, some of them trying to outdo each other.' He laughed. 'It was wet last year, remember?'

'Vaguely,' she said in a perfunctory manner.

'I must say you're looking lovely today. That outfit is quite something,' he persisted breezily. 'You'll outshine all the other mums.'

'Parents' day isn't meant to be a fashion parade,' she informed him in a blistering tone.

'Why are you looking like something out of *Vogue* then?' he asked lightly.

'Natural pride in my appearance . . . and for Joey's sake,' she snapped.

'There's nothing wrong with a spot of healthy competition, you know,' he said with a smile in his voice.

'If you say so,' she replied with studious indifference.

He concentrated on the road ahead in thoughtful silence for a while, then said, 'Look, Nina, I know you'd sooner walk to Dorset than travel there with me, but since that isn't possible how about us trying to get along during the journey? We usually manage to play happy families when we're actually at these school events so as not to embarrass Joey in front of his friends, so it shouldn't be impossible for us to behave like normal civilised people on the way.'

In reply she stared determinedly out of the window.

'Let me put it another way then. I don't fancy a long drive with you giving out bad vibes all the way,' continued Baz, who had hardly been able to believe his luck when Nina had phoned to ask if she could travel to Joey's school with him because her car had gone on the blink just as she was about to set off and it had been too late for her to take the train.

His candour forced her to admit her behaviour *was* somewhat churlish, since he was doing her a favour. 'All right, point taken,' she said. 'I'll try to behave.'

At thirty-four she was less censorious and more able

to see that she had not been blameless in the breakdown of their marriage. If she'd been more understanding about his ambitions it might have worked out. It was surprising that he wanted her back considering how bad things had been between them.

But Baz was asking her what she thought of his new car.

'Very smart,' she said, comfortably ensconced in its soft upholstery. 'You're getting to be a real high flyer.'

'I've no complaints.'

'Four dance halls is it now?'

'Yes. Two in London, one in Brighton, and we opened a fourth in Margate a couple of weeks ago.'

'Yes, I heard all about that from Mum. She had a lovely time when you took her down to Margate for the day to see the new place.'

He smiled at the memory. 'Yes, we had some laughs. We always do. It's good to see Tilly looking so much more like her old self again, isn't it?'

'It is indeed. She'll never be the same as she was two years ago, though.'

'Maybe not. But she's a damned sight better than when she first came home from hospital,' Baz pointed out gravely. 'She was very low then. I was really worried about her.'

'Weren't we all?' said Nina. 'But she's taking an interest in life again, thank goodness!'

'She seems to be involved with things at The Willow again too.'

'In a very much lesser way than before,' explained Nina. 'But . . . yes. Her helping out with the paperwork and going down into the bar for an hour or so during a session just to mingle with the customers has made a lot of difference to her frame of mind. She can even serve the odd punter now, as long as she doesn't stand for long. She gets dizzy if she does too much.'

'Yes, I know. She's had one or two bad turns when she's been out with me,' he said, 'though she seems to cope better than she used to.'

'I suppose you get used to anything in time. I think she's accepted her limitations now too,' said Nina. 'She knows she can't carry on like before . . . rushing up and down the stairs . . . working all hours. She's come to terms with the fact that she'll never physically run The Willow again, that she has to stand back and allow me to take the responsibility.'

'Still, you two always were a good team.'

'Oh, yes. And while we're on the subject of Mum, Baz,' she said thoughtfully, 'I really appreciate your taking the time to come over to see her and take her out in your car. I know you must have a busy schedule, so thanks.'

'Don't thank me, I enjoy her company,' he said. 'Tilly and I were always good mates before . . . well, you know.'

The past created an instant wall of tension between them. 'Yes, I know you were.' Nina swiftly changed tack to lighten the atmosphere. 'How are you getting along with Joey, these days? He never says much about his meetings with you.'

'I'm not sure, to be perfectly honest,' he confessed. 'We seem to get on better than we used to. Sometimes I even think he quite likes me. But then he goes all moody and I guess he's still bearing a grudge.'

'It might not be anything personal,' she suggested thoughtfully. 'Moodiness is all part of growing up. He'll be fourteen soon.'

'I think there's more to it than just adolescence,' he told her solemnly. 'At times it's almost as though he won't allow himself to like me.'

'Well, he'll be on the nursery slopes to manhood soon,' she pointed out. 'Maybe the two of you will find it easier to sort out your relationship when he's a full-grown adult.'

'Perhaps.'

'Going away to school seems to have been good for him, I think,' she said. 'He's so confident now . . . he can really handle himself in company.'

'Yes, I've noticed.'

'It hasn't broadened his career aspirations though,' she said with a rueful smile. 'He's still talking about working with me in The Willow when he leaves school.'

'There'll be a place for him in Paxton Leisure if he wants it too,' said Baz, 'but let's wait and see how he feels when the time comes.'

'Mm . . . it's still a long way ahead,' she said, adding lightly, 'who knows? I might have expanded The Willow by that time and have a more challenging career opportunity to offer him.'

'Oh, I didn't realise you were thinking of expanding?'

'It's just a germ of an idea I'm playing with at the moment,' she explained. 'I haven't even mentioned it to Mum yet.'

'Sounds intriguing,' he said. 'Tell me more.'

'Well, actually, I've been thinking of having an extension built and opening a restaurant,' she told him.

'Change The Willow into a Steakhouse, you mean?' he said, looking doubtful. 'They seem to be springing up all over the place.'

'No, not a Steakhouse,' she corrected speedily.

'Haute cuisine then?'

'Well, something like that. I visualise a small, intimate restaurant providing first-class cooking . . . something in keeping with the character of the place.'

'Ah, that's more like it.'

'As long as we keep it to a reasonable size, we won't have to build over any of the gardens or lose any of the car park.'

'I can see the sense in that,' he said. 'You'd hire someone to do the cooking, of course?'

'Oh, yes. A qualified chef.'

'Good.'

'So what do you think?'

'I think it's a terrific idea,' he said enthusiastically.

'You do?'

'Sure.'

'Oh, that's really encouraging, Baz. You're the first person I've spoken to about it,' she confessed. 'Perhaps I'll talk to Mum about it now. And of course the bank. It'll cost a bomb to set up.'

'Phew, not half!'

'Anyway, the whole thing needs to be looked at in much more detail before we make any sort of move.'

'Your first step will be to get some plans drawn up so

you can apply for planning permission to build, won't it?'

'Yes. I don't think permission will be a problem, though, do you?'

'No, not as you're expanding your existing business and you're already in a branch of the catering trade.'

'We have car parking facilities too,' she pointed out.

'Yes. The council can't possibly have any objection to your building,' he said. 'Though they'll probably insist that the new extension is built in the same style as the original building.'

'I'd want that too,' she told him. 'But anyway, like I said, it's only an idea at the moment. Mum might not share my enthusiasm and it's her name that's above the door.'

'That's just a technicality these days though, isn't it?'

'Oh, yes. I'm the landlady in every sense but legally,' she confirmed. 'But I still respect Mum's position and discuss everything with her.'

'I can imagine.'

They were too busy chatting to notice the passing miles and suddenly found themselves in the leafy grounds of the school where parents strolled under the trees with their offspring. They pulled up at the front of a dignified old grey stone building with wide steps sweeping up to a portico on which stood a gathering of pupils waiting to greet their parents.

As they got out of the car, Joey was already bounding down the steps towards them. Clearly inhibited by the presence of his peers, he gave his mother a rather restrained hug and shook Baz's hand.

There was nothing reserved about his reaction to the car though. 'It's terrific,' he said exuberantly. 'I didn't expect you both to arrive in it, though.'

'Mine's out of action,' explained Nina, feasting her eyes on her beloved son. 'But let me look at you.' She held him at arm's length, observing a tall, lanky adolescent with warm brown eyes currently hot with embarrassment. He looked so wholesome in his black school blazer and grey trousers, his hair neatly combed into place, she just couldn't resist another embrace. 'My, but you've grown since I last saw you!'

'Mum!' he admonished, glancing cautiously around to see if this display of affection was being noticed, a strawberry blush suffusing his face and neck. 'I'm fourteen . . . not five years old!'

'We can see that, son,' grinned Baz. 'You're nearly as tall as I am.'

'Shall we go for a walk before lunch?' suggested Joey expediently. 'And you can tell me what's been happening at home.'

After a stroll through the grounds they attended a buffet lunch in the dining hall, a huge room with a polished oak floor and panelled walls hung with portraits of past headmasters and dignitaries associated with the school. Some of the guests stood around chatting while they nibbled, others sat at the small tables with their food. Staff and parents mingled while the boys stood around looking somewhat superfluous.

Nina and Baz had finished lunch and were lingering over coffee at one of the tables with Joey when a woman in a pink and white spotted dress worn with a white

290

picture hat swept on to the scene with a man and a boy of about Joey's age.

'Mr and Mrs Paxton,' she said, offering her hand with such vigour they had no option but to rise. 'I'm Felicity Mayhew and this is my husband James . . . and my son Miles. Miles and Joey are such good chums I just had to come over and say a few words.'

Miles Mayhew wasn't a name Nina had heard Joey mention but she said, 'I'm delighted to meet you.'

Introductions were completed while the two boys stood aside from the adults looking apprehensive.

'I see these school events as an opportunity for us parents to get together as well as meeting the staff, don't you?' said Felicity. 'It's so important to meet the parents of one's children's chums, don't you think?'

It wasn't one of Nina's priorities but she said, 'Well, I suppose . . .'

'James is a consultant,' cut in the effusive Felicity. 'Rooms in Harley Street, you know.'

'How nice,' said Nina.

'Do family members get special rates when they need medical advice?' said Baz with a wicked grin.

Felicity's glare was a real killer before she turned her attention back to Nina. 'Miles said something about you being in the licensed trade.' She turned to her husband as though needing confirmation of this rather astonishing fact. 'Didn't he, James?'

'He did indeed, my dear,' said James, an immaculate man dressed traditionally in a blazer and flannels which made Baz's stylish Italian suit look rather showy in comparison. 'I believe he said something about your having an interest in some sort of riverside establishment.'

'Yes, that's right,' said Nina, bracing herself for battle.

'A public house is probably quite a good thing to invest in, I should think,' said Felicity, adding with a laugh and twisting her mouth wryly, 'as long as one doesn't have to be there. Physically, I mean.'

'I live on the premises as a matter of fact,' said Nina evenly.

'Oh, I see,' said Felicity with a shrill laugh. 'You mean that your husband is keeping a personal eye on his investment and you're helping him out.'

'Not at all,' said Nina, beginning to enjoy herself. 'I mean that I run the place.'

There was a shocked silence. 'Oh, really . . . how quaint,' managed Felicity at last.

'I'm in a different branch of the leisure industry,' put in Baz, catching Nina's mood of devilment. 'Dance halls actually.'

'So you help your wife with the public house when you're at home? What fun,' said Felicity, in a manner suggesting that hell would be preferable.

'No, I live in a flat in Bayswater,' Baz explained.

'My husband and I split up some years ago,' Nina informed her brightly.

'Oh.' There was an awkward silence until Felicity said, 'Miles will go to medical school when he leaves here, of course. If all goes well with his exam grades.'

'Good for him if it's what he wants,' said Baz.

'Has Joey any thoughts for the future?' asked James.

'He's talking about going into the licensed trade with me actually,' said Nina, who thought James had a certain warmth in his eyes and was probably a very nice man away from the dreadful Felicity.

'Yes, well, I suppose he would do.' Felicity exchanged a disapproving glance with her husband. 'Anyway, we must mingle. After all, that's what these things are put on for, isn't it? For us to mix. It's been so nice meeting you.'

'Likewise,' chorused Nina and Baz, collapsing into giggles as soon as the Mayhews were out of earshot.

They received a wigging from Joey who told them that parents were expected to behave in a dignified manner when they visited the school . . . not roll around laughing like a couple of hyenas. However, he did admit that Miles Mayhew was new to the school and no friend of his, and he thought his mother was probably vetting all the parents of the boys in his form.

The rest of the afternoon passed pleasantly enough. A formal discussion with Joey's teachers confirmed what they already knew: that he was no Einstein but he could hold his own with the work and was a popular member of the school. Fortunately they didn't encounter any other parents like the Mayhews though most were from the professional classes.

After tea in the garden, they said goodbye to Joey and left, bursting into renewed laughter as soon as the car turned out of the drive.

'I bet the boys are glad that's over,' said Nina. 'They embarrass so easily at that age.'

'Everywhere you looked there were young faces at

various degrees of scarlet because of some unstudied parental remark.'

'We were in the doghouse with Joey on several occasions,' said Nina.

Howls of laughter filled the car as they recalled the Mayhew incident. Then they talked more seriously about Joey, united in their pride in him.

As the shadows began to lengthen, Baz said casually, 'Actually, I'm feeling quite peckish. Do you fancy stopping for a spot of dinner, or do you have to get back early?'

'No, the staff can manage without me for once.'

'Good.'

They found a pretty old thatched pub near Box Hill with a restaurant at the back overlooking the gardens where squirrels and rabbits went about their business unworried by their audience.

'Aren't they tame?' remarked Nina, as they sat at a table in the window watching a squirrel flash up a tree and disappear into the foliage. 'Different to the wild life we get in The Willow gardens – sparrows and pigeons fighting over the crumbs from cheese rolls and crisps.'

'You've the ducks and swans on the river to look at, though,' he reminded her.

'Oh, yes, I'm not complaining . . . far from it.'

'Is this the sort of thing you have in mind for The Willow?' asked Baz, looking round the restaurant at the small tables with white starched tablecloths and fresh flowers as a centrepiece.

'Something similar,' she said. 'Though I would aim for a more intimate ambiance. Candles on the tables . . .

a pianist playing in the background . . . you know the sort of thing.'

'Sounds good.'

'Yes, you've really got me excited about it now,' she said, the warmth of her smile matching her mood.

'I'm glad to have been of some help to you.'

Their eyes met and she found it hard to look away.

'You do have your uses,' she said jokingly, seeking escape in humour. She was glad when the waitress brought their food because the interruption dissolved the strong sexual chemistry that was still there between them.

They chatted about general matters over Brown Windsor soup followed by roast lamb and mint sauce served with a delicious assortment of home grown vegetables, all washed down with a bottle of wine. They got talking about his new dance hall in Margate and how Baz's brother George and his wife were there at the moment.

'Is he managing it for you?' she asked with genuine interest.

'Oh, no, I can't spare George to manage just one hall. He's too useful helping me to run the whole operation,' he explained. 'I've put a manager in there but I've sent George and Marge down to give him support for a couple of weeks, iron out any teething troubles.'

'Has his wife gone with him to help, or just to keep him company?' Nina wondered aloud.

'To help,' he said emphatically. 'They're a team, those two. Marge will turn her hand to anything at all: office work, the cloakroom. She'll even do the cleaning if we're really desperate.'

'Sounds like a real gem.'

'She is. In fact, they're a smashing couple,' he told her. 'I hope the weather is as good in Margate as it is here. I've told them to take some time off while they're at the coast and make a bit of a holiday of it.'

'It's so important to have people you can trust working for you, isn't it?' she said. 'Neither you nor I would be here now without good back-up staff.'

'That's a fact.'

She smiled into his eyes. 'It's been a lovely day, Baz. I've thoroughly enjoyed myself.'

'Me too.' He reached for her hand across the table and she didn't have the strength to resist. 'I've missed you, Presh,' he said softly.

'Oh, Baz.' Hearing his pet name for her after so long moved her unbearably. 'I've missed you too,' she heard herself say, mellowed by the romantic atmosphere.

'We're right for each other . . . no matter what happened in the past.'

'Yes, I know.'

She wanted him so badly at that moment all she could think of was a notice she had seen on her way in saying 'Rooms to Let'.

'We could make it work, you know, Nina,' he said softly, putting her hand to his lips. 'I'm sure of it.'

The emotion she had tried to suppress all these years rose like a physical pain, reminding her of the agony she had suffered for a long time after he'd left. The vividness of it brought her to her senses.

'Don't spoil it, Baz,' she said. 'We've had a super day

out together . . . let's just leave it at that.'

'I still love you.'

'Don't, Baz . . . don't!' she begged him, snatching her hand away.

'You've just admitted that we're right for each other.'

'Yes, I must have allowed myself to get carried away.'

'It's still there for you, though, isn't it? The feeling . . .'

'Sure. I want to go to bed with you,' she admitted with brutal candour, 'but I'm not going to turn my life upside down because of it.'

'Nina . . .'

'Leave it, Baz, please.'

'But . . .'

'Honestly,' she implored him, her eyes shining with tears, 'I'd rather you didn't bring it up again. If you really care for me, please do as I ask.'

There was a brooding silence. 'All right,' he sighed miserably at last.

Their mood was subdued as they drove back to London. Although Nina congratulated herself on having stood her ground she was left with an aching sense of disappointment after she had said goodnight to him.

'This is the life, eh, Marge?' said George the following afternoon as he settled in his deck chair in the sunshine on the beach at Margate.

'Mind you don't overdo it and get burnt,' she warned. 'You're still sore from yesterday's sunbathing.'

'Don't worry, I'll cover the tender bits up in a minute,'

he said, lying back and closing his eyes. 'You ought to watch it an' all.'

'Yeah, I'll have to be careful,' agreed Marge, carefully smoothing some cream on to her skin. 'My legs are feelin' a bit raw. Still, it's worth sufferin' to go home with a suntan.'

'Mm,' agreed George sleepily.

'I think it's really nice of Baz to put us up at a luxury hotel and tell us to mix business with pleasure while we're at the seaside.'

'Yeah, my brother's a good bloke.'

'I could get used to all this good livin'.'

'I reckon we're gonna be getting more of it in the future too,' said George, ''cos Paxton leisure is going from strength to strength.'

'Well, you won't hear me complaining.' Marge smiled, lying back in her chair with a blissful sigh. 'Ooh . . . the sun feels so lovely and warm on my face.'

'Mine too.'

'I reckon us Brits must have a sunshine deficiency,' she said, 'that's why we go mad and overdo it when we do get a spell of decent weather.'

'Maybe we should think of going abroad for a holiday?' he suggested. 'Everyone else seems to be doing it.'

She sat up and stared at him. 'Oh, George, do you really mean it?' she said excitedly.

'Yeah, why not?'

'When?'

'Later this year, perhaps.'

'How thrillin'.' She reclined again and closed her eyes. 'I'll just lie here and think of exotic places.'

'Yeah . . . you do that while I have forty winks,' he said fondly.

They snoozed in perfect contentment, their skin turning salmon pink around their swimming costumes.

'Phew, it's hot,' said Marge after a while. 'Fancy coming in the water to cool off, George?'

'No, thanks.'

'Why not?'

'I'm feelin' lazy. Anyway, the sea'll be freezing.'

'Oh, don't be such a spoilsport. I really fancy a swim and it'll do you good to get some exercise.'

'Getting up in the morning is enough exercise for me,' he laughed.

'Aw, come on, George,' she coaxed. 'It's more fun with two.'

'All right, love,' he sighed reluctantly. 'You go on down to the sea. I'll join you in a few minutes.'

'You'd better,' she warned playfully. 'Or I'll come back and drag you down there by your ears.'

'You can warm the water up ready for me,' he said, smiling at her tenderly.

'The way my legs are burning, that might not be impossible,' she giggled.

She dragged on a white rubber bathing cap over her hair, her yellow and black striped swimming costume fitting tightly over her ample proportions.

'Does this costume look all right, George?' she asked, holding her stomach in as she pulled the legs of the costume down over her fleshy thighs. 'Doesn't make me look too fat, does it?'

'No. You're the best-looking wasp in Margate,' he

teased affectionately, running his eyes over the striped costume.

That remark earned him a swipe with her towel. 'Be serious, will you?' she urged him.

'Okay . . . seriously . . . you look really smashing, love,' he assured her.

'Right. I'll see you in a minute then,' she said.

She picked her way through the crowded beach to the water's edge which was alive with squealing children. Men with shins bared and women with skirts pulled up rinsed their toes. She shrieked as the icy water lapped over her feet and winced and shivered as it reached her waist.

'It's lovely once you're in,' called a woman who was on her way back to the shore. 'Doesn't feel cold at all once you start swimming . . . it's great fun riding on the waves.'

Marge took the plunge, the cold water taking her breath away initially. Oh, this was heaven, she thought when the shock had worn off. She struck out through the water then floated back on the waves. It felt so invigorating yet relaxing too . . . her body seemed to sing with a feeling of well-being. Life was so good for her and George. They were so lucky to have each other, work they enjoyed and enough money to live in reasonable comfort.

Finding herself back in shallow waters, she swam further out and waited to be swept back with the tide. That was odd . . . the shore seemed to be further away instead of nearer. Breathless now, she aimed back towards the beach, swimming hard, only to find the current pulling her out to sea. Her limbs were aching and her chest causing her pain as she struggled for breath. Panic-stricken, she raised her arms and tried to scream but her voice was taken by the roar of the sea.

The freezing water crept over her face and closed around her head. Trying frantically to tread water, she managed to reach the surface and raise her arms again. But she just couldn't stay up . . . Her body sank deeper and deeper.

George fully intended to follow Marge down to the sea but dozed off instead. He woke up with a start, feeling disorientated and confused. Something seemed to be happening around him. People were running down the sand to the water's edge or standing in groups, talking in hushed voices and staring towards the sea.

'What's going on, mate?' he asked a man who was standing near him with a handkerchief knotted over his head. He was shading his eyes from the sun with his hand and staring seawards.

'Someone's drowned, I think,' the man informed him.

'Ooh, blimey!'

'There's always some joker who does it, every summer, ain't there?' said the man in a doom-laden voice.

'Does what?' asked George, still feeling muzzy from his sleep.

'Swims out too far,' he explained. 'I mean, they ought to know how dangerous it is to get out of their depth.'

'Yeah, I suppose so,' mumbled George.

The man craned his neck, peering into the distance.

'Looks like a woman to me . . . they're bringing her in now.'

George was instantly awake. A woman! Marge had gone swimming! How long ago was that? Oh God! He tore across the sands, demolishing a child's sandcastle and tripping over a bucket and spade in his haste. There was a small gathering at the water's edge. He pushed his way to the front just in time to see a man in swimming trunks in the centre turn towards them.

'She's dead,' he told the shocked spectators.

George couldn't move or speak as he stared at the yellow and black striped swimsuit gleaming wetly on the sand.

Chapter Nineteen

It was just after ten o'clock in the evening and Baz was enjoying a rare moment of relaxation at home in his Bayswater flat. With his supper on a tray on his lap, he was ensconced in an armchair in front of the television set watching a news report of the inauguration of the youngest ever President of the United States, forty-three-year-old John Fitzgerald Kennedy, who had been sworn in earlier in the day as the thirty-fifth US President.

The nocturnal nature of Baz's business meant he could be called upon until the small hours to solve some crisis or other within his company. Tonight he hoped his staff wouldn't find it necessary to dial his number because he was a great admirer of the dynamic American and wanted to see the full coverage of this historic occasion. Almost as the thought came, his peace was shattered by the telephone.

However, the call was not from Paxton Leisure Ltd. It was the landlord of The Rising Sun at Acton.

'It's George again, I suppose?' said Baz gloomily.

'I'm afraid so,' confirmed the other man. 'I've managed to take his car keys off him but I daren't let him leave here in the state he's in . . . he'll be arrested for being drunk and disorderly on the streets.'

'Thanks, mate. I'm on my way,' Baz assured him, stopping only to switch off the television set and grab a coat before going out into the bitter January night, leaving his supper half eaten on the tray.

It was over six months since Marge's tragic death. Having known her for so long, Baz too had been shaken by it. Even now he couldn't get used to the idea that she was no longer around. He still expected her chirpy presence to fill the offices of Paxton Leisure Ltd at Acton.

You'd expect George to be devastated by such a blow, of course. But he'd been completely destroyed by it – he was now a lost soul seeking solace in the bottle. Baz was at his wit's end to know what to do about him. As much as he sympathised, his brother was fast becoming a downright liability. He rarely turned up for work until the afternoon and even then he couldn't be relied upon to carry out his duties efficiently.

This state of affairs put Baz in a real quandary because his position at the head of a large company depended on his having a dependable general assistant. If George didn't pull himself together soon he'd have no option but to find a replacement.

But how could he dismiss his own brother? Especially when he was so low. It would be too cruel and Baz just couldn't do it. But neither could the firm afford to carry a passenger indefinitely, so a solution had to be found.

Arriving at The Rising Sun, he found George slumped

at a table in the corner, staring blankly into space with a soppy smile on his face.

'Time to go home, old son,' Baz said authoritatively.

'Oh, wotcher, bruv,' said George in a slurred voice. 'What you havin' to jink, mate?'

'Nothing, George. It's time to go home now.'

'You'll . . . have to . . . to . . . get the jinks in . . . though,' he said, as though his brother hadn't spoken, ''cos . . . they won't serve me in here . . . bloody cheek.' His speech was indistinct and he flapped a limp hand towards the bar staff. 'My brother'll soon sort you lot out . . . no trouble.'

'Come on, mate, up you get,' said Baz, and in one swift movement grabbed his brother under the arms and lifted him, draping his arm around his own shoulders. Assisted by the landlord, he dragged him outside to the car and bundled him into the back where he immediately sank into a stupor. Rather than deliver him to an empty house, Baz took him back to his own place.

George was still comatose when Baz went to the office the next morning so he decided to go home at lunchtime and have a serious chat with him. George was sitting at the kitchen table, smoking and drinking black coffee when Baz walked in.

''Ello, what you doing home at this time o' day?' George asked dully, peering at his brother with half-closed eyes.

'I've come home to talk to you,' he explained.

'Don't talk too loud then,' said George, frowning with pain. 'My 'ead feels like a bus has hit it.'

'I'll come straight to the point,' said Baz, pouring himself a cup of coffee and sitting down opposite his brother. 'This heavy drinking has got to stop.'

'Not so loud, mate,' said George, wincing. 'I've told you, I'm feeling delicate this morning.'

'Never mind sitting here feeling sorry for yourself,' Baz admonished sharply, 'you're due at our Wembley ballroom today.'

'Ooh, Gawd . . . am I?' he said, putting a hand to his brow. 'Later, mate. I'll go over there later on.'

'Give us a break, George,' Baz said with a weary sigh. 'I've a business to run and you're not making it easy.'

George looked at his brother with bloodshot eyes, his skin the colour of porridge, a growth of stubble darkening his chin. 'Sorry, bruv. I just can't get myself together,' he said, his eyes glistening with tears. 'I still miss her something awful.'

Assailed by pity, Baz took a sip of his coffee. 'I'm sure you do, mate,' he said in a gentler tone. 'It seems hard, I know, but life has to go on and you'll feel better once you get back into a routine.'

'I wish life didn't have to go on for me,' said George, drawing on a cigarette.

'Now that's enough of that sort o' talk!' warned Baz. 'Marge will be turning in her grave.'

'We were so close . . .'

Realising that his brother needed to talk about his beloved wife, Baz let him ramble on while he made them a snack lunch. While he did battle with cheese and pickle sandwiches, George waxed sentimental about his life with Marge.

When he seemed to have talked himself into a calmer frame of mind, Baz said, 'I feel for you, I really do.'

'I know you do, bruv.'

'The trouble is, George, I need you to do some work. You're making life very difficult for me with your drinking habits.'

'Sorry.'

'It's like this,' Baz continued, determined to get through to him. 'If you don't get yourself over to Wembley today, I'll have to go instead and I really don't have the time.'

'Why does one of us have to go?' asked George, worrying Baz even more by having forgotten what his duties were.

'The manager there has some idea about booking some star bands for his summer programme. Don't you remember?'

'Er . . .'

'It needs a thorough discussion with one of us before a final decision can be made. Well-known bands don't come cheap. You and I have talked about this . . .'

'Yeah, of course,' muttered George in a manner suggesting he'd forgotten the whole thing. 'I'll go over there.'

'Are you feeling up to it?'

'Well . . .'

'Oh, forget it. I'll do it myself,' said Baz with more than a hint of impatience. 'I want this thing properly sorted.'

'Sorry.'

'Don't keep saying sorry,' said Baz, clinging desperately to his temper. 'Just try to get your act together, mate. Because we can't go on like this.'

'Okay, bruv,' he said, but Baz wasn't convinced.

Tilly enjoyed visiting different pubs when Baz took her out. He often teased her about it . . . told her it was a busman's holiday. She said she liked to watch other people work as well as keep up to date with the competition.

They were in a newish pub near Richmond a week or so later when Baz confided in her about George.

'Try not to be too hard on him,' urged Tilly kindly. 'He has to go through the grieving process. I know I did when I lost Joe.'

'You didn't let yourself go though, did you?' Baz pointed out. 'He seems to have given up on life completely. The drink is making him lazy and unreliable. I just can't trust him to do anything in the business these days.'

'Work was my salvation,' confessed Tilly. 'Without that I think I would have gone to pieces. It obviously isn't like that for George.'

'It certainly isn't!'

'He'll come out of it, Baz,' she said encouragingly. 'Just give him a little more time.'

They were sitting by an artificial log fire in a spacious, well-appointed lounge-bar with contemporary furniture and brightly patterned carpet. It was warm and comfortable but completely lacking in atmosphere, as Tilly was quick to point out.

'Some of these new pubs are just like posh railway station buffets, aren't they?' she said. 'Comfortable enough but they don't have any feel about them.'

'Perhaps that comes with time,' he suggested.

'Mm . . . but it doesn't happen on its own. It has to be worked on,' she told him thoughtfully.

'I'm very pleased that your plans for expansion aren't going to alter the character of The Willow,' he remarked, for Tilly had told him that they had recently submitted plans to the council for permission to build a restaurant.

She frowned. 'I was just going to tell you about that. Our expansion plans are finished . . . kaput!'

'Why?'

'The council turned down our application,' she informed him.

Up went his brows. 'I don't believe it,' he exclaimed. 'Why on earth would they do that?'

'They reckon we don't have enough parking facilities to accommodate the additional cars that a restaurant would attract,' she informed him. 'They say it'll cause inconvenience to local residents with extra vehicles parked on the streets.'

'There's restaurants and pubs in London with a lot less parking space than you have. In fact, some have no car park at all.'

'Nina queried that with them,' she told him. 'They say they can't do anything about those that are already in existence but they can limit new ones opening up with insufficient facilities because of the dramatic increase in cars on the road since the end of the war.'

'Seems a bit fishy to me.'

309

'That's what Nina said. She's furious.'

'I should think she is. I know I would be.'

'She wants to appeal against the decision,' said Tilly, sipping her Guinness. 'But I don't know if it's worth the trouble. I mean, once these government departments have made up their minds about something, there isn't usually any shifting 'em, is there?'

'No.'

'Damn' bureaucrats!' she complained. 'It isn't as though they're consistent with their rules and regulations either.'

'Oh, what makes you say that?'

'Well, there's a newish restaurant that opened a year or so ago about a mile downriver,' she explained. 'He doesn't have any car park at all but that didn't stop his application going through.'

'What sort of place is it?' Baz asked thoughtfully.

'One of these new style arty places with a continental flavour,' she informed him, 'run by a man called Charlie Webster. He's as much a Londoner as you and me but he's doing all this French food . . . a bistro I believe they call it. Goes by the name of André's.'

'And you say he doesn't have a car park at all?'

'That's right. He built the place on an infill plot among houses and factories.'

'Mmm . . . that really is interesting,' Baz said, stroking his chin meditatively.

'It's hardly fair, is it?' said Tilly hotly. 'I mean, if they turn one application down for that reason, they should reject the others too.'

'I couldn't agree more.'

'He probably gave someone on the planning committee a back-hander to get his application through,' she snorted.

'Or paid someone to stop yours?' suggested Baz.

Tilly's eyes widened. 'You're not being serious, are you?' she exclaimed. 'I was only jokin'.'

'I know you were,' he said, 'but think about it, Til. This bloke has just set up in business and is building his reputation nicely . . . then you apply to open a restaurant on his doorstep. The last thing he wants at this stage is competition.'

'But we wouldn't be competition for him,' she protested. 'We aren't planning to serve continental dishes.'

'He doesn't know that, though, does he?' Baz pointed out.

'Well, no, I suppose not,' she agreed. 'But even if we were there's still room for us both. We weren't put off by his restaurant being there so why should he feel threatened by ours?'

'A mixture of greed and fear, I should think.'

'But that's downright ridiculous,' she exclaimed. 'The Willow will always be a pub. The restaurant was only going to be a small addition to it.'

'It could still seem like a threat to a competitor.'

Tilly sipped her drink slowly. 'Are you sure you're not letting your imagination run away with you?' she suggested. 'I mean . . . I've always been under the impression that planning decisions are made democratically, by a committee.'

'That's what's supposed to happen.'

'So how could one of them persuade the others to block an application unless there was a really good reason?'

'By convincing them it's the wrong thing for the area,' he said. 'Some of these committee people can be very persuasive . . . which is how they got the job in the first place. Especially if it's being made worth their while.'

'You really think that's what happened?'

'I certainly think it's worth looking into.'

'Neither Nina nor I would know where to begin though.'

'You just leave it all to me, Til,' he told her in a sanguine manner. 'Don't do anything about an appeal until you hear from me.'

The next morning Baz went round to George's place, dragged him out of bed and fed him black coffee and Alka Seltzer.

'I need you with me on a special job,' he explained.

'I'm in no fit state . . .'

'You don't need to be,' said Baz. 'All that is required of you is that you're alive and vertical.'

'What's all this about?' asked George, looking pained.

'We're going out to lunch.'

'Ugh . . . no!' groaned George. 'I can't face food.'

Baz gave him a hard look. 'You won't have to eat anything.'

'Just the smell will be enough to turn me up,' whined his brother. 'You'll have to count me out on this one.'

'For God's sake, George,' boomed Baz in a tone that

made his ailing brother look up sharply. 'You're getting to be so selfish lately. I hardly recognise you as my brother.'

'Me, selfish?' he objected. ''Ere, you wanna watch what you're saying . . .'

'It's true,' growled Baz, 'and despite what you may think, you're not the only person in the world with problems. Other people have their fair share too.'

'I've never said otherwise.'

'You've thought of no one but yourself for months,' said Baz.

George remained silent.

'Anyway, I've not come here for an argument,' said Baz. 'I want to sort out a problem for some people who mean a lot to me – Nina and her mother – and I need a pair of broad shoulders with me for support.'

Still there was silence from his brother.

'If you can't be bothered to drag yourself out of your trough of self-pity to help me on this one, then I'll do it on my own,' barked Baz. 'But I really think it's about time you pulled yourself together and thought about someone besides yourself for a change.' He looked straight into his brother's face. 'It's really important to me that I get this right because I've nothing to go on at all but instinct.'

'Oh.'

'Well, are you with me on this or not?'

George sighed deeply, then slowly stood up, holding his head and wincing. 'All right, bruv. I'll go and get myself smartened up,' he grunted. 'You'd better tell me what this is all about while I get shaved.'

* * *

'Nice little place you have here,' said Baz, looking around the crowded restaurant at the knotty pine walls hung with strings of onions and wine bottles, the green and white checked table-linen, the handwritten menus.

'Thank you,' said Charlie Webster who was about thirty-five, a weedy poseur of a man with a protruding chin and goatee beard. His mode of dress was studied casual – blue jeans and a navy and white striped sweater. 'Have you booked a table?'

'No, we're not here to eat,' said Baz with a sangfroid that belied the fact that he was about to play the biggest hunch of his life. 'We're here to talk . . . and I think what my brother and I have to say would be better said somewhere private.'

'Yeah, somewhere private,' echoed George, dropping his voice by several tones and adopting the threatening look of a gangster's henchman.

The man narrowed his beady eyes. 'I don't think I care for your attitude,' he said haughtily.

'Somewhere private,' repeated Baz.

'You 'eard what the man said,' commanded George, really beginning to get into the part now.

'I demand to know what all this is about.'

'It's about a friend of yours at the Town Hall,' Baz informed him crisply. 'In the planning department.'

'I don't have any friends at the Town Hall,' came the swift denial.

'Well, that's strange,' Baz told him, 'because we've heard different. Isn't that right, George?'

'Not 'alf, bruv.'

'Okay . . . okay,' conceded Charlie, in a whisper, glancing furtively around. 'So I have a nodding acquaintance with Peter West. What has that to do with you?'

'Let's go into your back room and we'll tell you,' said Baz, triumphant at the success of his bluff.

They followed Charlie through some beaded curtains at the back of the restaurant, along a passageway past the kitchen and into a small living room furnished in the modern style.

'Has something happened to Peter?' asked Charlie, looking worried.

'Not so far as we know, but it soon will if you don't co-operate with us,' said Baz.

'Yeah,' snarled George, in a ludicrous caricature of James Cagney.

'Don't you threaten me,' warned Charlie, moving towards the telephone on the window sill, 'or I'll call the police.'

Baz walked over to the phone and picked up the receiver. 'Go ahead,' he said, offering the instrument. 'I wouldn't mind a word with them myself. I don't know if corruption in the Town Hall comes under their jurisdiction but I'm sure they'll be interested to know about it.'

The man turned pale and chewed his lip anxiously. 'I don't know what you're babbling on about.'

'Oh, I think you do,' said Baz with the superior attitude of a man who knows he is right. 'I'm referring to the little matter of the rejection of an application by the landlady of The Willow for permission to build a restaurant.'

'What has that to do with me?'

The Paxton brothers could seem an awesome pair when they really put their minds to it. They stepped towards Charlie and each slapped a hand on his shoulder. The man turned from white to a delicate shade of green.

'All right . . . all right . . . so what if I did pay Peter West to put a spoke in their damned application?' he said defensively. 'They make a good living with the pub. They're just being greedy opening a restaurant and getting their fingers into someone else's pie.'

Baz and George stood back, laughing.

'Well, if that isn't the pot calling the kettle black I don't know what is!' said Baz. 'Since *you* have a licence to sell alcoholic drinks!'

'Only so that people can have a drink with their meal,' he said. 'I'm not likely to steal custom from a pub.'

'And they're not likely to steal business from you,' Baz told him. 'Theirs will be an entirely different sort of operation . . . in fact, I should think one restaurant will complement the other. People will get to know that there's more than one decent place to eat on this stretch of the river and it'll act as a magnet.'

'You're speaking as though it's going to happen,' snorted Charlie. 'But their application has been refused, remember?'

'Yes, but they're going to appeal and that appeal is going to be granted,' Baz stated categorically. 'They are going to get permission to build their restaurant, do you get my drift?'

'Nothing to do with me,' said Charlie, shrugging his shoulders and seeming to gain a little in confidence.

Baz pushed him down into an armchair and stood over him. 'This is the deal, mate,' he said in a tone that didn't invite argument. 'You tell your friend Peter West to make sure that the appeal goes the right way for the landlady of The Willow or I'll go to the council and tell them what I know and demand an investigation.'

'You can't prove anything,' blustered Charlie.

'I don't need to,' said Baz. 'Just a hint of corruption will be enough to have him investigated.'

'I can't make Peter do anything,' said Charlie.

'You got him to block the application. Now it's up to you to get the decision reversed,' demanded Baz calmly. 'I don't care how you do it . . . bribe him . . . threaten him . . . do what you like . . . but if the landlady of The Willow doesn't get permission to build, you and Peter West are going to wish you'd never been born. We'll make an awful lot of noise if necessary.'

'Yeah, we will,' echoed George.

'If the appeal is granted you won't hear from us again,' said Baz. 'If not, competition for business in your restaurant will be the least of your worries. Come on, George, let's go.'

'Righto, bruv,' said George, and the two men marched from the restaurant.

They were still laughing when they drew into The Willow's car park, their breath steaming in the cold air.

'You're wasted working for me, George,' chuckled Baz as they walked towards the entrance. 'I think we'd better try to get you into films.'

'Did I do all right then?' he wanted to know.

'You were brilliant,' enthused Baz. 'All that brainless heavy stuff was pure magic. Great stuff, mate. I tell you, Hollywood had better watch out.'

'Someone's happy,' said Nina, as they faced her across the bar. 'You look like a couple of schoolboys who've just pulled a fast one on the teacher.'

This sent them into fits again.

'I only wish I was as cheerful,' she said wistfully.

'I think we can arrange that, don't you, George?' said Baz grinning.

'I sure do.'

'Having had our planning application turned down, I very much doubt it,' she told them.

'You can put your appeal in as soon as you like,' Baz said with a broad grin.

'I can?'

'Yeah. We can guarantee that you'll get permission to build this time,' he said, beaming.

She narrowed her eyes and gave an uncertain smile. 'What have you two been up to?'

'Oh . . . this and that,' said Baz enigmatically.

With a cautionary glance around to make sure they couldn't be overheard, she leaned towards them and said in a low voice, 'Mum said something about your suspecting dirty dealings at the Town Hall?'

'I was right about it too.'

'No! Why, the rotten buggers,' she exclaimed.

'It was pretty low.'

'I hope you haven't been involved in anything that will get you into trouble on our behalf? No rough stuff?'

'Better ask James Cagney here about that,' said Baz.

'No rough stuff, I promise you,' George assured her.

'How then . . .?'

In low tones he gave her a brief outline of what had happened.

'Well, thanks very much, boys,' she said, looking from one to the other, her eyes lingering on Baz for a moment. 'Have a drink on the house.'

'That's very civil of you,' said Baz, grinning. 'Thanks very much.'

He was feeling particularly pleased with himself. Mostly because he'd been able to help Nina and Tilly but also because he'd heard his brother laugh for the first time in months.

It would probably only be a temporary upturn in George's spirits, something that had happened because he'd been forced into a situation which had taken his mind off his own troubles for a few hours. He would soon sink into a decline when he got back home to the house without Marge.

But Baz was much more optimistic now because he knew how to deal with the problem in future. Sympathy was no use to George, that was obvious now. He needed a firm hand to help him out of the doldrums. It had certainly worked wonders for him today!

Chapter Twenty

'These scones taste good, Alice,' remarked Tilly.

'Mm, delicious,' agreed Nina.

'Er . . . oh . . . do they? Have another one then,' invited Alice absently, taking the plate from the tea-trolley and offering it to her visitors. 'Um . . . how about another cup of tea, too?'

'Please,' chorused her guests.

Having poured the tea with a shaky hand, Alice said, 'So . . . having the builders in at The Willow is beginning to get you down then, is it?'

'Not half,' said Tilly.

'It's a treat to come over here for an hour or so to get away from it,' remarked Nina.

'Still, upheaval is only to be expected when building work is being done,' said Tilly. 'We'll soon forget the inconvenience when we see the end result.'

'Have you had any complaints from the . . . the . . . er . . . customers?' asked Alice in a vague manner.

'No, everyone's been really good about it,' Nina told her. 'The builders have put sheeting across the opening to the extension in the public hallway so dust isn't getting through to the bars. It's just the noise that can get on your nerves.'

'So when are you expecting to open the restaurant?' asked Alice.

Nina and her mother exchanged puzzled glances. They had been talking to Alice about opening in time for the Christmas trade not five minutes ago.

'In time for Christmas we hope. We've just told you,' Tilly reminded her.

'Oh . . . yes . . . so you did,' she said, frowning into her tea-cup.

'Is everything all right, Alice?' asked Tilly.

'Of course. Why on earth shouldn't it be?' she snapped.

'You seem rather tense,' explained Nina.

'No, I'm not,' she said defensively. 'You're imagining things.'

It was September. Things had moved fast at The Willow since Baz's intervention in the building permission affair, and the place had been crawling with builders all summer. Nina was longing for them to finish the job so she could get started on the new project but at the moment she was more concerned about her cousin, who wasn't her usual self.

'The house is looking very nice, Alice,' she said, because this sort of compliment could usually be guaranteed to please.

'Thank you,' said Alice with a surprising lack of interest.

'Yes, lovely,' said Tilly.

It was too, thought Nina, glancing around the room. Shafts of sunlight filtered through the lace curtains, forming dappled patterns on the red carpet. There were good quality furnishings and a fine piano. Alice and Dudley considered contemporary furniture to be common, and favoured a more traditional look. Everything reeked of good taste and lavender polish.

A silence fell, unusual when visiting Alice who normally droned on endlessly about the escalating fortunes of the Harding family.

'How's Dudley?' asked Nina to ease the tension.

Alice threw her cousin a worried look. 'He's fine,' she replied in brisk staccato fashion. 'Why . . . why do you ask?'

'No particular reason,' said Nina, mystified by her cousin's reaction. 'I was just making polite conversation.'

Alice nibbled her lip nervously. 'Yes, of course.'

'How are the boys?' asked Tilly.

'They're all right.'

After another awkward silence, Alice drew the subject away from her own family, a rare occurrence indeed. 'So you hope to be opening the restaurant about December then?' she said, obviously forcing an interest.

'The beginning of the month, hopefully,' said Nina, her voice rising enthusiastically.

'Good,' said Alice vacantly.

'Perhaps you and Dudley might like to come along on our opening night . . . as our guests?' suggested Nina.

'Yes . . . yes . . . I'm sure we shall,' she said hurriedly, adding as an afterthought, 'er . . . thank you.'

'We'll make sure we put the red carpet down for you that night, won't we, Mum?' grinned Nina.

'Too true,' agreed Tilly, wondering what was bothering her niece.

* * *

'What's the matter with Alice, I wonder?' said Tilly on the way home.

'Something's up, that's for sure,' said Nina. 'It's a pity Alice doesn't find it easy to unburden herself.'

'Mm, she keeps everything bottled up inside,' agreed Tilly. 'Just like she did when her parents died.'

'It's probably something trivial. Some new item of furniture she can't get hold of or something,' said Nina, making light of it because she knew her mother worried so much about Alice. 'She'll be as right as rain when we next see her.'

'You're probably right.'

The traffic slowed to a standstill in King Street. 'What's going on here?' said Nina, craning her neck to see round the vehicle in front. 'Looks like some sort of a protest demonstration.'

'Ban the bomb,' said Tilly, catching sight of a banner.

'Might be a spin off from the big demo in Trafalgar Square yesterday.'

'Could be,' agreed Tilly.

'That was the biggest one so far in London apparently. They reckon there were fifteen thousand protestors there at one point,' said Nina. 'More than eight hundred people were arrested according to the papers.'

'Mm, some of them were from showbusiness too,' said Tilly. 'I saw it on the television news.'

'I reckon Joey would have tried to be there if he'd not been away at school,' remarked Nina.

'He certainly had enough to say about CND during the holidays.'

'Yes, his generation's very uptight about it.'

Nina got out of the car and looked into the distance. 'Looks like it's jammed solid right down to the Broadway,' she said. 'I'll turn off into the back doubles as soon as I can or we'll never get home.'

'Good idea,' said Tilly, but her mind was elsewhere. 'I do hope all is well with Alice and her family.'

'Yes, so do I,' said Nina. 'She'll not tell us if it isn't, though. That much I do know.'

Alice was in the kitchen washing the tea things after her visitors had left when she heard the doorbell. She was so startled, she dropped one of her best Royal Albert cups into the sink and smashed it. With uncharacteristic disregard for the breakage, she dried her hands and hurried to the door, her mouth parched with nerves. So great was her relief to see a kitchenware salesman on the doorstep, she almost took pity on him and gave him an order but was deterred by the Hardings' current economy drive.

Back in the kitchen she cleared up the pieces with trembling hands, admonishing herself for letting her imagination run wild. Recent happenings were probably nothing more than coincidence and certainly no cause for her to work herself up into such a state.

Even Aunt Tilly and Nina had noticed something amiss, and the last thing she wanted was the Harding image tarnished in their eyes. Her exalted lifestyle was her weapon against the world – it was her strength against those to whom she inwardly felt inferior. If it crumbled she would be nothing!

Looking back on the last few weeks she recalled the
first alteration to the genteel atmosphere of the Harding
household – a dramatic change in Dudley's personality.
He had never been a cheerful or affectionate husband
but neither was he given to sudden bouts of rage. But
recently the cool, unemotional man she had married
had become an irascible insomniac who was almost
impossible to live with. Her attempts to discover what
was bothering him had sent him into such a fury, she'd
been forced to let the subject alone.

Initially she'd thought perhaps his war wound was
troubling him. But when he'd suddenly demanded
drastic economies in their domestic budget she'd guessed
the problem was financial. He'd muttered something
about having to take a temporary cut in salary which
seemed very odd at this time of general affluence. But
since she and Dudley had never discussed money
matters and the details of his bank account and salary
were unknown to her, Alice knew better than to pry.

The thing that had really set her nerves jangling had
been a visit to the house by one of Dudley's superiors
one afternoon when her husband had been out at work.
The man had claimed to be just passing through the
area, and paying a courtesy call on the wife of one of the
staff. But he'd asked rather too many questions about
Dudley and the way they lived for that to ring true. She
got the distinct impression that Dudley was being
checked out. When she'd mentioned it to him later, he
had dismissed it as unimportant but she'd seen the
worry in his eyes.

There was obviously some problem with his job.

Maybe he wasn't working hard enough or was making too many errors. Alarming prospects indeed. Supposing he lost his current position and had to take a job with a lower salary permanently? It just didn't bear thinking about!

She took herself in hand, told herself she was being ridiculous. Steady, reliable people like Dudley didn't get fired, especially with so many job vacancies around at the moment. Whatever was wrong would blow over and everything would revert to normal. She certainly hoped so because she was becoming a nervous wreck with things as they were.

As the glorious autumnal riverside became leafless and bleak with swirling mists and icy drizzle, the cement mixers and builder's rubble that had cluttered the landscape around The Willow all summer were replaced by a smart new white-rendered building that blended in beautifully with the old.

They had kept to their original plan of creating a homely restaurant ambiance and had limited seating capacity to fifty at the very most. The intention was to earn a reputation as one of those places that necessitated booking well in advance.

With the builders gone it was time for the really interesting part – the furnishings and interior decor.

'We're still agreed on a colour scheme of pale peach and green, are we?' asked Nina of her mother with whom she had had many similar discussions over the last few months.

'That's fine with me,' said Tilly, who trusted her

daughter's judgement rather than her own on such matters.

'With the wood panelling and the soft wall lighting, it should have a relaxing feel to it.'

'Definitely,' said Tilly.

'Peach table linen and curtains, green carpets. Okay?'

'Smashing.'

There was so much for Nina to do and organise. The place bumped and creaked with activity as kitchen equipment was installed, decorators worked with wallpaper and paint, a department store measured the windows for curtains and potential restaurant staff arrived to be interviewed. In addition to all this the pub still had to be run. Nina was on the go from morning till night, organising, planning, serving behind the bar.

One misty morning she was outside talking to the delivering draymen when a familiar Morris Minor drew into the car park.

'Alice,' she muttered in surprise, going over to meet her cousin. 'Well, this is unexpected.' As the other woman drew close and Nina saw her lurid pallor against her camel-coloured coat, she put a comforting hand on her arm. 'Alice love, whatever's the matter?'

'Arrested!' gasped Nina a few minutes later upstairs in the living room. 'You mean that Dudley has been carted off by the police?'

'That's right,' Alice told her cousin and aunt in a tight little voice. She'd been driven here by instinct, the depth of her trouble too much to bear alone.

'I don't believe it!' exclaimed Nina.

'Me neither,' said Tilly.

'I can hardly believe it myself,' admitted Alice.

'So what's been happening, love?' asked Tilly kindly.

'Oh, I've known something was wrong for ages,' she explained, all fear of her relatives knowing the truth banished by the severity of the situation. 'I've been worried sick.' She sighed, shaking her head. 'I suspected he was doing badly in his job and that was worry enough. I never dreamt it was anything so awful as this.'

'I don't suppose you did,' said Nina.

'It will be all over our neighbourhood by now,' said Alice. 'The police came to the house last night to tell me they'd taken him in. I had to leave the boys with a neighbour while I went to the police station so everyone will be talking about it.' Her face was bloodless. 'They've got him locked up in a cell just like you see in the films, like a real criminal.'

'What exactly has he done?' asked Tilly, sad that her gut feeling about Dudley had been proved to be correct.

'He's been stealing money from his firm for years,' she told them gravely, 'since before I knew him even. He's taken thousands and thousands of pounds from them over a very long period. They're going to take everything we own to get their money back. The house . . . the car . . . everything.'

'Can they prove it?'

'Oh, yes. Anyway, he's admitted everything.'

'Bloody hell!' said Tilly, whose look of astonishment was emphasised by a shock of back-combed hair standing out in mid-style like starched mohair. She'd been doing her hair when Alice had arrived and thrown them into chaos with her news. 'Who would have thought it of someone like Dudley?'

Alice told them about the events of the last couple of months and how much he had changed. 'That's why I've been so uptight,' she said.

'You should have talked to us about it,' said Tilly. 'At least you wouldn't have felt so alone.'

'I just couldn't bring myself to . . . you know.'

'It's understandable,' said Tilly.

'Do you know what started him on this road?' asked Nina.

'Yes. He talked to me about it when I went to see him,' Alice said. 'Apparently when he went back to the firm after being invalided out of the army and they put him into a position of trust because there was no one else to do the job, they didn't pay him what he considered to be a decent wage for such responsibility. So he decided to help himself.'

'I bet he doesn't half regret it now,' said Tilly.

'No, that's the peculiar thing. He doesn't seem to feel any compunction about it at all,' she said. 'Seems to think the money he took was no more than his right.'

'Get away.'

'I think he's bitter about losing his health,' said Alice. 'Apparently he was quite robust before the war.'

'How did he get found out after all this time?' asked Nina.

'Ironically, after all those years of outwitting his employers and the auditors, he was seen by another member of staff – one of his subordinates, a new junior

330

clerk fresh from grammar school. A go-getter with an eye to promotion, according to Dudley.'

'So what happened?'

'The new clerk left his umbrella in the office one evening and when he went back for it saw Dudley putting money from the takings into his pocket.'

'Did he accuse Dudley there and then?' asked Nina.

'Oh, no. He pretended not to notice anything,' explained Alice. 'But he went to the management with the story. They've been keeping Dudley under surveillance, waiting to get proof. They had to catch him in the act because there was nothing on paper to incriminate him.'

'So Dudley thought he'd got away with it for a while then?' said Tilly.

'He wasn't sure. He had an idea the clerk was on to him . . . something about his attitude made him suspicious,' she explained. 'That's why he's been in such a shocking mood. He thought they might be watching him and was worried sick.'

'So he stopped stealing. Hence the supposed drop in salary?' said Nina.

'That's right. He was bringing home his normal salary without his ill-gotten gains.'

'He must have started thieving again or they wouldn't have caught him,' remarked Tilly.

'Yes. When nothing happened he thought he was safe,' she told them. 'He thought he must have been imagining things . . . which was exactly what his employers wanted him to think. They had the clerk and another man watching him through a skylight in the roof. Dudley's office is on the top floor. As soon as they saw him taking money and putting it into his pocket, they confronted him with it. The police were called and he was arrested there and then.'

'Blimey,' said Tilly.

'There wasn't much point in him denying it since his pockets were stuffed.'

'It's a wonder he wasn't rumbled long ago,' said Tilly.

'His position of trust was his protection,' said Alice. 'No one thought it unusual for him to stay on in the evening after everyone else had gone . . . to make sure the books balanced before the takings were put into the safe. All the money was checked against the till receipts from the different departments by him. He used to enter the day's takings in a ledger. He'd take what he needed and enter a lesser amount in the book. The receipts were destroyed after he'd checked them and no one ever checked the checker because he was in a trusted position.'

'Didn't you ever wonder how he could afford to give you such a comfortable life on the salary of an unchartered accountant in a store?' asked Tilly.

'Not really. I thought he earned well because he'd been there so long.'

'Nina and I have often wondered how you could afford to live like toffs,' admitted Tilly.

'I feel stupid now, for not realising what was going on and not doing anything to stop it,' said Alice. 'He'll go to prison for a very long time and it will kill him, he isn't a strong man.' She put her hands to her head. 'And, oh dear, the shame.'

'Bugger the shame!' retorted Tilly. 'There are far more important things for you to worry about now. Those boys of yours, for instance.'

Alice looked at Tilly helplessly. 'Oh, what am I going to do, Aunt Tilly?' she said, tears rolling from her eyes in an uncharacteristic loss of control. 'Please tell me, what I am to do?'

'For a start you can come here,' said Tilly, opening her arms to the younger woman who joined her on the sofa with tears streaming down her cheeks. Tilly held her close. 'Then, when you've calmed down a bit, the three of us'll work out what can be done. Together.'

Moistening her dry mouth with strong tea, Alice said, 'God knows what's going to happen to Malcolm and Teddy . . . there'll be no money to pay their school fees.'

'That's the least of your problems,' said Tilly. 'They can go to the ordinary local school like most of the other kids round here.'

'Oh, but what a terrible come down,' wailed Alice.

'You're gonna have to forget your upper crust life now, Alice,' advised Tilly with brutal candour. 'It's time to come down to earth.'

'I know that,' she said miserably, brushing her brow with the back of her hand. 'But there's so much to take in all at once. I mean, not only are the boys to be deprived of their school but their home too. We've nowhere to live. Without Dudley I'll have no income. We'll be out on the streets.'

'Stop being so melodramatic, for Gawd's sake,'

reproached Tilly. She looked across at Nina who nodded in agreement at the question in her mother's eyes. 'You know perfectly well that Nina and I would never let that happen to you. There'll be a home for you and the boys here with us at The Willow for as long as you need it.'

Alice had never thought she would be so pleased to hear those words. For the second time in her life these people had opened their hearts to her without a moment's hesitation. She was stripped to the bone of all pretensions, and the love that had been growing for them all these years rose to the surface in a tide of gratitude.

'Oh, thank you both . . . thank you,' she said with genuine feeling.

The Hardings moved into The Willow a couple of days later. The directors of Dudley's firm said there was no need for such haste but Alice no longer felt comfortable living in a house that had been paid for with stolen money, and among people to whom she was now an outsider. Bail was refused for Dudley because of the seriousness of his crime and Alice had to face up to the possibility of living without him for a very long time into the future.

Nina and Tilly let her potter about in the flat, helping with the chores and adapting to her new life. As a temporary measure they put the boys in Joey's room until the attic room could be made into sleeping quarters for them, whilst Alice shared a bedroom with Nina. Nina wasn't thrilled to lose her privacy but felt duty bound to do so with a good grace. And, to be fair, Alice did seem very grateful.

Malcolm and Teddy seemed to accept their changed circumstances, including their new school, with a quiet pluckiness. Almost too quiet, Nina thought. They were very close – more like twins than just brothers – so she guessed they found comfort in each other.

Life was even more hectic for Nina now because, in addition to the extra work involved in getting the new restaurant up and running, the flat seemed to be in a permanent state of chaos while Alice and Co. settled in. When two weeks had passed, Nina decided it was time a few practical matters were faced.

'Now that you've had time to settle in, Alice, I think the three of us should have a chat as regards your living here in the long term,' she announced to her mother and cousin one morning after the boys had gone to school.

'I'm pulling my weight with the chores,' said Alice defensively. 'And I've asked the boys to keep their room tidy and not to make too much noise. We don't want to be a nuisance.'

'And you're not being. Mum and I have told you that you're welcome here,' said Nina assertively. 'But helping in the house just isn't enough.'

'Oh dear,' said Alice, who had never really got used to her cousin's tendency to speak her mind.

'Don't look so worried,' said Nina in a moderate tone. 'I've an idea for the future that I think will suit us all.'

'Oh . . . and what is it?' asked Alice warily.

'Well, although you're welcome to stay on here rent

free for as long as you like, obviously you're gonna have to start paying for your keep eventually.'

'Yes, of course,' she said, breathless with nerves, 'but I don't know what with . . . unless I try for National Assistance.' She gave a half sob. 'Oh God, the shame of it.'

'You can spare yourself the shame if you get a job,' suggested her cousin.

Alice looked grey with worry and Nina felt bad about being so blunt. But these matters had to be resolved in the interests of domestic harmony as well as for Alice's own self-esteem. 'There's no need to look so stricken,' she said lightly. 'I suggested you get a job, not throw yourself under a train.'

The latter seemed almost preferable to Alice who had only bad memories of her job at the bank, mostly because she'd never felt equal to her colleagues. Now, having been away from the workplace for so long, she was terrified at the prospect of returning.

'Don't worry,' she said with a touch of her old hauteur, 'I've no intention of sponging on you.'

'No one is suggesting you would, love,' said Tilly with her usual concern for her niece's feelings.

'I should hope not,' she said testily.

'If you could come down off your high horse for a minute,' said Nina, 'I've a suggestion to make.'

'Oh?'

'Why not work with us here at The Willow?'

'Now that really *is* a good idea!' enthused Tilly.

'No, I couldn't do that,' said Alice looking extremely doubtful. 'Bar work isn't my thing.'

'I know you didn't used to like it but your circumstances are different now,' Nina pointed out. 'Compromise might be no bad thing.'

'No, I really don't think so.'

'That's a pity because we could really do with an extra pair of hands while we're getting the restaurant ready to open,' said Nina. 'We're already taking bookings so it's imperative that we open on time. And once it's open . . . well . . . I'm taking on extra staff anyway so why don't we keep it in the family as far as we possibly can?'

'Well . . .'

'Another point in its favour,' persisted Nina, 'is living on the premises. You'd be on hand for the boys after school.'

'No, Nina, it just isn't for me,' insisted Alice.

'Oh, well, it was just an idea,' said Nina, oddly disappointed by her cousin's negative reaction. 'I know you're not cut out for our sort of work. I thought you might adapt now . . . but perhaps you'll be happier going for something more suited to your personality. Fortunately, there are plenty of jobs around at the moment.'

Alice lapsed into a worried silence. 'Were you offering me a proper job with a wage?' she asked.

'Of course,' said Nina.

'Surely you don't think we expect our staff to work for nothing?' said Tilly lightly.

'On the staff, eh?' Alice's thoughts were beginning to slot into place. Working at home with her aunt and cousin had to be better than going out into an unfriendly world to find a job among strangers. The thought of facing the public on the subordinate side of a bar counter scared her, but not half as much as trying her luck in some office, having to lie about her husband's whereabouts the whole time. 'I think I might rather like working here after all.'

Uneasy about her sudden change of heart, Nina said, 'I hope you don't see it as a soft option, Alice, because it won't be. We'll want you to give everything you've got to the job. Just because we're all family doesn't mean we won't expect you to work for your money. On the contrary, we'll probably expect more commitment from you than if you were just an ordinary member of staff.'

'I understand that.'

'Working in a family business entails team spirit, mucking in wherever you're most needed, especially in times of crisis,' she explained. 'Even rotten jobs like cleaning the toilets fall to us if our cleaner goes sick.'

'I still think I'd like to give it a try,' said Alice.

'Just as long as you realise what's involved. And another thing . . . you're going to have to learn to get along with people,' Nina went on. 'Making people feel happy and welcome in our pub is what our business is all about. Airs and graces are out.'

Alice looked suitably sheepish. 'I can hardly have those now, can I?'

'They might be a bit incongruous,' smiled Nina.

'At the same time,' put in Tilly, 'you mustn't be a doormat to the customers, or anyone else for that matter.'

'That's perfectly true,' agreed Nina.

'In fact, confidence in yourself is going to be vital to you over the next few months,' continued Tilly. 'It's no good your walking about with your head down just because your old man is banged up. Dudley committed the crime, not you, and it's important you remember that for your own sake and your lads.'

'Mum's right,' said Nina.

Alice was deep in thought. No one was more surprised than her to feel a tingle of excitement in the challenge that lay ahead. To her amazement she found herself feeling genuine interest in her new job. 'I understand everything you say about mucking in and working as a team, and I'm prepared for that,' she said. 'But I've had another idea too. There's something I know I could do as well.'

'Well, let's hear about it then?'

'You said something once about having a pianist playing background music in the restaurant,' she said, her eyes unusually bright.

'Yes, that's right,' said Nina.

'Well, I can't claim to be a great musician but I'm a competent pianist and a good sight reader,' she said. 'Perhaps I might be suitable?'

Nina and Tilly exchanged grins.

'Consider yourself hired,' said Tilly.

'I'll second that,' said Nina.

'Right. Now that everything's sorted, perhaps we can get some work done?' suggested Nina.

'Well, I can't be such an active member of the team as I'd like to be,' said Tilly. 'But I reckon we'll be a threesome to be reckoned with.'

'The Willow Girls,' said Alice, experiencing a moment of guilt for feeling so positive about the future when her husband was locked up in a prison cell.

Chapter Twenty-one

Coming downstairs from his bedroom to the living room, where the family were gathered for breakfast, Joey stopped to answer the telephone in the hall.

'That was Raymond's wife on the phone,' he announced, sitting down at the table next to his mother. 'Apparently our chef's gone down with the dreaded stomach bug and won't be coming to work today.'

'Oh, no!' cried Nina dramatically, pushing her food away and rising to her feet in agitation. They had just had a similar message from Raymond's second-in-command which meant they now had a kitchen staff of nil, the rest having fallen victim to the bug at various intervals during the last few days. 'Having the chef go sick is a crisis. Having the entire kitchen staff away at the same time is a ruddy disaster!'

'Specially today,' said Tilly.

'Yes, today of all days,' echoed Nina.

Today the restaurant was booked for a private party – the annual Christmas luncheon for the executives of a local engineering firm.

'Whatever are we going to do?' asked Alice.

'We'll have to get some temporary kitchen staff,' said

Nina, pacing up and down. 'I'll get on to the agency right away.'

She was out of luck. A combination of seasonal functions and sickness had created such a demand for temps, they didn't have anyone available.

'The menu is traditional Christmas fare . . . turkey with all the trimmings . . . and Raymond has already made the Christmas puddings,' said Nina, looking at her mother and cousin meaningfully.

'You mean . . .' began Tilly.

'Yes. There's only one thing for it, we'll have to do the cooking ourselves.'

'Cor, what a laugh,' said Joey, who was home for the Christmas holidays and rather fancied the idea of a nice healthy crisis to liven things up. 'I'll help.'

'That's the spirit,' said Nina. 'We'll put you on potato peeling to start with.' She turned to his cousins. 'Malcolm, can you do the sprouts, please? And Teddy, can we leave the carrots and parsnips to you?'

'Sorry, we can't help,' said thirteen-year-old Malcolm. 'We won't be here this morning.'

'Where are you going?' their mother wanted to know.

'We're meeting some pals from school in the Broadway.'

'Oh no you're not!' declared Alice emphatically. 'You know very well I don't allow you to hang about the streets.'

'But, Mum,' protested Teddy who was twelve. 'We're only going to have a look round the shops.'

'Yeah, we wanna look at the records,' put in Malcolm rudely. 'We're entitled to have some fun in our holidays

342

so we're going and that's that.'

'Just do as you're told, you little twerps,' said Joey, who by virtue of his seniority felt entitled to adopt an imperious attitude towards his cousins.

'Shut up, you. You stuck-up boarding school prig!' said Malcolm.

'Cor! Hark who's talking,' retorted Joey. 'You two were the biggest snobs in London when you were at Grove House.'

'Boys, boys,' shouted Nina. 'We've enough problems without you quarrelling among yourselves.'

The meek young boys who had moved into The Willow less than two months ago hadn't stayed that way for long. The deportment they had had hammered into them throughout their formative years seemed to have disappeared altogether lately. In fact, they had become positively unruly. Nina put it down to an overly sheltered existence before the dramatic upheaval. Being plunged into a more liberated environment for the first time, and suddenly finding themselves with a mother who didn't have quite so much time to smother and protect them, had gone to their heads.

Poor Alice didn't seem able to control them at all. 'You are staying home this morning and helping us,' she ordered.

'We're not,' retorted Malcolm.

'Yes, you are,' she tried again, looking red-faced and fraught. 'That's my last word on the subject.'

'You can't stop us . . .' began Malcolm.

'You two lads will do as your mother tells you while you're living under my roof,' intervened their Great-

Aunt Tilly decisively. 'She says you're staying home so that's what you'll do. Now, let's have no more of your lip.'

They both turned pink and stared into their laps.

'Right. As soon as you've all finished your breakfast, we'll get cracking,' said Nina. 'Everyone downstairs to the kitchen . . . except you, Mum, of course.'

'I'm not missing out on this,' said Tilly cheerfully. 'I might not be able to do as much as you others but I'll make myself useful somehow.'

For the next few hours the restaurant kitchen hummed with activity. Glorious aromas began to emerge: turkeys roasting, potatoes and parsnips baking, vegetables cooking steamily and the savoury scent of gravy being carefully stirred by Tilly.

'Stop it, young Teddy,' she rebuked as he picked a roast potato out of the dish and popped it into his mouth.

Having been so firmly put in their place by her, Malcolm and Teddy had decided to make the best of things and were joining in the general camaraderie as the preparations progressed on schedule.

Fortunately, they had lost none of the bar staff to the bug, so Nina was able to leave the pub side of things to them after opening time, and remain in the kitchen herself.

'We're not quite out of trouble yet, though,' she said, as the sizzling turkeys came out of the ovens.

'Why's that?' asked Alice who had surprised everyone by really knuckling down to her new job these last two months. She particularly enjoyed her musical work but was less confident behind the bar. Pulling a decent pint was no longer a problem but she found it hard to respond to the sharp badinage of the punters in the same way as her cousin and aunt. Quick-fire wit was as natural as breathing to them.

Oddly enough, Alice felt less conspicuous at the piano than she did behind the bar, probably because the instrument was discreetly positioned in the corner of the restaurant partly hidden by a small forest of pot plants. Here she did battle with light classics and popular songs played pianissimo, to avoid being too intrusive. Sometimes she wondered if any of her repertoire was heard against the clatter of crockery and conversation.

But her cousin was answering her question. 'Because both Mum and I are hopeless at carving and we need the turkeys to be thinly sliced to make the meat go round. Are you any good with a carving knife, Alice?'

'I'm afraid not,' she confessed. 'Dudley always used to do it in our house.'

'Carving is usually left to the men,' said Nina. 'Which is why they're often so good at it.'

'That's no problem,' said Tilly, trudging slowly across the room to the door. 'Because men are one thing we're not short of in this establishment.'

The Paxton brothers were in the area on business and had popped into The Willow for a quick one. And they were at the bar when Tilly hobbled in.

'Ah, just the men I want to see. I've got a little job for you two boys,' she said, and led them into the kitchens.

By the time the waiting staff had reported for duty

and got busy laying the tables, the turkey meat was neatly sliced and ready to go on the plates.

'Thanks, boys,' said Tilly.

'Hear, hear,' said Nina. 'You've helped us over our first major crisis.'

'Glad to help,' said Baz, his eyes smiling into Nina's across the steamy kitchen.

'Come and have a drink with me,' said Tilly. 'The girls can do without me for a while.'

'The restaurant seems to have got off to a good start,' said Baz, as he and George sat at a table in the corner with Tilly. 'You certainly don't seem to have any shortage of takers.'

'It's the staff we're short of,' she said. 'We're gonna be run off our feet right up until Christmas Day.'

'You'll be ready for a day off then, I bet?' remarked George, who was much more his old self these days.

'Not half!'

'There'll be quite a crowd of you for Christmas dinner in the flat this year, won't there, now that Alice and the boys have moved in,' remarked Baz who was kept up to date with events at The Willow by Joey and Tilly.

'That's right,' she said. 'Still, you know me, Baz. I like plenty of people around me, especially at Christmas.'

'That's a fact.'

'What are you two single blokes doing on Christmas Day?' she asked chattily.

'We haven't really thought about it,' said Baz. 'We'll probably go out somewhere for Christmas Dinner . . . to one of the hotels up West.'

'Why not come to us?' she said impulsively. 'It'll be a bit noisy with three healthy boys about, but you'll be very welcome.'

'We wouldn't want to impose,' said Baz, doubtful as to how Nina might feel about sharing her Christmas Day with him.

'Nonsense . . . the more the merrier,' she assured them. 'It'll be my thank you to you both for sorting out our little problem at the Town Hall earlier in the year.'

Baz looked at George. 'What do you say, mate?'

'Sounds like a good idea to me.'

As Tilly had predicted, Christmas Day at The Willow was not a sedate affair. The Paxton brothers arrived at midday in their best suits, laden with bottles and chocolates and gifts.

'I know it's a bit like taking coals to Newcastle, Til,' Baz said as he put the bottles down on the kitchen table, 'but Happy Christmas, love.'

'Thanks dears . . . and Happy Christmas to you,' said Tilly, hugging them both.

Had Nina been given any choice in the matter, she would probably have objected to her mother inviting them because of the emotions Baz still aroused in her. But since it was a fait accompli she entered into the spirit of the occasion wholeheartedly.

The guests were entertained in the sitting room by Joey and his cousins while the women prodded, stirred and tasted till at last the food was taken to the table in the living room where a lighted Christmas tree stood in the window.

Crackers were pulled with a great deal of hilarity while Baz carved the turkey. Everyone was talking at once: reading out cracker mottoes, commenting on the deliciousness of the meal, until cries of delight were eventually replaced by groans of overindulgence. At that point they all staggered into the sitting room to watch the Queen's Christmas message on the television.

Even George, who was much less outgoing than his brother, had no trouble feeling at home in such cordial company. 'Okay, fellas, and that includes you boys,' he said as Billy Smart's circus burst upon the television screen in a fanfare of noise and colour. 'The girls cooked the meal so it's only fair that we should do the washing up. Shirt sleeves up and out to the kitchen, pronto.'

Baz agreed with him but there were predictable groans of objection from the youngsters who claimed they were too full to move. Joey was eager to go to his room and try out his new record player.

'No arguments,' said George with a broad grin. 'You girls relax with the sweets and nuts while we clear up.'

He received no argument about that. Nina and Alice settled in the armchairs while Tilly went to her bedroom for a nap. A bit later on, over tea and Christmas cake, the tree presents were opened. Cuff-links and cigars for the guests, records for the boys, toiletries for the ladies, all of whom had received a special gift from the visitors. Perfume by Chanel for Nina, a long playing record of classical music for Alice and a leather handbag for Tilly. Thanks were exchanged and things quietened down while everyone had a good look at their presents.

'I think I could do with some fresh air to liven me up,'

remarked Nina. 'Anyone fancy coming for a walk? It's already dark but a spot of exercise will give us all an appetite for tea.'

'We've just had tea,' said George, patting his stomach.

'That was just tea and cake,' said Tilly. 'You'll get the full works later on.'

'In that case I'd better go with Nina or I'll not be in a fit state to manage another thing,' said George.

'Come on, you lazy lot,' laughed Nina. 'Stir yourselves and come with us.'

There was a lot of yawning and humming and hawing. But eventually the boys agreed to go, Baz and Alice went to get their coats, and Tilly said she'd stay and watch the telly as long winter walks were a thing of the past for her.

The waterfront was cold and bleak, the black waters splintered with gold from the street lights. The stars were diamond bright in the bluish-black sky above the amber haze of a million town lights just above the rooftops. The silence was eerie. Their footsteps echoed in the stillness as they walked along The Mall towards Hammersmith Bridge.

There wasn't another soul about . . . no rumble of trains or throb of traffic on the road. Everyone was inside during this quiet period between afternoon tea and nocturnal partying. A lighted Christmas tree in the window of an imposing Regency house shone through the winter limes; undrawn curtains in a row of ancient cottages revealed paperchains roped across the ceiling; holly wreaths decked front doors; tree lights glowed in porches.

'The atmosphere outside on a Christmas Day has a feel all of its own, doesn't it?' Nina remarked to Baz as they walked side by side on the bridge behind Alice and George who had fallen into step together behind the boys.

'Sort of spooky, you mean?'

'Mm,' said Nina. 'Almost as though the earth has stopped turning for a day.'

'It has for some of your regulars. The Willow is closed and that amounts to the same thing to them!' he laughed.

'You fool. Seriously though, it feels almost as though some ethereal force is causing the stillness . . .'

'When in actual fact it's just that everyone is at home at this time on a Christmas Day and everything is closed down for the holiday.'

'How very down to earth.'

'You used to accuse me of being a dreamer, remember?'

'Yes, I remember.'

Pausing, they leaned on the guardrail and looked across the dark river flanked with lights at either side – little yellow squares in serried urban ranks. In the distance the glow of The Willow Christmas tree could be seen. She pulled her coat collar around her ears.

'George seems to have come to terms with his wife's death now,' she remarked.

'He's much better than he was . . . especially since I persuaded him to move out of the house and into a flat near me,' Baz explained. 'It was depressing for him, rattling about in the house on his own.'

'Yes, it must have been.'

'I don't think he'll ever get over losing her, though,' said Baz. 'They were such soulmates, you see. Even when they were kids. She'd always been a part of his life and that's what made it such a wrench for him.'

'It's a damned shame.'

'Still, at least I don't have to go and drag him out of some pub every night now and that has to be progress.'

'He seems to be enjoying himself today, anyway.'

'Yeah. I haven't seen him in such good form for ages.'

'Christmas is a bad time for the lonely.'

'Not 'alf.'

'Alice is the one who's amazed me,' Nina told him. 'Not that Dudley has died or anything like that but she's had a terrible shock and has had to learn to manage without him. Frankly I thought she'd be hell to live with and dead miserable over Christmas. But – and I know it's not a very nice thing to say, Baz – she seems more cheerful than she ever was when Dudley was around. She's certainly easier to get along with now.'

'Ah, yes, the notorious Dudley,' he said as they walked on, his hands sunk deep into the pockets of his overcoat. 'That was a real turn up for the books, wasn't it? I couldn't believe it when Tilly told me what had happened.'

'Mum and I never really took to him, you know,' she confessed. 'We'd wondered vaguely over the years how he had so much money but we never gave it any serious thought . . . we certainly never dreamt he was a crook.'

'That it should happen to Alice of all people!'

'Yes, she's really had adjustments to make.'

'She seems to be coping.'

'Yes. Alice is all right,' said Nina with sincerity. 'Her trouble has brought us closer together. After all these years, my cousin and I are beginning to get along.'

'Her sons seem a bit . . . er . . . um . . . exuberant.'

'Wild is the word I think you were looking for,' she laughed.

'Well, I didn't want to be rude. They are your relatives, after all.'

'It's amazing how they've changed,' she said. 'Before all this blew up with their father, there was never so much as a peep out of them.'

'They've had a lot to contend with,' he said. 'They've probably had to learn to defend themselves against the other boys at school. Word's bound to have got round about their dad being in the nick, and you know how cruel kids can be. They'll settle down in time.'

'I hope so, but Alice certainly has her hands full with them at the moment,' said Nina. 'They were kept on such a tight rein before, you see. Never allowed to go anywhere without their parents except school, and even then Alice took them in the car. She monitored their every movement. She had time then because she wasn't working. Now it's all very different and they're making the most of it.'

'It's just youthful high spirits, I expect.'

'Frankly I think it's high time they were allowed out of the house without their mother, don't you?'

'Not 'alf. When I was their age I was doing a paper round and helping in the market on Saturdays.'

'Alice wrapped them in cotton wool. It's hardly surprising a bit more freedom has turned their heads.'

Ahead of them the three boys could be seen in the glow from the street lights. They had dropped back behind Alice and George. Joey was in the centre, the tallest of the three.

'Joey is like an elder brother to them, isn't he?'

'He tries to be,' she said. 'But they won't always wear it.'

'Our son's growing up fast . . . he'll be as tall as me soon.'

'Don't remind me,' she said. 'Every time he comes home he seems to have shot up another foot. He's getting fashion conscious too. He wants all the modern gear to wear when he's not in school uniform.'

'I noticed his tight jeans.'

'Yes. A fraction baggier is really square and he refuses to wear them,' she grinned.

''Struth!'

'Kids of today aren't like we were.'

'I know, it's a different world,' Baz chuckled. 'It doesn't seem five minutes since he was keeping us awake at night.'

'He's even got a bit of fluff on his chin now too.' She sniffed with affected sadness. 'My little boy . . . oh dear!'

They both giggled and Nina felt very close to Baz at that moment. 'He was thrilled with the record player you bought him for Christmas,' she said.

'Was he really?'

'Oh, yes. Couldn't you tell by his reaction?'

'I'm never sure where I stand with Joey,' he admitted ruefully. 'He still blows hot and cold with me.'

'Bear with it. One day the two of you will sort yourselves out.'

'Maybe . . . Anyway, today has been lovely,' he said. 'I'm really enjoying myself.'

'Me too,' she said, turning to him and looking into his face, the pale light from the street lamp gleaming on his strong features.

'I'm glad we've learned to be in the same company as friends at last. It makes it so much easier for everyone else.'

'We'll never be just friends,' he said, his warm breath brushing her face. 'And you know it.'

'Maybe I do,' she admitted with a familiar ache in her heart. 'But at least now we can go through the motions.'

'I love you, Nina.'

'Don't start all that again, Baz,' she said quickly. 'Or you'll create an atmosphere and ruin the day for the others.' She linked her arm through his companionably as the headlights of a solitary car came into view. 'Come on, let's make our way back now before we freeze to death.'

'I sometimes wish Marge and I had had a family, you know,' remarked George to Alice as they followed Nina and Baz back to The Willow. 'I think it might have been a comfort to me now.'

'Did children just not come along or did your wife not want any?' asked Alice surprising herself with the impudence of her question.

'They just didn't happen but we weren't really

bothered . . . we always felt complete in ourselves,' he told her. 'It's only now that I'm on my own I've got to thinking about it. I expect you find comfort in your lads, don't you?'

'I'm not so sure about them being a comfort to me at the moment,' she confessed ruefully. 'They're being absolute horrors. But I wouldn't be without them.'

'They're probably just reacting to what's happened,' he said.

'Yes, I know. Allowances have to be made. Their lives have been turned upside down,' she agreed. 'I'm hoping they'll revert back to the reserved, well-behaved children they were before Dudley's arrest . . . eventually.'

'It can't have been easy for you either,' said George. 'It must have been a terrible shock . . .'

'To find out my husband is a villain?' she finished for him. 'I'll say it was! I still keep thinking I'll wake up to find it's all just a bad dream.'

'When does his case come up?'

'February.'

'Perhaps they'll go easy on him,' he said, in an effort to comfort her.

'The solicitor says we must prepare ourselves for a four-year sentence at least,' she explained gravely. 'It wasn't just one petty crime, you see. He'd been at it for years.'

'Poor you.'

'Poor Dudley,' she said sadly. 'I know he must be punished for what he's done but it will be very hard for him. He isn't a strong man . . . he's still got shrapnel in him from the war.'

'Really? How's that?'

'It would have been more dangerous for the doctors to remove it than leave it where it is apparently,' she explained. 'It's quite close to the lung.'

'They might take that into consideration when sentencing him.'

'I hope so,' she said. 'Of course, you could say that I'm as guilty as he is because I've been living comfortably off the fruits of his dishonesty.'

'That's ridiculous. You wouldn't have wanted that lifestyle if you'd known how it was being paid for, now would you?' said George.

'Good God, no!' she exclaimed emphatically. 'My middle name is respectability. That was what attracted me to Dudley . . . the fact that he was so upright and respectable. Or so I thought.'

'I see.'

'I'll be honest with you, though, George. I wanted a comfortable life and I was determined to get it somehow. But not that way. Oh no. Had I known what Dudley was up to when I met him, I'd never have got involved with him.'

'If material things are so important to you, it must be hard to adjust to having less?'

'It isn't as bad as I thought it would be, actually.'

'You seem to be managing, anyway,' he remarked.

'No one is more surprised about that than me,' she admitted. 'I suppose it's just a question of having to put up with the way things are. Nina and Aunt Tilly have been a great help though. I don't know what I'd have done without their support.'

'Mm . . . I know the feeling,' said George. 'Baz has been very supportive to me since Marge died. It's taken me a long time to come to terms with it and I still haven't quite . . . not yet.'

'It's a lot worse for you,' she said with genuine compassion. 'I mean, at least Dudley is still alive.'

'Yes.'

'I feel as though my life with him is over though.'

'Really?'

'Yes. Dudley is part of a way of life that's gone,' she explained, beginning to see it clearly for the first time herself. 'It will be hard to pick up with him again when he does come home because I realise now that I never knew him. The man I thought I knew never existed. He was a fake.'

It was odd to be speaking to a relative stranger with such candour. Maybe it was because she only had a casual acquaintance with him that she was able to unburden herself in this way. With George there was no need to pretend – he knew she was the wife of a criminal, with barely a penny to her name. It was wonderfully relaxing. She felt as though she could talk to him about anything.

'I can understand your feeling like that,' he said. 'But I'm sure it'll work out . . . it's still early days.'

'Yes. There'll be plenty of time to worry about that later on,' she said. 'I've enough to do just surviving for the moment as the mother of two energetic young boys.'

'I can imagine.'

They approached The Willow. The boys had overtaken them and were following Nina and Baz inside.

'I've really enjoyed our chat, George,' said Alice at the door.

'So have I,' he said with a slow, thoughtful smile.

After a traditional Christmas tea of cold turkey and pickles, sausage rolls, mince pies, chocolate yule log and tinned fruit and cream, the youngsters departed to Joey's room to play records while the adults sat around talking and half watching the Max Bygraves television show. The visitors left about midnight, claiming to have had a wonderful day.

'This is going to sound really awful . . . with my husband spending Christmas in prison,' said Alice as she slipped into the bed next to her cousin's, 'but I've really enjoyed myself today . . . isn't that terrible of me?'

'Don't be so daft,' admonished Nina. 'You're entitled to some pleasure. You need it to take your mind off the trouble than man has left you with.'

'You and Aunt Tilly have never liked Dudley, have you?' said Alice.

'He was always a bit too smug for our taste,' Nina confided. 'Still, so were you for that matter. If Dudley's arrest has done nothing else, at least it's made you into a reasonable human being!'

'You don't think I should feel guilty for enjoying myself today then?'

'Of course not,' said Nina, yawning. 'You've enough on your plate. Dudley has done wrong. Don't make him into a hero because he's in prison and you're not. Life is going to be hard enough for you bringing those lads of yours up without a father through the teenage years.

Save all your strength for that.'

'I suppose you're right.'

Nina yawned again. 'Well, it's been a smashing day but we'd better get some sleep. Boxing Day is always busy at The Willow.'

'Is it?'

'Phew, not half. We'll be packed to the doors at lunchtime. People will be glad of a break from the house by then.' She turned on to her side. 'Goodnight, Alice. Happy Christmas.'

'Goodnight, Nina.'

Tilly was lying awake mulling over the events of the day and coming to the conclusion that it had been a very happy Christmas Day for them all. Her decision to invite the Paxton brothers had proved to be the right one for all her fears about Nina and Baz creating a tense atmosphere. They hadn't put a foot wrong – had even seemed to enjoy each other's company.

Those two were still a pair, separated or not. You could see it in their eyes, feel the electricity sparking between them. It was a pity they didn't give their marriage another chance because they were so right for each other.

Her thoughts became more introspective. Although she had enjoyed the day with her family, she was conscious of an aching loneliness. Turned fifty or not, there was still a need within her that could not be satisfied by family or friends, as much as she loved them.

Chapter Twenty-two

Immersed in the task of running The Willow in its extended form, the time passed quickly for Nina in the New Year.

While the world marvelled at the achievement of Lieutenant-Colonel John H Glenn, who became the first American to orbit the earth in his Mercury capsule, Alice learned that her husband was to spend four years in prison.

Nina wasn't surprised to see her cousin accept the news with such stoicism. Even though Dudley's arrest had removed many of her inhibitions, she was still not given to excessive shows of emotion. With dutiful regularity she visited him in Wormwood Scrubs and seemed to concentrate all her energies on her work at the pub and trying, unsuccessfully, to bring her wayward sons to order.

When Dudley had served only six months of his sentence, he was taken ill with a collapsed lung and died in the prison hospital. It was a shock to them all and Nina's heart went out to Alice. She was glad that her cousin was more able to share her troubles than she used to be.

'It's sad that a war hero like Dudley should have ended his life under such a cloud,' she confided to Nina.

'Yes. He wasn't one of my favourite people but I'm so sorry it's ended this way,' said Nina. 'It must be very hard for you, losing him so prematurely.'

'I'm sorry for him, of course, but I think I lost Dudley the day he was arrested,' she confessed. 'In fact, looking back on it, I'm not sure I ever had him . . . not really. We were two people living our lives side by side but not together.'

Nina wasn't at all surprised to hear this.

Nina and Baz received a shock that summer after Joey's O levels when he told them that he wanted to leave school and train to be a chef. He was hoping to get a place at one of the West End hotels as a trainee.

'Well, it certainly isn't what I had in mind for him,' Nina confessed to Baz as they discussed it at a corner table in the lounge bar.

'Nor me. I was hoping he'd go on to university.'

'Me too,' she said, 'but we've always known he wasn't academic. We shouldn't be surprised by his decision because he's become very interested in cooking since we opened the restaurant.'

'He can build quite a good career as a chef, I suppose?'

'It isn't the sort of thing you go into just because of its career possibilities, though, is it?' she answered. 'It's a creative thing . . . something you want to do because you have a feel for it.'

'He could go far though,' said Baz, 'if he works his way up in a big hotel.'

'Yes. Anyway, as he's made up his mind, there isn't much we can do about it, is there?' she pointed out.

'Not really, except give him our blessing.'

So Joey left school and started work in the kitchens of a big London hotel. The hours were long and unsocial but as The Willow was within easy reach of the West End, he was able to live at home, albeit he wasn't there very often. Much of the spare time that he did have was spent helping out in the restaurant kitchen. He had become a real culinary enthusiast and was keen to gain additional experience.

The Willow flat often resembled a busy railway station with three teenagers coming and going. The whole place throbbed with the new Mersey sound that was the latest teenage craze. The loud, compelling beat of Gerry and the Pacemakers and The Beatles blared out from the record-player Joey shared with his cousins, whenever any one of them were at home.

Although Nina and Alice had become good friends, there was one subject on which they were fiercely opposed. Nina thought Alice was far too soft with Malcolm and Teddy who became more rebellious with every day that passed. Disobeying their mother on practically every issue, they would slam out of the house when she'd told them to stay at home, her attempts at reprimands producing only a stream of the most foul invective from them. Their manners were simply appalling, and all Alice ever seemed to do was to make excuses for them.

Nina respected her maternal instinct to defend her

young; she herself was ferocious in Joey's defence. But the Harding boys were out of hand and if something wasn't done they would get worse. Since the entire household was affected by their atrocious behaviour, she felt she had a right to speak her mind to Alice.

'If you don't put your foot down with them now, you're going to have a couple of real villains on your hands later on,' she told her one night in the autumn after Malcolm had been abusive to his mother after a mild rebuke.

'Don't be so melodramatic,' snapped Alice. 'It's just youthful high spirits, that's all.'

'Maybe, but if it isn't nipped in the bud now . . .'

'They've had a hard time,' protested Alice. 'With everything that's happened.'

'I know that. But they can't do just as they please indefinitely because they've had an upheaval,' said Nina. 'They need some strong discipline.'

Alice brushed her short hair vigorously in front of the dressing table mirror, her blue eyes dull with worry. 'It's just an adolescent phase . . . they all go through it . . . I don't suppose Joey's always been an angel.'

'He certainly hasn't,' admitted Nina. 'He thinks he knows better than me about practically everything – that's just the arrogance of youth. But I think Malcolm and Teddy are completely out of hand.'

'What do you suggest I do about it then?' Alice asked wearily. 'I made them join a youth club but they roamed the streets instead of going. I've tried to bring them up to be decent people. I've taught them the difference between right and wrong . . . what else can I do?'

'Stand your ground with them,' advised Nina. 'Don't back down every time they give you a hard time. For instance, they know you'll give them more pocket money even though you've already said no. They know you'll take their side against Mum and me when they're rude to us.'

'They don't mean it, it's just their age.'

'It still needs to be sorted,' persisted Nina.

'You're making a mountain out of a molehill.'

It didn't seem like a molehill to anyone a few months later when the boys stole some spirits from the bar and emerged legless from their bedroom.

Although shocked and apologetic, Alice still tried to make light of it.

'They're just experimenting,' she said. 'All youngsters do that.'

'I know one youngster who didn't,' said Tilly. 'And that was you . . . your mum and dad must be turning in their graves at all this. Experimentation or not, they mustn't be allowed to get away with it.'

Their pocket money was stopped to pay for what they had taken and they were grounded for a month. For a while things seemed to calm down and Nina heaved a sigh of relief. Until one evening in the spring of 1964 when the police came to The Willow to say that the Harding boys had been taken to the police station for causing a public nuisance.

Malcolm and Teddy stood up straight and faced the magistrates, hair combed, faces scrubbed. Nina and

Tilly sat either side of Alice in the public gallery with Baz and George.

'Well, you two have been behaving in a most antisocial way, haven't you?' said a woman magistrate sitting between two men on the bench. 'You've caused a breach of the peace by breaking a window, smashing milk bottles in the street and using foul language to a member of the public and the police. So what do you have to say for yourselves?'

The boys studied the floor in silence.

'Well?' she prompted.

'It was just a bit of a laugh, madam,' said Malcolm at last, addressing her formally as instructed beforehand.

'You call throwing a large stone through someone's window a laugh?' she said with asperity.

'That was an accident,' he explained.

'Yeah . . . we didn't mean that to happen,' put in Teddy.

'Perhaps you'll be good enough to tell the court how it came about then?' she said briskly.

'Well . . . we were playing on this bit of waste ground, you see, with some other boys.'

'Yes,' she said with thinly veiled impatience.

'We were lining milk bottles up and aiming stones at them.'

'Where did you get the bottles?' she asked.

'From front doorsteps,' said Teddy. 'There was nothing in 'em . . . they were only empty bottles.'

'They are still the property of the dairy,' rebuked the woman. 'So technically you were stealing.'

Nina gave her cousin's arm a supportive squeeze as

things seemed to go from bad to worse.

'Sorry, madam,' said Malcolm.

'So how did the stone end up through Mr Brown's window?'

'We put some bottles on his front wall.'

'And you misaimed your stone,' she finished for him.

'Well, it wasn't my stone actually . . .'

'One of your pal's then?'

'Yeah.'

'Who ran away as soon as Mr Brown came out of his house, I suppose?'

'That's right.'

'Why didn't you two run away with the others?' she asked, staring at them thoughtfully.

'Dunno.'

'We wanted to make sure the stone hadn't hit anyone inside the room,' said Teddy.

She narrowed her eyes for a moment. 'All right, I'll give you the benefit of the doubt and accept that you were concerned for the occupants of the house,' she said. 'So why, having proved that you are not completely without human decency, did you then use insulting language to Mr Brown?' She consulted her notes. 'You called him an effing old fart who ought to be put down . . . and that was one of the milder insults.'

''Cos he was doing his nut,' replied Malcolm. 'He wouldn't stop ranting . . . he went on and on . . . he just wouldn't listen to us.'

'And then you started to insult the policeman who had been called by Mr Brown's neighbour.'

'Yeah, well, the fuzz were really stroppy. They just wouldn't let us get a word in,' said Malcolm.

The magistrates conferred in low tones.

'This is a very serious matter,' the chairwoman said at last. 'You have caused damage to property and distress to Mr Brown, not to mention the worry you have given to your poor mother. In view of this we feel that . . .'

There was a sudden interruption. 'Might I have a word, please, madam?'

She frowned at the speaker. 'Is it relevant to this case?'

'Yes.'

'What is your involvement with these boys?'

'I'm their uncle by marriage,' said Baz, having received a frantic phone call from Tilly last night. 'My name is Baz Paxton.'

'Can we hear what you have to say then, please?'

'The boys are from a good family but they have had rather a traumatic experience.'

'Yes, yes. We are fully aware of their background, Mr Paxton. Please get to the point.'

'It's this,' he began. 'Malcolm will be leaving school quite soon and I'd like to suggest that he comes and works for me. I am the proprietor of a large leisure company.' He explained his line of business. 'I would be prepared to keep a close eye on him. I can also find something for him and his brother to do after school until then, to keep them off the streets.'

'Are you saying you'd be prepared to take responsibility for them?'

'I certainly am, madam. In conjunction with their mother, of course.'

'Me too, madam,' said George, rising and giving his details.

There was another hushed confab on the bench.

'My colleagues and I have decided,' announced the woman, gravely addressing the accused, 'that in view of the fact that you have such good people willing to take responsibility for you, and also because this is your first offence, we are not going to take this matter further.'

Nina felt weak with relief.

'Thank you, madam,' chorused the boys solemnly.

But the magistrate hadn't quite finished. 'You will pay for the damage to Mr Brown's window and his expenses,' she said. 'And if we ever see you here again, you will not be treated so leniently. Is that clear?'

'Yes, madam,' they said in unison, sounding humble . . . almost.

Alice was effusive in her thanks to the Paxton brothers. 'I'm so grateful to you,' she said. 'I'm sure your speaking up for them got them off.'

'So am I,' agreed Nina.

'It was no trouble,' said Baz.

'The least we could do,' echoed George.

'Don't you boys have something to say to your Uncle Baz and his brother?' said Alice.

'Thanks a lot,' they chorused in unusually subdued tones.

They were obviously very shaken by the result of

their latest prank, Nina was pleased to note. Perhaps it was just what they needed to make them toe the line.

'I'm not sure if you'll still want to thank us when you get to know us better,' said Baz with a grin.

'Neither am I,' said George, exchanging a meaningful glance with his brother.

Chapter Twenty-three

One Saturday lunchtime a few weeks later, a stranger came into The Willow, a florid Australian with an expensive suit and a big cigar.

Making polite conversation while she served him with a scotch, Nina asked what had brought him to these parts.

'I'm looking for someone, as a matter of fact,' he explained in a slow drawl, his broad grin splitting his leathery tanned face into a mesh-work of lines.

'If it's someone from round here, I'll probably be able to help you. I've lived here all my life.'

'It's a lady called Tilly,' he said. 'I've been asking around and I'm told I'll find her at this pub.'

'You certainly will,' said Nina, eyeing him curiously. 'She's my mother.'

'Well, I'll be buggered.' He seemed taken aback by this and peered at her oddly. Recovering quickly, he beamed and thrust a calloused hand across the bar. 'Good to meet you, love. I'm Monty Marsh. I was born not far from here . . . emigrated to Australia when I wasn't much more than a boy. Your mum's a friend of mine from the old days.'

She shook his hand, deciding she liked this craggy man with dancing brown eyes and a shock of white hair.

'Is Tilly about?'

'Yes, she's upstairs,' said Nina. 'I'll pop up and tell her you're here.'

She flew up the stairs eager to tell her mother that an old friend had come to see her. She was therefore astonished at Tilly's reaction to the news.

'Get rid of him,' she said in a wobbly voice. 'Tell him I'm not here.'

'But I've already told him you are,' Nina pointed out.

'Well, you damned well shouldn't have done without referring to me first,' snapped Tilly, her face ashen. 'Now you'll just have to tell him you were mistaken.'

Nina chewed her lip. 'But why don't you want to see him?' she asked. 'He seems a nice enough chap.'

Tilly seemed very flustered, cheeks pink, her rapid breathing making her bosom tremble. Alice was doing her musical stint in the restaurant, Joey was at work, and Malcolm and Teddy had gone out with George delivering advertising handbills, so the two women were quite alone.

'I'm not saying he isn't,' she snapped. 'When I last saw him he was just a lad of seventeen so I don't have the faintest idea what he's like now.'

'You've never said anything about having a friend who emigrated.'

'You don't mention every single person you've ever known in your life, do you?' said Tilly abrasively. 'He was just a boy I knew, that's all. He lived in the next street to me.'

'He seems very keen to see you,' Nina told her. 'He's gone to trouble to find you too.'

'That wouldn't have been difficult,' she said huffily. 'My whereabouts are hardly a secret in our old neighbourhood.'

'Why don't you just come downstairs and say hello to him?' Nina suggested. 'You needn't get involved in a long drawn out conversation.'

'No,' she insisted. 'I don't want to see him . . . not even for a second . . . so you make sure he's gone by the time I come down for my lunchtime hour in the bar.'

'I can't very well order him off the premises if he wants to stay, can I?' said Nina. 'I mean, it is a pub we're running here after all. How can I bar him if he's done nothing wrong?'

'He'll probably leave when you tell him I'm not in.' She looked at her watch. 'I'm planning to come down at one o'clock. If he hasn't gone by then, make sure you come up and let me know and I'll stay away.'

'He'll come back another time if he really wants to see you.'

Tilly tutted. 'Mm, that's a point. Tell him I've gone away for a long time or something. He's probably only in England on a flying visit. He won't bother to come back to The Willow.'

'This is a ridiculous way to carry on and you know it!' exploded Nina. 'All you have to do is come down and say hello to the man, then he'll go away.'

But Tilly wouldn't be moved. 'Just do as I say and get rid of him.'

'Oh, all right,' agreed Nina with reluctance. 'But I

think you're being very childish. You wouldn't let me get away with such silly behaviour.'

'One of the perks of being a mother,' said Tilly, throwing her daughter a warning look, 'is that you make the rules.'

With a parting look of disapproval, Nina went downstairs to embark upon deceit, wondering what all the fuss was about.

Tilly was still feeling shaky from hearing that Monty was back when she sat at her dressing table to make herself presentable for her visit to the bars. An hour or so downstairs during each session had become routine. She chatted to the customers and made sure they were being looked after – she even pulled an occasional pint if the staff were busy. Just enough to keep her involved without overdoing things. It had become the highlight of her day and the last thing she wanted was a ghost from the past popping up to spoil things.

Powdering her face in the mirror, she wondered if the fear of disappointing someone was the same thing as vanity. People who knew her now accepted her how she was today, with a walking stick, her shoulders slightly hunched as she fought against unsteadiness.

But she couldn't face Monty seeing her like this. The pull of gravity on her person would be enough of a shock compared to the flowering young girl he would remember. But to see her hobbling around like a feeble ninety year old would be too depressing for him. Better he keep his youthful memories of her, as she remembered him – a strong, handsome boy with black hair and sparkling brown eyes.

With her make-up complete, blonde, bouffant hair looking well with a plain black dress with satin trimmings, she made her way slowly and laboriously down the stairs and into the counter area of the lounge bar.

'A good crowd in,' she remarked to Nina, who was busy at the optics.

'About the usual for a Saturday.'

Much to Tilly's relief there was no sign of any dark-haired Australian.

'You got rid of him then?' she said but her daughter had already turned away to pay attention to her customer.

There was quite a gathering at the counter, but deciding that another pair of hands this side of the bar would only hinder those already serving, Tilly made her way towards the flap with the intention of having a chat with old Albert whom she'd spotted in his usual seat. She was deterred, however, by a white-haired man with a face like a deflated leather football.

'A scotch please, Tilly,' he said with a wide grin.

'Certainly, sir. My daughter will be with you in a ...' She stopped in mid-sentence. He was a stranger yet he'd known her name. She looked at him more closely. This old man couldn't be him, could it? But she'd know those eyes anywhere even if they no longer sparkled in a smooth young face surmounted by a mop of dark hair. 'Monty, is it really you?'

'None other,' he beamed. 'Cor, you're a sight for sore eyes, Til. Just as good-looking now as you were over forty years ago. You always were a classy bird.'

Blushing with girlish modesty, she said, 'And you always did have more flannel than a draper's stockroom.'

Now that the meeting had happened, she was so pleased to see him she didn't even bother to rebuke her daughter for not warning her that he was still here ... something she guessed was a deliberate oversight on Nina's part.

Sitting at a table by the window with him, Tilly said, 'I told my daughter to tell you I was out.'

'So she's a lousy liar,' he laughed. 'I hung around. The regulars told me you usually put in an appearance at some point during opening hours.'

'I see.'

'Why didn't you want to see me?'

'It was the other way around. I didn't want you to see me ... as I am now,' she confessed.

'None of us stays sixteen forever,' he pointed out.

'We certainly don't. I still pictured you with dark hair,' she laughed. 'But don't worry, white hair suits you.'

'You still look good.'

'It wasn't the being older I was worried about,' she explained. 'It's my being slow and doddery beyond my years.'

'It's only in the way you move ... not in the way you are,' he told her earnestly. 'Anyway, I knew you'd been injured in an accident. I did my homework before I came looking for you ... just in case you'd been killed in the war or something.' His eyes shone with tears of pleasure. 'Oh, Tilly, it's so good to see you again.'

'Likewise,' she said, swallowing a lump in her throat.

'It was cruel what they did to us,' he said.

'Yeah, I thought I would die at the time.'

'Me too.'

'We survived though, didn't we?' she said, her eyes glistening.

'Yeah, we did.' He dragged a hanky from his pocket and blew his nose. 'It's a nice place you've got here,' he said when he'd composed himself. 'I had a look in the restaurant too ... very nice indeed. I like the idea of a piano in the background. It creates a nice soothing atmosphere.'

'The pianist is my niece Alice, my sister Winnie's girl ... remember Winnie?'

'Will I ever forget her?' he said. 'All that raw disapproval ... she terrified me.' He paused thoughtfully. 'Does this mean that Alice is—?'

'Yes, that's right.'

Tilly went on to say that her sister was dead and gave him a general update about herself. In fact they were still chattering after the pub had closed. He told her his wife had died two years ago and, although he was only here on a visit, he intended to settle back in England. He'd put his garage business and his house in Sydney in the hands of an agent out there. He was staying in an hotel in Kensington at the moment.

'I'll go back to Oz just to tie everything up out there, but once my properties are sold, I'll buy a place here.'

'Will you buy another business?'

'Not likely,' he said. 'I'm looking forward to being able to please myself and take things easy.'

'I'd be lost without my involvement in this place.'

'You're not so involved with it that you can't find time to come out with me, I hope?'

'Well, no. But I can't walk far,' she warned him.

'You won't have to,' he assured her. 'I've a hire car for the duration of my stay.'

'What can I say then but that I'd love to?'

'How about going for a drive right now?'

'Smashing!'

Malcolm and Teddy were pounding the West London streets with delivery bags slung over their shoulders. Up and down garden paths they trudged, pushing handbills printed with details of forthcoming attractions at the Lilac Ballroom through letterboxes. They worked on opposite sides of the road and at the end of the street they met for a discussion.

'How many have you got left?' asked Malcolm.

'Millions of the bloomin' things by the feel of this bag,' complained Teddy, peering inside.

'Yeah, me too,' said Malcolm. 'Let's dump 'em, shall we?'

'I'm all in favour of that.'

'We'll chuck 'em in the bushes on that bit of waste ground in the alley we've just been down,' said Malcolm.

'Okay.'

Grinning at their inventiveness, they made their way back to the alley and were about to turn into it when someone appeared in front of them.

'Lost your bearings, have you, lads?' boomed George.

Four eyes goggled at him.

378

'You're supposed to be doing Brook Street next,' he reminded them.

'Er . . . we were just gonna . . .' began Malcolm.

'You were just gonna dump what you've got left and take the money from your Uncle Baz for completing the job,' accused George.

'Er . . .'

George clapped a hand on each shoulder in an iron grip. 'Look here, you pair of toe-rags, you might as well accept the fact that you can't win against my brother and me . . . 'cos whenever you try to pull a fast one we'll be at least two steps ahead of you. Baz and I have been there, you see. We've been horrible little boys like you. We know every trick in the book. Unlike your mum who's a real lady, we were brought up in a tough school. We're hard men and we're gonna make decent human beings out of you, whether you like it or not.'

'You can't tell us what to do,' objected Malcolm, but he wasn't very convincing.

'I can and I will,' stated George in his deep gravel tones. 'My brother and I have your mother's permission to do whatever we feel is necessary to keep you in order. So go and finish delivering those handbills – pronto. I shall be behind you in the car, just in case you're thinking of putting them anywhere except through letter boxes.'

They didn't move.

'Go on. Chop chop.'

'It's boring,' whined Teddy.

'Not half as boring as Borstal which is where you'll end up if you don't start behaving yourselves.'

'Our feet ache.'

'Don't be so soft.'

'We'll get blisters.'

'And corns.'

'I don't care if your toes drop off. Now, get going. When you've posted every last one, then I'll take you to the office for your money.'

With a grin on his face, George watched them stomp sulkily down the road.

'All done then, boys?' said Baz, when they arrived back at his office.

Malcolm gave George a wary look, wondering if he was going to mention their intended misdemeanour.

'Yeah, they're all finished,' said George. 'As soon as they've got their wages I'll run them home.'

'Righto.' Baz looked at the boys. 'I can use a spare pair of hands tomorrow morning . . . if you're interested?'

'Not delivering more handbills?' said Malcolm without enthusiasm.

'No, not that,' said Baz with a wicked grin. 'Painting the walls of the gents' dance hall toilets actually.'

'Ugh!'

'Take it or leave it,' he said. 'It's worth a few shillings though.'

'Oh?' Now there was a flicker of interest from Malcolm.

'You'll have to get up at the crack of dawn if you take the job,' Baz pointed out. 'I want it finished early enough for the paint to be dry before we open in the evening.'

The discussion was interrupted by the telephone ringing.

'Hello? Yes, Baz Paxton speaking . . . You do? . . . They will? That's terrific . . . Yes, we'll confirm all the details nearer the time. Cheers, mate.'

'That was The Soundmen's agent,' Baz told George, looking enormously pleased with himself. 'They're booked to top the bill at our charity summer Gala Night at the Pearl Palace in Margate.'

'Cor, that's a bit of all right,' said George.

'I'll say it is,' beamed Baz. 'It'll be a sell out.'

'Anyway,' he said, turning to the boys and handing them both an envelope containing the money they'd earned, 'are you on for this painting job tomorrow or not?'

'Okay, we'll do it,' said Malcolm miserably.

'Don't do me any favours, son,' said Baz firmly. 'I'm sure I can find another couple of lads only too eager to make a few bob, if you don't want to do it.'

'We'll do it,' said Malcolm with a bit more zest.

'Yeah,' echoed his sidekick.

As they left the room and made their way down the stairs, George said to Baz, 'I didn't know the gents needed painting?'

'It doesn't,' he laughed, 'but if it'll keep those two buggers out of mischief, I'll have it painted every week.'

'Nice one, bruv,' grinned George.

'You'd better get after them, mate, before they try to drive your car away . . . or rob a bank or something.'

'I wouldn't put either of those things past them,' he

said as he hurried from the room.

Baz leaned back in his chair, smiling. If he was any judge, George was thoroughly enjoying the job of bringing those lads into line. In fact, he hadn't seen such a spring to his brother's step for ages.

On the way home in George's Ford Zephyr, Malcolm asked, 'Why didn't you tell Uncle Baz about us trying to dump the handbills?'

'I didn't think it was necessary . . . as you didn't actually do it.'

'You don't have to protect us, you know,' protested Malcolm with an affected display of nonchalance.

'We can look after ourselves,' pronounced Teddy.

'If I was protecting anyone it was my brother,' he informed them. 'He has quite enough to do running his business without having you two tearaways to worry about.'

'Fancy Uncle Baz having The Soundmen playing at his dance hall,' remarked Malcolm, clearly impressed.

'They're fab,' said Teddy.

'Will he actually . . . you know . . . talk to them?' asked Malcolm, impressed.

'Of course. So will I, come to that. We're both going down to Margate for that special night,' said George.

'Cor, you lucky thing! They're brilliant,' said Teddy. 'They were on the telly the other night . . . on "Ready Steady Go".'

'Must be great to be in charge of a business like Uncle Baz's,' said Malcolm. 'You can order everyone about all day and get to meet pop stars. He doesn't have to do boring jobs like painting out the men's room, either.'

'Baz has done his share of that though. He's only where he is today because he did boring jobs when he was young,' George explained. 'No work was too hard or dirty for Baz. He grafted every hour God sent to get enough cash together to get started in business.'

'Cor, is that right?' said Teddy.

'Yeah.'

'And now he's made it to the top,' said Malcolm.

And lost the thing that meant most to him in the process, thought George, but he said, 'He certainly has. So you just think of your Uncle Baz when you're splashing about with your paint brushes tomorrow morning.'

It was only half-past four when they got back to The Willow so the pub wasn't open. Tilly had gone out with Monty, Nina had gone shopping and Joey was at work so Alice was in on her own. She invited George up to the flat where he explained about the painting job and said he would collect the boys first thing in the morning and take them over to Acton in his car.

'It's ever so kind of you and Baz to take all this trouble with them, George,' she said, as her sons disappeared into their bedroom and immediately filled the flat with the sound of The Rolling Stones. 'I really appreciate it.'

'They're not all bad, those boys of yours,' he said, 'and Baz and I intend finding the good in them and bringing it to the fore.'

'Fancy a cup of tea?'

'I'd love one.'

He sat on a chair at the kitchen table while she made the tea, chatting to her companionably.

'Don't breathe a word to them or I'll lose all my authority,' he said, smiling at her and thinking how attractive she was in a quiet, genteel sort of way. She dressed too frumpishly for his taste in her twin sets and pearls but they suited her somehow. 'But I quite enjoy being with Malcolm and Teddy . . . I suppose it's because I've never had any kids of my own.'

'Whatever the reason, I'm very grateful to you for taking such an interest in them,' she said. 'They need a man to keep them in line. It's such a difficult age. They think they're grown up but they're not. Not quite.'

He studied his large square hands to avoid her eyes and gave a nervous cough before looking up. 'Um . . . but as they are almost grown up and off on their own some of the time . . . er . . . I was wondering if you might like to come out with me sometime? On your next night off perhaps?'

'I'd like that George,' she said, surprising herself. 'I really would.'

Chapter Twenty-four

'What, no customers!' grinned Monty Marsh, breezing into the saloon bar of The Willow one Saturday morning in August to find the place almost deserted. Nina and Alice were engaged in conversation behind the counter while the bar staff chatted among themselves to one side of them.

'Give them a chance . . . we've only just opened the doors,' riposted Nina. 'Come one o'clock you won't be able to move in here and we'll all be longing for the chance of a breather like this.'

'Only kidding.' He ordered a pint and embarked on light conversation. 'So, Alice, are you gonna be tinkling the ivories today?'

She nodded. 'Later on, when the restaurant gets busy.'

'I can knock out a tune on the piano myself, you know,' he informed them chattily.

'Really?'

'Mm. I enjoy a bit of vamp now and again.'

'We know where to come if we ever need a replacement for Alice then,' said Nina lightly.

'Oh, no. I'm not in that sort of league,' he corrected.

'I just do it for fun. I play by ear, can't read a note of music.'

'I can play by ear too but I was taught not to by my piano teacher when I was small,' explained Alice. 'She liked things done by the book.'

'I reckon she knew what she was talking about,' drawled Monty. 'I've heard you play . . . you're very good.'

'Why, thank you,' she said graciously.

'You can't beat the sound of a joanna well played, can you?'

They all agreed then lapsed into comfortable silence as he took the head off his beer.

'You're looking very smart this morning, Monty,' remarked Nina, with a note of surprise in her voice. Not a man of quiet tastes, he usually dazzled them in apparel more suited to sunny Sydney than a grey-tinged British summer. Today, however, he was a model of sobriety in a blazer and grey flannels, worn with a plain white shirt.

'Thanks very much,' he said, sounding pleased. 'I want to look the part for Tilly . . . she's always so neat.'

'I understand you're off to Brighton for the day?' said Nina.

'That's right. A breath of sea air and a plate of whelks. Just what the doctor ordered.'

'Let's hope the Mods and Rockers keep away from there,' said Alice, referring to rival teenage gangs who had hit the headlines this summer by pouring into coastal resorts on motor bikes and scooters in weekend orgies of hooliganism.

'The seaside does seem to be a magnet for those ruffians lately,' said Nina. 'Still, as it isn't a Bank Holiday, they'll probably stay away.'

'I hope they keep away from Margate, too,' said Alice.

'Ah, yes. That's where Joey and his cousins have gone for the weekend, isn't it?' said Monty.

'Yes. They've gone with Baz and George for a special Gala charity night of pop music Baz is putting on at his dance hall there this evening,' explained Nina.

'There was no end of trouble at Margate over the Whit weekend back in May,' commented Alice gravely. 'A couple of the louts got stabbed.'

'Still, you can't let yobbos like that frighten you into staying at home, can you?' said Nina.

'Too right,' agreed Monty.

The conversation was halted by the appearance of Tilly looking fresh and smart in a pale blue Crimplene dress with matching jacket.

'You look nice, Til,' he said simply.

'Ta, dear,' she replied, smiling.

'If you're all set then, love, let's go.'

The couple left with Monty holding Tilly's arm supportively.

'It's good to see Mum enjoying herself,' Nina remarked to Alice.

'She certainly seems to be having a whale of a time.'

'It's about time she had some fun after all she's been through,' Nina went on. 'I don't think I've ever seen her as happy as she is now . . . even when Dad was alive. She seems positively radiant.'

'I know.'

'She has more time to go out and enjoy herself now too instead of being tied to this place morning noon and night. At least the accident gave her that much.'

'Monty's nice, don't you think?' remarked Alice.

'Oh, yeah, a smashing bloke,' agreed Nina with enthusiasm. 'Just like one of the family. Even more so now he's sold up in Australia and living so near in a flat in Acorn Court.'

'That's true.'

'He's obviously serious about her.'

'No doubt about it,' said Alice.

'In fact, I'm beginning to feel like the odd one out around here,' laughed Nina. 'What with Mum going out with Monty and you spending all your spare time with George. Are you two a couple or what?'

'I don't know about that,' said Alice. 'I enjoy his company a lot but I'm taking each day as it comes for the moment.'

'Very wise.'

Nina and her mother had been astounded when Alice and George had started dating. Surely few people could be less suited than a rough diamond like George and Alice who was still very refined, even without the swank?

But, oddly enough, they seemed right together somehow, and George was wonderful with Malcolm and Teddy. He couldn't do more for them than if he was their father. Firm but friendly, he joked and sparred with them, went with them to watch football and cricket, let them go so far – and no further.

Nina guessed that the Harding boys saw George as the streetwise hero they admired but could never be. Their behaviour was still not perfect but since Malcolm had left school and started full-time work at Paxton Leisure, learning the business from the bottom with a view to management in the future, he seemed more sensible and less inclined to hang about the streets, often because he was simply too tired to go out when he got home from work. Since Teddy was influenced by his elder brother he had quietened down too.

Nina was genuinely pleased to see Alice looking so cheerful because she'd had more than her share of tragedy.

As for Nina herself . . . well, if she wasn't happy, at least she was reasonably content with her single status. If she missed the joy of sharing her life, at least she was secure in the knowledge that there was no one to disappoint her. She was always too busy for introspection anyway, for The Willow was no longer a small-time establishment. The restaurant had put them on the map. People came from all over to eat here which in turn increased the pub trade. The proof of their success in retaining a homely atmosphere was the continuing presence of their regulars in the bars.

The biggest problem on the restaurant side was keeping a decent chef for any length of time. If they had any sort of flair they were usually ambitious and soon moved on in search of better things. Staff in general changed frequently in the licensed trade because of the unsocial hours. Some part-timers only wanted temporary work to earn money for a particular reason.

Joey was a great help around the place in his spare time but he was going to France in the autumn on a three-year contract, to work in a restaurant under a chef who was much admired in cooking circles. She'd miss him terribly for at eighteen he was great fun to have around.

But Alice was saying, 'I hope all goes well in Margate . . . it's a big night for Baz and George.'

'Yes, I hope so too,' said Nina, with genuine concern, for tonight's event was Baz's most adventurous project yet and she knew it meant a lot to him.

The fans came in their thousands to the Pearl Palace that night. Mini-skirted dolly girls with beehive hair styles, and boys in high-fastening Beatle suits. In contrast to the heavily lacquered raised coiffeur, the soft, well-cut Vidal Sassoon look was also very much in evidence.

Girls came in skinny rib sweaters and dresses with chain belts worn on the hip; in short loose frocks with pale tights and buckle shoes. Boys wore elastic-sided Chelsea Boots and collarless jackets. Long after every last ticket was sold, crowds of unlucky youngsters waited outside hoping for a glimpse of The Soundmen.

As relatives of the owner, Joey and his cousins enjoyed certain privileges and had been here all afternoon watching the equipment being set up. Now the first half of the show, featuring several lesser known groups, was in full swing and the three boys were upstairs in the cafeteria looking over the balcony on to the dance-floor where a seething mass of humanity wiggled and twisted beneath the coloured lights that changed to the beat.

After the interval when The Soundmen took the stage, all hell broke loose. The crowd stamped and screamed – some of the girls were almost hysterical.

'Imagine having all those girls fancying you,' said Malcolm.

'Yeah,' said Teddy wistfully.

'And imagining it is all we're ever likely to do, boys, unless we learn how to play the guitar,' joked Joey. 'That's what gets 'em going.'

'That and having a hit record,' laughed Malcolm.

As the last notes of the group's final number died away, the whole place erupted. Determined not to let the musicians go, throngs of people swarmed on to the stage, shouting for more. It took a team of bodyguards to get the performers safely out of the ballroom.

The foyer was jammed solid. Instead of leaving, the fans lingered in the hope of another glimpse of their heroes. Banks of people stretched right out through the doors and into the street. Outside they were chanting, 'We want The Soundmen . . . we want The Soundmen . . .'

Joey spotted his father by the ticket office to the side of the wide glass doors that opened on to the street. He was with Uncle George and the manager of the ballroom, all three looking the part in dark evening suits. The boys elbowed their way over to them.

'You lads all right?' enquired Baz.

They nodded.

'You'd better stay here, out of the way, till we can

shift this crowd. Don't want you getting crushed,' he said.

'The crowd won't leave till The Soundmen do,' said Joey.

'They've already gone,' Baz informed him. 'Their manager whisked them off in his car immediately they came off stage. Their assistants are going later in the pantechnicon with all the gear.'

'Somebody's gonna get hurt in this lot, boss, if we don't do something quick,' said the manager worriedly. 'The police are expecting a crowd so they'll be doing what they can outside, but we need to clear this lot – sharpish.'

'We could speak to them on a megaphone . . . tell 'em the boys have gone,' suggested George.

'We'll never make ourselves heard above this racket,' said the manager.

'Leave it to me,' said Baz, and disappeared into the crowd.

Baz pushed his way into the thick of the crowd. 'The Soundmen have left the building,' he said directly into the ear of a girl with long straight hair.

'Who sez?'

'I do . . . and I own the ballroom,' he told her.

'You're having me on,' she said, but there was doubt in her voice as Baz's appearance registered for he was obviously not just one of the crowd.

'No, I'm not. They went out of the back door and straight into a car right after the show. I saw them myself.'

'Aah, what a rotten trick.' She turned to the girl beside her. 'They've gone, mate. We're wasting our time 'ere.'

He repeated the process with a few other fans and let the crowd do the rest. The message rushed through the ranks like a cooling wind, lowering the emotion and the volume of noise until it faded almost to nothing and the crowd began to disperse.

'I don't know how you did it, boss,' said the manager when Baz returned to the foyer, 'but well done.'

'I'll second that,' said George.

Almost despite himself Joey was impressed by the ease with which his father had handled the situation. Seeing him at the hub of his empire today had illustrated to Joey the esteem in which Baz was held. Everyone looked up to him.

'All in a day's work,' he said. 'Anyway, as it's quieter here now, I think we'll make our way to our hotel.'

Goodbyes were said and they walked along the brightly lit seafront, chatting companionably about the show. Groups of lads stood outside the amusement arcades and cafés, their noisy presence creating a sense of danger.

'Did you boys enjoy yourselves?' asked Baz.

'Fabulous,' said Teddy.

'It was quite good,' said Malcolm, who thought that too much enthusiasm showed a lack of 'cool', 'but The Soundmen aren't a patch on The Beatles.'

'They're every bit as good, I reckon,' said Joey.

'All those screaming females got on my nerves,' said Malcolm.

'Only because they weren't screaming for you,' laughed Joey.

The conversation came to an abrupt halt as the air became fraught with shouts and the thunder of running feet. Joey was pushed aside by a gang of marauding youths. Chaos ensued as Baz and his group became embroiled in a brawl between rival gangs armed with sticks and bottles. The thuds and screams of violence could be heard all along the seafront. Innocent bystanders were yelling for help as they found themselves caught up in the vicious crossfire of gang warfare.

In an effort to stop the violence, Joey tried to drag the brawlers apart only to find himself on the receiving end of their aggression. He was shoved to the ground and held down by four of them while another thrust the jagged edge of a broken bottle close to his face. Powerless against their numbers, he closed his eyes and braced himself for the worst.

'Leave him alone, you bloody hooligans!' said Baz, dragging the one with the bottle away from Joey while George and the Harding boys took on the others.

Baz pulled Joey to his feet and was about to get him and the others out of this mayhem to safety when one of the yobs drew a flick knife on Joey.

'Out of the way, old man,' he said to Baz, pushing him aside and moving in on Joey with the knife ominously poised.

Before Joey had time to move out of the path of the blade, Baz placed himself between his son and the weapon.

'Get out of here quick, get the police,' Baz commanded breathlessly before slumping to the ground, overpowered by a searing pain in the side of his chest where the knife had gone in.

Alarmed by the sight of blood seeping through their victim's white dress shirt in the neon lighting, the youths made a hasty retreat.

'You bloody fool!' growled Joey, leaning over his father who lay unconscious on the ground. 'What did you do a stupid thing like that for?' Tears trickled down the young man's face as the love he had denied himself all these years welled up inside him like a physical pain. 'Don't die . . . please don't die . . .'

'Why don't you go back to the hotel and get some sleep, Joey?' said Baz a few hours later from his hospital bed in a cubicle in the casualty ward. 'No sense in your hanging about here all night.'

'I will in a minute,' he said. 'I just wanted to make sure you were going to be all right before I left.'

'Are the others still waiting outside?'

'No . . . they went back to the hotel once they knew you weren't going to die on us,' he explained. 'I wanted to see for myself.'

'Of course I'm not going to die.' Baz glanced at his chest. 'It's nothing very much.'

'I don't call twenty stitches nothing much.'

'It's just a flesh wound, that's what I mean,' explained Baz. 'It isn't life threatening.'

'Why are they keeping you here overnight then?'

'Just to make sure there are no complications, I

suppose,' said Baz wearily. 'Who knows what goes on in the minds of medical people?'

'They know what they're doing.'

'I don't doubt it. Anyway, are George and the boys all right?' Baz asked, yawning. 'They were fighting the buggers off just before I blacked out.'

'They're fine. And the police seemed to be making a lot of arrests.'

'Do you know if they got matey with the knife?'

'I doubt it,' said Joey furiously. 'He had it away on his toes, the miserable coward! If I ever get my hands on that bast—'

'That's enough of that sort of talk,' admonished Baz firmly. 'No point in sinking to their level. It's all over now and best forgotten.'

'Humph.'

'You'd better go now, son,' said Baz woozily. 'I think they're gonna move me into the main ward for the night . . . what's left of it.'

'Okay,' Joey said, rising.

'I think I'm about to fall asleep anyway,' said his father drowsily. 'The tablets they've given me to kill the pain must have some sedative in them or something. They're making me feel sleepy.'

Joey looked grey with the strain of the last few hours. His father couldn't possibly know what he'd been through tonight. He would never forget that terrible moment when Baz had fallen to the ground and lain there so ominously still, or the terror that had gripped him at the possibility that he might never come round. Joey had not realised he was capable of feeling anything in such depth. Through fear and anguish, the confused emotions he had suppressed for so long out of a lingering sense of loyalty to his mother had finally come to the surface and were clarified.

Whatever mistakes his father had made in the past, he was basically a good person; a man willing to put his own life at risk for his son. Joey's love for him knew no bounds. To come right out and say so, though, would embarrass them both so he had to find another way of letting him know.

'It should be me in that bed,' he said, swallowing the lump in his throat. 'The knife was meant for me.'

'Don't talk wet.'

'You saved my life,' said Joey, choking back the tears.

'Leave off.'

'It's true. You could have died if the wound had been an inch either way on your chest, the doctor told me.'

'I didn't die though, did I? So it's all theoretical,' said Baz, his lids drooping as the sedative took effect.

Joey stood for a few moments watching his father drift off to sleep. Then he gently rested his hand on that of the sleeping man. 'Thanks anyway . . . Dad,' he said, and slipped quietly out of the cubicle.

Baz had almost dozed off. But he was not too far gone to have missed that one word which said so much and which he had despaired of ever hearing. Joey had called him Dad . . . for the first time. It certainly was an ill wind, he thought, as he fell into a contented sleep, a joyful tear sliding from under his eyelid.

* * *

Nina was beginning to think everyone was deserting her as the year drew to a close. No sooner had she got over Joey's departure to France than Alice announced her engagement to George. Although that relationship had seemed the least likely match of the century originally, no one was surprised when they decided to make a go of it, having watched them get on so well together over a number of months.

Although Nina was pleased for her cousin, she knew she would miss having her around.

'So I'm about to lose a cousin and gain a bedroom, am I?' she said, making light of it. 'But seriously, the place will seem empty when you and the boys move out.'

'Don't worry, you won't get rid of me altogether,' Alice laughed. 'I'd like to stay on at The Willow part-time after I'm married.'

'Oh, that's a surprise.'

'I think the place must have got under my skin.'

They both knew it was Nina and Tilly to whom she was really referring for they had all become such good friends since she'd come to live with them for the second time.

'George is going to sell his flat and buy a house,' Alice continued. 'I shall make sure it isn't too far from here.'

The wedding was in the spring of 1965, and the couple set up home just down the road in Chiswick. As Alice only worked part-time now, Nina employed a freelance pianist to fill the gap for live music was a popular feature of the restaurant.

Also at this time, she hired a new full-time barmaid to replace Mary who retired. The new girl was a Twiggyslim eighteen year old, a mini-skirted brunette called Samantha Briggs with huge brown eyes, a lovely smile, and oodles of vitality. She was new to the licensed trade, having worked in an office since she left school.

'I want a change, Mrs Paxton,' she told Nina at the interview. 'Feel like doing something entirely different, know what I mean?'

'Why not tell me about it?' suggested Nina.

'Well, I never wanted to go in an office when I left school . . . it was what Mum and Dad wanted me to do.'

'I expect they thought it would be a good job for you.'

'Oh, yeah, they did. But I'm fed up with being stuck at a desk all day, never meeting any new people,' she explained. 'When I saw your advert in the local paper for a barmaid, I thought, now that's something I really do fancy.'

'Can you tell me why it appeals to you?'

'I enjoy meeting people. I get on well with 'em.'

'Yes, I can imagine.'

'Anyway, here I am. Mum and Dad aren't too pleased though, seeing as they paid for my typing classes.'

Her youth and lack of experience made Nina somewhat wary of taking her on, but being desperate for staff in this time of near full employment, she decided to give Samantha a try. After ten minutes it was obvious she had made the right decision. Rather than letting the fact that she was a novice be a handicap, Samantha turned it to her advantage. She flattered the customers by asking their advice in such a charming manner most of them would willingly have got their own beer to help her out if that were possible.

In Samantha, Nina saw the quality with which she and her mother had been blessed. Anyone could learn to be an efficient barmaid but Samantha had that extra something which made people choose The Willow as their venue for the evening rather than any other pub in the area. She was attractive without being intimidating, nicely spoken but not affected, and friendly without being pushy. An absolute Godsend to Nina, she quickly endeared herself to the customers and became a friend of the family.

She was very much a Sixties girl, a devotee of pop culture who travelled to work on a motor scooter. Such was her devotion to The Beatles, one day in the autumn she stood outside Buckingham Palace with her girlfriends to watch the Fab Four arrive to receive their MBEs.

'We saw 'em go in through the gates,' she said excitedly when she came on duty that evening. 'They were in a Rolls Royce with their manager Brian Epstein. We actually saw them – in real life . . . I just can't believe it.'

Joey first met Samantha when he came home for a month's holiday, having developed into a handsome and polished young man, the image of his father at that age without the rough edges. Nina and Tilly were delighted when he and Samantha took an instant liking to each other and embarked upon a romance.

'They make such a lovely couple,' said Tilly. 'It's a pity he has to go back to France.'

'Mm . . . still, they can write to each other,' said Nina. 'And he'll be back for holidays. If they're that keen on each other they'll get together when he comes back to London for good in two years' time.'

'Let's hope they're both patient enough to wait that long,' said Tilly. 'And that one of them doesn't find someone else.'

'If that happens then it can't be that serious,' said Nina. 'It'll be a very good test.'

Samantha showed no sign of finding anyone else after Joey left. She seemed to be more interested in pop music and the latest clothes than men. As well as being up to date with fashion, she was also very much in tune with the views of the modern generation which she expressed with a lack of inhibition unheard of in Nina's day.

Whilst she was effusive in her praise of the contraceptive pill, she was less enthusiastic about the other big social issue of her age group.

'You won't catch me taking purple hearts,' she said one day when she was bottling up and Nina was doing something at the till, ready for opening.

'Do any of your friends take drugs?'

'No, not in my close circle,' she said. 'But a few of the people we see at the discos do.'

'But not you?' confirmed Nina.

'No. I don't need drugs to give me a high . . . the music does that on its own,' she explained. 'Anyway, I wanna stay in control of the way I feel.'

'Quite right too.'

'Joey feels the same way as me about it,' she said. 'Neither of us wants to get into that scene. No way!'

'Thank God for that,' said Nina.

Joey and Samantha stayed in close touch throughout his time in France. They lived for his holidays at home when they spent every moment they could together. When he had completed his contract and was back for good they announced their engagement.

With all the experience he had gained he didn't have any trouble finding a well-paid position in a West End hotel. So Nina was surprised and delighted when he told her it was only temporary.

'I'd like to be chef in The Willow restaurant when you get a vacancy,' he told her. 'It wouldn't be fair to get rid of the chef you have to make room for me, but I'd like first refusal if he leaves.'

'There's nothing I'd like better than having you work with us, son,' she said. 'But you can earn more money in a big London hotel.'

'I know . . . but The Willow is our family business,' he said with sincerity. 'And I'd like to be a part of it. It's what I've always wanted, you know that.'

'Yes, I do. I just want what's best for you.'

'I reckon I'm old enough to decide that for myself now.'

'Yes, son. I think you are too,' she agreed.

Just after Joey's twenty-first birthday, Nina's chef announced his intention of opening his own restaurant on the coast and offered his resignation. After a thorough discussion Tilly and Nina finally decided to hand over the entire responsibility for the restaurant to Joey: the choice of menu, staff control, everything.

He was delighted and threw himself into the job, stamping his own individuality on the cuisine whilst teaching his cooking skills to his subordinates and allowing them practical experience. He and Samantha seemed to grow ever closer now that they were working on the same premises. Nina and Tilly thought of Samantha as one of the family and eagerly awaited the wedding.

Then a girl called Linda came to work at The Willow as a waitress and everything changed.

Chapter Twenty-five

Samantha's spirits plummeted on entering the restaurant to see Joey and Linda ensconced at one of the tables in the otherwise deserted room. Innocent enough, perhaps, the chef relaxing over a drink with one of his staff after a busy lunchtime in the kitchen. But Samantha's instinct had been telling her differently for weeks.

She saw Linda as a formidable rival by whom she herself was threatened. A stunning blonde of the Monroe ilk with an amazing figure and skin like porcelain, every sensual nuance of Linda's body-language was a declaration of war to Samantha. Added to her personal fears, too, was the suspicion that Linda's interest in Joey was motivated by his being the boss's son.

The couple hadn't noticed Samantha come in and were laughing softly when she approached their table.

'Just popped in to tell you that I'm going home now,' she said to Joey, forcing a smile.

Looking flushed and sheepish, he scrambled to his feet. 'Oh . . . okay, darling,' he said with a smile, as though still amused by some private joke he'd shared with Linda.

An uncomfortable silence hung heavily around them.

'I hope I'm not interrupting anything?' said Samantha curtly.

'Of course not,' he was rather too quick to deny. 'Linda and I were just talking about a difficult customer we had in this lunchtime. Honestly, some of them would try the patience of a saint.'

'She was a right old crow,' Linda said with a laugh in her voice. 'She said to me, she said . . .' There was a pause while she shook with laughter. 'She said, "You ought to put a skirt on, young lady, instead of waiting at table in just the hem."' Another yell of mirth. 'Cor dear! Talk about the dark ages. The silly old trout ought to be in a museum.'

To Samantha's annoyance Joey was unable to suppress his mirth.

'The woman's entitled to her opinion,' said Samantha tersely.

'Ooh, hark at her,' said Linda with a snigger. 'And you with your skirt up to your bum, too.'

'That's got nothing to do with it,' said Samantha, reddening. 'That woman is of another generation . . . they didn't wear short skirts in her day.'

'And that gives her the right to criticise me, I suppose?' sneered Linda.

'She paid good money to come here and eat and that's what pays your wages,' Samantha pointed out. 'It isn't right to mock the hand that feeds you.'

'All right, no need to come out in a rash over it,' snorted Linda.

Samantha ignored that and turned to Joey. 'Well, I'll

be off then. I'll see you later.'

'I'll take you in the car,' he said, referring to the MGB his parents had given him for his twenty-first birthday.

'Suit yourself.'

In the car he slipped his arm around her, only to have it firmly removed.

'What's got into you?'

'Don't play the innocent.'

'Look, all Linda and I were doing was talking.'

'This time, yes.'

'Meaning that other times we do more?'

'I'm not saying that.'

'What are you getting at then?'

She could feel him slipping away from her and didn't seem to be able to regain control. Nagging him about Linda wasn't the answer but she couldn't just ignore what was going on.

'I'm saying that Linda is after you . . . and you're not exactly discouraging her.'

'Don't be ridiculous,' he snapped. 'She's just good fun, that's all. She doesn't mean anything to me.'

'You promise?'

'I promise.'

She turned to him with a contrite smile. 'Sorry. I've behaved like a jealous neurotic.'

'I forgive you.'

'I've been so happy since we've been together, Joey. I don't want anything to spoil it.'

'And nothing will,' he said, kissing her. 'I promise you that.'

* * *

But a few days later Samantha witnessed a further display of the growing attraction between Joey and Linda. This time they were whispering together in the porch of The Willow when Samantha arrived for work one morning. They sprang apart, flushed and giggling, on noticing her presence. Their actions spoke volumes to Samantha. They had the distinct air of a couple who fancied each other like mad.

After the lunchtime session was over, Samantha caught Linda on her way out. 'I think you and I need to talk,' she said, falling into step beside the girl as she made her way along the waterfront.

'What about?' asked Linda, stopping and turning to her.

'You know what about.'

'Oh, you want to assert your exclusive rights to the boss's son, I suppose?' she said, chewing gum slowly.

'I *am* engaged to him, you know.'

'So what?'

'So keep off!'

'Oh, do me a favour,' came the cynical retort. 'You sound like some second-rate actress in a B-movie.'

'He'll soon see through you,' said Samantha.

'I wouldn't be too sure about that,' was the confident reply.

'And don't you dare get Joey into your habits,' she went on, for Linda didn't hide the fact that she was into drugs. In fact, she boasted about it.

'Oh, for God's sake. He's a grown man. Quite old enough to make up his own mind.'

'You dare . . .'

'Grow up, will you?'

'You're the one who needs to do that,' retorted Samantha.

'You should try a little something yourself,' suggested Linda coldly. 'You need something to loosen you up, put a smile on that sour face of yours.'

'I'm not that much of a fool . . . and neither is Joey.'

'Joey isn't your puppet. You can't speak for him.'

'You just leave him alone!'

'Hey, are you sure you've got this the right way around?' asked Linda with a cynical smile.

'You're making all the running,' said Samantha.

'I haven't noticed him backing off, though, have you?'

She couldn't argue with that so she said, 'You're using him to try to get into his family's business.'

'And you're not, I suppose?' was the sharp retort.

'No, I'm not.'

'Oh, come down off your high horse for Gawd's sake,' demanded Linda. 'You're just a barmaid here . . . you're no better than I am . . . don't tell me you don't want to be one of the family with all their money and prestige. The fact that Joey is the sexiest thing on legs is a bonus.'

'You *are* after his money then?'

'I like the idea of having access to his chequebook, yeah,' she admitted. 'And as I fancy him like mad too, it's a perfect combination.'

'You bitch!'

'Get real,' said Linda, chewing gum in a slow, relaxed

manner. 'He might be engaged to you but he fancies me rotten.'

'He doesn't!'

'You don't really believe that,' said Linda, shaking her head. 'Anyone can see he's panting for me . . . that's why you're so worried.'

'You just leave him alone,' repeated Samantha as a parting shot before hurrying away.

She wasn't the type to be easily defeated but felt out of her depth and powerless against Linda whose words had a definite ring of truth about them. She decided to have a chat with Joey that evening – try to make him see what Linda was up to. It was their night off and they were going out for a meal together.

'Honestly, Sam, you're getting to be really boring about Linda,' admonished Joey that evening over dinner in a restaurant at Richmond.

'She'll get you into drugs if you're not careful.'

'Don't be ridiculous.'

'I'm not being. She's a very persuasive girl.'

'You really think I'm that stupid?'

'It isn't a question of that, Joey, but . . .'

'But nothing,' he interrupted hotly. 'Look, Sam, I think Linda is a fool to do what she does but what she gets up to in her own time is her business and, frankly, I think you've got a bloody cheek to suggest I'm weak enough to be persuaded into anything by her . . . you *really* are out of order on this one.'

'That girl can do no wrong in your eyes, can she?' said Samantha, hitting out wildly in desperation.

He frowned darkly. 'What a silly thing to say. You seem to have a vendetta against her.'

'She's trying to break us up, Joey,' she warned.

'Oh come on, Sam, now you're getting paranoid.'

Samantha sensed that she'd gone as far as she dared, that to continue along these lines would only serve to distance them further.

'Let's talk about something more interesting, shall we?' she said, forcing a smile.

'Yes, I think we'd better.'

The tension eased slightly with the change of subject and they chatted about things in general. Over coffee, Samantha said, 'Your mother has been nagging me about a date for our wedding. I think she and your gran are keen to get things moving.'

'Mm . . . I suppose it's time we did something definite about that,' he said, sounding quite keen.

'An autumn wedding would be nice,' she suggested, heartened by his interest, 'then we would be back from our honeymoon well before the Christmas rush gets under way at The Willow.'

'Yes, that's a very good idea.' He smiled.

He looked across at Samantha, so smart and pretty, her shiny dark hair slightly raised at the crown and falling loosely to her shoulders. She had everything. She was beautiful, intelligent and caring, a woman any man would be proud to have as his wife. So why didn't the fact that he was in love with her protect him from Linda's compelling sexuality?

Linda was callous and self-seeking – she amused herself at other people's expense. But she excited him almost unbearably. His brain told him to beware. His biology said different. Now, observing his beloved fiancée across the table, he was consumed with remorse for his lecherous thoughts towards Linda. He wasn't proud of the fact that his guilty conscience caused him to deny all knowledge of her evil intent, either.

'The sooner we get married the better,' he said, reaching across and taking Samantha's hand. 'I do love you.'

All her fears melted away and she felt happy for the first time in ages.

A date in October was set for the marriage of Joey and Samantha and wedding arrangements were set in motion. Feeling very much more secure in Joey's affections now that they had set the date, Samantha was able to be more objective when she saw him and Linda talking or laughing together. She told herself, They work together in the restaurant. It's important they get along. There's no more to it than that . . .

On Sunday afternoons, Samantha and Joey usually managed to grab a few hours alone together before the evening shift. When the pub closed after the midday session, she would go home for lunch with her parents and he would come round to her house later. They normally went for a run out somewhere in the car or for a walk by the river.

One Sunday in August, however, Joey said he had a thumping headache and didn't feel like going anywhere. They agreed that he would see Samantha when she came on duty at The Willow that evening.

Knowing that his grandmother was going out with Monty, and his mother was spending the afternoon with his Aunt Alice in Chiswick, Samantha decided to go back to the pub a couple of hours before they opened to try to cheer him up.

She'd been given a key to the private entrance on her engagement to Joey, so that she could come and go as she pleased when the pub wasn't open. Now she opened the door and made her way upstairs, quietly in case he was asleep. Reaching the first floor, she became uneasy as she received a whiff of something unmistakable. On her way up to Joey's bedroom on the next floor, she stiffened at the sound of voices.

With dread in her heart she opened the bedroom door and froze at what she saw. Joey was sitting up in bed with Linda who was smoking a joint which she handed to him while Samantha stood in the doorway in a state of shock. The sweet, pungent smell of dope was overpowering.

'Hi, Sam darling,' Joey said in a slow voice, clearly incapable of comprehending the situation.

'Hi,' echoed Linda, and they both erupted into fits of laughter.

With terrible calmness, Samantha removed her engagement ring, walked slowly into the room and put it down on top of the chest of drawers.

'When you're not stoned out of your mind, Joey, this will help you realise that you're a free man again,' she said in a tight little voice, then turned and marched stiffly from the room.

* * *

413

Nina and Tilly tried hard to persuade Samantha to change her mind and stay on at The Willow. But she couldn't even be coaxed to work until the end of the week. She left after that Sunday evening shift, explaining that she and Joey had split up and she would rather not have any future contact with him.

'It's obviously something to do with that Linda,' said Tilly. 'A troublemaker if ever I saw one.'

But since Joey was completely unapproachable on the subject and his foul mood didn't invite persuasion, the wedding plans were cancelled and Nina and Tilly had to accept the fact that they had lost a dear friend and future member of the family as well as a damned good barmaid. They also lost a waitress because Linda left suddenly, soon after Samantha. Linda and Joey had fallen out, apparently, but he wouldn't say much about that either.

One morning in September, Tilly asked Alice if she would stay on after the pub closed for a spot of lunch with herself and Nina in the flat. She said she wanted to have a chat with them. She also asked Joey to make himself scarce.

'I bet this'll be a wedding announcement,' said Nina, as she and Alice made their way upstairs to the flat. 'Though I don't know why she wants Joey out of the way.'

'Wants to make it a hen party, perhaps?' said Alice.

'Maybe . . . anyway it's about time she and Monty tied the knot,' said Nina. 'They've been seeing each other for long enough.'

'I couldn't agree more,' smiled Alice.

Their speculation proved to be correct – Tilly and Monty were going to get married.

'He's been trying to persuade me for ages,' Tilly explained as the three of them ate cheese omelettes at the table by the livingroom window overlooking the river. 'I've kept the poor bloke waiting for an answer because of my obligations to The Willow. I know I don't do anything like what I used to about the place but I've stayed closely involved. I don't think it would be fair to Monty to be so deeply committed to something else besides him. It would be different if we were both involved, like Joe and me were.'

'Monty wouldn't want you to give it up, surely?' said Nina. 'He isn't the possessive type.'

'You're right, he isn't,' Tilly explained, 'but he thinks it would be nice if I was free from work commitments altogether – the same as he is – and I agree with him.'

'So what's all this leading up to?' asked Nina.

'I've decided that I'd like to have an ordinary home life with Monty,' she explained gravely.

'Oh.'

'So we're gonna buy a house. Don't worry, we won't be leaving the area so we'll be popping in and out all the time. But I don't want to have responsibilities in the pub any more.'

'That's perfectly understandable,' said Nina. 'I'm happy to relieve you of the paperwork and so on.'

'There's a bit more to my plans than that,' said Tilly enigmatically.

Both younger women looked puzzled as they waited for her to continue.

'What I propose to do,' she explained, 'is to legally hand over the pub now, while I'm still alive, rather than have you inherit after I die.'

'Oh, Mum,' said Nina, shaking her head doubtfully. 'Are you sure that's wise? It's a very big step and I'm quite happy to carry on as I am, managing the place for you.'

'Monty and I have discussed it at great length,' Tilly went on in an assertive manner, 'and he thinks it's a good idea for me to hand over now. He isn't short of cash. He's got more than enough to keep us both in comfort for the rest of our lives.'

Nina tapped her thumbnail on her front teeth meditatively. 'Well, as long as you're quite sure,' she said.

'I am.' Tilly seemed to become uneasy. She pushed her plate aside and studied her fingernails with intense concentration. Then she cleared her throat several times and said, 'Um . . . actually . . . what I have to tell you now will come as a very great surprise to you both.'

An expectant hush filled the room as Nina and Alice waited.

'To be fair to both my daughters,' she announced, her voice wavering slightly, 'I propose to hand over ownership of The Willow to you jointly with Nina to have the larger share since she is the mainstay of the place and has worked so hard in it for so many years.'

There was a bewildered silence while the significance of her words registered.

'Both your daughters?' echoed Nina at last. 'You mean . . .'

'Yes, you're actually sisters, not cousins,' she said, biting her lip, her shrewd blue eyes darting worriedly from one to the other.

'But how?' muttered Alice, stupefied.

Tilly took a deep breath . . . then she began again.

'When I was a young girl I was in love with a boy I'd grown up with. We'd been childhood sweethearts and we . . . er . . . well, to cut a long story short we became lovers. We didn't know very much about contraception back in the nineteen-twenties and I found myself pregnant when I wasn't quite sixteen. It was considered the worst sin a girl could commit in those days and my parents were horrified when they found out. There was no question of my keeping the baby. My parents got together with his. He was sent away and I was kept out of sight until the baby was born, when my elder sister Winnie and her husband Cedric took you, Alice, and registered you as their own child. Winnie had already been married for several years and hadn't conceived so she was delighted. In fact, the arrangements suited everyone except your father and me, and we had no say in the matter whatsoever. It probably seems unbelievable to you now but that's how it was in those days.'

'My father?' said Alice with a question in her voice. 'Is it . . . ?'

'Yes, I expect you've guessed. Monty was the boy, he's your natural father.'

She looked at Nina. 'I was very fond of your father

and we had a good marriage. Joe was a lovely man but Monty was my first love and I didn't forget him through all the years we were apart.'

'I always knew there was something special about your feelings for Alice,' said Nina thoughtfully. 'The way you've always defended her . . . worried about her.'

'Yes, it was the empathy of a mother you saw, not an aunt,' Tilly explained.

'Well, it certainly takes some getting used to,' said Nina.

'Why bring it out into the open now?' asked Alice. 'Having kept it secret for so long?'

'It seems right you should know the truth . . . now that Monty's come back into our lives and the people you know as parents are not around to be hurt by it. I promised Winnie I would never tell you the truth. But now I feel I must.'

'I see.'

'Well, how does it feel to have a sister?' asked Nina.

'Bewildering,' said Alice, still in shock. 'How about you?'

'Likewise,' said Nina.

'I'm sure about one thing though,' said Alice, looking at Tilly.

'Oh?'

'The Willow must go to Nina in its entirety,' she said. 'It's nice of you to think of me, but we all know that morally it belongs to her.'

'Now I can tell you something,' said Tilly, smiling mistily. 'That was the reaction I was hoping for from you but I didn't want to put words into your mouth. Now I know I have two daughters I can be proud of.'

'It might take a while for me to get used to your being my mother,' said Alice, looking very flushed and worried.

'I'll probably always be Aunt Tilly to you,' said Tilly sagely. 'And that's only right and proper. I didn't bring you up. Winnie did that.'

'You and Nina have been there for me for most of my adult life though,' said Alice, feeling deeply emotional now that the initial shock was beginning to wear off.

'And what a madam you were in the early days too!' teased Nina in an effort to moderate the strong feelings that were flowing between them.

'Now I know we're sisters,' said Alice, hovering between laughter and tears. 'Isn't it traditional for siblings to insult each other?'

Suddenly they all seemed to be laughing and crying and hugging each other. Nina said tearfully, 'One thing we've forgotten in all this . . . we haven't drunk a toast to Mum's engagement.'

'Well, that's easily rectified,' grinned Tilly, hobbling over to the sideboard and producing a bottle of sherry. 'Get the glasses then, girls.'

'So it's just the two of us now, Joey,' said Nina on the night of her mother's wedding day in November when she and Joey were alone in the flat after everyone had gone and the pub was closed.

'Mm.'

'And you'll soon be moving out too, I expect?' she

419

said, adding laughingly, 'And then there was only one.'

'I've no plans to move out,' he told her. 'It's handy living on the job.'

'For the moment, yes. But you'll want a place of your own eventually,' she said, 'when you meet a girl and want to set up home with her.'

'I can't see that happening,' he said gloomily. 'I blew it with the only girl I wanted.'

Sensing that he needed to talk, she encouraged him to do so.

'I was weak,' he said, having told his mother the story of his attraction to Linda and what it had led him to do. 'I thought I'd sample the drug . . . just to see what it was like, you know. Well, one thing led to another. I was right out of my head when Sam found us.'

'Did it continue after that?' she enquired.

'No, it was just the once, on both counts.'

'That's a relief.'

'The thing with Linda was purely physical,' he explained, 'but she didn't seem nearly so attractive when I realised I'd lost Samantha because of her.'

'Is that why Linda left . . . because you cooled off?'

'Yes. She didn't have an incentive to stay after that. I didn't want her around.'

'Have you told Samantha all this?' asked Nina.

'Yes, over and over again. I've begged her to give me another chance but she won't,' he explained. 'She says it wouldn't work because now she won't ever be able to trust me again.'

'I can understand how she feels.'

'I hurt her deeply, Mum.'

'Yes. It must have been dreadful for her to find you with Linda like that.'

Painful memories were reawakened in Nina. Different circumstances but the same feeling of betrayal she herself had experienced when Baz had left. Nina knew, more than anyone, how unforgiving Samantha must be feeling at this time.

'Like I said,' Joey sighed, 'I really blew it.'

'Yes, I'm afraid you did, son,' she agreed sadly.

Early in the New Year of 1969, The Willow's centenary year, formalities were completed with regard to Nina's becoming the legal owner. But the plans she was making for celebrations in July to mark the pub's first opening a hundred years ago were unexpectedly overshadowed by something her solicitor said when she was in his office one day tying up a few loose ends.

'I've been thinking about your legal affairs, Mrs Paxton,' said Mr Jenkins, a small, diligent man, 'and I feel duty bound to point out one aspect of them that is bothering me now that you are officially the owner of The Willow.'

'Oh, really?'

'You are perfectly at liberty to tell me to mind my own business, of course,' he said, leaning back in his chair and placing his fingers under his chin, 'but now that The Willow is yours, I think it's a bad idea to stay legally married when you and your husband are separated.'

'Do you?' was all she could utter, completely taken aback.

'Is there any particular reason for this unsatisfactory state of affairs?'

'No, not really,' she informed him. 'It's simply that we've never bothered to do anything about it, since neither of us has wanted to remarry.'

'Mm, I see.' He pondered for a moment. 'Well . . . it might be a good idea to consider divorce now, in the light of your new circumstances.'

'But why exactly?'

He cleared his throat. 'Well, not to put too fine a point on it, in case your husband tries to make any sort of claim on The Willow in the event of anything untoward happening and your meeting an untimely death.'

'But Baz would never do that,' she said, aghast at the suggestion.

'The Willow is worth a lot of money now, Mrs Paxton. It's no longer just a small pub.'

'Yes, I know that, but Baz is a rich man in his own right,' she pointed out. 'He doesn't need anything of mine.'

'You must think of your son,' he warned her.

'The Willow will go to Joey when I die, I've made that quite clear in my will,' she informed him. 'And that is what Baz would want. He's as devoted to our son as I am.'

'Now, maybe. But what about in the future?' persisted Mr Jenkins. 'Anything could happen. Your husband's business could fail and he could fall on hard times . . . or he could take up with a woman with an eye to the main chance who could influence him. People live together without marrying these days. As long as he is still legally married to you, he could contest the will. I'm not saying he would be successful but it could be most unpleasant for Joey.'

It was odd how the idea of Baz and another woman still hurt, after all these years apart. 'I can understand your concern but there is no need for it in this case,' she told him. 'Even if Baz was destitute he wouldn't take anything of Joey's. And as for your second point . . . well, Baz has had girlfriends over the years, naturally, but I don't think there has ever been anything serious.'

'It might not always be like that,' said Mr Jenkins. 'He's still a relatively young man, isn't he?'

'Mid-forties.'

'Still young enough for a serious relationship then.'

'Well, yes, I suppose so.'

'I'd be failing in my duty if I didn't point out the irresponsibility of leaving your affairs in such a vulnerable state,' he told her in a sober manner. 'Obviously whether or not you take my advice is entirely up to you.'

'Of course.'

'Is there any reason why a divorce should not be sought?' he persisted. 'I mean, is there a possibility of your getting back together again, perhaps?'

'None at all,' she said without hesitation.

'Then I must reiterate the potential risks of leaving things as they are,' he said gravely.

'Divorce is really unpleasant . . . so I've heard.'

'Not necessarily. Especially not in your case. I mean, you've been separated for a very long time.'

'Oh, yes. And it was a clear case of Baz deserting us,' she said.

'There you are then,' he said firmly. 'It should be fairly straightforward. Anyway, think about it and let me know what you decide to do.'

Although she knew there was no chance of Baz's ever behaving in the way the solicitor had suggested he might, Nina was forced to admit that it was most unprofessional to leave her affairs in such a state. Maybe it was time to put things in order and make that final break with the past?

The question of whether or not to divorce Baz was not something she felt able to discuss with anyone, not even her mother or Alice. Nor was it something she could treat lightly. It should have been just a formality. After all, she and Baz had been apart far longer than they had been together and making it legal would make no difference to the way they lived their lives.

But it was with deep regret that she came to her decision. Not wanting Baz to hear about it from the solicitor, she arranged to visit him at his Bayswater flat one evening to break the news.

Chapter Twenty-six

'Well, don't look so shocked,' said Nina at Baz's obvious devastation. 'Surely it can't be *that* unexpected?'

'It damned well is. I didn't expect to be dragged through the courts after all these years,' was his gruff retort. 'You know perfectly well I wouldn't use our legal bond for personal gain.'

'Yes, I know that.'

'Why do this then?'

'I've already told you,' she said, having gone to great pains to explain why she thought the time had come for them to divorce. 'It's simply that Mr Jenkins made me realise how stupid the present situation is, that's all. I mean, here we are, separated for over twenty years, and we still haven't made it legal.'

'It doesn't matter.'

'It does. It's untidy. Like leaving a cupboard door open when you've finished with it.'

Which was exactly why Baz wanted the situation left as it was. While things were incomplete there was still the chance of a reconciliation. 'But it's so final, Nina,' he said gravely.

'Mm, I know,' she said, her voice tinged with regret.

425

They were sitting by the fire in his sitting room with
a fluffy black hearthrug at their feet. The room was
distinctly masculine with black leather armchairs, plain
cream-coloured carpet, soft lighting created by simple
table-lamps and wall lights.

Baz went slowly over to the cocktail cabinet and
poured them both a drink. 'I'll be honest with you,
Nina. I've always hoped that we might give it another
try one day,' he said, handing her a gin and tonic and
standing with his back to the fire, staring into his glass.

'Even now, after all this time?'

'Yes, even now.'

She sipped her drink, glad of its soothing bitterness.
'You're clinging to the past, Baz,' she told him. 'We
were just kids playing at marriage, forced into it by the
circumstances.'

'That doesn't mean it has to be written off as
meaningless.'

'Of course not. But it didn't work out so let's just put
it down to experience and stay friends.'

'I love you.'

'Baz, stop it.'

'Why do you want me to stop?' he wanted to know. 'Is
it because you don't want to face up to the fact that
there's still something between us?'

'No. It's because sentimentality could lead us into
trouble . . . the second time around,' she told him.

'But we're mature people now, sensible enough to
consider each other's feelings, to give each other space.'

'Maybe. But it's still time to move on,' she said. 'You
should find someone else, remarry.'

He sat down on the edge of his chair and leaned towards her earnestly. 'I don't care how many times you deny it, Nina, you and I are right for each other. Why do you think I've stayed single all these years? It certainly wasn't for lack of takers.'

'You're too modest,' she quipped.

'There's no need to be sarcastic,' he countered. 'I wasn't boasting. It's a fact of life that money and success are a turn-on to some people. It has nothing to do with me as a person. But, anyway, I've never wanted anyone but you.'

'Please don't do this to me, Baz,' she begged.

'We're still young enough to have a future together,' he persisted. 'Let's not throw away something that some people never find in the whole of a lifetime.'

She felt as drawn to him as she had over twenty years ago. It was incredible the effect he still had on her. In danger of losing control, she said firmly, 'If I'd known you were going to make all this fuss, I wouldn't have come to see you. I'd have just told the solicitor to go ahead with the divorce.'

'Why didn't you do that then?' he asked, eying her shrewdly.

'I was thinking of you,' she informed him. 'It seemed so horribly cold and impersonal to have you hear about it in a solicitor's letter.'

He narrowed his eyes at her. 'I'm not so sure that was the reason,' he said thoughtfully.

'Oh . . . so you're claiming to know me better than I know myself now, are you?' she said acidly.

'Perhaps. I think it was because you don't want a

divorce any more than I do, and subconsciously you want to be talked out of it.'

'Don't be ridiculous!'

'If you really wanted to finalise things you'd have done it years ago . . . you wouldn't have needed some bloody solicitor to inspire you.'

'Oh, this is hopeless,' she sighed. 'I wish I hadn't come.'

'You haven't wanted to get married again for the same reason as me,' he went on, his voice rising, 'because neither of us wants anyone else.' He rose and crossed to her chair, pulling her to her feet and kissing her roughly. 'That's why you came to see me.' He moved back, his voice ragged with emotion. 'Because you still want me every bit as much as I want you . . . even if you won't let yourself admit it.'

She was shaken to the core. 'Trust you to reduce everything to basics,' she said in a trembling voice.

'That's where you'll find the truth,' he said. 'It's what brought us together in the first place.'

'Oh, really,' she said breathlessly. 'I think we're both a bit beyond that kind of simplistic philosophy.'

'Come back to me, Nina,' he entreated, his voice quivering.

'No.' She walked to the door. 'I didn't want it to be done this way. I was hoping we could have been adult about it. But you'll be hearing from my solicitor, as they say.'

'Okay.' He was suddenly composed. 'If it's what you really want, you'll get no more argument from me.'

At the front door he helped her on with her coat.

'Goodbye then, Nina,' he said coldly.

'Goodnight, Baz,' she said, and hurried out to her car.

It was over a month before she could bring herself to take the plunge and instruct her solicitor to start divorce proceedings. The right thing or not, she still felt like hell about it, and was surprised by how upset Joey was.

'I've always hoped you'd get back together eventually,' he said. 'Even when I thought I hated Dad, I still wanted that.'

'Why?'

'When I was a kid, I suppose it was because it would have been easier for me,' he admitted thoughtfully. 'But since I've been older I've noticed that you still seem fond of each other.'

She decided not to comment on that and just said, 'You get on well with your father now, don't you?'

'Yes,' he said promptly. 'He's a really good bloke.'

One day in March Samantha telephoned Nina to ask if they could get together for a chat. As she wanted to avoid seeing Joey they arranged to meet in the park on Saturday afternoon.

'I'm so pleased to see you, love,' said Nina, hugging her when they met by the bandstand. 'The Willow hasn't been the same without you.'

The young woman looked as smart as ever in a red coat with a black velvet collar and long black boots. She was very pale though and less exuberant than Nina remembered.

429

'I've missed you a lot, too,' she confessed.

'Where are you working now?' Nina enquired.

'In an office in the West End,' Samantha told her gloomily.

'Pounding the typewriter again, eh?' said Nina. 'I'm surprised. You were a natural for the pub trade.'

'Mm, I know. Typing invoices all day drives me nuts.'

'Why didn't you get a job in another pub after you left us, then?'

'I thought it might be easier to forget Joey if I went back to the work I was doing before I met him,' she explained. 'Working at The Willow was an interlude ... a really happy one until Linda came. I felt alive when I was there.'

'Yes, I could tell.'

'Anyway, I thought a return to my other kind of life might help to put the whole episode behind me.'

'But it hasn't worked?'

'No.'

They walked on arm in arm. Dark clouds rolled across a mottled grey sky with occasional shafts of light shining through. A chilly wind blew specks of rain into their faces and roared through the trees, mocking the fresh green shoots burgeoning on the branches.

'Joey wants me back,' announced Samantha sadly.

'Yes, I know. He told me what happened between you.'

'I'm so miserable without him,' admitted Samantha. 'But I feel as though I can't take him back ... and I just have to talk to someone about it.'

'Is it because you can't forgive him?' suggested Nina.

'That's right. I can't forgive or trust him,' she said. 'I want to, but every time I think of him and Linda together I just flip . . . it makes me want to hurt him back . . . and that's not the way to make a new start, is it?'

'Not really.'

'Oh, why did he have to spoil everything?' the girl said in anguished tones. 'It was so perfect between us.'

'Nothing stays perfect forever,' said Nina sadly. 'We're all subject to the frailties of human nature. He's genuinely sorry for what happened, you know.'

'So he tells me. He swears he'll never do anything like that again,' she said, 'but how can I be sure of that?'

'You can't,' said Nina. 'There's no absolute guarantee on human behaviour. If you do take him back, you'll have to accept that and take him on trust.'

'That's the problem,' she explained. 'I don't think I can . . . I feel so terribly betrayed.'

'I know how you feel,' said Nina truthfully.

'It won't be much of a marriage if I'm going to be throwing up the Linda episode to him every time we have a row.'

'You're right, it won't.'

'But I can't face the thought of life without him,' admitted Samantha, biting her lip. 'I just can't.'

'Then my advice to you is to take him back as he is, with all his faults and weaknesses,' said Nina. 'Obviously it will have to be on your terms but he can't be absolutely certain that he won't *ever* let you down again, any more than you can, since no one is entirely predictable. All both of you can do is to try your best.'

'Do you really think we could make a go of it, after what happened?'

'That depends on how much you want it . . . but, yes, I think so.'

'I wish I could be more confident about it.'

'Why not consider the alternative for a moment?' suggested Nina. 'You could turn him away and regret it for the rest of your life. There'll be other men, you'll probably even marry someone else, but he'll never match up to Joey. Not for you.'

'You could be right.'

'Only time can tell,' said Nina. 'All I can do is give you my opinion. Frankly I think you'd be a fool to throw away something as precious as the feelings that you and Joey have just because of past mistakes.'

'You make it sound so simple.'

'I certainly don't mean to. That's the last thing it is.'

'Anyway, I really appreciate your opinion,' said the young woman. 'I'll think seriously about what you've said.'

'It'll be up to you in the end.'

'I know.'

'Let's go and have tea somewhere, shall we?' suggested Nina. 'It's starting to rain heavily now.'

When Nina got home from the meeting with Samantha she was deeply preoccupied with her own thoughts. As it wasn't quite time to get ready for opening, she sat in the living room with a notepad and pencil, trying to turn her mind to the centenary celebrations they were planning for July. Should the first drink of the evening and the refreshments be free to every customer, or just the drink? Should they supply a bottle of wine free to every table in the restaurant? What about a firework display?

Her concentration was severely impaired by her vivid recall of the advice she had just given to Samantha. 'You'd be a fool to throw away something so precious because of past mistakes.'

What a hypocrite she was! She'd advised Samantha against something that she herself had been doing for a very long time. Ever since Baz had come back into her life, fourteen years ago, and made it obvious that he wanted her back, she'd gone against her instinct and fought hard to keep him at a distance. Would those years not have been much happier spent with him?

In this mood of introspection she could admit that he had more than made up for past misdemeanours. He'd been there with comfort and practical assistance when her mother had been so ill; he'd come to the rescue when Alice's boys had been in trouble; he'd taken up the cudgels on her behalf to get building permission for the restaurant. He'd even put his own life at risk for his son at the hands of thugs. In fact, he was always there when she needed him.

With the benefit of hindsight she could see how difficult she must have been to live with when she'd had the responsibilities of motherhood thrust upon her prematurely. When she recalled how she had nagged him, forced him to stop working to benefit his family, it was no wonder he had walked out.

Whilst being brutally honest she could also accept

the fact that Baz had been right about her not wanting a divorce. As he had said, if she'd really wanted to make the final break she would have done so long ago.

The truth was that she hadn't wanted to let him go even though she hadn't the courage to have him back. She'd been so obsessed with self-protection she'd lost a potentially happy fourteen years for them both. What a terrible waste!

Dazed by this revelation, she went to the telephone in the hall and picked up the receiver. With a sudden change of plan she replaced it and went to find Joey who was in the kitchen. Asking him to take charge of The Willow if she wasn't back by opening time, she left the premises.

'Hello, Baz.'

'Nina?' he said, opening the door to her with a puzzled look. 'Well . . . this is a surprise.'

She looked at him uncertainly. 'You know that chat we had a few weeks ago . . .'

'Yes,' he said slowly.

'Well, what would you say if I were to tell you I've had a change of heart?'

'I'd say come inside,' he said, beaming broadly and opening the door wide for her to enter.

The Willow was awash with brightly coloured flags and bunting, flapping in the breeze on the roof and strung across the gardens. Red, white and blue satin banners had been placed above both public entrances carrying the words: THE WILLOW – JULY 21 1869–1969.

Inside the building on this summer evening, the crowded bar also had a festive look about it. As well as an abundance of flowers and balloons there was a trestle table at one end laid with the remains of a buffet spread. In the centre stood a square centenary cake, cleverly decorated by Joey in the style of the pub sign complete with an iced impression of a willow tree.

The party was well under way. Another momentous event had added to the celebratory atmosphere for in the early hours of this morning American astronaut Neil Armstrong had become the first man ever to set foot on the moon.

'My Joe's great-grandfather could never have dreamed that one hundred years to the day since he opened The Willow, man would walk on the moon,' said Tilly, who was sitting with Monty at a table near the bar with Alice and George and Malcolm and Teddy.

'Or that we'd be able to watch it in our own living rooms,' said George.

'They didn't even have cars, let alone space rockets and televisions,' remarked Tilly.

'It makes me feel peculiar to look at the moon now,' remarked Samantha, who was on duty behind the bar. 'I mean, to think that someone is actually up there walking about on it . . . that it isn't just a shiny round thing but another world with a surface like a desert.'

'But we knew it wasn't just a shiny round thing before,' teased her husband, who was now the overall manager of The Willow, giving his wife an affectionate smile as he appeared at her side.

'Yeah, but actually to see it.'

'I know just what she means, Joey,' put in Nina from behind the bar. 'I came out in goose pimples watching telly last night when I saw Neil Armstrong step off the ladder of the lunar module on to the moon.'

'When he said that bit about it being "one small step for a man, one giant leap for mankind", I was quite overcome,' confessed Tilly.

There was a murmur of agreement from others who had been similarly affected by the astronaut's eloquence.

'Well, folks,' said Joey, raising his voice to be heard throughout the room, 'if you're not too tired from staying up all night to watch the moonwalk on the box . . . perhaps you'd like to make your way out to the garden where my father is ready to let off some fireworks. When we come back in we'll cut the cake.'

Cheering and chattering, the assembled company followed Joey outside where fairy lights shone through the trees around the floodlit garden which was packed with people. Many local families with children had come along to join in the fun and were seated at tables at a safe distance from the space that had been cleared for the firework display.

As a multitude of bangs, bumps and whooshes had the crowd 'oohing' and 'aahing', and Baz and Joey handed out sparklers to the children, Nina stood aside from the gathering in reflective mood.

Seeing Joey performing his duties with such aplomb confirmed her good judgement in handing over the management of The Willow to him when she'd decided to give her marriage another chance.

She and Baz had moved into a house on the river just a few minutes' walk from the pub, so she was near enough to be closely involved without having sole responsibility. She had thought it only fair to Baz and their marriage to give themselves some time together and privacy.

The arrangement was mutually beneficial. Joey and Samantha had a comfortable home in which to start their married life as well as an interesting challenge and a decent income. She herself was free to have a life outside whilst being on hand to give them support. Most days she was here for a few hours helping out.

In fact, the place acted like a magnet to all the family. Mum and Monty were regulars on the public side of the bar. Alice still played the piano in the restaurant a few times a week. Malcolm and Teddy, who seemed to have shed their bad behaviour along with their teenage years, often called in. Still twin-like, they worked together at Paxton Leisure Ltd, training for management.

She looked at Baz, his tall form visible in the luminous glow of the floodlights. He was still a fine figure of a man and the dusting of silver in his hair suited him. A born showman, he introduced each firework with humorous banter.

It occurred to her that he was the embodiment of the working-class dream – the poor boy made good. He'd done it with no help from anyone too, not even his young wife. She was so proud of him, albeit belatedly.

'And now for our grand finale,' he was saying as he went over to a trellis frame on which he'd spent hours arranging fireworks in a set piece. 'The highlight of the evening, folks . . .'

Touch-papers were lit and the crowd waited. A small crackle of light grew until colours fizzed and sparkled in all directions, climbing and spreading across the frame to form the words THE WILLOW in a shower of golden rain over the top of the figures 100.

Squeals of delight quietened into an awed hush as the spectacle glittered against the night sky under a moon which had lost some of its mystique that very morning.

The simultaneous timing of the moonlanding and the centenary seemed symbolic to Nina at the moment. It brought to mind the rapid advancement of civilisation since her ancestors had first opened the doors of The Willow to the public. Society had progressed from horse transport to space travel; from the total suppression of women to the sexual revolution; from workhouses to the welfare state.

Change had touched The Willow too. From a small riverside inn it had become one of West London's most popular social venues. For all its expansion, though, it remained a cosy family pub, a part of English tradition. And as long as there was a Dent descendant's name over the door, it would remain that way.

The fireworks fizzled out and people began to drift back inside for the last treat of the evening, the cutting of the centenary cake. Some of the children searched the grass for burnt-out fireworks while waiting for parents to deliver them their slice of cake.

In a mood of deep contentment, Nina made her way

over to her husband who was clearing up the debris in the floodlights. He looked up and smiled when he saw her coming towards him.